GOOD GRADES & MYSTERY GAMES

NORTH UNIVERSITY
BOOK 2

JANISHA BOSWELL

❀ Created with Vellum

For those who desperately crave academic validation.
You don't need a grade to determine your worth.
You are worth more than any letter or number. So much more.

AUTHORS NOTE / CONTENT WARNINGS

You do not need to read the first book in the series to read this. But I would highly suggest you do to see where Scarlett and Evan's story left off at the end of book one. Any major scenes are described briefly, so you will not be missing out on too much.

As much as this book deals with sickly sweet romantic scenes and the joys of female friendships, it also takes a slightly darker route dealing with death which is described slightly on and off page in light gruesome detail.

This book is also an open door romance, meaning it contains explicit sexual scenes that are described on page. Mentions of grief journeys, anxiety, obsessive compulsive disorder are also topics that are discussed in this book. If any of these may upset or cause any distress to readers, I encourage you to seek help from family, friends or a professional.

All your feelings and journeys are valid ones.

Playlist

Only Angel by Harry Styles
Mastermind by Taylor Swift
Sweet Disposition by The Temper Trap
Woman by Harry Styles
Fade Into You by Inhaler
In My Life by The Beatles
Jackie and Wilson by Hozier
Fearless by Taylor Swift
Tread Carefully by SZA
Delicate by Taylor Swift
Space Song by Beach House
Fantasy by Bazzi
High Enough by K.Flay
Carolina by Harry Styles
Call Out My Name by The Weeknd
The Beautiful Dream by George Ezra
California by Lan Del Rey
Treacherous by Taylor Swift
Stupid by Lizzy McAlpine
Bloom by The Paper Kites
Your Needs, My Needs by Noah Kahan
Everybody's Crazy by Olivia Dean
It'll Be Okay by Shawn Mendes
I Can See You by Taylor Swift
I Know You by Faye Webster
Cinnamon Girl by Lana Del Rey

The lie was the weapon, and the plot was empty. Darkness was the dictator.

Charles Bukowski - 'Let it Enfold You'.

1

SCARLETT

"ONE MORE TIME." I roll my eyes and push his sweaty body off mine. It takes me a few blinks to register the room again without my head spinning. The dark blue walls blink back at me as I focus on the framed Marvel posters on his bedroom walls that I forgot about. I groan as I sit up, my legs and back feeling sore.

"Not today. I've got to go," I sigh, twisting my body to the side of the bed to fish up my underwear from halfway across the floor. God. Did I really get that desperate that I couldn't even make it to the bed?

I ignore the warning bells that are going off in my brain as I pull on my dress, trying to look presentable. I feel his hot large hands wrap around me from behind when I'm close to the door and his chin rests on my shoulder. If I wasn't so eager to get back to my own home and my own bed, I would let him take me again. And again. The three times we did it last night are enough for me. "I'm being serious. I do have to go."

"Are you going to do this every time?" he groans into my skin. I shut my eyes tight before turning to him and stepping out of his grasp. His huge hands fall limp at his sides as he stands naked in front of me.

"There's not going to be a next time, Charlie. This is the first and the last time we're doing this," I smile, and he groans, throwing his head back. "C'mon. You knew that going into this."

"I thought you'd change your mind." He smirks.

"I didn't. You're not as good as everyone makes out." I shrug.

"Ouch," he groans dramatically, clutching his heart. I don't let my eyes travel any further down than his chest as he stretches.

There's something so undeniably hot about a naked man stretching in front of me. If I don't keep myself in check, I'll do yet another stupid thing I'll regret.

He smiles as he says, "You could have left me with some dignity, God."

"Sorry," I say. For one of the first times, I actually am sorry. Charlie's a nice enough guy and the sex was...okay. I just don't want to see him again in case he figures out who I am and realises he'll want more or nothing at all. Instead, I lie. "I'll see you around."

I slip out of his room and do the walk of shame through his frat house. This is my favourite part of this whole routine.

Kidding of course.

It's not as bad as it used to be. Sure, my friends say having sex with random college guys is not healthy for me, but who cares anymore? At first it was nice for the thrill. The escape. Then it became edged into my routine. School at 8:30, lunch, homework, hang out with the girls, more homework and then do something a little reckless. A little out of control. Over the last few days, I've needed that out-of-control feeling a lot more.

I could get any of the nice, well dressed, and well-mannered guys that my mom keeps handing me off to, but I don't want that. I want something messy. Rough. Dirty. Quick enough that they don't register my surname. With the proper men I'm exposed to at weekly family events, it makes my stomach turn thinking of how they'd treat me in bed. And not in a good way.

There's something exhilarating about the boys at NU or nearby, with little to no common sense, that makes my nerves sing. They can expect a little sex and nothing more. Plus, most of them are too eager to even ask any of the important questions. The few guys I've been with that attend the Bailey Foundation event every year always expect something more. They would get down on one knee on the first date if they wanted to just to expand their businesses. Hell, I've known some people that got engaged at eighteen from that shit. That is the last thing I want or need.

Instead, I force myself to walk across campus and down to my apartment. It's a few weeks into September, and I'm still not used to the winter air in Salt Lake. I should've brought a jacket with me. Or drove. But no. I have to walk in the cold in a black minidress and flats.

My best friends and roommates, Wren, and Kennedy, are used to these weekly antics, so they're not surprised when I walk through the door in the same clothes I had on when I left yesterday.

Kennedy blinks at me from the kitchen counter, her spoonful of Cheerio's pausing at her mouth when she raises one eyebrow up at me. I shrug at her before searching the fridge for a drink.

"Fun time?" she asks around a mouthful. I grab a water and lean against the sink, drawing my face into a puzzled expression as I stare at her. I slowly pull the bottle to my lips and take a sip silently. "From the state of your dress and your hair I'm going to take that as a yes."

"Do we have to do this every time?" I ask, bored. I take another gulp, setting the drink down onto the counter.

"I guess not. I just like to piss you off sometimes. You're easier to wind up than Wren," Kennedy says, spooning more cereal into her mouth. Her brown curly hair drops down into her face and she flicks her head dramatically to push it out of the way, her brown skin glowing a deep red from the sheer effort she's putting into making sure she eats. Nothing can get between this woman and her food.

"Yeah, where is she?" I ask, looking over her shoulder into the empty living room.

"She says she has practice, but we both know what that means," Kennedy murmurs, wiggling her eyebrows.

For the past year, our best friend and favourite NU figure skater, has been dating Miles Davis, a hockey player at NU, who has been head-over heels for her since day one. At the beginning, she was only dating him to regain her social status and to help him get back on the hockey team, but then things got real, and they fell for each other. Hard. Since then, they've been all over each other and fucking like bunnies.

It's starting to get disgusting being around them or just being in my own home. I've walked into my own living room too many times to them doing stuff while watching the TV. Our whole friend group knows how they are, yet Wren still tries to hide it by claiming she's going to 'practice,' when really she's going to his house.

"Right," I whistle, draining the last of my water before

throwing it in the trash. "I need to catch up on work for class. Are you going into the studio today?"

Kennedy's face lights up at the mention of her safe place: the art studio. The same way I'm obsessed with numbers and spreadsheets, Ken loves to draw and create. Studying art and photography at NU has been the best thing to ever happen to her after her dad passed away.

The studio has become her sanctuary and when we're lucky enough, we're able to see some of the projects she creates.

"Yeah, I'm going soon, but aren't you meant to be meeting your mom, like, now?" Kennedy mentions, checking the time on her phone.

My gut twists. I forgot. "Shit, Ken, you could have told me to come back earlier. I need to shower and get the smell of sex off me," I exclaim, rushing around to the other side of the kitchen to grab my towel out of the airing cupboard.

"Oh, let's all blame Kennedy," she mocks before adding, "I didn't want to interrupt your sexy time. The last time I did, you threatened to burn my Jasmine James shrine," she shouts to me from the kitchen when I get into my room down the hall.

"Yeah because you worship her like an insane person," I shout back. "Next time, at least text me. My mom is going to freak out."

THE VOSS HOUSEHOLD has one rule: don't be late but if you are, come bearing gifts. After a quick shower and replacing my minidress with a dark blue pantsuit, I stopped off at *Cane's* and bought enough chicken sandwich meals to feed a pack of lions before pulling into my family estate.

Maybe it's always been in the air, and I forgot about it. Or maybe it's intensified since my dad has been in the hospital — but there's been something deeply unsettling about the Voss mansion.

Growing up here, the deep brown stone walls became comforting. It felt normal as our family assistant, Mia, greeted us in the entryway and pestered us with reminders or refreshments. Even the larger-than-life portrait, of my great-great-grandfather Carlo Voss, that hangs over the dining room table has become welcoming. But moving out is still one of the best things to ever happen to me. Not only has it given me the chance to hang out with my best friends 24/7, but I'm no longer being ridiculed by my four older brothers who were lucky enough to have access to the family business the second they turned eighteen.

I've always known I'd have to work for my spot in the family, the second I realised that I'm the only woman - apart from my mother - who has ever been involved in the Voss family business. My eldest brother, Alexander, moved to London a few years ago and is managing our designer clothing brand on that side of the world. The twins, Arthur, and Leo have taken comfortable positions as customer service managers. While Arthur chases after the role as the eldest Voss son, Leo is usually off in a corner smoking weed. Henry is working his way up to help with graphic designs.

It's bad to have a favourite, I know, but Henry has always understood me more than my other brothers. We're only two years apart and since he has a six-year age gap with the twins, he understands what it's like to be out of the loop sometimes. As much as I like to believe that I know him better than anyone, I should have seen it coming when he captured me in a hug the second I walked through the door.

"Hey, you're going to squash the sandwiches," I muffle before pushing away from his embrace. I almost topple back on my heels when I register his face in front of me. He has the same set of dark features I do – dark arched eyebrows, slick black hair that falls onto his forehead and a lined dimple on his right cheek. I swear he looks older every time I see him, which makes *me* feel old.

"I'll take those out of your hands," he teases, trying to pull at the bag. I put the bag behind my back as I brush past him. I walk down the mile-long foyer until I reach the kitchen, placing the bags on the counter.

"Are the twins home?" I ask Henry who has eagerly followed behind me. I pull out some plates from the cupboard and lay them onto the glass countertop. He reaches over into the bag, and I swat his hand away. He pouts.

"No, Arthur is visiting dad and Leo's *somewhere*," Henry replies, drumming his fingers onto the table. I finally tear open the bags of food and start to share out Henry and I some food. I swear the boy's mouth starts to water.

"And why aren't you there?" I ask, pulling a seat out from the island and sitting down. Henry props himself up on the counter.

"I could ask you the same question," he challenges.

I don't bother to fight him on it. Since our dad, the current heir to the Voss dynasty, randomly fell into a coma, it's been hard to see him.

My dad and I were always close. When I was younger, my dad would tell me tales of how the clothing business came to be and all the scary stories that stemmed from his family back in our small town in Italy. He would tell those stories to frighten me. To scare me away from the business. To see it as this evil thing that I'd never want to be a part of so I could watch from the sidelines with my mother when it eventually burned to the ground. That only excited me more. It challenged me. It made me want to work harder than ever to prove that I'm as good - or better - than my brothers. *It is a dirty and filthy world, amore mio,* my dad would say, *it's not for perfect people like you.*

My dad is a healthy man, so when he mysteriously got ill, I knew it wasn't an accident. Everyone has been too afraid to even humour the fact that he could have been attacked. But not me. I may have no proof, evidence, or any sort of motive, but I'm working on it. Sort-of.

"I'll see him soon," I say, disguising my guilt with a bite of my sandwhich. With a flourish — and I swear I see glitter falling — our mom rushes into the kitchen with her arms wide.

"Oh, Scarlett, love," my mom announces, sauntering towards me in a purple gown. If having four brothers isn't enough overprotectiveness, I also have my mother.

I shoot Hen a look to intervene because I don't want my mom on my case right now.

"Mom! Fancy seeing you here," Henry exclaims, jumping off the counter and placing his arms on our mom's shoulders, intersecting her path to me. He turns back and grins at me. I furrow my eyebrows at him and tell him to tone it down a notch. "Scarlett doesn't feel like embracing you right now, but by all means, act as if you haven't seen her in years. From a distance."

"Why? What's wrong? Is she sick?" my mom quizzes. She pushes Henry out of the way and comes to face me, placing her hands on my cheeks. "Are you sick? What's the matter with you?"

"Jesus, mom, I just didn't want you all up in my face," I groan, prying her hands off me. She pushes her dark brown hair over her shoulder. Considering the fact that her husband is in the hospital, she seems pretty put together. As always.

"First you want to move out and now you don't even want to hug me. What's next? You're going to run away and elope," she sighs frantically, dropping into the chair beside me. I laugh as I nudge the food towards her, and she grins.

"I'm sorry but you've got to forgive me because I have food," I beam, popping a fry into my mouth. "Why did you want to see me?"

"It's your dad…" she begins dramatically, poking at the tray of food. Henry comes around to the other side of the island, his forearms leaning on the table.

"What? Is something wrong?" he asks, his eyebrows knitted together with concern. Mom shakes her head, dipping her fry into some sauce before chewing thoughtfully. If there is one thing about Lara Voss, she will create tension wherever she goes for no reason at all.

"No, he's fine as he can be, honey," she replies reassuringly, patting Henry's arm. "I just had a bad dream. One of *those* dreams."

"What do you mean?" I ask.

My mom is one of the most spiritual people I know, and she has really vivid dreams. Nearly every time she has a dream, they come true. Good or bad, they *always* come true. She had a dream when I was four that I would be my high school's valedictorian. She wrote it down in her diary and never told me until the day I graduated as - you guessed it - valedictorian. So, when she says she has a dream, we all listen.

"The dream wasn't like the others. It wasn't predicting the future," she starts. We wait for her to continue, afraid that interrupting will only draw out the torturing process. "I can't place the time, but all I know is that it was before the coma. I walked into his office, and he was signing some contracts and he didn't look happy about it. Which is weird because he is always in control. He caught my eye and then the door slammed. Next thing I knew, I was sitting next to him in the hospital, and he looked just how he looks now."

"Do you think someone did this to him? On purpose?" Henry asks exactly what I'm thinking. Sure, I wanted to believe there'd be some cool mystery I could uncover, but the fact that it could be true makes my stomach twist.

"I don't know what to think. It looks too suspicious for it to be a coincidence," mom says quietly.

We all let the idea settle over us for a minute. Why would anyone be after my dad? He might have done some shady stuff back in Italy, but for the most part, he's a decent guy. He would never do anything to put us, or himself, in danger.

"Anyway," mom chirps. Mine and Henry's heads snap up at the sudden liveliness in her tone. "Scarlett, a friend of mine has a son who I need to introduce you to. He crochets! How cute is that?"

And my chance at a mystery lasted thirty seconds.

2

EVAN

"WHY DO you look like this on a Wednesday night? I'm starting to think that you don't have any friends, Branson."

I ignore Miles' comment for the hundredth time because he can't let it go. Having housemates that are hockey players has one perk: they're always practising. They're out on campus for a few hours and then they usually hang out with their girlfriends. Except for today. Instead, both Xavier and Miles are up my ass as I try to get ready to go to my dad's house to *talk*. While they get to sit topless on the couch and play ridiculous sports games all evening, I have to face the wrath of my dad in a tux.

"Just because I have plans with my family, doesn't mean I don't have any friends," I retort, fixing the sleeves of my suit again. Tailored suits are all fun and games until you have pulsing anxiety running through your body while you feel like you're sweating buckets. "Besides, I'd much rather have a professionally cooked meal in a mansion than sit around all day like you slobs."

"If you're jealous that we're comfortable, just say it," Xavier calls from the couch.

"Real question, Z," I begin, looking at myself once more in the reflection of the refrigerator. I brush my hand through my blonde hair that is in desperate need of a cut. Another thing I've been putting off. I turn around and lean my forearms on the kitchen hatch that overlooks the living room.

"Shoot," Xavier replies, not tearing his eyes away from the screen as his fingers fly rapidly over the controller.

"Do you ever do any schoolwork? Like, seriously. I only see you train or sit here all day and I'm genuinely curious as to how you manage to stay on this scholarship," I ask with a head tilt.

"Are you being for real or not? I can never tell with you," he responds, flickering his confused gaze to me for a second before turning back to the screen. "I'll take your silence as a no. I do work, but you're just never here when I'm doing it."

"Huh," I say disbelievingly, walking out of the kitchen to the entryway to grab my jacket. As I'm about to say bye and leave, I hear Miles call my name as if I've forgotten something important. I turn back to him, and he pauses the game before looking at me. "What?"

"Don't you want to know how *I* manage it all? How I'm so incredible at going to school, playing hockey, *and* managing a relationship," he grins.

"This feels like a trap, so, I'm going to say no. I don't really want to know," I groan, trying to suppress my laugh.

I don't think I've ever met a man as dramatic as Miles Davis. I seriously don't get how Wren has put up with him for the past year. This is my third year living with him and I can't stand him most of the time. The only tolerable thing about him is that he's a loyal friend.

"You're right. It was a trap. I don't know how I do it either. It's exhausting. Every time I go to study, I just think about Wren and boom," he gestures to his lap. "It's over."

"Good to know, Davis. The next time I want to know your sexploits, I'll let you know in advance," I say. Neither of them are listening to me anymore anyway. They both turn back to the game, grunting and shouting at each other as I slip out of the door.

As expected, my family's driver, Charles, is waiting in the black Escalade outside. Charles has been a good friend to our family for years. He and my dad, Samuel, grew up together in a small town in Vermont and he'd always been in the loop with the Branson business that my great-great grandfather founded.

Branson & Co is one of the biggest clothing brands in the states right now, and it has been for decades. I still don't know the inner workings as to how the business came to be and how it became such a hit here, but all I know is that my family is loaded for life.

My dad says that Charles was never interested in being a part of the business. Not only is it mostly family-run, but it's also very competitive to even land an internship working at one of our branches. Charles got his licence before my dad did and he drove them around for years until my dad finally got a licence as well. Even now, after I was put on probation from the business, he's stuck by me.

Charles rolls down the window and nods at me to get in. He's dressed plainly in a black Pal Zileri suit and dark glasses, looking ever so serious. I can't take it seriously when I know he's the same guy who once leaned against a chocolate fountain at one of our events and ended up covered in chocolate without realising it. The same guy who embarrassed the hell out of me when I tried to go to second base with a girl in the back of the car in high school.

I slide into the backseat, picking up a bottle of water and downing most of it before leaning back in the chair. Is it cringe to have a playlist that Charles plays every time I go to my dad's house? Maybe. As much as I know the guys would bully me for it, there is nothing better than listening to dark pop songs and driving on the interstate to the other side of town.

The fifth The Weeknd song is about to play before we stop outside of the Branson estate. Great. I take a deep breath, thank Charles, and climb out of the car, dusting off my suit.

I throw my head back before adjusting my collar and start up the gravel pathway. Growing up here was a dream. A ridiculously privileged and insane dream. We had weekly charity events in the backyard, we spent Easter's doing huge treasure hunts around the whole house, Christmases with a tree almost as big as the one in Rockefeller. It was perfect for fourteen glorious years until my mom left. Then shit got really bad. Everything became about money, B & Co, power, and more money.

All the stupid family traditions ceased to exist when my mom couldn't handle it anymore and she left. Since then, coming back home has felt like a chore just to be caught in another petty argument with my dad.

I'd be lying if I didn't say he's a great dad; he's funny and he's kind, but beneath it all, I can tell he's not happy with me after the stunt I pulled two years ago. The man knows how to hold a grudge.

I was transferred from Drayton Hills to NU in the first few weeks of my first year after a very public break up with my ex-girlfriend and high school sweetheart Catherine Fables. Without the excessive details that I'm constantly replaying in my mind, let's just say that there was a public screaming contest on campus which ended up with me on the doorstep of her dorm, sobbing into an empty packet of Oreo's.

Although some girls dig the idea of the soft, cry-baby side of me, for the business, it was a PR disaster with popular gossip sites taking the issue into their own hands. It also meant that I was stripped from my usual privileges from the company and thrown into NU to gain some responsibility and to learn how to present myself better, meaning I keep my head down and I keep myself to myself. I think I've been doing a pretty good job at that so far.

When I slip into the sleek, black three-storey house the first thing I can hear is my dad's voice echoing down the hallway. He's on the phone.

I don't get much time to process it before our family Labrador runs up to me. She's a chubby girl named Mila. She's pretty low maintenance after growing up with her, but she still tries to intertwine herself with my legs like she's still a puppy while I try to get closer to my dad's voice.

"Not now, Mila," I whisper to her, scratching her ears before shoving her off to the side and she listens, whining softly.

As I inch closer towards the noise, I figure out who he's talking to. It's Damon. He's only a few years older than me and has been my dad's assistant for the last five years. Assistant is a bit of an understatement. Damon is the whole reason why my dad's house is still on all its legs and the only reason he's still breathing. He does a lot more than assist my dad on a day to day basis. Like right now, as he gets called a motherfucker for something that probably wasn't even his fault.

I lean against the wall in the family room behind the

kitchen. If I press my back against it hard enough, it can turn in on itself and it'll swivel around to face the larger-than-life kitchen area, but I try and keep my weight off it.

"I told you to do one thing for me, Damon. One fucking thing. If you can't do that, I'll find someone else to do it and you know I can," my dad threatens over the phone. There's a muffled response from Damon which he grunts and sighs to before continuing. "If you don't come back to me by the end of the week with a solid plan, I will cut you off and you can kiss that Lamborghini you wanted goodbye."

His phone slams onto the table and I jump, almost knocking over the bronze statue on the mantelpiece to my right. I let out a sigh of relief when the statue teeters before falling soundly back into place.

"If you're going to eavesdrop, at least be less obvious, boy," my dad says cooly on the other side of the wall. He always catches me out somehow. I don't have the energy to continue this stupid game, so I turn and push my hands against the wall until it opens to the kitchen.

My dad is sitting with his back to me, his greying blonde hair cut short at the nape of his neck which pinches as he throws back a glass of bourbon before slamming it down onto the bar. I walk cautiously towards him, trying my best to uphold any sort of composure that I used to have before I got kicked out.

"Eavesdropping has become my last resort as I have to find out all of the news from TMZ or a very cryptic message from Charles. And you know how he is with technology," I say with ease as I stand across from my dad, taking in his tense features and furrowed eyebrows. He shakes his head.

"I'm glad you find this situation so amusing, Evan. Truly. When really you should be ashamed of yourself for getting yourself in this situation," he responds, pouring himself another drink, but I snatch it up and drink it before setting it back down. He doesn't flinch. Instead, he pulls himself a clean glass, pouring yet another drink.

"Whatever," I say. "I have two questions, dad. One: what have I done to be summoned here again? And two: what did Damon do for you to rip him a new one?"

He blinks at me for a second, sipping his drink before placing it back down. "Damon is acting a fool, as per usual, but surprisingly you've done nothing particularly wrong."

"'Surprisingly?' What's surprising about me being the perfect kid I've always been?" I beam, pushing a hand through my hair for extra emphasis as I puff out my chest proudly.

He laughs a little at this before painting on his serious expression. He's susceptible to my charm more often than not nowadays. Only because he doesn't have to deal with it as frequently.

"You have *not* always been perfect, Evan."

"I have. You were just too dumb to realise it, old man." I push off the counter and rest my hands on the bar table, trying to regain control of the conversation. "But, really, what am I doing here? I'm sure you didn't force me to come just to eavesdrop and have a good drink. I actually have classes and shit to do."

He hums, sipping back the last of his bourbon as he thinks. "You have good grades, don't you?"

"Perfect grades." Straight A's in fact. As much as people my age don't give a shit about school, it's one of the only things I'm actually good at. Plus, my classes are pretty easy.

"Right," he replies cautiously. "I have something I'd like you to do, as long as it doesn't mess with your studies. This is a perfect opportunity for you to earn your way back to B & Co since Damon is too damn slow."

My heart almost leaps out of my ribcage. I have to take a step back and grip my chest for a beat before letting my heart rate settle. I've been trying to get my dad to trust me again to get back to how my life used to be. When I'm done having a mini freak-out, I finally focus back on my dad.

"Yes. Yeah, sure. I'll do anything," I say quickly, feeling the way my face burns. I clear my throat as my dad's mouth lifts up in a smirk before smothering it with his glass.

"I heard the youngest of the Voss kids still go to North. Is that true?" he asks, his eyebrow arched.

Fuck me.

Why did the mention of Scarlett make me tense up and he didn't even say her name?

I've gotten to know her a lot more in the past year with our friend groups being so close, but she would cut off my balls if I tried to look at her outside class or when our groups are forced to hang out.

She seems to hate me whenever we're in the same room, but it's hard to take her seriously when she tried to kidnap me a few weeks ago and accused me of stealing her ridiculous whiteboard.

It doesn't help that our families have been deep in competition for decades. She's a smartass and is always trying to one-up me in class but I let her. She hates me and I act like I hate her too. It's how we work. What she doesn't know is that we're a lot more alike than she wants to admit.

"Yeah," I say finally, swallowing the ball in my throat. "Only their daughter, though. She's in my class, and one of her best friends is dating my housemate."

"Great," he begins. He pauses, murmuring to himself

before meeting my gaze. "I'm sure you know that her dad's in the hospital, don't you? Well, he has been for weeks."

I nod but he doesn't follow it up with anything. "You… We…We didn't have anything to do with that, did we? I know he's seen as a threat, but I once caught him shrieking over a bee at an event. So, he seems harmless."

He cuts my rambling with a wave of his hand in the air. "No, Evan, we – or anyone we're associated with – didn't have anything to do with it. That's the problem. We're his biggest competitors so it *seems* like we had something to do with it. I can assure you that we did *not*. It's too much of a coincidence that around the time things started getting heated with their family, he mysteriously fell into a coma, but none of us were responsible."

"And what do you want me to do about it?" I ask wearily.

"If you know his daughter, try, and get closer to her and find out what she thinks. If we can get a lead in this, we can find a way to take him down *before* it hits the press," my dad explains, his eyes lighting up with the same fire and intensity as it always does when competition is in the mix.

"I, uh, I don't know if I can do that," I respond, taking a generous sip of my drink.

"Why not? You want to be back in don't you?"

"Yes. Of course, I do. More than anything. But isn't there a way we can do this without hurting anyone. Scarlett's…" God, how do you describe the same girl who threatened to punch me in the dick when I spat out her cookies which she forced us eat at the BBQ we had in summer. The same girl who shoved bacon in my face last Christmas, yet still had it in her to drive my drunk ass home afterwards. I can't tell my dad that. So, I lie. "She's different from them. She's a handful, she's snarky and competitive. But, beneath that… she's nice is all I mean."

"*You* don't have to play nice, Evan. If you want this badly enough, you'll find a way to get more information without breaking her heart if that's what you're worried about."

It's one of the many things I'm worried about when it comes to her.

AFTER CHARLES DROPS me off back home, I try to rack my brain for some sort of game-plan. I can't just start texting her out of nowhere to get her to speak to me. Fuck. I don't think Miles would even trust me with her number. Z probably has it, but he can't keep a secret to save his life. Instead, I settle for the easiest option which is to wait for Miles and Xavier's next hockey game, which Wren will drag her to and ambush her then.

"Do you know how to play the game, dude? How are you losing with the best squad in the game?" Miles shouts to Xavier as I walk behind the couch to the kitchen.

They continue shouting at each other until I sit down on the couch across from them with my tie loosened and a bottle of water in my hand. My dad and I had a huge steak dinner and I'm exhausted. Xavier shoots me a glance then turns back to the screen. Then back to me.

"You're back already?" he asks, turning back to the screen again as his fingers fly over the buttons.

"I was gone for three hours, you idiots," I retort.

"Oh," Miles says.

"Have you really been playing this entire time?" I ask. They both nod in unison before Miles turns to me for a split second while Xavier takes a penalty on the screen.

"It's a no-breaks-allowed kind of game," he replies, howling at the screen when Xavier 's goal goes in.

"What if one of you needs to take a leak?"

"That's what the buckets are for," Xavier replies, nodding his head to a bucket I hadn't noticed was there and I grimace. "I'm kidding. That's where we catch our trick shots with the ping-pong ball, obviously."

"Right. *Obviously*," I respond sarcastically. Every day I learn something new about the people I live with. The game ends and Miles sighs heavily at his defeat as he turns to me.

"Wanna play?"

I pause for a second before nodding. Why the hell not? He throws the controller at me and walks me through the first few steps of the game.

I look from the controller to the screen every few seconds as I watch the avatar move around in a zigzag. I try to gain control, but Xavier is not going easy on me, and he tackles me as he shoots into the net, earning me a loud whoop in response.

"Jesus, Evan, you really can't play for shit," Miles hollers, laughing as he sinks back into the couch, folding his arms across his chest. "You need to have better coordination than that. Don't you play the guitar or something?"

"Piano," I correct, trying to think of the last time I sat in front of a Steinway. It's been too long. I try to concentrate on the screen, my player running down in the wrong direction. "And they're really not the same thing."

"Potato, potahto," Miles grumbles. "You're too stressed out for a twenty-year-old. Just chill. When was the last time you slept with someone, seriously?"

"I dunno," I say, not ready to engage in this kind of conversation with one of the most talkative people I've ever met. I don't know how Wren copes.

"It might help you loosen up," Xavier chimes in.

"Yeah, maybe," I murmur, still trying to figure out how to play this fucking game. I throw the controller back to Miles who has been itching his hands like he can't deal without playing for a few minutes. "Hey, Miles. How's, uh... how's Scarlett?"

Miles' head whips around at me, his eyebrows drawn together as his lips pull up into a smirk. "Why are you asking me? Didn't she hold you hostage when Wren and I were at her sister's wedding?"

"Yeah, but not much talking happened. Kinda hard to ask how she's doing when it was more her shouting at me and trying to get me to confess to something I didn't do. I haven't spoken to her since then."

"She's fine...I guess," Miles says, shrugging. "Wait? You're not asking because of what I said about needing to get laid, are you?"

My breath catches in my throat. "No!" I'm practically yelling. *Jesus. This is going great.* "No," I say more calmly. "I was just wondering. You know, mutual friends and all that."

"Good. You guys hate each other. And if you ever touched her, Wren would have an aneurysm and I would somehow get blamed for it. So don't think about it," Miles warns, and I nod. "Plus, she has, like, four brothers. That's a disaster waiting to happen."

"People love me," I say proudly. Miles and Xavier throw each other a glance before bursting into a fit of laughter. It's not long before I join in on their hysterical screams.

3

SCARLETT

HAVING a break between second and third period doesn't mean taking a well-deserved break like the rest of the class, it means running across campus to meet in the middle where Kennedy's art classroom is.

I have ten minutes to catch up with the girls like we do every time between our double periods but this time we were summoned by Ken for an emergency meeting. The rink that Wren practices at is at the other side of the campus so the art studio is the middle-ground from my business class.

I run through a dark corridor past the school's dark room, towards the art classroom and I make my way through stressed out students until I find *my* stressed out student, basically ripping out her low pigtails.

Kennedy is sitting in the corner with a sketchbook in front of her, her blue denim dungarees covered in paint splatters, tugging at the band of her pigtails letting both bands break in half as her curly hair springs free.

I inch closer to her, not sure which Ken I'm about to interact with right now. As I take a step closer, I feel a hand on my shoulder, pulling me back into the corridor which I just exited. I recognise the hand immediately because we just got matching manicures a few days ago.

"She's freaking out," Wren says when we're face to face in the corridor, both of her hands on my shoulders, shaking me like an insane person.

"Yeah, I can tell. Why are *you* freaking out? You're scaring me," I say, removing her lethal grip from my shoulders. She brushes her blonde hair over her shoulder and exhales deeply, her green eyes searching mine. God, I swear I have the most dramatic friends to ever exist.

"She's got a deadline for a project and that empty canvas in there is all she's done. I've tried to help, but I think I'm making it worse," she replies.

"That doesn't sound like her. She's usually on top of these things," I say, trying to figure out how this could have happened.

When we were all freaking out about our exams at the end of last year, she was ahead of us all and helped Wren with her creative writing course. As chaotic as she is, her work always comes first for her and it's a trait of hers I've always admired.

"Yeah, I know," Wren says. She blinks at me for a minute, not saying anything. Kennedy is the literal glue to our group — if she's freaking out, we're all freaking out. "Can you try and talk to her? Darcy will have my head if I'm not back in two minutes."

I nod and take a deep breath before entering the room again. Her hair has become a wild mess of curls and coils as she runs her hands through it nervously, tapping her pencil on the empty sketchbook. She looks up at me. A faint smile paints across her face before returning down to her book.

"Hey," she says quietly, not tearing her eyes from the blank page. I check the time quickly, realising I only have a few minutes before I need to make my way back to class.

"Hey."

"Are you here to give me a pep talk? I really don't think I can deal with that right now. Wren's one was really shitty," she mumbles, finally drawing faint lines with her pencil. I pull out a chair across from her and laugh.

"I'm not here to give you a pep talk, Ken. I am, however, here to tell you that you can, and you *will* finish the project before the deadline."

"This is starting to sound like a pep talk," she murmurs. I shoot her a stern look. "The deadline is in three days."

"Three days? Shit. I thought it was like a month or something," I say, and she groans loudly, pushing the sketchbook away from her as she drops her head onto the table. "Okay, okay. Listen, you are one of the strongest, coolest, funniest, and most talented people I know. I'm not just saying that cause we've known each other forever. I'm being dead serious. Your work is insane and so much better than half of the stuff I've seen around the department."

She lifts her head up, resting on her forearms as she mumbles into her skin, "Thanks, but that isn't going to help."

"It better help, Ken. You *can't* give up on this. This is your dream. You're not working your ass off at Florentino's for nothing. And we all know coffee gives you a stomachache, so don't act like you can justify it."

"You're right."

"Of course, I'm right," I say, and she smiles. I push out my seat to stand up. "I have to go back to class though. We'll talk later, okay?"

She nods and I have three minutes to get back to my class. The only thing I forgot was that this break clashes with the freshman lunchtime, meaning that everybody and their mothers are out in the corridors. Fucking hell. This school needs to invest in bigger hallways because there is no way I'm getting back to my class in time.

Sometimes if Mr Anderson is in a particularly shitty mood, he locks us out, making us catch up with notes in our own time. Still, this is my third year here at NU and I still don't get how he's legally allowed to do so.

I make the brave decision to cut across the football field instead, finding this route to be more effective to get back to class. The first semester of this year only started a few weeks ago so the football team isn't exactly paying much attention to me cutting across their field, except for the one boy who does a double take when he realises that my red-bottoms are sinking into the muddy pitch.

I'm clearly not paying attention either because that's why I collide with the body standing at the top of the stairs, in front of the doors to the business building.

"Jesus. Can you watch where you're going?" the boy grumbles, pushing me away from him. I take two steps back, almost falling down the steps, but he latches onto my elbow, steadying me.

"My bad. I was just-" I say, the words falling out of my mouth automatically before I look up and of course it's him.

Evan fucking Branson; the literal bane of my existence.

He enjoys getting under my skin just as much as I enjoy getting under his. He's spent his last two years at NU torturing me, turning every class game into a competition and not to mention, he's rich as hell, as his family's clothing brand is one of the top in the States, rivalling mine. Also, I think it's very important to mention that he's blonde, which speaks for itself.

I yank my arm out of his grip as he stubs out his cigarette

on the railing. I brush past him, pushing through the doors and into the corridor. And obviously, we're walking to the same class, so I can hear his footsteps a few paces behind me.

"God, if you're going to smoke, at least do it off campus," I mutter, pulling my bag up higher on my shoulder. He steps in beside me, walking with me. For once, he's not that dressed up and has ditched his usual tailored suit for baggy light washed jeans and a white tee. It makes him seem more human. Interesting.

"Thanks for the advice, Angel," he replies. I take a quick glance at him, glaring at his insistent use of that stupid nickname. "*You're* awfully late for someone who cares so much about this class."

"And so are you," I retort, trying to pick up the pace so I don't have to look at him.

"Why?" he asks.

"Why, what?"

"Why are you late?"

I always try my best to keep conversation with him to a minimum because the more we speak, the closer I get to ripping his head off. He stops outside the door to the lecture theatre, arms across his chest, waiting for me to say something.

"Do you always ask this many questions or are you choosing to be extra irritating today?" I ask curiously.

"Do you always have something to say or are you incapable of shutting up?"

I match his stance, pinning my arms across my chest, narrowing my eyes at him. He has the tendency of making every single thing that comes out of his mouth sound like an insult, it's almost like he's begging me to strangle him. I can't last a day at school without his stupid comments on everything that I do, disguising it as 'constructive criticism.' He stares back at me, and I still can't tell if his eyes are blue or green.

I lean back on the class door, slightly pushing it open behind me as I whisper to him, "For the record, I'm not being quiet because you told me to. I simply don't want to waste anymore of my breath on you."

Then, because I'm petty and seeing his face pisses me off, I slip through the door, shutting it on him before walking up to my seat in the half full room.

I make it halfway up the stairs before Evan finally appears through the door and I smirk.

"Miss Voss and Mr Branson, I'm glad you didn't get lost on your way back to class," Mr Anderson says when I get my laptop and notebook out of my bag, pushing it onto my desk. He's one of the greatest teachers in our department, even if most of our lessons end with a forty minute rant about his ex-wife.

I watch as Evan takes a seat at the front of the class because like me, he doesn't exactly have anyone waiting for him in here.

As embarrassing as it is to admit, I don't have many friends in this class. Well, I don't have many friends in general. It's always just been me, Wren, and Kennedy since we were kids and I like it that way. I've always been fine with solitude. I've had to be, growing up with all brothers and feeling like the odd one out.

People either don't care about my existence or hate me because they think I've got everything handed to me, which couldn't be further from the truth. I worked hard for my spot at North University, and I've never once taken that for granted. I've accepted the way I'm going to be perceived and I'm fine with it. But it stings that I have to sit here and play the *"I hate you so much that it makes me sick"* game with Branson while everyone else can laugh and talk with their friends.

That's why it sucks when I swear I hear Anderson introduce a new project for this year. I raise my hand, almost knocking over my water bottle in the process. *This can't be happening.*

"Yes, Scarlett?"

"Uh, sorry, but could you repeat that? I think I just missed the end of that," I say nervously as slowly, one by one, people in the rows below me turn towards me, snickering. I swear it's like high school all over again. I sit up straighter, pushing my dark brown hair over my shoulder, feigning confidence.

"I've been talking for the last hour, but you only missed the end of it?" Anderson asks. I shrug. "You need to start paying more attention. I want to do something a little different to incorporate productivity and fun for this year. So, I'd like everyone to pair up with someone else in the class and I want you to create a hypothetical business. It can be anything from clothing to food, to an app; I'm not fussed. As long as you can present to me a project by the end of the school year on how you would market your business, your target audience, and the realistic ways you would build it from the ground up. It might come more naturally to some more than others, but the whole point is for this to be some fun before we…"

That's about where I start to drone him out.

I'm confident in all the ways that matter, but not with talking to people my own age, especially those that make it no secret that they don't like me. I've always found it hard to make friends, but the friends that I do have, I hold them dear to my heart and I appreciate them more than anything. It's the making of them that sucks the most and is the hardest.

The sound of Evan's annoying voice draws me back to the

class. "Do we get to choose our own partners?" Anderson nods and the strangest thing happens: Evan turns back to me, looks me dead in the eye and he smiles. Not a sweet, genuine smile, but one that holds mischief. Danger.

No. *No.*

He wouldn't.

Oh, but he would. He'd do it just to torture me.

I raise my hand this time. "Can we also reject offers of partnership?"

Anderson sighs, pushing his glasses up his head. "I don't care. As long as you come to me with a project before summer break, then it's fine."

With that, everyone in the class rushes around, yelling and finding their partners and I sit there, hoping that someone will be left without a partner and lead me to pair up with them. I don't think I could handle the rejection right now if I tried to ask someone.

When my row has cleared, people partnering in different sides of the lecture theatre, Evan turns back around, leaning on the table behind him with a lazy smile hanging off his lips.

"Then there were two," he drawls.

I roll my eyes. "There's one: you. I would rather drop out of this class than work with you for the next few months."

"We're really carrying this on, huh?" Evan says, chuckling low. I'm glad he finds this so amusing because I cannot work with him. "Our housemates are dating, the least we can do is be civil with each other."

"This *is* me being civil," I retort. He raises his eyebrows at me, tilting his head.

"Really? 'Cause it looks like you're ready to gauge my eyes out."

"Listen, Branson, this is not going to work out."

"Why not?" he asks, scratching his eyebrow, not taking his eyes off me as if he can see right through me. "It's not like people are exactly lining up to work with us."

I pin my arms across my chest, suddenly feeling defensive. I know he doesn't have many friends in this class either, but admitting it aloud, watching everyone else being paired up, makes it seem more real.

"What's in it for you?" I ask.

"You're the smartest person in here, second to me, and I could do with some extra credits. It turns out that going on vacation during the semester isn't always the smartest idea," he admits. Of course, he believes he's the smartest person in every room he walks into.

I try to mull over the idea. In reality, it could work, but that would mean having to speak to him nearly every day and interact with him when I don't need to. It also means putting up with more competition than usual, purposefully letting him get under my skin.

"Just being in your presence gives me a headache," I mutter, rubbing at my temples for extra effect. It can't be a coincidence that since I've seen him and his snobbish self, my head has started to hurt.

"Oh, 'cause you're such a delight, aren't you, Angel?" My body automatically shivers, and he smirks when he watches the way I squirm. "Believe me, I don't want to do this as much as you do. I need the grade and you're my best shot at getting it. Are we clear?"

I roll my neck before nodding, adding, "Fine."

4

EVAN

SOMETHING DOESN'T FEEL RIGHT.

Since that conversation with my dad, I've been feeling on edge. Well, more on edge than usual. And I hate it. I especially hate that Scarlett spent the entire lesson ignoring my proposals and glaring at me with her killer hazel eyes.

This all feels like it's too easy. My dad told me to get more involved with her and then Anderson's project just fell into my lap. I'm lucky that neither of us are well-liked in this class. Still, I know I'm the last person she would want to work with.

I wasn't lying about spending most of my money on short getaways during the semester, so my grades have started to slip. Being good at school always came pretty naturally to me, but that doesn't mean I haven't been working hard at NU. With or without my family's money, North University is an expensive place to get into and I can't exactly risk my spot when I'm slowly being cut off from my family. I was planning on slowly inserting myself into Scarlett's life, finally getting her to see me as a friend, let her open up to me and *then* do what my dad needs me to do. I wasn't expecting to have to see her all the time so suddenly, especially when I don't have a plan. And I always plan.

As soon as Anderson dismissed the class, Scarlett practically bolted away from me, not giving me any chance to ask her any follow-up questions. Not like she would answer any of them anyway.

Since Miles and Wren have started dating, I've had to see her more than usual and you'd think she would've warmed up to me by now, but she hasn't.

Since first year, we've had this weird competitive thing going on which I thought she would drop after a few weeks, but she is relentless and if she wants to continue to play this game, I'm happy to play by her rules.

Most of the time, she says things that make me want to cover her mouth and tell her to shut up, but other times, her insults are so out of pocket that I have to stick my tongue in my cheek, so I don't laugh. If she wants to pretend she doesn't like me, I can play along. I've always been good at acting.

After that painfully awkward and irritating class, I was left alone with my thoughts to think of a game plan. Which lasted about three seconds before Miles and Xavier came back from practice.

They've been sitting in front of the TV, watching the football highlights for the past hour while I cook in the kitchen. I might have had chefs at my house growing up, but I know my way around a kitchen. Cooking is one of those calculated, put together things that I can do when I've had a long day that makes me feel more in control, which is exactly what I need right now.

I don't know why this whole situation is getting me so riled up. If I had more time to think about a plan, maybe I wouldn't be feeling this way. I want more than anything to get back in on the business, having more access behind the scenes, for my dad to stop looking at me like he's disappointed in me, waiting for me to fuck up again.

A civil relationship with Scarlett could also be a benefit to both of us. It would make group hang out sessions less awkward and with both of our intelligence, we could create an outstanding project. If only she would let me in.

I finish preparing the vegetables, placing them in a pan for the stir-fry, grabbing some seasonings to add to the pot, loving the smell that wafts off them. This is what I need. Just me, the kitchen, and the smell of homemade chicken stir fry.

"Did you talk to her?" Miles shouts from the living room. At first I think he's talking to Xavier because he has no volume control, but he doesn't respond.

"Who?" I ask, turning down the heat on the food.

"Scarlett, you idiot," he replies.

"Oh. Yeah. We have to work together on a project for class."

Xavier and Miles laugh and when they come down from their hysterical laughter, Miles says, "Oh, I bet she's loving that."

There must be some sort of inside joke I'm missing. I get it. She doesn't like me. She's not necessarily my favourite person either when she's being mean to me. I know people pick up on our animosity, but I can't shake the feeling that there's something going on behind closed doors that I don't know about.

"Do you actually know why she doesn't like me, or what?" I ask, scratching the back of my neck, a nervous tick I have had since I was a kid that I haven't been able to get rid of.

"It's a mystery," Miles says dramatically, sighing. "Mostly,

I think she just doesn't like your face," he mutters, and I throw him an evil look, narrowing my eyes.

"Carry on, Davis, because I know a few ways to poison food," I retort.

"Hey! The food doesn't deserve that," Xavier adds in, and I roll my eyes. "Well, if it's completely necessary, poison Miles's food only."

I'm about to thank Xavier for his basic decency to not piss me off, but Miles interrupts. "Do you remember that time when Scar was dating Jake and they came over and she accidentally threw a beer can at you?"

It was not accidental at all. Based on the way she smiled at me afterwards, flipping me the bird as she drank from her cup, it was a planned and calculated move to piss me off. For whatever reason, that is not the part of the sentence that I caught on.

"I thought she didn't date," I say and the way I sound like I actually care is pathetic. I don't care if she dates or not because I know her reputation. It's typical of girls with her status. She meets someone, sleeps with them, and never sees them again. I've met Jake a few times and it still baffles me that she ever let that rat anywhere near her for longer than a one-night-stand.

"She doesn't," Miles says.

"But you just-"

"Anyway, she's a violent one," he says, cutting me off as he shovels popcorn into his mouth, still watching the TV. He swallows, dusting the crumbs off his shirt, adding, "I'd sleep with one eye open if I were you."

"I just don't get it," I mutter, turning off the cooker completely, rounding the wall into the living room, taking a seat across from them. "What is there not to like about me?"

Miles doesn't miss a beat as he says, "You think you're

better than everyone else." *That's because most times, I am.*
"You're always calling people out on their mistakes." *It's*
important to do so. "And you care too much about stupid
things like school and money."

I snort. "Miles, those are two very important things."

"See," he says, gesturing to me as he gets up, wandering
into the kitchen. "That's what I mean about you thinking you
know everything." Then he mumbles something about how
money and school won't matter when he's in the NHL.

Great.

So, I'm back at square one. I still don't know why Scarlett
doesn't like me and I don't know how I'm going to get her to
trust me and open up to me.

It's easy enough to use the project as a front to talk to her,
but she's stubborn enough as it is. I need to think of a plan, and
I need to think of one fast. Finding out what happened to her
dad needs to be my main priority.

If she cracks in the process, I can pick up the pieces
afterwards.

5

SCARLETT

IT'S all fun and games when you go to a party on a Thursday night, forgetting you have a lecture the next morning and you have to turn up hungover. It's already one thing to be hungover – my head is throbbing; my back is sore, and my thighs are aching for reasons it hurts too much to explain. It's another thing to be hungover *and* listen to Evan Branson talk shit all morning.

Friday morning lectures are the one time of the week where I decide to switch my brain off for two hours. It's the seminars where I am more interested in arguing with this fool, but today he's been trying to get on everyone's nerves for reasons I can't find. He's been arguing back and forth with the lecturer for the last five minutes about different marketing techniques that huge cities use to increase sales. It's a topic that interests me as much as a jar of peanut butter. A total snoozefest.

I'm not the only one who has had enough of his bullshit. Everyone in the room is sighing quietly, scribbling aimlessly and Evan doesn't seem to notice. Or maybe he does, and he just doesn't care. The old professor, one of the most experienced and interesting teachers we have on the course, is reluctantly trying to change the slides, but Evan doesn't give him a minute of leeway.

I finally try to put an end to it and raise my hand. "I actually have a question for Evan, if that's okay, professor," I say, a bored expression falling across my face. Evan turns around from his seat in the row below, the top of his cheeks a tiny shade of red, his green-ish-blue eyes rolling as he looks at me.

"Go ahead," the professor murmurs, probably giving up on teaching. I give him a sympathetic smile before locking my gaze with Evan's displeasing face.

"Is your head really that far up your ass that you think people will be dying to buy products just because a half-decent male is on the cover of a billboard?" I ask in the most serious tone I can muster. A few snickers scatter around the room and I cross my arms against my chest, titling my head to the side in challenge.

Despite the insult, he smirks. "It's classic. Old school. It's what works."

I scoff. "Yes, fifty years ago when you'd have to sell your lung to afford a cell phone. I don't know if you've noticed, but technology has advanced since then. And if your family's business knew that you'd be getting a lot more monthly sales than you are now."

It's a low blow and embarrassing to admit that I constantly check B&Co's statistics. They're almost too easy to access and sometimes when I'm having a bad day, it makes me feel better that they're also doing just as bad.

Evan opens his mouth to speak, his eyebrows knitted in confusion, but the lecturer cuts him off, shaking his head. "You make a valid point, Scarlett. What would you suggest is a better marketing tool?"

"That's easy," I say to him. "Video advertising. It's the best-"

"Of course," Evan mutters under his breath, cutting me off.

I roll my eyes. "Think about it for one second before cutting me off, you moron. You've already had your moment," I bite out. His eyes widen at the sharpness in my tone before another mischievous smirk spreads across his face. I swear he just loves to piss me off.

"Language," the professor warns.

I take in a deep breath. "Right. Sorry. All I'm saying is that no matter how annoying they can be, a good commercial, a funny one, draws people in more than a billboard you pass by on the way to your grandparent's house upstate. I'm sure everyone has those adverts from their childhood that they'll never forget. It's all about being memorable, something that'll draw you into a particular brand."

The room fills with hums of agreement, and I feel satisfied with my answer. Everyone except Evan seems to agree with my answer as he just frowns at me.

"And you don't think a billboard could do that? Be memorable, I mean," he argues, and I shake my head. "Not even with a naked man on the cover?"

"Something so in my face just puts me off more than anything," I say with a shudder, remembering the amount of posters and billboards I've seen with huge men on them. I can admit it draws you in, but not in the way you want to be drawn into a brand or product.

Evan tilts his head, leaning his forearms on the desk, the skin on his arms a golden and weirdly intriguing colour. He catches me looking at his arms and I snap my eyes up to his face. "You're telling me you wouldn't want to see Chris Evans in an underwear campaign on a huge poster that you could see from your apartment window?"

I actually laugh at that. "Of course, I would, but do I want to see his bulge when I'm having a bad day and it's right in my face? No way," I say, shaking my head again. I turn back to the professor, unable to look at his ridiculous face any longer. "I think some of us are forgetting that it's not always the size that matters."

TRYING to nurse a hangover with your two best friends hovering around you as they very loudly tell you about their day is the worst thing in the world. I've been trying to get some peace and quiet in our apartment for the last hour since I came back early from campus. I thought that hiding in my room would work, but these girls will find a way to find me and annoy me.

I'm snuggled under my covers in sweatpants and a tank top, planning to hibernate for the rest of the day while I mentally prepare myself for having to meet up with Evan at some point to get started on our project. Just the thought of it makes me pull the covers around my head tighter.

Kennedy yanks them off my head, sitting beside Wren at the end of my bed.

"How was your day then, Scar-Scar?" Kennedy asks me, her whole face lighting up at the nickname she knows I hate.

"Great, until you two came in here," I mutter, playing tug of war with Ken as she tries to pull the covers away from me. "You went out too last night. How are you not dead?"

She laughs, giving up on our fight. "Because I know how

to handle my drink," she says easily. I roll my eyes, jealous of her unique talent to constantly stay tipsy throughout the night and can only get drunk if she really *really* tries to. I, however, don't have that luck. And neither does Wren, which is why she stayed in with her boyfriend last night instead of coming out with us.

"You're coming to the game today, by the way," Wren says, her voice chipper as always as she stands off my bed, opening my closet.

"Am I?" I groan. I've gotten to the point where these girls make my decisions for me, and I just go along with them. I don't mind it for the most part, but going to hockey games stresses me out more than I enjoy it. The NU Bears are notorious for causing fights and always having some sort of drama with either their own team or whoever they're playing against.

"Yep," she says, popping the 'p' as she reaches into my closet and pulls out the practice jersey that her boyfriend so generously gifted to Kennedy and I so we could represent their team at the games. She throws the shirt at me. "It's only a friendly, but you know what Milesy's like. Every game counts."

"Fine," I say, not wanting to argue over it. Wren's face lights up when I agree, her cheeks turning the cutest shade of pink. If it means making her smile like that, I'd go to as many games as she wants me to. Plus, this also means I'll won't end up with a hundred texts from Miles asking why I didn't go to one of his games.

Her smile twitches into a frown and I crook an eyebrow. "And, uh, I think Evan's coming too. So, you know, prepare yourself."

The minor – and I mean *minor* – excitement I had about

going to the game completely dissipates. "Consider me prepared."

EVAN

You know it's bad when your friend gives you a two hour notice before letting you know that the only seats left in the small stadium are the ones with your rival and her friends. I'm trying to be a better 'friend' to Miles and Xavier, and they've been complaining that I don't go to their hockey games enough even though the season hasn't started properly.

I don't particularly like hockey games.

I don't understand it and I don't get why Greyson and Miles are constantly in and out of the penalty box like it's a personal game between the two of them. They're constantly fighting the other team, whilst Harry, the youngest one on the Bear's team, stands with his head in his hands, embarrassed. At least it's entertaining.

What they didn't prepare me for was how fucking sexy Scarlett would look.

I've always been attracted to her – I mean, I have eyes and I'm not a complete idiot – but it's always been her wonderful and complicated mind of hers that drew me in. But seeing her here in a NU Bear's training jersey, a blue cap on her head and her ponytail threaded through the back as she rocks the sexiest fucking leggings I've ever seen.

"If you look any longer, she's going to notice," Kennedy whispers. I don't think I fully register that Kennedy is sitting on one side of me while Wren, and Scarlett walking down the aisle to our seats until I hear her voice. I'll be honest, Kennedy scares me sometimes. She's always sneaking around, trying to push me and Scarlett into the same room, the same way she used to scheme to get Wren and Miles together before they started fully dating.

"I don't know what you're talking about," I mutter, turning to Kennedy. She narrows her brown eyes at me, and I notice the blue face paint she has on her cheek with Harry Butler's number nineteen on it. Weird.

"Yeah, sure you don't," she mocks, "you know, you could just-"

"Shhh," I say to her, cutting her off with a wave of my hand. "The game is starting."

Her eyebrows pull together in confusion as she glances to the ice and then back to me. "It's not."

I turn away from her as she sulks, crossing her arms against her chest and turning back to the ice. I feel bad for cutting her off, but she's up to something, or she knows something she shouldn't. And that fucking terrifies me. I know how close those girls are and if she caught me staring at her, she's going to think more of the very subtle looks I've been sending Scarlett.

She takes her seat next to me, her fresh and crisp smell reaching me. She doesn't even look at me as she says, "Branson."

"Scarlett," I greet, smirking to myself. I feel her gaze on me as I turn my head away from hers. It was only a few hours ago when she tripped me up in class, wanting to make a fool of me and like the idiot I can be, I let her.

"It's a pleasure as always," she says.

"I wish I could say the same," I murmur. I turn to her then, and I can see the way she's biting her cheek, trying not to laugh or smile. "I bet you're proud of yourself, huh?"

"Oh, extremely," she says, turning to me, a huge grin taking over her face. "You should have seen your face."

I grunt in response, dying to roll my eyes. "Has anyone ever told you how insufferable you are?"

"No, but you must really love to suffer then," she says.

I open my mouth, a witty comeback on the edge of my tongue, but the lights in the stadium dim and the blue lights light up the rink and everyone's attention is turned to the ice. As the players skate onto the ice, the student commentator announcing each player, the girls jump up out of their seats, cheering them on. It baffles me how easily Scarlett can switch from being a complete ass towards me and then becomes this loveable ball of energy when she's with her friends. Beats me.

For once, I let myself get engrossed in the game, desperately trying to understand the rules of the game. Miles and Harry both manage to get a few shots in, and Xavier too. They make it look so easy. So effortless. Either the other team is really shitty or they're just that good. I can see why it interests people so much – the chants, the music, the fighting, the celebrations. Something about watching a hockey game turns the least competitive people into complete animals and it's hilarious.

I watch Scarlett sulk and groan when the other team catch up in points with the Bear's and I hate myself for finding it so fucking adorable. The team finally gets back up in points as Miles scores a goal which seems humanly impossible.

When the shot lands, Wren jumps up from her seat, screaming and yelling like a complete mad woman. Miles sees her and points his hockey stick at her before making a heart with his hands. Kennedy lets out a dreamy sigh and Scarlett gags beside me.

When the second period ends with the teams tying, Kennedy and Wren talk across me as they converse over tactics I can't seem to understand. Scarlett must get the same out of place feeling I do because she jumps up from her seat, smoothing out her shirt.

"I'm going to get some snacks. Do you want some more popcorn, Ken?" she asks, and Kennedy shakes her head, still talking to Wren.

"I'll come," I say, standing up out of my seat too. She rolls her eyes at me, walking off without me, but I chase after her, almost tripping down the steps. How is she so fucking fast? I'm practically panting when I reach her, but by the time I get there, she's talking to a dark haired guy by the vending machine.

This is not how I saw this going. Really, I don't know why I said I'd come with her, but I also didn't want to sit in the middle of Wren and Kennedy's conversation either. Instead, I'm torturing myself, watching her openly flirt with this guy who hasn't stopped dropping his gaze to her chest when there's nothing really to see.

I try to tune out their conversation as I watch her fiddle with her ponytail, leaning against the vending machine. I hear the word flowers and a few other sickly sweet things that make my stomach turn. I can only imagine how she's looking at him as her back is to me. I know what she's like. She's a playgirl, she'll probably get his number, fuck him once and never speak to him again, but that doesn't make this whole thing any less painful.

When he's finally gone after giving her his number and she slips it into her pocket, I finally stand closer to her next to the vending machine. She doesn't even look at me as she punches in the code to get the snacks she wants.

"Are you seriously that easy to win over, Angel?" I mock as the machine whirs. "A few flowers and some sweet words are all it takes, huh?"

"Hm," she hums, picking up her chips from the bottom of the machine. She steps aside as she twists the packet in her hand. "Not really."

I scoff, punching in the code for some M&M's and push a few pennies into the machine. "Really? What more could you possibly want?"

"Flowers and sweet words are a nice start," she begins. The packet of chips opens with a pop as she adds, "Throw in a couple orgasms and I'll be good."

A lump in my throat forms at her words, but I style it out with a cough. "Oh, so still easy to get?"

She barks out a laugh as I pick up my M&M's. "You have a lot of faith in the male species, Branson. You'd be surprised how many boys our age have no idea what to do with their hands."

"I play piano," I blurt out. *What the fuck am I doing?*

Abort.

Abort.

Abort.

Don't talk about your hands when she just mentioned how guys can't get her off. What are you doing, you fool?

Her eyes connect with mine and my face feels like it's on fire. She seems unfazed, as always, and I probably look like a prepubescent teenager who has never spoken to another girl before in his life.

"I know," she whispers, almost to herself. Her eyes drop to my hands which are tight around the poor candy packet as my veins become clearer on my hands. My breathing quickens as she looks at them and then back to my face. Before I can question it, she starts to ramble. "I mean, I already knew. Greyson told me right after New Years. I was planning on using it against you. Well, that, and I could just tell. I mean, your hands are-"

"Scar!" Kennedy's voice booms as she appears out of thin air into the corridor. "They're fighting *again*. You're going to miss it."

She doesn't even say anything as she turns away from me and walks towards Kennedy, leaving me absolutely dumbfounded and dying to know what she was going to say. When Scarlett reaches her, Kennedy turns back and she fucking winks at me like this is a huge game.

Rambling is one of Scarlett's many annoying yet endearing traits, so I'm not surprised she was talking a lot. She does it all the time in seminars or lectures or when we get forced to hang out by our friends.

Today was the very first time she has ever rambled like that with me.

6

SCARLETT

USUALLY, hanging out with the girls is one of the things that can smooth out any tense feelings I have, but today it's not working. I shouldn't feel so on edge after one disastrous class with Evan, but I do. We argue all the time, that much isn't new. But we argue from afar, over stock prices and over who is reading the graphs wrong. Now, we actually have to have real conversations to make this project work. Craving academic validation has always been my weakness and I don't think I'll ever get out of it; this project is no different.

My mom thought it was just a phase that I'd grow out of, especially growing up with all brothers. When you grow up with four boys who get praised for pissing in the toilet bowl or for tying their shoelaces, you need to work extra hard to be noticed.

You'd think that since I'm the only girl, I'd get special treatment, but no. Instead, you realise more than ever that you're not special because your brothers could do everything that you do, when they were five years younger.

My mom thought that I just wanted to prove myself in a world where men dominate, but sometimes I think it's deeper than that.

I know my worth. I know I'm smart. I know I'm good at what I do. And I know I don't need a grade to determine that. But I've always had a strong relationship with numbers, so having it on paper helps. It makes it feel real. People can only assess your worth on what they see in stats.

Oh, she's got a clothing brand that sells thousands per week: perfect. *She has straight A's and a 4.0 GPA:* amazing. *She works and studies three hundred and sixty-five days a year, striving for that perfect A at the top of her report:* fan-fucking-tastic.

My friends think it's something that I will eventually grow out of when I finish college. Still, when I close my eyes, I can see myself, ten years from now, still wanting to pin my report card on the fridge.

Wren, Kennedy, and I have been sitting on the floor in our living room for the last hour, in our usual spots. Which means Kennedy is sitting in her bean bag next to the coffee table, Wren's back is against the sofa with her laptop in her lap, while I'm on my stomach next to her feet.

We have our own mini book club. Every time Wren writes a new chapter of her romance novel, "Stolen Kingdom", she reads it out loud to us.

She's become shy with her creative writing, even though she's been taking the course for over two years, as well as figure skating. I can tell that she's been in a slump since our friend Gigi got signed with one of the top publishing agencies in the Midwest. We've been trying to lift her up, hyping up every chapter, but I can tell something is wrong.

"Just stop getting in your head about it, Wrenny," I suggest, resting my hand on her knee reassuringly so it stops shaking. She nods, pulling her bottom lip between her teeth.

"I know. I know. I'm trying," she responds, staring at her laptop screen. Sometimes I think she's too hard on herself, always trying too hard, but she needs to realise how brilliant she is. Even when it's all we and her boyfriend tell her, but she can't get it into her head.

"Try digging deeper," I press. I know I sound harsh, but this girl is incredible if she'd realise it. Kennedy throws a hard candy at me, hitting me right in the back of my head. I flinch, rubbing that spot. "Hey! What was that for?"

"You're being mean, Scar. You're going to make her cry," Kennedy whispers as if Wren isn't sitting right there.

I snort. "Come on, Ken. She isn't going to cry. I'm just being honest," I say and Wren nods, smiling at me. I don't think I'd be able to cope if she cried right now. Kennedy gets up abruptly, the wrappers she had in the pouch she created with her shirt dropping to the floor as she does. "Where are you going?"

She shrieks as she runs down the corridor. "Stress-induced pee break!" she squeals. Wren and I laugh, knowing her and her bladder problems.

"You don't think I was being too harsh, do you?" I whisper, poking Wren in the knee. I've known her longer than I have known anyone in my life, and we've always worked like this. We met Kennedy in high school and since then we've been inseparable, but Wren and I have literally been glued to the hip since we were in diapers. "I'm not trying to sound like a bitch. I just care about you, and I know how happy writing makes you and I don't want you to lose that. You're an incredibly talented writer, Wren."

She turns to me, tears brimming her eyes. "Thank you, Scar. It's just a little hard right now, but I am trying."

"I know," I say back, squeezing her hand and she squeezes back. There is nothing that I want more than my friends' success. Especially Wren's. God knows she deserves it.

She nudges my knee. "What's going on with you? I haven't seen much of you since you left that party with that guy. What's his name? Charlie?" she quizzes, and I laugh at the change in subject. "He was cute."

"If you mean his dick size, sure," I mutter and she nudges me again, chuckling as she tucks her blonde hair behind her ears.

"Oh. So, small, I assume," she replies, nodding.

"*Tiny*."

She laughs again, shaking her head. "Yikes," she mutters. "I don't want to dick-shame, but if Miles' dick was smaller than it is, I don't think we'd be dating. It just wouldn't do the job."

The way this girl has grown in the last year shocks me. She would hardly ever speak openly about sex like this. Well, because she hadn't had much experience before dating Miles, but still, I find it funny.

"I know, right? I mean, not with Miles's dong, but in general. I just don't see how-" I start but I'm interrupted by Kennedy's loud entrance into the room, sitting down onto her beanbag.

"Okay, okay. Enough talk about penises. Two updates, go!" Kennedy says, pointing at the both of us.

We've been doing the 'Two Updates' game since freshman year where we have to give two updates on what our life has been like when we haven't been able to hang out. Most of the time, I'm out at some event, Kennedy is in the studio until late and Wren's at the rink. So, when there's a time we're all together, we have to give updates.

"I'll go first," Wren says, shutting her laptop and pushing it onto the coffee table. "Okay, so I got new skates from my mom as a pity gift for missing my birthday. Classic Hacks. And I got to use them while I went skating with Miles and his sister. Boring updates, but I've got a boring life now."

Wren sulks and we clap, like we always do. "Still great, Wrenny. Still great," I say, patting her arm. "My first update is that I got that Buelli painting I've been eyeing for a while. *But,* I have to work with Evan for our class project, so that's fantastic."

"There it is," Kennedy whistles, beaming at me. "You can't get through an update without mentioning him."

"I do not," I retort with a gasp.

"You do," Wren adds and Kennedy nods. "I still stand by what I said. I think you need a good fuck to get it out the way. Hate-sex is much better, according to my readers."

"The only thing Evan is getting from me is a slap to the face," I mutter, rolling my eyes. "Anyway, Kenny, what are your updates?"

She smiles wide, her lined dimples popping out. "You know that project I was stressing out about? As soon as you guys left, I cracked it and it's done. It's not perfect, but my teacher said it's probably going to be the best in the class. Not that it matters, of course, but it felt amazing. And I alsohadaonenightstand."

Her last few words blend together, not making sense as she pulls her hair into her face, a thing that she does when she's nervous. "Didn't quite get the end of that, babe."

She sighs, blowing her hair out of her face. "I had a one

night stand!" she shouts and mine and Wren's mouths hang open.

Kennedy does *not* do casual. Ever. Mostly because she doesn't date and gets the ick too easily. If she wants to be in a relationship, she'll be in one. She hates the uncertainty of situationships, so her sleeping with someone randomly is insane.

"Who?" Wren and I gawk at the same time, looking at each other and then back to Kennedy.

"I will neither deny nor confirm if it was someone from the hockey team," she whispers. Wren's hand goes to her chest dramatically.

"Kennedy, you wouldn't," she mutters and then Kennedy very slightly, it's barely noticeable, but she nods, and we both know who it was.

Harry Butler, the guy she's been on and off with since the start of this year. They never actually dated, but after a kiss during a game of seven minutes in heaven, I'm sure they're not strictly best friends, as much as Ken likes to hide it.

"We were both sad and emotional and he was there, and I kissed him, and he felt good and the next thing I knew we were naked," she explains, doing a poor job at trying to hide her blush.

"Oh, my fucking God, Ken," I whisper.

"I know," she mutters back. "It's terrible. But we're just friends, so it's never going to happen again."

"Just friends, huh?" Wren mocks. Kennedy tries to nod, showing that she's telling the truth, but the way her face looks like it's radiating heat is enough of a giveaway.

Wren tackles her to the ground, pestering her with excited questions and I'm about to join in, but my phone lights up with a text.

> **UNKNOWN:** Hey, we should meet up soon to start working on the project.

My heartbeat triples in pace. Evan and I never text. If I ever needed to contact him, I've only done it through Miles or if I'm desperate, it's through Instagram. I don't like the thought of him having my number. It feels like we're crossing some sort of invisible line. The kind of line that has been put up for several reasons.

> **ME:** How did you get my number, u weirdo?

> **EVAN:** Miles gave it to me under strict conditions.

> **ME:** Which are....?

> **EVAN:** Not to piss you off because then you'll tell Wren and Wren will tell Miles and Miles will tell me and I'll never hear the end of it.

Huh. I'll have to give Miles some brownie points for that one. Even when I was fooling around with his dickwad of a teammate, Jake, Miles was the only one I could tolerate, which is why I'm glad Wren is dating him.

> **ME:** And how well is that working out for u so far?

> **EVAN:** You're still texting me, so I'd say pretty well.

I *almost* cracked a smile.

Apparently, he's more bearable over text, which is probably because I can't see his smug face and I can have more than five seconds to think of a reply. Being in his presence makes me nervous and not in a good way. But texting him feels easy. Easier to insult. Easier to talk to. It's a win-win.

The girls must have caught onto whatever stupid grin is on my face because they've stopped the interrogation and they're both staring at me. I raise my eyebrows at them.

"Who are *you* texting?" Kennedy asks, leaning over to look at my phone and I let her have a peek.

"Evan," I say, grimacing.

"And he's making you laugh," Wren mentions, tilting her head to the side.

"Yeah, at his stupidity," I retort.

"*Riiiight,*" the girls say in unison, sounding like Kronk from *'The Emperor's New Groove.'* I get up, interrupting their overanalyses of a stupid half-smile that doesn't mean anything.

"I've got to go. I need to go see my mom," I say, brushing off my long skirt, readjusting my white top.

"If you're going to meet Evan, you can tell us," Wren says quietly. "We don't hate him as much as you do."

They don't have a reason to. When they met him, he was his charming self that he puts up when they're around. Opposite to our first interaction.

I KNOW that every time I walk into my house, my mom is going to be on some sort of new rant. I don't know why I get surprised anymore. This time, she's going on about how she won't know what to do if my dad doesn't pull through: immediately going to the worst case scenario. My dad will pull through. He has to.

My parents had the picture-perfect wedding, all five of

their kids being able to attend. I had only just learnt to walk, so I was a little wobbly going down the aisle in the pictures, but there is no doubt that my parents are so sickly in love with each other. You'd think that after twenty years of marriage and thirty-five years of being together, they'd dial it down, but no. They remind me of a modern day Morticia and Gomez Addams, constantly all over each other, never being afraid to show off their love to us kids.

That's why it hits so hard that my dad isn't here to be the rock for my mom. She is an independent woman, and she always has been, but there's a certain light in her eyes that can only be lit by my dad. She has been with my dad before *Voss* got popular and that grounded both of them, knowing that they always chose each other, no matter what.

As the brand grew from clothing into designer accessories, you start to realise that the numbers on the spreadsheets you come across in your parents' bedroom aren't just little figures. The dollar sign means power and not everyone knows what to do with that kind of power.

My dad never lied to us about our competitors, and as a business student now, I know how important competition is, but I didn't realise the dirty truths behind why some companies are so desperate to take the other down.

"You need to stop worrying, mom," I say, stopping her pacing as she stalks around the coffee table in the living room. I guide her into her favourite plush violet chair, letting her settle in it before taking a seat across from her. "Gio is going to be there *if* things fall through. Which they won't because dad is the strongest person I know."

The mention of my uncle soothes her somehow and she nods, tapping her foot rhythmically. "Can I worry about you instead?"

"Why would you need to worry about me?" I laugh.

"Because you don't have a partner yet," she says, sounding genuinely frightened that I won't ever settle down. I'm twenty, for God's sake. I do not need to be settling down. She adds with a pout, "Even Henry has a girlfriend."

"Yeah, because he's a manwhore," I say through another laugh.

"Don't call your brother a manwhore."

"It's true," I mutter, and she swats me on the arm. Honestly, I've called Hen a manwhore to his face and he just laughed at me, telling me he's going to use that insult in the future and thanked me for my service. My mom doesn't seem so happy about it though. Her deep brown brows are furrowed and she's gnawing at her bottom lip. "I'm fine, mom. I don't need a relationship right now. Dad's not here and you're doing okay, I think I can manage."

She sighs deeply. "Yes, because I have years of marriage to fall back on. Don't you want someone to take care of you? The same way me and your dad look out for each other. The way he took care of me when I was going through chemo."

The mentions of my mom's battle with cancer sends a dagger straight through my heart. Those two years were probably the worst two years of my life, watching my mom slowly fade away while I couldn't do anything to help. But she pulled through. She always does. And she's been cancer-free for almost two years now.

"I don't need someone to look after me, mom. I have you, dad, myself and four brothers to do that," I say proudly, holding up my chin.

"Scarlett, my love, we're going in circles here." I've been playing this game for too long, so I just smile, letting her project all of her worries onto me if it distracts her from thinking about my dad. For a minute, it distracts me too.

7

EVAN

IT ONLY TOOK my dad twenty-four-hours to call me asking for an update on the situation with Scarlett after the game, even though we just started working together on the project. Well, 'working together' is a bit of a stretch. It's more of us sitting in silence so we don't piss the other one off.

My dad has given me nothing to work with, meaning I have to coax some starting information out of Scarlett when I get the opportunity.

All I know is that her dad, Mateo, has been in the hospital for a few weeks now in an intense coma, meaning he's been hooked up to machines to keep him alive. It's worrying for both of our businesses since he is the head of *Voss* and right before he fell ill, there were a few dodgy articles about the business and a new drug called Tinzin that had been linked to the Voss' clothing and accessories.

It alarmed both of our companies because even though we sometimes play dirty, drugs and smuggling are something we don't mess around with. *Ever*. It's too much of a coincidence that he suddenly can't speak on the matter the second that it starts to gain more popularity in the press.

Scarlett and I are sitting in the school library in one of the collaborative study sections on a long brown bench. There are not many people in this section as people prefer the silent study zones. She's sitting across from me, her posture scarily straight, her deep brown hair slicked straight down her back, with one of those black ribbons in her hair tying half of it back. She always has one of those and I can't figure out why. Is she secretly a ballerina or some shit? Because considering her basic outfit choices, the ribbon that she sports and her posture, I would not have pegged her for a business student. Obviously, the *Prada* loafers say otherwise.

We've been sitting in this uncomfortable silence for almost half an hour. I've tried to concentrate on the homework I've needed to finish up for most of that time, but I've been spending my free seconds glancing up at her instead. I don't think she's looked at me once since we've sat down.

"Are you going to read the textbooks or just stare?" she asks, not looking up from her laptop.

"As much as you think I'm annoying, I think the same about you," I say, because two can play that game.

"Awh thanks," she says, finally looking up at me.

Maybe it was better when she was looking down because now she's got one of those fake smiles plastered across her face, those hazel eyes staring straight at me.

"Wasn't a compliment."

"Sure, it wasn't, big guy," she replies, looking back down at the laptop. She huffs, typing angrily. "How long is it going to take you to do your homework? You always hand it in early."

"Didn't know you paid such close attention to me," I say back, tilting my head.

"I don't," she retorts, looking up again and holding my stare. "I only know because Anderson doesn't let me hear the end of it when you hand in your work before me."

I always hand my work in early. It takes off the stress of trying to rush it before the deadline. I'm a mess as it is, I don't need unnecessary anxiety about deadlines and grades on top of that.

"I've just got a lot going on right now. So, excuse me if it takes me a little longer to finish my work before starting on the project. I was being serious when I said my grades have slipped," I admit, finally finishing the sheet I've been staring at for nearly a week. I shove it away into one of my textbooks, glad that I don't have to look at it anymore.

"Oh," she says, closing her laptop. Unlike the aggressive texting, she gently closes it, looking up at me. "Is the last assignment why you're stressed? Everyone was raging about it, but I finished it last week and it wasn't too much trouble. Maybe you're losing your touch." She shrugs innocently, glancing around the room. If I knew any better, I'd think that was her trying to be nice. She has an annoying tendency to talk too much to anyone.

But I don't know any better, so I smile.

Big mistake. Because our eyes connect and when she sees the grin on my face the faint, barely-even-there sort of smile on her lips fades and she presses her mouth into a thin line, rolling in her pink lips.

"Thanks for the concern, but I'm fine. It's just family stuff. You can understand that, can't you?" I say and I know I hit a nerve when her body goes rigid. Her hands freeze for a few seconds before she clears her throat and continues to write something down. "Oh, come on, Angel. You can drop the act and stop pretending you don't know."

We've never openly discussed what has happened with her dad. Not many people were supposed to know about Tinzin-gate and if you do, you clearly have a bias.

My family thinks it was Mateo, using the coma to cover up the smuggling, while others in the company continue supplying it, hoping that when he wakes up everyone has forgotten about it. I'm sure her family don't think it was him. Especially with the big Papa-Bear energy he gives off, you wouldn't suspect him. I've seen him squeal like a little kid before, but if it's not him, then who could it be?

Scarlett keeps her gaze on her paper, not looking up at me. I almost miss the way she mutters, "So what if I know? It doesn't mean anything."

Good. At least she's talking. I lean further in, ensuring that there is no one else nearby. Most of the people in here are zoned out with headphones on and wouldn't be disturbed even if the fire alarm went off. "I'm not going to tell anyone. If that's what you're worried about."

She drops her pencil, folding her arms across her chest against the thin black top she's wearing. "I'm not worried about that." But from the shift in her body language, there's something else that she's not sharing.

"Then what's your problem?" I ask.

"Nothing," she says, sighing as she drops her arms from her chest, fiddling with the sheet of paper. I know we've spent the better half of two years verbally attacking each other, but I can tell that talking about her family is a vulnerable thing and I almost feel bad. *Almost.* "You're just going to think I'm crazy."

I snort. "I already think you're crazy, Angel."

"Gee, thanks," she mutters, adding, "Why am I even talking to you about this?"

"Scarlett," I press. The use of her full makes her freeze up. I hardly ever say it, but from the way that she is about to deflect, I need to draw her back to the conversation.

Just keep her talking, Evan.

"Listen, I'm only telling you this because none of my friends would understand and it's all hypothetical anyway. Just a hunch," she begins, pinning me with a defiant stare and I nod. "I don't think my dad getting 'sick' was an accident. I don't know how I'm going to prove it since I have no evidence, but I need to find out what happened. It's probably nothing, but I can't let it go."

She's confirming what I thought I knew. The Voss' don't think it's an accident either, but they don't know if it was self-inflicted or if someone purposely poisoned him.

"And you have no leads?" I ask.

She shakes her head. "None." When I don't say anything, she blinks at me before her face becomes panicked, her eyes widening. "What? What do you know?"

"Nothing. I swear," I say quickly and I'm telling the truth. I'm having to figure this out alongside her. "But, you know how this looks, right?"

"Yeah, I know," she says, almost frustrated as she groans. "But it wasn't him. I *know* it wasn't him. He would never try to put our family and his business at risk."

"Are you sure?" I ask.

"What are you getting at, Branson? My dad is a good guy and he's a lot nicer than yours. So don't try and act like he isn't."

God, she's so defensive about her family. I love my family

too. I'm protective over them when I feel like it, but, the truth is, we haven't felt like a family in years.

After my mom left and it became just me and my dad, everything just felt.... cold. Nothing has felt like the warmth that my mom had. Where everything just felt okay and I didn't have the heavy darkness is my chest, constantly weighing me down.

"I- I wasn't. I was just-" I sigh, shaking my head. With the pointed look she sends me, that wasn't going to get me anywhere. "Forget it. We should start to get to work on this."

"Yeah. Forget I said anything," she mumbles, opening her laptop again.

"Great."

"Good."

"Perfect."

"Fan-" She hits the key on her laptop extra hard. "-Tastic."

Jesus, this woman is going to be the death of me.

We get through an hour of being in each other's presence without screaming at each other. This is a good start. At least now what I already thought has been confirmed and I feel a little less on edge. Still, I need more. We manage to brainstorm a few ideas for the project, disagreeing on most things, until she calls it a day and I'm grateful to have some alone time to think of a plan.

Should be easy, right?

8

SCARLETT

THE START of the school year always ends in a series of stupid decisions for me. It's something I can't get rid of. It's almost like a canon event that has to happen or else the rest of the year will turn to shit. Well, either way, it will turn to shit.

At the start of first year, I was the only person in my class to turn up in a pantsuit, believing it was smart to look my best. Of course, when Branson wears a suit every day, everybody thinks it's hot, but when I do it, I'm trying too hard.

Then I realised how easy college boys are. Like, a little too easy. Then I dated Jake, finding solace in warm bodies instead of being alone.

Then, in our sophomore year Evan and I's competition went off the scales. Every lesson turned into an aggressive board meeting and after the *Christmas 2021 Incident*, where I revealed that I had sex with someone in our classroom as part of truth or dare, I don't think he's looked me in the eye since then. And now this year, my dad is in the hospital and I'm stuck working with Branson for the project, which I'm already anticipating will be months of torture.

See? Canon events of stupidity.

After spending the last few nights tossing and turning about what could have happened with my dad, I was relieved when my uncle Gio called me. I'm hoping that seeing him will give me some peace of mind; he usually does.

Growing up, as the business has always been a family thing, I got to see the different perspective that Gio brought to *Voss*. While my dad's ideas were typically old-fashioned and he was stubborn in accepting new ones, Gio always managed to persuade my dad into new additions whether that be on the website, promotional advertisements, or the actual clothing.

Unlike many members of the team, Gio actually went to college, gaining a degree as an economist and in design and technology before joining *Voss*. Even though my dad would freak out if he knew, some of the ideas Gio has pitched have actually come from me too. It's not that my dad doesn't think I'm smart enough or capable to get involved, he just wants to keep me safe and there are lots of risks with joining a multi-million dollar business like ours. So, I keep my designs and plans to myself, waiting for the opportunity after I graduate to finally show my dad what I'm worth.

Gio and I have always been close. While the boys and my dad had a strong relationship, I gravitated more towards Gio. He always listened to me and took the time to get to know me. He understands what it's like to be the youngest sibling in a family full of entrepreneurs and surrounded by insane amounts of money. We got even closer when his wife, Sara and their good friend Lucas died in a plane accident, which inevitably led to bad press for *Voss* with rumours speculating that Lucas and Sara were having an affair.

After losing Sara three years ago, Gio submerged himself into working closer with the business and brought about new changes in honour of his late wife. It's been a tough journey for all of us, but that's why I need to go and see him today. We've not spoken much about what has happened with my dad, but after talking to Evan, finally vocalising my fears out loud, I realise that I'm ready to dive into this. Whatever *this* is.

I walk up to Gio's front door, taking in the surroundings of his secluded modern home in the mountains. He moved out here after Sara's passing and the piece of land he has for himself here is gorgeous. The house gives off a natural, woodsy vibe and a gallery-like aesthetic on the inside, unable to tell if it looks straight out of a horror film or a cute family vacation home.

I knock twice and it takes all but five seconds for Gio to pull me inside, dead bolting the door behind me. He's only a few inches taller than me, still a lot shorter than my dad. His face is rough around the edges, his olive skin a little paler, as the trees around this house hardly let any sun in. He's been growing out a rugged beard over the last few weeks and he resembles Bruno from the movie *'Encanto'* with his shoulder length dark brown curly hair.

"Jeez," I mutter when he spins me around, walking us over to his huge kitchen. "Someone is in a rush today."

He basically pushes me into the high, white glossy stool that rests next to his breakfast bar, and I hoist myself up onto it as he rounds the island, closing the blinds on the kitchen window.

It's only then that I realise that his house is practically in darkness. Where the light usually shines from the floor to ceiling windows, it's blocked out by thick black curtains. I notice the record player in the corner of the open living room which usually plays 50's and 60's Italian music is cut off, records lining up behind it. Just looking at the lifelessness in here makes me shiver.

"What's going on?" I ask. Gio tenses, turning around from the blinds and leaning down on the breakfast table, pulling up his long sleeved shirt to display his sleeve of tattoos, most of them that match with my dad and Lucas.

"Did they follow you up here?" he asks.

"Who?"

"The press. They've been hot on my heels for weeks," he murmurs, pulling up two glasses from the cabinet beneath the island. "Want a drink?"

He reaches for a bottle of whiskey, pouring some into one glass. "Just juice, please." He nods, opening the fridge to pull out my favourite tropical juice. "What's going on, G?"

Gio sighs again and it sounds a little shaky this time as he pours the juice into my glass, pushing it towards me. "I don't know. I've just had the feeling I'm being watched all week. I took the plane to LAX on Monday and when I landed, there were reporters everywhere, bugging me with questions."

There are always reporters when it comes to my dad and Gio, so I'm not surprised. Especially in California, since that is where HQ is. I've lived in Salt Lake my whole life, but the boys had to live in LA for a few years before I was born. My mom says we moved to get away from the busy and non-private lifestyle. Still, there is an odd reporter here or there when we go out as a family here.

It's definitely better here, it's quieter and I get recognised less. But when I join them on business trips to LA, it's hell. They like the drama there way more than they do here. There are a million different things to do and a million different scandals to get caught up in. But when I'm here, I feel safer.

"What were they asking? Was it about dad?" I quiz, taking a sip of my drink, loving the familiar taste.

"Yes," he confirms, pausing as he glances back to the closed blinds and then back at me. "Scarlett, *tesoro*, I don't know what to tell you." He takes in a deep breath, running a hand through his hair. "Something doesn't feel right. It hasn't felt right for a long time."

My whole body goes rigid. The more I hear my family addressing it out loud, it makes it seem more real. As if this isn't something I've just made up in my head but a real, possibly life-threatening thing that is going to affect us.

"Do you mean about the whole thing with Tinzin?" I ask, whispering the last word as if we're talking about Voldemort. "Because we don't actually know anything about it, do we? It's all speculation. A coincidence that it somehow traced back to *Voss,* right?"

He shakes his head, not in a way of disagreeing, but almost in a way to shake his head of the thought. As if there is something I'm completely missing. "It's probably nothing, *amore*," he says. If it's stressing him out this much, it can't be nothing.

"G, you can tell me. I'm not like Arthur. I'm not going to narc. I just want to understand the situation better. You know how it feels to be out of the loop," I say, playing the youngest sibling card that gets him every time. I watch as his features soften, his jaw unclenching as he leans against the sink, arms dropped to his sides.

"Like I said, it's probably nothing," he says, trying to downplay it again and I raise my eyebrow, urging him to continue. "When I was at HQ, I heard a few of the shipping managers discussing the next import for solitaire diamond pendants and where they were getting it from just didn't seem right to me. We always, and I mean, *always*, use imports from

Canada or Botswana that are ethically sourced. We never get local imports. As much as it would be better for the small businesses, we don't do that with the diamonds. It's just not the way things are done."

I blink at him, trying to make sense of it. "So, these shipping managers were thinking of getting it from somewhere else?" He nods. "Why is this a problem? Aren't they just changing it up a little? It would be better for the small businesses, no?"

"I have never seen those shipping managers before in my life, Scarlett," he explains, and it sounds like a punch to the stomach. This is not good at all. God, I think I'm going to be sick. "When I asked them who signed them on, they said it was from Mateo. I checked the records, and they were right. They were signed the day before he went into the hospital."

"Oh my god," I mutter. "What do you think they were doing? I mean, isn't it always better to have the best product for us to sell?"

"Yes, of course. That's what worried me. They said Mateo gave them the orders, but he and I never spoke about it. It's making me wonder if I was spaced out during the meetings. If maybe I was in on this too and I've just forgotten. The store name sounded too familiar for me to have never heard of it before," he explains.

"Which store?"

"'Julia's' in Provo. Almost an hour from here," he says before shaking his head again, looking at the ground. "Like I said, Scarlett, it's all speculation. You know how hard it's been for me. I wouldn't be insulted if you thought I was going a little bit crazy. Maybe this was the plan for this rota, and I just missed out."

"I don't think you're going crazy, G," I say quickly. "You're the furthest away from that. I believe you."

He looks up at me, a small smile on his lips. "Don't tell your brothers about this yet, okay? I need to figure out a few things before I talk to your mom too," he warns, and I nod. I would never tell them anything. Henry, maybe. But Arthur has been an uptight prick since Alex left and Leo's too high to care. "We're going to figure out what happened to your dad, Scarlett. I promise you."

"I know," I say, and I believe him because one way or another, I'm going to figure it out. I have to. I need to. I've been second best to everyone my whole life, if I can figure this out, they'll finally see how special I am.

WHEN I WALK OUT of Gio's house a few hours later, taking the long route down to my black Lamborghini Urus, I pull out my phone, texting the group chat with the girls in it. They don't know much about what is going on with my family, other than my suspicions with my dad's hospitalisation. I'm sure they've picked up on the true crime documentaries I've been watching recently too.

Maybe that's why I swear I hear a branch snap from a nearby tree. My brain tells me that someone is here, lurking somewhere. Watching. But my heart tells me that isn't true. If I can tell myself over and over that it will be fine, I'll start to believe it. I know I will. I take a quick look around and it's all woods. No one is coming for me. I'm safe.

I glance back down at my phone.

STARBUCKS LOVERS

> ME: OMG. Guys. I feel like I'm in an episode of HTGAWM!!

> KEN: Who did you kill?

> ME: No one. Jesus, Ken. Just LOTS of family drama. Wanna come investigate?

> KEN: Can't. Shelbia has us under a ball and chain.

> ME: Boooo. What about Wrenny?

> KEN: Dunno. Check her location.

WHEN I'M STRAPPED into my car, driving the twenty minute drive from Gio's house to our apartment near campus, I hook my phone up to the speaker, double checking Wren's location. She's at home, which means I'll be able to coax her into coming with me to stakeout the store. I know Gio didn't tell me to go, but he also didn't tell me *not* to go so...I'm going to go.

Wren answers on the fifth ring.

"Wren!" I basically squeal when the call connects, stopping at the stop sign. "Oh my god, you're not going to believe this."

"What is it?" she asks. She's breathing really fast and hard, like she sprinted up the stairs instead of taking the elevator. Weird. But I'm too excited, so I continue.

"You know when I was saying that I hoped the stuff with my dad could turn into a real mystery? Well, I think it just has," I say, my voice an octave higher than usual.

"*Oh,*" she says. Strange. She takes in another deep breath. "That's- That's really great, Scar."

This time I don't jump at the chance to speak and that's when I hear it. The rhythmic sound of squeaking followed by the sound of thumping like something is banging against a hard surface. No way...

No.

Way.

"Wren, darling?" I ask sweetly, smirking when I get a sharp inhale as a response.

"Mm hm?"

"Are you having sex right now?"

"*No,*" she cries, and it sounds awfully similar to a moan. She's panting harder now. "Of course, I'm not...*Fuck,* Mi-"

Anddd, that's my que.

I end the call, shuddering. Unfortunately, that is not the first time this has happened. She'll deny it every time, but I'm not that stupid.

I'm happy though; she's really grown into herself this past year and I love to see it. I'm still smiling when I pull into my parking space outside the apartment, hoping that they've finished so I can grab my friend and take her on this adventure.

My smile drops when I get to my apartment door. Not only can I still hear the bed hitting the wall, but Evan is also standing outside my door.

He's dressed in his usual attire; black dress pants, a crisp white shirt and a black tie hanging lazily from his neck. It's never actually tied and it pisses me off every time. If you're going to wear a tie, *tie it.* I can't tell if he enjoys dressing like he goes to a private prep school or if this is his only choice in outfit. Either way, it's ridiculous. Almost as ridiculous as him standing outside the door, ankles crossed, and his hands shoved into his pockets.

He's been here a few times since our Friendsmas meal that he was invited to by proxy and countless game nights that bring out the worst in us.

He's not said anything since I appeared in front of him, just staring because apparently that's his thing now. Great.

I cross my arms against my chest, raising an eyebrow at him.

"What are you doing, you perv?" I ask, nodding to my apartment door, which is basically shaking at this point. I swear, they are absolute animals.

"What?" he gasps, blinking at me. Then the realisation dawns on him as he sighs. "Oh. 'Cause they're...Yeah. It's worse at my house. Try sharing a wall with Miles' room and you learn to tune them out."

"What are you doing here?" I ask again.

"Waiting for you, obviously," he says and my chest pinches. I hate feeling so nervous around him. He has no reason to make me feel like he can see just straight through me. Like every thought in my brain is just on display for him to have a pick at.

"Why?"

He groans, rubbing the back of his neck. "For the project... Why else would I be here?"

I tilt my head. "Oh, so you're not here to listen to our friends have sex? I totally misread the situation," I say in a mocking tone, loving the way his eyebrows pinch together.

He pinches the bridge of his nose with his thumb and fore-finger, sighing. "Miles is hardly my friend," is his pathetic excuse.

I snort because I can imagine the argument they would get into if Miles could hear him right now.

Miles Davis is friends with everybody. He's been living with Evan for almost three years, I'm sure he would be insulted if he heard this blasphemy.

"I saw the pictures he posted from Wren's birthday. And in case you're forgetting, I was there too. So, the memory is forever etched into my brain." Then, making my voice sound extra sweet, I add, "The matching outfits were cute."

It was Wren's 20th birthday in June, and we all had to come in matching outfits. Wren, Kennedy, and I came as the Chippettes while Evan, Miles and Grey went as Alvin and the Chipmunks. I almost peed myself laughing at Evan in a blue shirt, glasses and freckles scattered across his nose.

"It was Miles's idea, not mine," he mumbles.

"And yet, you let him," I retort. He's got to drop this grump act. His roommates can be annoying, but I know he loves them deep down. I shift my weight from one foot to the other, not sure what to say now the small talk has died down.

When I look up, his eyes are still on me, and I can't stop the words that come out of my mouth. It's either this or interrupting my best friend doing *it* with her boyfriend.

"Wanna help me with this mystery?"

His eyes practically light up. Well, I think so. I'm still undecided if his eyes are blue or green. Still, his features smooth out a little as his eyes widen. "You got a lead?"

I shrug. "Sort of. Let's go."

9

EVAN

WHEN I TURNED up outside of Scarlett's apartment, I wasn't going there to work on the project. I actually don't know why I was there.

I asked Charles to take me for a ride around the city to clear my head and it was either going there or going to my dad's house. As soon as I remembered that Miles was there, I realised that I'd be better off waiting outside. Still, I don't know why I was shocked that she turned up as if she doesn't live there. I definitely wasn't expecting her to have a lead.

Well, from what she explained and her uncle Gio's explanation, it could be nothing. They think that something is going on with the imports of diamonds from a local dealer which is not what they have been doing for years.

Just finding out that alone is more than I need to know. It feels dirty knowing these things as a Branson. We never trade secrets like these, but I can tell that she needs help in some way and I'm going to give it to her. I knew I hit a nerve asking her about it during our study session, but it seems to have broken down a piece of a wall that she's had up for years.

Obviously, because she's a Voss, she has the coolest fucking car. I'm a guy. I can admit when a car looks good, even if the person driving it drives me insane.

She has a black Lamborghini Urus with red stitched seats. *Red,* I thought, *like her name.* It's beautiful. It has been on my car wishlist for a few years, but I didn't want to invest in one since I don't drive as often as I should, and my Range Rover is collecting dust in the garage.

I know I wanted to admire it, but since she explained the situation on the elevator ride down and since we got into the car, she's not said a word. She's been staring out at the parking lot and I'm pretty sure she's spaced out.

"Are you going to drive or what?" I press, looking at her and then the empty parking lot.

"I don't know yet," she whispers.

I sigh, unbuttoning another button on my shirt. Why do I suddenly feel nervous? I take another deep breath. "What do you mean you don't know? You know where we're going, don't you?

"Yes, I'm not an idiot," she murmurs, looking at me now, those brown eyes piercing me with a look so fierce it could cut glass.

"Okay...? Then what's the problem?" I ask again, looking out into the near darkness. It's getting close to 8PM. "I don't want to get there when it's too late."

She turns away from me, facing the steering wheel while she shakes out her hands as if she's about to run a marathon, twisting her neck to the side. "I don't know," she groans as if it's my fault. "I'm too excited or nervous. Or both. I can't sit still."

God, does she want to find out what happened or what?

"Then get out," I demand. She turns back to me, eyes wide.

"What?"

"Let me drive. Move seats," I explain. If she's not going to get us to where we need to be, I'm going to have to be the one to do it. Trying to contact Charles is not an option. You try hiding an Escalade outside a random shop in Provo and see if you don't get caught.

She throws her hair over her shoulder. "Branson, I *hope* you take this the wrong way, but I've never seen you control a vehicle a day in my life. You're always being chauffeured around everywhere like some sort of fucking prince. What makes you think I'm going to let you drive my car?"

I huff. "Why are you making this difficult?"

"Because I don't trust you to drive my car. Do you know how much this thing costs?" she says, gesturing to the gorgeous car.

I roll my eyes. "I have a licence and I have never had a ticket or any type of violation in my life. If you're not going to drive, let me do it. We're wasting time. If I crash it – which I won't – I'll just buy you a new one. You know I can afford at least three of these."

She considers it for a second, pulling her full bottom lip between her teeth. "Fine," she says finally, unbuckling her seatbelt. "But be kind to *Bellezza Nera*."

I don't know why her Italian catches me off guard. It shouldn't. Especially when I've heard her speak it a million times, but here, in this dark and confined setting of this car, the way she rolls the 'r' almost makes it sound filthy.

Jesus.

If I'm getting turned on by Scarlett Voss speaking Italian, I *really* need to get laid.

She lets me take over her seat, switching around to the other side, settling in the passenger seat, one leg hanging down and the other pulled up to her chin. How in the world is she comfortable like that? I flick my attention from her and to the road, following the instructions that the GPS has set up.

Unlike most people I know, Scarlett doesn't change the music ten times before settling on one song. She knows exactly what she wants and settles on a playlist and the first song that plays is '*Sweet Disposition*' by The Temper Trap. It's not a bad song, but it could have been better. The only upside to this is that she's relaxed more now, and she doesn't look like she's about to bolt out of the door or stare into space.

We drive mostly in silence as the playlist continues to play more songs, similar to the one that played first.

When we get to the street in Provo, as I imagined, it's mostly deserted. It's never extremely busy here, but there is the odd person wandering around as all the buzz lies within the bar at the corner. It's lively down there, loud cheers and music playing, but from where we need to be, the lights on the stores are the only thing keeping it lit. There's a laundromat, a record shop, then the jewellery store, Julia's, wedged between an antique store and a convenience store.

We park in a side alley, giving us a side view into the shop because of the way the streets have been designed. It would be too obvious if we parked on the main road, so this is our best shot. The store looks normal from here, a typical white, sterile looking place with a silver sign. It must be close to closing time now because there's only one person behind the till, sitting on their phone.

"Are we going to go in?" I ask Scarlett as she stares out of her window at the shop.

"No," she replies, her voice quiet.

"So, now what do we do?"

"We wait, obviously."

Wait for what? I don't know, but I'm terrified to ask any questions because she'll either get angry at me or start to freak out again and I can't deal with either of those things right now.

She's still staring out the window and I'm still staring at her, and I can't fucking move my eyes.

Okay, I have a problem.

Not like that.

Sometimes, when I get too in my head, (which is often) I stare. Not because something is particularly fascinating or drawing my attention. I just need something to focus on so my brain can just shut up for two minutes. Most of the time I'm aware I'm staring, and I probably look insane and even when I tell my eyes to move I just... Can't.

My therapist calls it 'compulsive staring' as part of my OCD diagnosis, but I hate the label and I just let people comment on it the way they want. There is no use trying to explain it to people who wouldn't understand.

But this time feels different. Most times I space out and I don't actually know what I'm staring at, but this time I do.

It's her and *only* her.

It's her long dark brown, slightly curly hair and that fucking ribbon that she always wears. It ties up half of her hair in a cute bow and it makes her whole look seem innocent. It drives me crazy every time I look at it because it draws people into this false innocence. But she is the furthest thing from that. She's lethal and dangerous and-

"Any theories?" she asks, still looking out the window. I shake my head, averting my eyes to the steering wheel in front of me. Could she sense my eyes on her? God, I hope not. I clear my throat.

"What?" I croak out.

"What do you think is going to happen? I can't sit here in

silence, Branson," she explains. I don't know how long I was spaced out for, but I'm surprised she didn't fill that with her talking. She talks a lot. A lot of it is nonsense. But it's a lot.

"I never said you had to," I whisper, picking at the cuffs on my shirt.

"Well, it didn't look like you were starting a conversation anytime soon," she murmurs with that sarcastic undertone that makes me want to shake her shoulders.

"Do you always give this much attitude?"

"Do you always say the most stupid things?" She turns to me now, raising an eyebrow. I narrow my eyes at her, not sure what to say and she backs down with a smirk, turning back to face the store. "Just tell me a theory."

I sigh, trying to think of something. It's what I should have been thinking about instead of her. I say the most basic, typical thing that comes to mind. "I think whoever is in there is someone in *Voss* and is probably connected to Tinzingate in one way or another."

She blows a raspberry. "Boring," she says, dragging out the syllables. "Next."

I groan, scratching at the back of my neck as I try and think of something more substantial. "Okay. I think that whoever we were supposed to be looking out for has been using the change in strategy for the diamonds as a coverup, steering you away from where the real source is; the source that leads you to finding out who started the rumours with Tinzin and *Voss*."

"Ooh, that's not bad," she says, turning to me and she actually smiles. Not at me, but at the idea. And it's sort of... endearing? I don't know. But the way her face lights up does something to me.

"Are you a true crime junkie or something?"

She shakes her head. "Not at all. Only about this. I'm

getting more of an adrenaline rush from being here than I could from a documentary."

"Why do you care so much? Aren't you supposed to want to rebel or some shit if you're not even a part of the company?"

I finally say what I've been thinking all day. About what this means to her. Why is she so set on finding out what happened when no one else is? Most of the press has made up their minds, not digging into what has happened, waiting for her dad to recover. Meanwhile, *my* dad thinks it's *our* place to find out what happened to expose them.

"I don't have to be a part of the company to care about my dad," she argues. Fair. But I want to know more. There is more than that. Especially because she's letting me help her. She must be desperate.

"Come on. What are you trying to prove, Angel? This seems like more than just trying to help a situation that doesn't need you meddling with it," I say, shifting in my seat to get more comfortable, leaning in closer to her. She glances out the window hesitantly and when she catches no more movement from the store she turns back to me.

"Not like I need to tell you any of this, but I'm hungry and I'm tired and I don't know what I'm saying," she begins.

"Strong start if you want me to listen to you," I mutter, and she pins me with a look. *The* look. The one that my dad gives me when I'm being a little shit. The one that when she gives it, it's extra fucking terrifying. I wave my hand between us, adding, "Continue."

"You know that my mom was sick for a really long time, right? Well, of course you did. Everyone knew. Because we couldn't get a moment of fucking privacy, even when we switched to private care, we were still followed everywhere," she explains. I don't say anything, not wanting to break whatever has led her to open up to me. "I was useless. Absolutely fucking useless. I was scared and all I could do was stand and watch. I couldn't help the company because I didn't have enough experience. I couldn't succeed in school because of the pandemic, so none of it even mattered. I couldn't help my mom and she was literally *dying* right in front of me. Do you know what that feels like, Branson? To watch someone you love almost disappear right before your eyes?" I shake my head, almost frozen to the spot. I do know what that's like, just not in the way she means. "She managed to pull through, luckily. And now we're going through it again, but this time, I can have a handle on it. I'm going to find out what happened, and my dad is going to be *fine*."

She ends her last sentence almost with a growl, as if she's trying to convince herself that that is what is going to happen. I swear the more I speak to this girl, the more I learn about her and how fucking wrong I've been. She has layers. Tons of them.

"That's…A lot," is all that my stupid brain can come up with to say. She blinks at me for a second, slightly shaking her head at me in disbelief before dropping my gaze and turning back to the window.

"Gee, thanks for that analysis," she mutters. "Like I said, I'm hungry and tired, so don't let me telling you that go to your head."

"I wasn't going to," I argue. I totally was.

"Right," she says sarcastically. She leans off from the window, resting her head against the headrest with a sigh, giving me the prettiest fucking view of her throat. *No.* We're not going there. "Do you know how long this is going to take?"

"You're asking me?" I say. "You're the one with the lead that got us here."

"Yeah, but I didn't think we'd actually just be sitting here," she retorts, her eyes still closed. I watch as the guy inside the shop finally slips his phone into his pocket, turning off the back light as he walks towards the door. "I'm just going to come back on my own tomorrow."

That's a terrible idea. There is no way she's going back here alone. It's a fine enough place, but everywhere becomes sketchy at night. The guy from the shop stands outside the door now, hands in his pockets as he looks around. I slouch down further, trying to hide myself from view.

"Don't you think that-"

"Stop talking," I mutter, watching as another dark figure appears, walking towards the Cell Phone Guy. They nod at each other, their mouths barely moving, and my heartbeat picks up.

"Okay, that's a bit rude," she replies. "I was just going to-"

"Scarlett. *Stop*. Talking," I bite out and she opens her eyes, ready to rip me a new one. She sees that I've lowered my gaze from just above the steering wheel and her eyes widen as she looks between me and the two figures.

"Oh shit," she murmurs.

"Yeah, oh shit."

She leans down closer to where I'm looking since I have the better view. She's too close to me now and I hate it. I can smell her *Chanel No. 5* and the coconut scent of whatever she uses in her hair as some strands tickle my forearm.

"Why are you so close to me?" she groans as if she isn't the one that came to *my* side of the car. She tried to reposition herself, but her elbow ended up wedged into the inside crease of mine.

I nudge her with my arm, but she doesn't move. "Why are *you* so close to *me*?"

She ignores me, huffing, "Can you just move your arm?"

"I would, but your elbow is right in my-"

"*Jesus*, Branson. Just move your-" She pushes me again and she's practically wedged between me and the steering wheel.

"Scarlett, for the love of god-"

"I can't see anything when you're in the way!"

There's a moment of brief - and I mean, *brief* - silence before the loudest sound I've ever heard starts to blare out.

Beeeep. Beeeep. Beeeep.

The fucking car alarm goes off and we duck our heads down, hoping that will shield us from the attention we've just drawn to ourselves. Could tonight get any worse? We've been going in circles, Scarlett's mood shifting like the weather, and now we've completely blown our cover.

I glance over to her, and her shoulders are shaking, her head tucked beneath her hands in a protective embrace. Is she crying? I really hope she's not crying. I'm fully convinced that it is only me who ends up in these kinds of situations.

When the car stops beeping, I look up to the store slowly, groaning when I see the lights are completely off and the two guys that were standing out there have gone. Fucking great.

"They're gone," I say, nudging Scarlett beside me and she lifts her head up.

She turns to me and our gaze locks. My lips part in exasperation. Honestly, I thought my life was about to be over just then. She blinks back at me, staring, her eyes wide and her cheeks a deep red.

Then the strangest thing happens.

She laughs.

Her face basically cracks open like the sun bursting through the blinds, her white teeth fully showing as she throws her head back, tears springing to her eyes as she clutches her chest. Her laugh is a high wheeze that I've never heard before. She only ever snorts or scoffs at me. *This* is her real laugh. It takes about two seconds of her contagious laugh before I start to join in with a low chuckle, shaking my head as I scramble to drive us away.

10

SCARLETT

HOLY SHIT.

Watching Evan Branson almost shit himself was single-handedly the highlight of my year. I don't think I've ever seen so much terror in those – yes, I confirmed it – green eyes.

The whole thing was too funny for me not to laugh. I have a habit of laughing in uncomfortable situations and that just happened to be one of those.

At first, I thought I insulted him before he started laughing too. It was low and barely noticeable, but it strangely felt good to laugh. With him. It lasted all of thirty seconds before he drove us out of there and dropped me off home while he walked back to his.

I'm more confused today than I was two nights ago. One minute I'm feeling like I'm being haunted by something in Gio's yard, the next I'm outside a sketchy jewellery shop, with Evan of all people.

I didn't tell him this because I'm still not sure how much I trust him yet: academic rival and all. But I'm *sure* I recognised the guy who was inside the store. I don't know what it was, but his posture was so familiar.

I know that's a weird thing to say, but that's the way I've always understood people. Wren almost always sits with her legs crossed, arms across her chest. Kennedy always womanspreads. My mom has naturally 'perfect' posture like me. But this guy was as straight as a door. He was standing with his phone in hand, his neck not seeming like a single kink was in it as he typed away. What was he doing, typing for so long? None of it made sense.

As I stared out that window, I tried to make sense of it all. I tried to let myself come up with some sort of theory, making myself believe that the change in shipments must be linked to Tinzin somehow and my dad unknowingly signed off on it.

It didn't help that I could feel Evan's eyes on the back of my head. It drives me insane not knowing what he's thinking, that's why I started the conversation. He makes me uneasy when he's not talking so I filled the space with useless conversation. I'd rather speak nonsense than not speak at all. I've been like that my whole life, no matter who I'm with.

Well, it's different with my dad, sitting here in this sterile room in a private hospital in Denver. I hate that he has to be so far from us, but this is the best hospital we can get and it's only an hour and a half flight from Salt Lake. We've tried to make this room homey for him, pinning up pictures of us, hanging an Italian flag above the bed, a small bedside table with rosemary's and prayer booklets my mom left but that doesn't change the fact that there's still the hiss coming from the heater, the rhythmic beeping of the machines and the gentle droplets of water coming from the dispenser in the corner of the room.

Even though I'm not supposed to, I've spent a few nights

here, curled up with a blanket in the chair next to my dad's bed. Most times I don't even speak. I don't go on my phone. I don't read my book. I just *think*.

And it's fucking terrifying. Being in your head all the time, feeling so utterly lonely whilst still feeling claustrophobic is the worst and most painful thing to experience. One minute I'm thinking about what I'm going to have for dinner, the next I'm thinking about oblivion. Even when I try to get the words to stop, they just keep coming, gushing towards me and I can't escape it.

I spent the better half of the morning trying to piece together moments from the night outside of the store before I ended up going in circles. Then I finally got my ass out of my room, called Arthur to make sure the jet was ready, and I got here.

I wish there was more to say to my dad. I alternate between apologising and thanking him. I mean, that's what you say to someone who gives you their everything and you can't do anything when they need someone the most. Just like I was when mom was sick.

A small part of me regrets opening up that part of me to Branson, but it needed to be out there. If he's going to be around more than usual, the least I can do is break a small barrier between us. If anyone is going to get what being in my situation is like, it has to be Evan, as annoying as that is to admit. There's only so far that the girls can comfort me when they don't fully understand what it's like to be in my position.

Surprisingly, Evan is a good listener. He didn't judge me or try to diminish my feelings like I thought he would. I can't tell if that should be a quality I like or should be afraid of.

"Who did this to you?" I whisper, tapping my knee. I know I won't to get a response, but it feels better to say my worries aloud. All there is in response is the rhythmic beep of the machine. "I'm trying, dad. I'm really trying. I don't want you to think for a second that I've left you like everyone else has."

I wait a few seconds. I don't know what for. He's only had two muscle spasms causing his finger to twitch, so I'm not expecting anything.

"Nothing is making sense to me. Why would you sign off on new imports when it doesn't fit the status quo? And mom's dream that you might have been forced into doing it..." I whisper, hoping that speaking it aloud will help me piece it together somehow. "That guy at the store was so familiar. I've seen him before. I must have. I'm going to figure this out, dad. One way or another, I'll find out what happened to you. I'm not going to sit back and watch anymore. I can't do that to you."

I'm startled by the knock at the door, turning to realise it's my dad's nurse Sylvie, an older woman with pink hair. When I nod at her, sitting up straighter in the couch, she opens the door, wheeling in a cart of my dad's food and other necessities.

I greet her and she updates me on how my dad is doing, telling me he's responding well to the medication. When she straps on her gloves and gets ready to feed him, I stand up and say goodbye. I don't like to stay for this part, and I know my dad would not want me to see him like this; so helpless and in need of help to feed himself. I give her my best smile before slipping out the door and catching an Uber to get the runway to get back home.

"THAT BOY WAS LOOKING for you again," Kennedy shouts from the kitchen.

There is nothing I love more than an out-of-context

conversation starter from Kennedy. I've been home for almost an hour after finishing up my homework at the library. The second I got in, I showered off the smell of hospital and school, snuggled into my favourite silk pyjamas and spread myself out on the comfortable white rug in the living room in front of the TV. Wren has a late practice today, so it's just me and Ken and we're about to watch a new episode of Love Island. That was until she ran into the kitchen to get us a refill of snacks.

I try to think of an answer to her weird statement. The only person I can think of is Charlie who I hooked up with a few weeks ago. Or maybe it was the guy from the night before the lecture on marketing strategies? I don't know. I've had a ton of messages from Charlie since then, which I've been ignoring. I wouldn't be surprised if he turned up here.

"What boy? If it was Charlie, I swear I'm going to-"

She cuts me off with her sing-song voice saying, "It was *Eh-van.*"

"Oh."

I've been slightly avoiding him since the stakeout. It feels like we're slipping into unknown territory, and I don't know how to act around him. One second we hate each other, the next we're staking out a potential murderer. I blew off our plans to study today so I could see my dad and he seemed fine with it.

Kennedy comes into the living room now, dressed in a set matching mine, except hers is in a dark blue opposed to my red. She flops down next to me lying on her stomach, her head in her hands as I lie on my back.

"What does 'oh' mean?" she asks curiously, tilting her head.

"It means I'm surprised that weasel is coming near our

home when he doesn't need to," I say, snorting. "I'm going to have to put some pest spray outside the door to keep him at bay."

Kennedy laughs and the sound is one of my favourites in the world. Unlike my wheezy laugh, she has the most child-like giggles ever. I don't think she'll ever grow out of it, and I love it. It's also extremely contagious.

"You're so dramatic," she concedes when her laughter dies down.

"Dramatically necessary," I correct, pinning her with a look before looking back at the ceiling. "Plus, you and Wren hardly like him, so don't act like it's just me."

"He's...fine," she says through a sigh. I turn to her again, raising my eyebrow, silently urging her to go on. "He's nice, okay? Like, *really* nice. And I know that you hate him because of your family feuds, and I respect that. You know, 'Romeo and Juliet' is Shakespeare's greatest play, but he's *nice* to me."

I snort at her rambling. "I'm happy for you, Ken, truly. You're just lucky you don't have to put up with his dipshittery every day at school."

She sulks, pouting. "I think you're refusing to remember that day he brought us home from the bar."

There is no way I'd be able to forget that day, no matter how drunk I was.

Wren had just found out some shitty news from her sister who had just told her she was pregnant, and we all went to a lowkey bar that didn't check our IDs. Before we knew it, we were drunk-singing Taylor Swift songs on the karaoke machine. Wren called Miles to pick us up and Evan was already out with him, so they both helped us up to our apart-ment. It's the bare minimum, but unfortunately, Kennedy's standards aren't the highest.

I distinctly remember frantically telling him not to dye his hair brown, no matter how much I loathe the fact that he's blonde. He didn't even seem to care. He told me that he'd basically do anything I asked him to and that confused the fuck out of me.

"Yeah, because he was there by proxy. If Wren hadn't called Miles, he wouldn't have been there," I explain, trying to justify it. She makes an exaggerated sigh, looking away wistfully. "What are you trying to get at, Ken?"

"He just seemed sad that you weren't here, that's all," she says. I really try to conjure up a picture of a sad or lost Evan and I come up with nothing.

"Evan Branson does not do 'sad.' He does a douche-bro face, stressed, and pissed. That's it," I say, almost laughing at the idea.

She shakes her head. "He also does a dreamy 'I-miss-Scarlett' face too," she adds, grinning like an evil genius.

"*Really*? You better take a picture next time," I mutter, hoping that's the end of the conversation about him. I get up, going into the kitchen for a drink because just talking about him gets me hot and bothered. And not in a fun way.

"Why don't you just sleep with him?" Kennedy shouts and I almost drop the glass I had to climb up onto the counter to get. We really need to reorganise these shelves.

"What?" I choke out.

"Yeah," she begins as if that solves everything. "Just bang out all that sexual tension and see what happens. You can get it out of your systems."

I bring my glass of water into the living room, sitting down next to her on the couch. "Ken, have you met me? I look like this and he's all *that*. I'm not letting any of *that* near me. Plus, there is no sexual tension to bang out. You're making that up."

"Boo. You're no fun anymore," she says, slipping further back into the couch. "When did you turn into such a prude?"

"When I realised that I'd rather sit naked on a hot grill then let him anywhere near my private parts," I say with a shudder for extra effect. Ken doesn't take the hint to end the conversation and instead takes another deep sigh, batting her long eyelashes at me.

"He's like a lost puppy trailing after you," she whines. Since when was she such an Evan supporter? They must have all hopped on the bandwagon that I've missed because I can't deal with this, as well as my already conflicting feelings about him.

"That's what it looks like to *you*. He's more of a leech, picking up on my every mistake and never letting me live it down."

"You do the same thing to him. Minus the leech part," she says, shuddering. She nudges me with her leg. "Come on, Scar. Just give in. I know you want to."

I laugh. "How much is he paying you to say this?"

"Not nearly enough," she murmurs, and I tilt my head, smirking. She barks out a laugh. "I'm kidding. I just think you guys could work well together if you weren't so set on hating him."

"We work together fine. Not everyone has to be best friends to make a decent team," I say, and she nods, flicking her eyes towards the screen. "Okay, let's see who is being voted off this week."

I get another infectious giggle from her and we're deep into our favourite reality TV show. This is how I want to spend my nights instead of worrying about what's going to happen. Sometimes all I need is a hyperactive best friend and a so-bad-it's-good TV show to laugh at.

11

EVAN

I'VE SPENT the last two hours listening to Anderson drone on about shit he probably has no idea about, followed by a twenty minute conversation with my dad on the phone. Today is going great.

My dad can never get straight to the point. He has to tell me everything that has gone wrong with his day, give me a ten page essay on the current state of the business that I didn't ask for *before* telling me why he's really calling me. Today's conversation has a little kick to it, though.

Every once in a while, my dad will talk about my mom, Junie Sylvester. She's not like a Voldemort situation where we can't say her name. If anything, talking about her brings the mood down.

As much as my dad has a hard exterior, I know he's a soft puppy on the inside. I was there with him when he cried over her. My dad misses her, and I miss her too. I usually save all my talk about my mom for a late night in the comfort of my bed when I'm missing her, but today my dad wants to poke some old wounds with his infected finger.

Unlike most cases with spouses in our family that latch onto a Branson for a sense of security and wealth, my mom decided to run the other way. Literally. It turns out that constant press about your relationship with a Branson CEO and anything else you do, isn't for everyone. I don't blame her. I know she loves me, and I know she still does, wherever she is.

Still, I wish she stayed and gave me a better goodbye than a stupid letter that I've had since I was twelve. If I really wanted to find her, I could. Similarly, if she wanted to find me, she could. I've never been good at making the first move and I feel like getting the 'closure' my therapist aspires for will only open more wounds that I don't need to deal with right now. As much as I miss her, I've moved on and matured. If in a few years from now, I'm desperate for her contact, I'll find her. Right now, I'm good.

That's why I'm shocked that my dad has been talking about her for the last fifteen minutes, talking about everything from her giving birth to me, their successful marriage until the moment it suddenly imploded. My dad made sure that all press would leave her alone as that was the one thing she requested when she left. In a weird way, his ego was bruised that she didn't even try to steal from him or ask for any money. She's probably started a new life, making her own money out of the spotlight.

I finally interrupt his rant on how my mom was too good for him.

"*Okay*, Sammy," I say, using her nickname for him to reign him back in. "What do you really want?"

He clears his throat. "Do I have to want something to talk to my only son?"

"When you're talking about mom, yes."

I push my back closer to the wall, sighing against it. Scarlett probably thinks I'm trying to ditch our study session, but I've been trying to put an end to this conversation for the last half an hour. It's a pretty busy day in the library with the freshmen panicking about their first assessments of the semester and I want to get as much work done as possible.

"I just wanted to see how things are going. You know, with the Voss girl," he says in a hushed tone.

"She has a name," I bite, hating the way he talks about her like that. I'd be like this with anyone. I know what it's like to only be known by a last name and when that name starts to mean something bigger than you could ever imagine, you realise that you're nothing without it. I don't want that to be the case for her. Or for anyone, really.

He ignores me. "I haven't heard anything from you since you said that the jewellery store stakeout was a bust."

"Yeah, because nothing has happened," I say truthfully. We haven't had time to discuss what happened that night and that was my plan for today, until my dad called me, a disruption as always.

"Well, you need to make something happen. And quick. We can't have the press finding out about this before we get a hold on it," my dad explains like I don't know this already. You try coaxing information out of a girl who only opens up to you when she's hungry and tired and spends the rest of that time giving you the stink eye. "Are we clear, son?"

"Crystal," I murmur. He's silent on the other end for a few beats. "Look, dad, I've got to go. These A's aren't going to get themselves."

"Good boy," he coos, and I roll my eyes, ending the call on him.

When I quietly slip through the library doors, Scarlett is

exactly where I left her. She's sitting at one end of a brown bench, tucked into the far corner of the bookshelves in the collaborative study area.

Because she's Scarlett Voss, she manages to pull off a black dress and an oversized blazer, her wavy hair tied back into a messy low ponytail, with small gold hoops in her ears. When she got up to use the bathroom, I got a look at the loose ribbon in her hair. This time it's a deep red one to add some colour.

Her style is so unique to her that I'm convinced that people are afraid to dress like her. It's not like it's so out of this world, it's just not what you usually get from girls here at NU. It makes me wonder why she doesn't have many friends when she has such a good sense of style, she's smart, she's pretty and is casually a millionaire at age twenty.

"You took your time," she mutters without looking up at me as she writes in her notebook.

I take my seat across from her, placing my phone face down on the table. "My dad can talk for the whole of America," I respond, pulling my papers back to me. "Have you got anything new yet?"

We are yet to make a breakthrough for this project. Which is concerning considering we're both from families that have their own clothing line that are famous internationally, but Anderson is being a dick and said we can't use our own businesses for inspiration and have to start from scratch. So, we've been circling around the same basic ideas for the last few days.

"Not yet," she says, finally looking up at me. "I can't really focus."

"Did Anderson drain you out, too?" I ask, sighing. She nods. "Ah, so you admit it?"

Her right eyebrow quirks. "Admit what?"

"That you're normal like the rest of us," I say, humour lacing my tone.

"What makes you think I'm not normal?" She pins her arms across her chest, leaning back in her chair. She tilts her head at me, nodding at me to continue.

"You always act like you're better than everyone in the class, Angel. You're the first one there and the last one out. You hand in your work early, but not as early as me, and when you do, you're always bragging about how easy it is."

She laughs quietly, the sound making all the hairs at the back of my neck stand up. "I can't tell if you're trying to compliment me or not, Branson," she says, grinning.

"I'm not."

"Right. You're just casually telling me how amazing I am," she replies. I swear she's one cocky motherfucker. "It wasn't just Anderson's lecture. I'm *still* trying to catch up on sleep after what we saw."

"And what exactly was it that we saw? Because I only saw two people talking before you hit the alarm and blew our cover. You should be grateful we left there in one piece. Who knows what weapons they had on them," I say, shuddering at the thought of them harming us in any way. Honestly, it was one of the most terrifying moments of my life.

She laughs again, sounding a lot like it did that night, wheezy and chesty. "You're so fucking dramatic. They weren't going to hurt us," she concedes through her laugh. I shake my head at her, not sure why she finds the possibility of death so amusing.

"Did you at least tell your uncle what we saw?" I ask, needing her to give me some sort of information. Anything that can tie this up.

"I can't exactly follow it up with my uncle because he

doesn't know that we went," she mumbles. The words are hard to make out as she strains her eyes on the sheet in front of her, avoiding my eyes.

"Are you being serious? We went there without anyone knowing where we were. What if something happened to us, Scarlett? Does that thought not terrify you a little bit?" I quiz, completely baffled as to how she would let us go out there in the night, alone, with no one knowing our whereabouts. When she told me about the lead, it seemed like her uncle had urged her to go out and see what was going on, not this.

"Can you chill?" she asks, and I can tell she's trying not to laugh. *I swear, this woman.* Then, she adds easily, "If it's any consolation, there's a tracker on my phone and on the car. If we were to get mauled, someone would have found us."

"No, that's not any consolation, you animal."

Now it's her turn to shake her head, desperately trying not to laugh at me. "Listen, there would be nothing to report anyway. I tried looking through some employee photos and I couldn't find him. It's a dead end."

The words sound like a punch to the stomach. I can't let this end before it's even started. The store, the diamonds, Mateo's signing of the documents and her uncle's lack of knowledge of this; there has to be something we're missing.

"Maybe you're not looking in the right place," I suggest with a shrug.

"Do you know something I don't, Branson? Because where else is there to look? All the records of the diamond exchange are official. Like I said, I don't know who the guy is, and I can't exactly go up and ask him," she explains with a huff.

"Then let me help you."

The words are out of my mouth before I can stop them.

Scarlett's eyes widen for a second, clearly taken aback by

my suggestion. What am I doing? I was going to need to ask her at some point. It's already enough to be working with her on this project, the last thing she wants to do is spend more time with me than necessary.

"Why?" she asks finally.

"What?"

"We barely like each other. Why do you want to help me?"

I tut, shaking my head. "No, Angel. *You* don't like *me,*" I correct for her, reminding her that it's not me that wants this. She raises an eyebrow. "Listen, I think we could be a pretty good team if we weren't fighting all the time. I've got nothing better to do and it doesn't seem like you have many options to help you either. I'm not going to let you risk your life for nothing. Not to mention, I'd be the first suspect in the investigation since we're doing this project together. I don't want my reputation to be tarnished because you'd be dumb enough to get killed."

She scoffs. "If anything, you'd be the one dying first. I have Final Girl energy," she says defensively.

"You think so?" I ask cooly. She nods, holding up her chin proudly. "I'd peg you more as the first girl, but sure."

"What have I ever done that makes you think I'm not Final Girl worthy?"

"For starters, you wear red bottoms for no other reason than they look good," I say, but her face doesn't crack. "You'd be out before the opening credits roll."

"Is that how little you think of me? That I'm just a pretty face, too dumb and easy to kill."

"You having a pretty face has nothing to do with what I think about you," I say, shaking my head at how this conversation has completely flipped.

She smirks. "So, you admit it? You think I have a pretty face."

"Scarlett," I press, ignoring her obvious comment. "Are you going to let me help you or do you want to keep running your mouth some more?"

She closes her eyes, taking a deep breath in and then back out. "Don't make me regret this, Branson."

"You're agreeing?" I ask, sounding like a kid on Christmas.

I need to learn how to control my excitement, but it's hard when it comes with her. She's starting to give me these little pieces of herself, and I want to cherish them all. Her head nods ever so slightly and I take it as a victory. I hold out my hand to her, ready to formally agree on this.

I'm used to shaking hands with people. It was pretty much my job for a whole year when my dad got sick of it. Still, I'm surprised my whole body lights up when Scarlett slips her hand into mine.

We never touch. Ever. When we do, it's completely an accident and we pretend it didn't happen. But right now, as I extended my hand, she put her hand in mine, no questions asked.

With her rough yet put-together exterior, I don't know what I was expecting when her skin came into contact with mine. Not only is her hand fucking tiny in comparison to mine that engulfs hers, but her hands are also just so...*soft*. They're all feminine and smooth, like a fancy silk sheet.

The way she shakes my hand is nothing like the way I expected it to feel. Her grip is firm yet gentle, like she's also had practice with this. She almost pulls me in a little, trying to see how far she can push me, as if this is another one of our games. When she finally lets go, I feel like I can breathe again and I get back down to looking at my work.

For the next hour, we spend it researching possible business ideas that haven't already been done. We've been added to a spreadsheet that has all the other students' ideas, so we know not to do the same as someone else. This project is a lot harder than Anderson made it out to be. I need to get a good grade on this project because I'm barely hanging on to an average grade of a 'C' after missing a few classes last year.

I've never really thought about what I would do if I had my own business. In my head, it's always had something to do with fashion since I've always had an eye for the designs and new ways to make basic clothes unique. Thinking outside that box has been a fucking struggle.

"Some kind of music site?" Scarlett suggests.

"Like there aren't already a million of those," I relay, crossing it off the list that we've been passing back and forth. "A laptop the size of a phone?"

"So, an iPad?" Shit. Why am I actually so terrible at this? "How about…A food chain that only sells quiche, but they're sponsored by a huge dairy farm company. We can do the whole climate and animal safety thing."

I shake my head. "Too complicated."

"Complicated is good, Branson. How else do you think we're going to get a good grade?" Scarlett questions, sighing frustratedly.

"With an idea that *we* can actually get our head around would be a good start," I say back. The project could be hypothetical, but I know if we think of a good one, we could turn it into a reality, easily bumping us up into the top grade boundaries.

She taps her pencil against her laptop rhythmically, gradually gaining a faster pace. It feels out of beat for a second or two before she matches the pace again.

God, she's going to drive me insane.

"I've got something," I say. The words leave my mouth before the idea is fully formed in my head. This is how most of my ideas start. They are out there before I can even register it and then they end up becoming a complete mess. She nods for me to continue, finally dropping her pen. "How about an app of some sort where you get to record, film, or type a message to someone, but it doesn't get sent until you say it does? But you can't edit it or change it once you've set who you want to set it to and the date. Once it's out there, it's out there forever."

"That's not a bad idea," she murmurs. "So, it's kind of like a confession page? No turning back sort of thing."

"Exactly," I say. "It doesn't always have to be people confessing their deepest darkest secrets, but it can even be a fun thing where someone can tell their family that they love them in a less serious way."

She nods, closing her laptop, resting her head in her hands. "I hate that idea a little less than the others. Keep talking."

It's crazy how she can switch from wanting to argue with me to actually listening to me. She manages to create this serious, businesswoman persona when she talks about the project. Even when she's trying to be nice, she's still in control, demanding.

So, when Scarlett tells me to keep talking, I do.

12

SCARLETT

"I'M GONNA BE HUNGOVER," Kennedy sings loudly, linking her arm into mine and Wren's as we walk along the sidewalk in downtown Salt Lake City, feeling the end of September chill rush through me.

It's not that cold out as it usually is, but I still regret wearing only a black mini dress and heels.

"*I'm gonna be hungover,*" Wren harmonises, tugging on my other arm. They both look up at me, waiting for me to finish the line. We've been singing this unironically for the last few months after the video the band *HAIM,* posted on TikTok. They get me singing the last line every time, yet they still look up at me like little puppies, waiting for it.

I finally put them out of their misery.

"*I'm gonna drink a bunch of different drinks and I'm gonna be hungover,*" I sing back to them, and they cheer, starting the catchy song all over again.

I'm sure people are staring at us, but I've done this too many times to care. Nearly every night we go out, the girls insist on singing a song to get us from one place to the other.

We once walked from our apartment to campus singing the 'All Too Well' ten minute version by Taylor Swift. No breaks. No interruptions. Just pure and utter chaos. There's something extremely cathartic about screaming *'Fuck the patriarchy'* while walking past the frat houses near campus.

Tonight, we're celebrating the first few weeks of the school year going surprisingly okay. It's nothing, but we can think of pretty much any excuse to go out. It's always hard to find a day when we can all go out together because our schedules are a mess again this year, so we're trying to make our rare night together fun.

We've started going to this bar because my family are friends with the owners, so we're able to get drinks without getting checked for ID. The bar staff always make sure we're safe and that we don't drink too much. Overall, it's a great place to go when we want to have a good time. I need a night off from thinking about everything with my dad and since we made a minor breakthrough with the project, I feel more at ease.

We finally make it to Kiwi, all of our arms linked together. It's a Friday night, so we're not shocked that it's packed in here. The bar has two floors, both resembling Nick Miller's bar in the show 'New Girl' with dark brown accents and burgundy furniture.

The upstairs is where most drinks are served, a jukebox in the corner and where most of the older, rich people hang out. Downstairs is where me and the girls usually go, where there's is a smaller bar, karaoke machine, booths, and tables full of people dancing and singing.

It reminds me of the kind of restaurant you end up at while on vacation with your family as a kid, when you're sleepy and tired, the floors are sticky, it's humid and you know that you'll be fast asleep on your way back to the hotel. It's by far one of my favourite feelings. Especially with these girls.

We make our way to the bar, each of us ordering a cocktail to start off, scanning the surroundings as we lean against the bar. These are the kind of places where I meet someone, we have a flirty chat, and it usually ends with me in their bed. I'm willing to see whatever the universe wants to throw in my way, as Kennedy suggested.

I've never been a relationship person and when that line started to blur with Jake, I vowed never to cross it again. Being in a relationship is a lot of work and I can't do that right now. After taking a Buzzfeed quiz with the girls, it confirmed the fact that I'm afraid of abandonment, realising that I won't be enough to make someone stay. It's a sickening and pathetic thought, but when you've been seen as nothing more than a spoiled millionaire your whole life, it's hard to convince people to stay because they actually like you and not your family's money.

I can do as many party tricks as I want, give amazing hand-jobs, pass every test at the top of the class and I'm still not seen as enough. Not something that people aspire for.

I'm great on paper but the second a guy realises that I've got more baggage than they're put out for, they run the other way. I'm the kind of girl a guy gets before settling down with the bubbly, fun, easy-going, Princess Sunshine girl. I've accepted my fate and I'm cool with it.

Mostly.

"Look! The karaoke machine is free," Kennedy says, pointing to the corner of the bar, which holds a modern karaoke machine and a screen. "Last one there has to do a solo."

Her last words come out of her mouth in a hurry as she

rushes off into that space of the bar, me following after her and Wren being the last one to catch up. It's not that far of a distance, but Ken loves to make things into a competition and I'm naturally very competitive. Wren's more of the chill one, not caring too much about having to sing a solo.

"What song should I sing?" Wren asks, looking through the small device attached to the screen. "I know the night just started, but I physically don't have it in me to go all musical theatre on you tonight."

"Milesy's gonna hate that," I say, laughing.

Her boyfriend is a *huge* musical theatre fan, which she found out on their vacation to Palm Springs last summer and the torture she gets put through whenever they carpool. Kennedy and Wren laugh before I say, "What are you in the mood for?"

"Something sad," she replies, and I raise my eyebrows. "I'm fine, before you ask. Sad music always hits differently." I nod and she scrolls through the list again. "I'm thinking Adele. I am *so* ready to serenade you."

Less than a minute later, Kennedy and I are slow dancing to Wren terribly singing *'All I Ask'* as the whole of the bar sings along with her. She misses nearly every high note and Kennedy and I try our hardest not to laugh, feigning sadness as we dance like two lovers going through a breakup. When she hits the bridge, we can't help it anymore and we start to laugh, falling apart in each other's arms.

Do you ever just look at your friends and think, *wow, I am so lucky to have them*? Because I think that every time I look at them. It's hard to even put into words the feeling that I get when I spend time around these two. I love watching Kennedy talk with her hands about fictional characters and watch Wren cry to Phoebe Bridgers songs. I love the childlike joy on

Kennedy's face anytime anyone mentions something she loves and the blush on Wren's cheeks when she talks about her boyfriend. They make the most mundane activities fun. We can spend hours talking about the same topic and I will never get bored. They turn a sweaty bar full of twenty-somethings into a concert and I love them for it.

Kennedy is trying to catch her breath as the song ends and Wren steps down from the elevated surface and embraces us as the crowd cheers her on.

"That was incredible," I say, hugging her tight to me. She's all sweaty and puffy-faced, looking how she does after a training session on the ice.

"Why, thank you," she says coyly, giving us a curtsy, but it's more of a bow since she's wearing shorts and a tank top. "I think I've traumatised people with that performance."

"The only person you've traumatised is Evan. He's looking over here like his life has just flashed before his eyes," Kennedy says, nodding her head back towards the bar. She nudges me. "*This* is closest to the sad I-Miss-Scarlett face you're going to get."

That's when I see him.

Jesus, how did I not notice him before? And he's staring right at us.

He's dressed casually in a white button down, some of his chest exposed, and black dress pants, his arms crossed against his chest and his ankles crossed. I shouldn't be surprised to see him here.

I've seen him around here a few times, but he never stays for long. He sits here on his own, staring at his drink for a couple of minutes before leaving. I can deal with ignoring him and having a good time, knowing that he's judging me from a distance. But tonight, his eyes are on us, and I hate it.

"How long has he been there?" I ask, turning back to Kennedy, feeling the heat of his gaze on the back of my neck.

"I saw him when we came in. He's kinda been watching us. No biggie," she replies, brushing it off as she scrolls through her phone. She turns to Wren who is downing a bottle of water. "I've *got* to show you the video I took. I've already sent it to Lover Boy, so don't worry."

Wren laughs. "He's going to think I'm drunk already," she says, pulling Kennedy's phone into her hand.

I turn back around, ready to tell Branson to bring his sad vibes somewhere else. What is it with him always scowling like somebody has personally offended him by having fun? I don't have any time to think about it before I collide into someone's chest.

"Jesus, can you watch where you're going," I mutter, pulling myself out of this stranger's weirdly comforting smell. It reminds me of Gio's house, woody and homey. Still, I don't exactly want to nuzzle my face in it right now.

"Clearly not," the guy murmurs, his voice deep and sultry that it runs through me like honey, feeling it low and tight in my stomach. I look up at him.

Holy shit.

He's gorgeous. Like, Calvin Klien model level of gorgeous.

He looks like a young Henry Cavill – all dark features, sharp jaw, but a kind and smooth face. His eyes are a bright brown colour that pairs well with the tight black shirt he's wearing. And his chest is hard and firm. Frankly, it's unfair for him to look this good.

"You alright?" he asks me, steadying me with his firm grip on my elbow.

I shake my head and when I see his head tilt with a smirk, I nod. How am I getting tongue tied over a guy I just met? I never get tongue tied. Ever. I'm not supposed to. It's undeniably out of character for me. I've got tongue tied over one guy, Jake, and well…you know how that ended.

So, I blurt out, "You can't just go around with all *that*," gesturing to his chest, "and not expect people to bump into it."

"You calling my chest an 'it,' darling?" he asks playfully.

He's British?

Game changer or game over? I can't decide. I shake my head again, trying to get rid of all the filthy things I can imagine him saying in that accent.

"'*Darling?*' Are you serious? *You* just bumped into *me*. The least you can do is apologise," I say, instantly getting defensive.

He clears his throat. "You're right. I'm sorry my *that* got in the way of your night," he says cooly. I can tell he's fighting a smile at how ridiculous this is, but I can't help but smile too. He holds out his hand. "Maxwell Grant, but most of my friends call me Max."

I take his hand in mine. I've learnt how to shake a person's hand. More like I forced my brothers to teach me the best way to do so to seem intimidating. So, I pull his large hand into mine and squeeze it and watch the surprise flash across his face.

"Scarlett," I say back, letting go of his hand.

"No last name?"

"Nope," I say. I've learnt that if they don't introduce themselves to me first, they're more likely to have no idea who I am. He's lucky he bumped into me on accident. I'd be damned if I ever give a man the satisfaction of thinking they know me by judging me off my last name. "So, Maxwell, is this a usual thing for you? Just bumping into girls and not apologising."

He lets out a short laugh. "I said you can call me 'Max' and I did apologise eventually."

"You said your friends call you 'Max,'" I retort, feigning confusion.

He holds my stare, a strange fire igniting in my lower stomach. I can't remember the last time talking to a guy has excited me so much. If Kennedy could hear this, she'd be all over it, believing that the universe sent him to me.

Fuck it.

He leans into me, and I have to crane my neck to look up at him because fuck, he's tall. He pulls out his wallet from his back pocket, twirling it in his hand. "Let me buy you a drink."

"I'll get it," I say, shaking my head. I know I just met the guy and it's a nicer gesture, but I know better than letting a technical stranger buy me a drink. Who knows what he could do to it. He quirks an eyebrow and he thinks it's better not to ask and passes me two twenties.

It's partly a pathetic excuse to collect my wits, but it's an excuse, nonetheless. I watch the smile creep on his face and it's fucking adorable as he nods over to the bar. Which is concerning contrasting his very bad boy, I'll-fuck-you-into-next-week kind of energy. I pat him on the shoulder, slipping past him to get to the bar and – of course – Evan is still there.

"New friend?" he asks when I reach the bar, nodding over to where I left Max in the crowd. Evan's leaning his back against the bar while I face the other way, waiting for a bartender to turn up.

"What happened to 'Hello?'" I ask, not sure why he wants to suddenly be involved in my personal life.

He shrugs. "Just making polite conversation."

"That's not how you make conversation, Branson. They usually start with nice greetings," I say sweetly, as if I'm talking to a baby. He scoffs. "We agreed to help each other with school and my family. What I do outside of that is none of your business. Plus, I'm with Kennedy and Wren, I don't need you babying me."

He turns to me, setting his dark green eyes on me, resting one arm on the bar. "That's even more of a reason for me to be here. If Wren's here, Miles would kill me if I didn't stay and watch over you."

I actually laugh at that. "'Watch over us?' God, Branson, what kind of mafia movie are you in? We're independent women in our twenties. We can handle ourselves."

"If I'm going to sit here and drink while you guys break everyone eardrums with the karaoke machine, the least I can do for the common good is make sure you don't break something or yourselves," he explains, nodding to where Kennedy has somehow wrestled the karaoke machine again. That woman needs to learn how to keep still. "I'll stay out of your way, but I'm not leaving."

God, why is he being such a party pooper? Before the project, I could have fun and mess about. Now he feels like a bodyguard. And not the fun, sexy kind.

I groan. "You need to loosen up, Branson. Why don't you turn your frown upside down and go find some girl to take home? You're ruining my vibe."

He swallows, thinking for a second and my drinks arrive, so I pick them up, one in each hand. "Maybe I will," he challenges.

"Maybe you should," I call, my back turned to him as I saunter back over to Max.

This is the kind of fun I need.

Don't get me wrong, I love a good night at home like the next girl, but being here, under the dark lighting with good music playing, I feel at home. It also helps that I'm dancing next to a really hot guy who hasn't tried to rip my clothes off yet. It's been a good night all around.

I ask Max what year of college he's in and when he tells me he's a junior like me, I feel myself start to relax. He asks me about school, and I ramble like a fool about my business classes, and he does the same about his literature degree. I find smart men so fucking sexy, so I don't miss the leap my heart does when he easily tells me some of his favourite authors.

I apologise for being rude to him when we first met and he assures me that its fine, and even when I blurt out my addiction to reality TV shows, he doesn't seem phased.

Instead, he pulls me closer into him, so our fronts are almost touching. "And here I thought you couldn't get any more perfect," he murmurs. God, these British guys really have a way with words.

Because my life is becoming more and more like a movie each day, the second the atmosphere shifts in our relationship from friendly to flirty, the music also changes to one of my favourite songs; 'She' by Harry Styles.

As Max tightens his grip around my waist, pulling me further into him, I lock my hands around his neck, loving the way our bodies fit together. We feel like two pieces of a puzzle, each open piece of us fitting to complete the other. And he smells so fucking good that I just want it all over me.

We're hardly even dancing anymore. We're just pressed against each other, my head resting on his shoulder as I close my eyes for a second, letting myself be taken away in the moment as the song builds. It's hardly a slow song, but as the song picks up, it starts to feel dirty, and I love it.

When I open my eyes I'm staring directly at Evan. He's moved from his spot next to the bar and is instead standing a few feet away from me as everyone dances around him. My heartbeat immediately picks up. He stands there, hands in his pockets, face emotionless as he stares directly into my eyes.

Our gazes lock. Hold. Burn.

I challenge him with my eyes to stop looking at me, seeing how far he's going to push it until he finally drops his gaze.

But he never does.

Even when my body is completely pressed to Max's and I can feel his bulge in his jeans, Evan doesn't look away. I grip onto the back of Max's head tighter, hating the way he's looking at me, but I can't stop looking back. Even as I try to tell my eyes to move, they just can't.

Max turns back, glancing over his shoulder, no doubt noticing the intense staring contest that is taking place and then he turns back to me and I lean up off his chest to move my attention to him, my front still crushed to his. "What's the deal with him? Does he fancy you or something?"

"No," I say quickly, looking up into his eyes that flash with something I can't quite place. "Are you jealous?"

"Scarlett," he presses, spinning me out and then he pulls me back in again, clasping his hand around my waist. "Have you seen yourself? You're fucking stunning. I wouldn't be surprised, that's all."

Am I blushing right now? No. I can't be.

I've been complimented by guys before, but I don't know why the way Max's says it runs through my body like honey and makes me feel weak in the knees.

"We're just working on a project for class," I say, my voice betraying me as it sounds shaky when he presses me into him again. "And my best friend's boyfriend is his roommate so we kind of have to see each other all the time."

He hums, murmuring, "That sounds awful."

"Yeah, it is," I say back. "I mean, just looking at him makes me mad."

"I can tell," he laughs. "You're squeezing my neck pretty hard."

"Shit. Sorry." I detangle my arms from around his neck, but he catches my wrists, pinning his darkened eyes on me, slowly easing them back up onto him and I clasp my hands behind his neck loosely this time. He smiles down at me, a dimple popping out on his right cheek, and it almost undoes me.

"It's okay. I like it when a girl's a bit rough."

"Yeah?" I ask, tilting my head to the side. I can tell he's about to kiss me, but I want to be in control, to be the person to make the first move. A reckless part of me knows that Evan's watching, and I want to push him again, see if he'll finally stop watching over us and I crash my mouth to Max's.

He wraps one hand around my neck, pulling me further into him until there is no more room for me to go. My breasts are flush against his chest now and I swallow the groan he makes as I rock my hips against his, loving the feeling that he has over me. He wraps his hand tighter around my neck, curling into my hair as he deepens the kiss and I open my eyes as I gasp at how good it feels.

When my vision clears I catch Evan just…staring.

What the fuck is his problem? I thought the kiss would at least scare him off a little, not spur him on. Instead, there's a little more emotion in his face this time. Anger, maybe? I flip him off behind Max's back, still kissing him, before tugging on Max's shirt because holy shit, he really knows how to kiss.

When I come down from the high, panting and staring up at him, his lips are swollen, his brown eyes dilated. This is how I like men to look; dishevelled and still hungry.

I look over his shoulder, hoping to catch Evan's reaction, but he's gone. I look back at Max and I can't help but smile at his shocked face, loving the fact that I did that to him.

"Do you kiss all of your new friends like that?" he asks, his hand still curled in the back of my neck, and I melt into his touch.

Maybe it's the shitty week I've had or the fact that I've been feeling out of control recently or the very weird encounter with Evan, but I lean up on my tiptoes, press another kiss to his cheek and whisper, "Just the ones I want to see again."

I can do this, right? I can have a no-strings-attached relationship with this gorgeous human as some stability over the next few weeks. I'm not expecting to fall madly in love with him. I know, just by looking at him and feeling him, that we'll be a good match for what I want right now.

Whatever the hell that is.

13

EVAN

THERE ARE many things that I love in the world. I love music and the feeling that I get when I get in front of a piano. I love my slightly dysfunctional family. I love school, numbers, and learning. I love money and power and the opportunities I get when I have it.

One thing I don't love; dinners with my dad on a random Saturday evening for no other reason than he "wanted to see me."

Apparently a half-an-hour conversation on the phone about my mom wasn't enough family time for him. This would be fine if I hadn't been under surveillance for the last two years and especially over the last few days as we navigate the Voss situation.

Samuel Branson is a nice guy. He always has been just that...*nice*. He's kept a clean public record and knows exactly how to handle the press the way his dad taught him. People cast him as the villain because he's a man with power and he might not be putting it in the best places, but he's trying.

Secretly, I think he's been trying to redirect B & Co for a

few years now, subtly creating more sustainable and environmentally friendly resources to help strengthen our brand and community. But once someone has one opinion on you, it's hard for them to change it. Especially in a day and age where public apologies are meaningless and cancel culture is so vehement.

That's why the Voss' are not my dad's biggest cheerleaders. It's understandable. My dad knows how to push the competition until it gets too far, until it's borderline unhealthy and some people are sick of it. Hell, I kind of hate it too, but business is business.

Especially with whatever happened with Scarlett at the bar last night, I haven't been able to sleep properly. After getting to know her a little more, watching her grind up against some rando is not something I exactly want to see.

I suddenly feel protective over her. It might be a little misplaced given my situation and my need for her to stay on track with the investigation, but I just couldn't stop watching her. If I couldn't tell her to stop, I could at least make sure it didn't get out of control.

Well, that was until it got too much and watching her felt like I was trying to kill myself. You try and watch someone you've been arguing with for two years straight grind up against someone without a care in the world and see if it doesn't alter your brain chemistry. The worst part of all? For a second – and I mean a *second* – I wished I was in his place instead.

Since we've sat down to eat, both of us at heads of the long table in the sleek, black dining room, my dad has hardly said a word. Am I supposed to say something? Is this how these check-ins are supposed to go?

We're just staring at our food without speaking. I push my

sprouts to the side of my plate; I've never really liked them, but my dad insists on making them with every meal. I clear my throat after taking a sip of the sparkling water beside me.

"Do you want a run-down, or... what?" I ask playfully. My dad drops his fork onto the table, the clanging sound echoing off the walls. There's no one else but us here, other than Mila wandering the halls.

"Do you have one?"

"Sort of," I begin. He nods for me to continue. "We know that shipments changed for the diamond imports and that the uncle was somehow unaware of this. We know that Mateo signed off the change in shipments and that the people outside the jewellery store must be the ones in charge of it from their end. My only question is why would he change it and why is Giovanni unsure as to whether it happened or not?"

My dad hums, the sound so deep that it's barely noticeable. "They have to be linked to Tinzin somehow. The dates of when they signed off the contract for the diamonds was around the same time Tinzin was starting to get discovered. Perhaps they're working together."

I nod, considering it for a moment. "Yes, but why? Why would Mateo do something so reckless? Scarlett said herself that he would never intentionally put their family at risk."

"Maybe it wasn't him," my dad mutters. My stomach drops a little at the suggestion. It has to be him. As much as he's a nice guy on the surface, an extra income through drugs and black market deals are common in major companies. Sure, they're not common with ones like ours, but it's a possibility. Some people would do anything for an extra bit of cash in their hands.

"Who else could it be? There's no one else that has any reason to try and go against the status quo. It just doesn't make any damn sense," I try to explain, huffing as I run my hand through my hair. Naturally, my hand latches onto the back of my neck, scratching like I have a bite. I can't keep getting worked up over this. I need to figure this out, tie it into a neat bow and move on.

"I don't know, son. For once, I really just don't know," my dad says, sighing and I can tell he's just as defeated as I am. "I'll keep pressuring Damon and you do what you can on your end. How are things with the girl?"

"Scarlett," I correct. "Her name is Scarlett. Can you remember that for future conversations or do I have to remind you every time, old man?" He holds his hands up apologetically, signifying that he's standing down. "Things are fine. She's just hard to talk to sometimes."

He nods understandingly, taking a sip of his red wine before placing it back down. "Don't get in your head about it, Evan. You worry too much. I know it's a hard task, but you'll figure out a way to get through to her."

When my dad puts it like that, it actually seems possible. He's always understood what it's like to be in my head sometimes, realising that it's not all sunshine and rainbows up in here. After starting therapy, even though I don't go as much now, it's helped me come to terms with it too. I used to blame my emotions and my sensitivity for the reason why I couldn't handle Cat's breakup, which ultimately led to my banishment from the company. But now I realise that it wasn't a weakness, it's a strength.

Being vulnerable, listening and caring for people has always been something I'm good at. I just wish people could see that side of me more, but when they get too close, I end up messing things up and pushing them away, the same way Cat and I did to each other.

Working on this whole thing with Scarlett is giving me the chance to be in control and prevent the worst situation instead of trying to cure it. Prevention is way better than cure.

"I know, dad," I say back. "I'm trying to-" My phone starts to ring loudly in my pocket, vibrating against my thigh and I pick it out, smiling as I see Scarlett's name on the screen. "Speak of the devil," I mutter, getting up from my seat and silently excusing myself to go into the corridor as my dad continues with his food.

Once I've walked as far as I can down the corridor, passing large modernist art pieces on the walls, I answer the phone.

"Hello?" I ask.

"Branson," she greets, followed by a huge yawn. Weird. "I need you to come over."

"A 'please' would be much appreciated," I tease, resting the phone on my shoulder so I can't adjust my sleeves. She doesn't say anything else. "What do you want?"

"We're working together. I can call you whenever I want," is her response. It sort of sounds like she's either slurring or really tired. I can't decide.

"That's not exactly how it works, Angel," I mock. She groans through the phone followed by another huge yawn. Yep, she's tired. Tired-Scarlett is like trying to poke a bear. Terrifying, but weirdly endearing. Which is why I'm edging her.

"I think I'm having a breakthrough with the project," she replies, her voice dropping to a whisper. The sound of her sleepy voice turns my mind absolutely feral, imagining her in bed or fresh out the shower. It's sickening, really, how quickly my thoughts turn something so innocent into something filthy. And for Scarlett Voss, for god's sake. That itself is a crime.

"Yeah?"

"Mm hm," she murmurs.

Fuck me. The sound goes straight to my dick, and I barely mutter a frustrated, "I'm on my way," before ending the call. I say a quick goodbye to my dad, ensuring him that I'm going to get information, but I know I'm not.

It's really fucking difficult to say no to things when she talks to me in that voice. It would drive me insane if any woman spoke to me like that, but actually knowing Scarlett, and knowing the way she would get pissed at me if I ever made fun of her for sleepily calling me, it spurs me on.

AFTER NEARLY PASSING the speed limit to get to her apartment, I finally made it up the steps and to her door. The elevator is out of service like always, so by the time I've got to the top I'm heaving, trying to make sure my white shirt isn't sticking to my back and chest. I get to number 407 and knock on the door three times. She doesn't answer it. In fact, nobody answers it until I knock again, a little harder this time, and the door swings open.

Holy mother of God.

It looks like a printer threw up in here. Her precious whiteboard is covered in printed sheets with green string tying points together with pins. The whole kitchen counter is decorated in sheets of paper, her laptop somehow nestled in there as I hear music playing faintly in the background.

♫ FADE INTO YOU - MAZZY STAR

Jesus, this girl, and her sad music is going to be the death of me. I can't even step into the place without scrunching up sheets beneath my shoes.

"It looks like a crime scene in here," I mutter, making my way safely to the kitchen, looking into the living room.

"I had a breakthrough."

Her voice sounds muffled at first and I don't exactly know where it's coming from and then I turn around and...*holy shit.*

Scarlett's in front of me now, clear as day, in nothing but a white tank top with a tiny bow and purple panties. Her hair is braided into two French plaits, her waves curling at the bottom, falling down her front and the brown strands are long enough to cover her breasts.

It takes me a few seconds to really put together what I'm seeing. This feels like I'm crossing some sort of invisible line for sure. The underwear isn't purposefully provocative, they're a simple cotton design with tiny white dots on them, but I'm a man and I've never seen this woman in such little clothing. She doesn't even seem to care, feeling so at home. I mean, it *is* her home, so I shouldn't be so surprised. She doesn't try to cover herself up. Instead, she looks at me like *I'm* the one with a problem.

"You...You've not got any clothes on," is the stupid thing that comes out of my mouth as she just stares at me, her brown eyes narrowed.

"You ever seen a woman naked before?" she asks cooly. I nod. I'm not a virgin. I just act like it sometimes because I'm, well, me and she's Scarlett Voss. "See, this is *just* like that except I *actually* have some of my clothes on."

"Barely," I mutter, giving her another once over. She rolls her eyes at me, moving past me into the kitchen and I'm struck with a sense of Deja vu. It was only a handful of weeks ago when she trapped me in here, me on this side of the island and her on the other side, interrogating me for the whiteboard, which she clearly found.

I lean my forearms against the marble island, watching as she moves into the cupboards. Maybe this wasn't the best angle to choose because now I can see her small, but round ass in those panties. She reaches up, her shirt that's already short as it is, lifting to reveal a small tattoo on her right hip.

Fuck me sideways, it's hot.

I can't really see it from here, but there are a few words dotted next to a small black butterfly.

It's hard not to stare at it.

At *her*.

When she's around, she's all I fucking see. She's just *there*. Constantly in my face, practically shoving her beauty down my throat without even trying. She's stunning and she knows it. Everyone knows it. Well, they better do or else I'm starting to think I can no longer justify whatever it is I'm feeling as a common thing.

When my eyes snap back up to her arms, she's still grasping at whatever she's trying to get and even though she's not short, she still can't reach. I push myself back from the island, walking over to her, ready to put her out of her misery. And because I can't stop myself, I put my hand on her hip, steadying her as I reach over her.

Well…*shit*.

I should have thought that through. I don't know which one of us gasps when we notice the skin to skin contact. I don't think we've ever been this close before. Never on purpose. She lets out a sigh, maybe grateful that it's only me and I grip onto her tighter, my hands flexing automatically as her back is basically pressed to my front.

I let myself touch her for a moment. I just keep my hand there for a few extra seconds, feeling the smoothness of her bare skin, the warmth radiating from it and the soft, almost buttery feeling I get from it.

"Evan?" she rasps.

"Hm?" Maybe it's not a good idea to form actual sentences right now.

"What are you doing?" she asks as if it isn't obvious. There's a strain to her voice that I can't place. Annoyance? Frustration?

"Getting the glass for you, obviously," I say back, her hair tickling my chin as I reach further over her. "I'm not that much of a monster that I'm going to painfully watch you struggle to get it."

"I can do it myself."

"Clearly, you can't," I huff, picking up the glass with one hand while slightly shoving her to the side with the other, ending our contact. I put the glass on the counter, sliding it to her side. "Why do you even have glasses that high? None of you are over five-seven."

She leans against the opposite counter next to the sink, crossing her ankles and placing the glass under the dispenser in the fridge. "I usually climb up onto the counter, but then you'd end up seeing my bare ass and I don't think either of us want that to happen."

She finishes filling her cup, waiting for her to bring it to her lips before I say, "I can see your ass perfectly fine like this." I wait for the words to register in her brain, seeing if I can push her into the reaction I want. But she's cool, calm, and collected as she swallows smoothly, as if she didn't hear me.

"Thanks for that analysis, Branson," she quips, placing the glass onto the counter, crossing her arms against her chest. "Why are you here?"

Is she being serious? She stares at me, those brown eyes

darkening, pinning me with a look that could send someone running.

"*You* called *me*, remember?" I say playfully. Realisation slowly dawns on her face as her defiant smile fades as her face knots in confusion.

"Did I?" she asks, and I nod, grinning at the way she might be admitting that she was wrong for once. "Shit. I must have fallen asleep. Again. I don't think I've been sleeping properly."

Now I'm curious. "What's keeping you up?"

She sighs dramatically. "Just the fact that I don't know who tried to hurt my dad and someone might be after me and my family."

"No one is coming after you," I say with a groan. This girl needs to stop stressing out before it rubs off on me. I'm already on edge. One of us needs to be the sane one here and we both know it's not going to be me.

"How do you know that? Did they personally let you know that? Because it feels like someone is watching me at all times, Branson."

"I just know," I say quickly, trying my best to convince her. "Just relax, okay?"

"Ah, yes," she mimics dryly. "My favourite thing to do."

"How was your night with- What's his face?" I ask, trying to turn the conversation into a safer topic.

Her eye twitches. "I never told you his name but-"

"Steve?" I say cutting her off on purpose. I love the way her face hardens. She knew I was watching her last night. I mean, she flipped me off while she was *this* close to fucking him in the bar. It was weirdly erotic while she stared directly at me while doing *that* with him.

"Max," she corrects, tilting her head at me. Of course, he

has a dumb fucking name. She brushes one of the braids over her shoulder, her hand locking back in place across her chest. "And you would know if you didn't run off."

"I didn't run off. I just didn't want to see you fuck him on the dance floor," I challenge. She raises her eyebrows in fake shock.

"Really? You look like the kind of person who would enjoy that sort of thing."

"Not when it's you," I say. Her lips part and her eyebrows raise, no doubt about to pick apart what I just said. Before she can have a chance to question it, I change topics again. "What's this big breakthrough?"

Slowly, her eyebrows soften, and she shakes her head a little, drawing herself back to the conversation. She drops her arms, her gaze flickering to the mess of a room she calls her kitchen and then back to me. "Yes, I'm glad you asked."

She pushes past me, walking towards her whiteboard and I get a great view of her ass. Her hips sway back and forth as she marches over to it basically in slow motion. I really shouldn't be looking but I've not touched a woman in over a year and it's safe to say that it's driving me a little bit crazy. She's got the kind of ass you want to get lost in. Spend weeks – no *months* – getting to know.

"Can you at least put on some sweatpants?" I groan, running my hand down my face when my cock hardens at the thought of her ass beneath my palms. She doesn't turn back to me. Instead, she fiddles with the whiteboard, readjusting the pins, continuing to flash me.

"Oh, cause I'm supposed to make *you* comfortable in my own home," she mocks.

"Doesn't it get tiring trying to argue with me all day?" She shrugs, but it turns into a shiver, and I can see the tiny bumps rise across her arms. "I can literally see the goosebumps on your skin. This is clearly more uncomfortable for you than it is for me."

She finally whips her head around, those brown eyes staring straight in mine. "I'm only doing it because since you came in the temperature has dropped at least twenty degrees." With that, she turns around, flashing me her ass once more, walking down the corridor to her room, mumbling, "You're like a bad omen or something."

Seriously? Since I've walked in here all I've felt is heat, heat, heat. And it definitely wasn't the sprint I did to get up the stairs to the apartment. While she's gone, I take a look at the whiteboard, and she's actually done more than I thought.

As easy as this project should be for two people at the top of the class, it's been surprisingly difficult. Especially with trying to keep up on extra credit homework that Anderson sets every day.

She finally materialises in a grey NU sweatshirt and matching joggers that are way too big for her. I think for a second if someone she slept with gave it to her or a boyfriend of some sorts. She would never keep anything of Jake's given how much of a dick he was. I don't know why I care. I *shouldn't* care but I have a strange desire to want to know who gave them to her.

God, I've been weird this week. I need to cut it out before she catches on.

"So…This project?" I ask, trying to keep myself on track.

"Right," she says, turning back to the whiteboard. "I was thinking about how we could actually tackle it. I actually liked your idea."

I tilt my head. "Really? Or are you messing with me?"

"It surprised me too," she whispers. "I just like the idea of telling somebody something and they won't know until you say it, you know? It's like holding onto a secret for so long and you feel free, but still restricted at the same time because it's on the app but it hasn't reached them yet. It's like sending a message to someone you know won't see it until they get home. *That* sort of anticipation."

I nod, feeling like everything she just said is exactly what I'm thinking. "That's exactly what I mean."

Her face softens a little, letting me see another piece of her as she sort of smiles at me. "Well, we've got some work to do then."

14

EVAN

WE GOT through a solid hour of working through the project before Kennedy came home. She sat in the living room, reciting her whole day to Scarlett who "Yeah" and "Mm-ed" her way out of the conversation and then Wren came home, defeated yet happy from skating all day and we called it a night.

I may have gotten little from her side of the Tinzingate situation, but finally putting energy into our project felt good. We finally got a basis for the app, naming it *Hard to Tell* and working out how it would run realistically.

I'm desperate to get deeper into this, so I invited her over to my house today to continue working on it. It's a dumb thing to do, allowing a Voss onto the property. But living with the boys is like a frat house. I know she's been there a hundred times, but I want to impress her for some stupid reason.

I care about what she thinks of me. I care about what everyone thinks of me. The house I share with Miles and Xavier shows nothing of my true character. It's messy, loud and it smells like BO. But I'm hoping that bringing her here will help me open up to her more and she'll feel more comfortable to do the same.

It's exactly 3:15 when she turns up outside the gates to the estate. She drove in her precious *Bellezza Nera,* and I buzz the monitor to open the gates and let her drive up. I watch through the security cameras as she steps out of her huge car in a red dress and black Louboutin heels.

There is no way she's that dressed up to come and study with me. Unless she's trying to impress me too. No, that would be crazy. She wouldn't need to do anything to impress me.

I wait by the door for her to knock and when she does, I swing it open. I was wrong. The dress isn't just red, it's fucking scarlet. Like her name. The silk material is wrapped around every inch and curve of her body, hugging her frame like a corset. The dress falls halfway down her thighs, exposing her long tanned legs. The top part of the dress scoops into a cowl neck, covering most of her chest but leaves enough up to the imagination. She's a few inches taller in those heels, but I'm taller, still towering over her.

"You gonna let me in or just stare some more?" she asks, peering up at me. Her brown eyes narrow and I can't think of a dumb enough excuse, so I open the door wider and let her in.

"Do you want a tour?" I gesture towards the large black hallway. She walks behind me, and I look back at her as she admires the minimalist black and white paintings that are hung modestly on the walls.

"Why? So you can show off?" She scrunches her nose at the painting before looking at me, taking a sweep of my outfit. "I'm good."

That's fair. I can't tell if she's playing one of those games where she pretends she doesn't care, or if she genuinely is not interested. It would be a waste of time anyway.

I've seen pictures of the Voss estate. It's not bigger than ours, but that doesn't matter when it seems like there's is full of love and family and warmth. Real security. The kind of security that actually matters. Here, the sadness practically echoes off the bland walls, showing everyone who enters that there is no real life here.

Well, except for Mila who comes rushing towards me now, all golden fur and chub rubbing between my legs. Scarlett's still beside me, her eyes scanning the walls and then down to Mila.

"Such a good girl, aren't you?" I say, scratching her behind the ears. As the words are leaving my mouth, I look up to Scarlett and she's looking down at me, almost smiling, more at Mila than me, but I take it as a win.

"Are you talking to me or the dog, Branson?" she asks, one of those lined dimples appearing on her cheek. Mila sniffs around her legs and Scarlett crouches a little, scratching her on the head before straightening. So she *is* a dog person.

I shrug and continue walking down the corridor, saying, "Not sure. Can't figure out if you're into the praise thing or not."

She barks out a laugh. "Hopefully we'll never know," she says as she steps in to walk beside me. "What are we doing for the project today?"

"I think we have a good base idea down. Maybe we can start to work on expanding it. Like adding the finer details, you know?"

She nods. "Sounds good."

And we do just that.

I bring us into one of the spare offices; a medium sized room with navy walls, an iMac on one of the desks, a black plush sofa against one wall. She took the seat at the desk, using the iMac to write up plans while I lounged on the sofa, using my notebook of ideas we've accumulated to form a more concise plan.

There's not much talking while we work. Some people wouldn't call it working together, but that's exactly what we're doing. We know what tasks we need to complete and she just does what she needs to do, while I do what I need to do. For once, this project seems to be something we actually agree on. I knew she would like my idea, but every time I look up, she's typing away furiously, completely invested in what she's doing.

I wonder if this is a good distraction for her. If this is what she needs to take her mind off everything going on with her family. That's what numbers and spreadsheets do for me; they allow me to keep my mind focused on something that doesn't contain emotions or words with real meanings. They just make sense together and when they don't, it's easy to find a mathematical solution as to how it went wrong. You can't do that with people.

We've not spoken for another long stretch of time until Scarlett sighs loudly, leaning back in the chair as it creaks low beneath her weight. "I'm going to see if I can connect with a software developer. I think this could be a real app."

"You think so?" I ask, sitting up straighter on the sofa. She nods, her eyes wandering a little. She must be tired. She's been staring at that screen for almost two hours. Maybe we should take a break.

"Yes. It would help us get more credits too. I doubt anybody else has thought of this," she explains. "I'll call someone this weekend."

"Yeah, that sounds good," I reply, about to go back to

writing but then a thought pops into my head. "Have you got any more leads on the stuff going on with your family?"

She raises one eyebrow, rolling in her lips once before pushing them back out. I know there's something she isn't saying and it's getting harder to mention it casually. We've hardly spoken about it since the stakeout, and I don't want her to think that us doing that was a onetime thing. I'm all in.

She swallows, looking out into the backyard that's a forest of tall pine trees as she says, "I think I found the guy that was outside the store. I recognised him and I managed to identify an ID badge that matches the description."

"That's good news right?" I ask, sensing the hesitancy. From the way she got excited just from thinking about driving to the stakeout shows enough of her character. That excitement isn't here anymore. Instead, in its place is worry and uncertainty.

"Yeah, I guess," she says, turning back to me, her brown eyes finally settling on my face. "He owns a restaurant downtown, but I feel like it's going to be another dead end. I just don't want to waste my time."

"Well, you won't know if you don't go," I suggest. She nods, shrugging one shoulder. I thought we agreed to work together on this, but she still seems hesitant. She's probably trying to dismiss the idea so I add, "I can go with you. I'm not busy."

"What makes you think I want you to go with me?" she retorts with that annoying as fuck head tilt.

"I think previous events show what a good partner in crime I am," I say proudly.

She laughs, the sound reverberating through my body. "Do you mean when you almost shit yourself?"

"We could have been killed!"

"You're so fucking dramatic. We were *fine*," she replies, still laughing. I shake my head at her, unsure as to when she became such a hurricane, practically begging for danger. "Fine. You can come. Only because I want to hear you scream again."

"I didn't scream," I mutter, but taking it as a win anyway.

We go through another round of comfortable silence, except for the song she chose to play through the computer. *'In My Life'* by the Beatles plays softly as we both work.

She's stopped aggressively typing now and is instead sketching out a logo for the app while I work on the boring parts of creating an app. We've been working so quietly together, listening to The Beatles and Fleetwood Mac that I don't even realise it's raining hard outside until Scarlett gasps, snapping out of her trance.

"Oh, shit!"

"What?" I ask, startled.

"I haven't been keeping track of time. I'm meant to be going to the Greyson Fauvel event today," she explains, starting to pack away her things. Well that explains why she's so dressed up.

"Oh yeah? I was going to go to that too."

I wasn't.

"Really?" she asks, taking a look at my outfit which is a pair of black baggy jeans and a white tee.

"Yes. I was invited." That much is true. Rich boys in the industry send out invitations like their parents have told them to invite everyone to their birthday party. People of our status want the most of us there as possible to slowly build an army of little rich boys doing what they want. I was never going to go. I always get invited to shit like this, but it would be a waste of time. I have no idea why she wants to go there. There's nothing good for her there. I'm just dying to spend more time doing anything that isn't being caught up in my head. "I'll come with you."

She pauses what she's doing. "What?"

"Yeah, I was going to go and you drove here so I might as well carpool with you," I suggest casually. I already convinced her to let me go with her to that restaurant. Maybe I'm pushing it too far.

"And you want to go in *my* car?"

I make a face. "That's exactly what carpool means. Why are you making this weird?"

"I'm not making it weird," she says defensively, pinning her arms across her chest. The defiant look on her face lasts five seconds before she turns to look out the window as the rain pours harder. "It's just.." She sighs and then adds, "It's raining."

"So?"

She doesn't look at me as she whispers, "I don't like driving in the rain. I was going to think of an excuse to leave my car here and get an Uber and now you've ruined my plans."

She's embarrassed about not being able to drive in this weather, but I don't know why. I get it. If this is something I have to do for her to chill out, I'll do it.

"Just let me drive then."

IT ONLY TOOK two lightning bolts to strike down for Scarlett to agree to let me drive her car. The rain is relentless. I changed out of my home outfit into black trousers and a white button down and of course, a black tie. I have gotten used to driving her car. It's comfortable and is doing okay on the road, despite the rain. The Greyson Fauvel event is held at the same place every year, but I've never driven there from my dad's house.

Unlike the drive to the jewellery store, she doesn't have her leg propped up and is instead sitting with her legs crossed, slightly exposing the tan skin of her thigh. Frankly, it's distracting.

All I can think about is what she would do if I placed my hand on her thigh? Would she let me? Would she let me slip my hand further and further up until she begs me to give her a release?

I'm doing fine until I take the wrong exit on the freeway, and I have no idea where we're going anymore. The signal starts to become weak, and the GPS is left blinking in the same spot that we were in twenty minutes ago. Now, we're on the edge of a forest, rain pouring heavily on the hood of the car as we both stare at the fucked-up GPS.

"Great. Just great," Scarlett mutters angrily. She turns to me, her cheeks red with anger. "How did you manage to do this? You said you knew where we were going."

"I did. I just got confused and I... spaced out for a few seconds," I say, not sure if that's helping my case.

"You can't space out while you drive, Branson. It's, like, rule number one of road safety," she argues, tugging on the car door and opening it to the windy atmosphere. More rain pushes into the car by the wind, covering the console and hitting me in the face.

"Where are you going?"

"Away from you," she shouts, slamming the door. I flinch when the sound hits me, watching her strut away in that red dress, practically hypnotising me. I watch for a handful of seconds before opening my door and trying to catch up with her.

Fuck, she's fast in those heels.

By the time I'm walking closer behind her, she's rambling about how this is all my fault. For the most part it's cute; watching her ramble and get flustered as he talks with her hands, stomping around like a child.

"Trust Evan Branson to get us lost in the middle of nowhere as he breaks my GPS. All I want is a fun night out, but someone has to go mess it up *again,*" she says, turning towards me quickly before continuing to walk deeper into the woods. I pick up the pace and I'm in front of her now, seeing how far she's willing to go until we get lost again. "And because *I'm* the stupid one, I let him drive my car."

Yeah, no.

We're not doing that.

I turn to her. Her outfit is drenched, sticking to her and her hair is soaking, her loose curls more defined as it drips onto her dress, looking blacker instead of dark brown and it's falling crazily on her face.

I grip onto her shoulders as she continues to talk about how I messed everything up, shaking her lightly as raindrops pour down my face.

"Can you stop talking for two seconds and let me think?!"

She blinks at me. "You don't have to shout at me!"

"I'm not shouting," I say back. I'm definitely shouting now. "Can you just let me think? *Please*?"

She stares at me again, her mouth parted as the rain streams down her face. Slowly, she nods, and I turn my back to her, running my hand down my face. Fuck. How did I let this happen? I shouldn't have let this happen. The woods are thick and muddy, it won't stop raining and this girl keeps looking at me like she's three seconds away from ripping my head off.

I turn back to Scarlett with no plan other than to get us back to the car and figure it out from there. She's not looking at me, her eyes are focused on the ground and from the practised way I can see her shoulders rising and falling, I can tell she's forcing herself to calm down, a technique I know all too well.

I inch closer towards her, reaching out my hand. "Hey, Scarlett. Look, we can-"

She slaps my hand away. "Don't 'Hey, Scarlett' me, you dimwit!" she mocks as she pushes me in the chest. Hard. "You got us lost." She pushes me again. "In the middle of fucking nowhere." She pushes me again. "My shoes are ruined and I'm going to miss the whole event because…" She jabs a finger into my chest. "Of." Another jab. "You."

This time I force myself to breathe because she looks like she's going to cry, and I don't know what I would do if she cried right now. If I tried to comfort her in any way, she'd probably come straight for my dick.

"Let me carry you," I say, the words out of my mouth before I can even register it.

"No."

"Come *on*, Angel," I press.

"No."

I sigh. "You're pissed as it is, and I just want to go. So let me carry you, salvage your shoes and leave so we can get on with our day."

"You're right. I *am* pissed, but I don't want you to carry me," she retorts, throwing her hands up. God, she's so stubborn. She turns back around, heading towards the car finally. I run my hand through my hair, feeling how soaked it is as I follow after her.

I didn't realise how far out we were until we walked in angry silence for ten minutes and the car was still far away. She's talking to herself again, sounding like an evil genius. Honestly, I want to laugh, but I don't see how that will help our situation. I almost fall straight into her when she comes to halt and screeches.

"Jesus. What is it?" I ask, peering over her. She's kneeling over now, hopping in the mud, holding onto her right ankle. "Hey. What's wrong?"

"I think I twisted my ankle," she groans, shaking her ankle out. *It was about time.* She places it down but the second it touches the muddy grass, she winces.

"You gonna let me carry you now, Angel?" I ask. She looks up at me, rain streaming between her brown eyes and she nods. It's barely noticeable, but it's something. I crouch down in front of her, already at peace with the fact my shoes and pants are ruined. "Get on my back."

She huffs, mumbling about how this is the last thing she wants to do, but slowly, she eases her thighs around me until I can feel her *everywhere*.

Even though we're both soaked with rain, her skin is still warm as she wraps her arms around my neck and settles her thighs around my back. We're *definitely* crossing some sort of invisible line here, but I need us back in the car and away from these cursed woods.

"You good?" I ask, starting to bring myself up from the ground. She tightens her arms across my neck, linking her hands together.

"Never been better," she mutters into my neck, and I shiver. As I stand, I instantly grip the underside of her thighs,

securing her on to me as best as I can. Her skin is just so...*soft*.
I fucking hate it. Actually, no. I don't hate it. I just hate the
way it makes me feel so out of control of my own body and
mind. She's not even doing anything and it's messing with me.
How is that even possible?

I managed to walk us to the car, trying so hard not to focus
on the way that nearly every part of her was touching me.
Having her touch me like that was just maddening. Thrilling.

"Do you have wipes or something in here?" I ask when
she's sitting in the passenger seat. The door is open, rain still
pouring as she holds her heels in her hand, her right foot
crossed over her lap.

"In the glove box."

I round the other side of the car, searching through her
glove box to find some wipes. When I get back to her side of
the car, she's trying to tend to her ankle, twisting it in all
different positions. I'm not a doctor, but I'm also not an idiot.
It looks swollen, it's got mud all over it and she isn't
impressed with it either.

I hand her the wipes. "Here's what we're going to do.
You're going to clean these, and I'll check out your ankle.
Deal?"

She nods, retrieving them and starting to clean off her heels.
I'm surprised she didn't put up more of a fight about it, but I
think we've got to the point where we're both too tired to even
fight it anymore. I'm going to help her and she's going to let me.

Her feet aren't particularly big, but they just feel like they
are when they are right in my face. Her toes are painted red,
matching her dress and there's a line around the top of her foot
from the imprint of the heel shape.

Gripping onto her ankle lightly, she winces, pausing her

scrubbing and I mutter a 'Sorry' in response. I don't know what possessed her to go out in the rain and try and run off from me because all she got out of it was a fucked-up ankle and dirty shoes. I put pressure on the spot I can tell is sore and I pinch one of the wipes from her and clean off her ankle. Cleaning it off has probably made it look worse because now it looks even angrier. I'm still staring at her foot when I hear her shoes landing in the backseat.

The rain has slowed now, and it doesn't feel like we have to shout just to hear each other. She peers down at me, swatting her hair from her face.

"What's the verdict? Am I going to survive, Doc?" she asks, yanking her foot from my grip and setting it down in front of her across her lap. I take it as a sign to back up from her, so I stand, leaning on the open car door.

I tut, shaking my head. "No, I think I'm going to have to amputate your leg," I joke, and she frowns, tilting her head to the side. "You'll be out of service for a few days."

She gasps. "A few *days*?"

"Yep. No strenuous activities for you."

"No strenuous activities," she mocks, her voice an octave higher than her usual one.

"None," I say.

"Not even dancing?"

"Not even dancing."

"Walking?"

"No walking."

She nods thoughtfully and I swear I catch the exact second her eyes light up with excitement. "What about sex? Missionary only."

I shake my head. "Especially not that."

She sulks. "So, what am I supposed to do? Just sit around all day and wait for it to magically heal?"

"I'm sure you can find other ways to entertain yourself," I whisper.

I do the dumbest thing I could possibly do and brush her hair behind her ear. It was wet and sticking to her face, driving me insane that she hadn't removed it. It was only fair for the common good to sort it out before my OCD had a field day. I've already touched her enough as it is today, but one more time won't hurt.

Our gazes lock as she realises what I just did. She tenses at the contact, her eyes going wide for a second. It's such an unnecessarily intimate move. I drop my hand, clearing my throat.

"We should go," she whispers. "I don't want to miss out on anything more than what I've already missed."

I blink at her, pulling back. "You still want to go to that?"

"I didn't wear this outfit to just sit around at home. You can drop me off at the club and I'll Uber home and pick up my car tomorrow."

"Fine, but I'm going to come in with you. I can't have my project partner breaking her leg. You'll be even more unbearable to work with," I say, my pathetic excuse to stay close to her and keep her from getting herself into trouble.

"Fine," she huffs, turning back into the seat.

When is today going to end?

15

SCARLETT

I DITCHED Evan the second we got in here.

I've had enough of him today already. He's been just *there*. There is only so much of him I can take. He's usually best in small doses, but it feels like he's been constantly shoved down my throat recently.

When I get really tired and hungry, I naturally start to go a little delirious. *That's* the only reason why I called him the other day. Caffeine does nothing to help me stay awake and neither do any type of pills. I was high on the rush that working on the project gave me and I needed to tell him before I lost the momentum. I wasn't concerned about him seeing me almost naked, rival or not, I'm comfortable enough with my body to not give a shit.

But when he's around, the temperature either goes below zero or scorching hot. It fluctuates every time he's near and it drives me insane.

At my house: freezing. Shouting at him in the woods: hot. Him carrying me and diggings his fingers into my thighs:

freezing. The simple, tiny touch that sent electric shocks across my body as he tucked a strand of hair behind my head: hot, hot, blazing fucking hot.

These types of feelings are easy to get rid of and ignore because Evan is the last person on earth to ever give me electric shocks.

To get rid of that feeling tonight, I found the first guy that gave me the 'fuck me' eyes and took him to the bathroom.

Still, when I'm walking out, readjusting my dress, and double checking my makeup is clear in my hand mirror, Evan's standing right in front of me.

Great. Just fucking great.

My hair is as good as it can look after being drenched with rain. My dress had dried after putting it under the hair dryer. Still, I don't want Evan to see me like this. I don't want *anyone* I know to see me like this. I came here for a little fun. A release. Not a lecture from the look of disgust on Evan's face.

"Done with Steve already?" Evan asks, an evil smirk on his lips. I scoff and brush past him. The guy that I just with, follows me too, both him and Evan hot on my heels.

"It was *Max* and not yet," I say, correcting him, knowing he's trailing behind me. I stop abruptly, wanting this conversation to die a quick death so I can get on with my night.

"But you were just…With him…" Evan splutters, gesturing towards the guy silently standing by my side. Jason, I think his name was. He's a cute guy; tall, brunette, buzzcut. My usual type.

Mason thinks it's his time to shine as he extends his hand to Evan. "I'm Henry."

Okay, *what*? I just fooled around with someone who has the same name as my *brother*. What the hell?

Evan looks down to Jaxon- *no*, Henry's hand and grimaces.

"Don't care," he says, and I try not to laugh at the way poor Henry's face drops. He disappears as Evan turns to me. "Well, does it mean you're done with Max if you were just…" He trails off again.

"I was just…what? Spit it out, Branson."

"You look like you've just had sex," he points out, lowering his voice as he gestures at my outfit.

"Oh, and who named you the judge of sex, Mr Branson? Because I don't remember that ever being your title," I say back, raising an eyebrow.

"Careful, Angel. Keep calling me that and I'll think you actually like me."

I scoff, rolling my eyes. *God, he's so infuriating.* He does one nice thing, like carry me in the rain and then he starts to be a jerk again. I swear it's just wired in him. It's only a matter of time before he acts up again.

"For your information, I spilled a drink on my - already recovering - dress and he offered to help me clean it up. You see, that's what gentlemen do, Evan. They clean up messes they don't even make," I argue. I leave out the part where he may have finger-banged me into next week because I don't think that would help my case.

He nods, crossing his arms against his chest as he leans against the pale blue wall. "Whatever you say."

For some reason, I don't believe that he's choosing to play this cool. He doesn't have any right to comment on how I look like I've fucked somebody or better yet, be rude to people I have fooled around with. Not like I'm any better, but it's weird when he does it.

I give him one last look before turning around and finding the reason I came here.

EVAN

It only takes Scarlett twenty minutes for her to ditch me again and find some other dude to warm up to whilst getting slightly drunk. I don't know how she's managed to salvage her wet-hair disaster and turn it into a pretty decent look. It's working like magic for her because she hasn't been left alone for over two minutes as guys circle around her like vultures.

She doesn't care though. Or maybe she does and she's enjoying it. Because her eyes are closed, her hands are in the air as she sways to the music. Some girls even come up to me to talk, like they always do at these exclusive events, but I can't even give them the time of day.

One girl slips her phone number into my hand after a minute of nonsensical small talk. Another girl dragged her nails down my forearm, telling me how good she would be in bed. And another girl grinded herself into me and called me a prick when I politely asked her to stop.

I can't even entertain it. Not when she's there. Dancing like *that*. How is she managing to dance with a messed up ankle? Beats me. But she's not acting like she's hurt. Maybe she made the whole thing up.

One of the guys in navy dress pants and a white button down that's untucked, comes up behind her. She's minding her business, dancing, and feeling the music. He places his hands on her waist, pulling her back into him, her ass right in his lap.

God, this is worse than the other night at the bar. It gets from worse to fucking unbearable when she opens her eyes, glancing at him for a second before smiling that sly smile that no doubt signals to him that she's thinking about doing more than just dancing with him.

I can't place what it is that comes over me when I see her like that. Before getting to know her, I wouldn't care, but being around her more often these last few days, I don't believe this confident act that she puts on for a second. I can tell on the inside she's scared, which is why she's acting out and doing dumb shit like this.

I watch painfully as she grinds her ass into him as he kisses her neck.

No. Not happening.

I storm over, reaching them in a few seconds. They must be caught in some lusty daze because neither of them sees me approaching. Hell, Scarlett's eyes are still closed. The guy looks drunk or high, or both as he stares at me, still moving against her.

"Are you done?" I ask her.

Her eyes open then. For a second they're filled with surprise until they soften, showing me that she's enjoying pissing off. If that's what her aim for this whole thing was, it's working.

"What do you think?" she asks, slurring as her eyes wander around my face. She smirks as she purposefully grinds her ass into the dude behind her. My cock aches at the motion, causing me to groan.

"You're done," I say to her, gripping onto her forearms and pulling her away from him and then into me. She melts into me almost instantly, her warm body pressing against mine. "Dance with me."

"Why?"

"Because maybe if I soften you up, you'll *finally* let me take you home," I say and her eyebrows crease. She looks like a little bunny like this: her eyes filled with wonder and curiosity, her nose a little red and her cheeks flushed. Honestly, it's adorable. "You're drunk."

She shakes her head. I can tell it gives her a headache from the way she shuts her eyes for a few seconds. "I'm sober enough to know I don't want to dance with you."

"Then let's skip the dancing and I'll take you home. There's no way you're driving your car and it's dangerous to get an Uber at this time. Please, Scarlett," I say, practically begging. If anything happened to her...God, I don't even want to think about it. She mumbles something about how she can't catch a break. I pull apart from her to lift her chin up with two fingers, urging her to look up at me. "Speak up, sweetheart."

She groans. "I said, *fine*. It's the least you can do after messing up my shoes, my dress, *and* my hair."

"You're the one who *insisted* on coming straight here," I argue.

"Yes, because why would I want to stay at home all night and sulk? Life is way too fucking short for that."

I snort. "Since when were you such a party girl?" I'm genuinely curious, but she doesn't answer me, as always. Instead, she answers my question with a question of her own.

"Since when were you such a dick? Oh, wait. You always have been."

"That's not true," I mutter.

I'm sick of this back and forth.

When will she finally see the kind of person I really am and not the facade that she makes of me every day? If me giving her a piggyback, tending to her ankle and driving her here wasn't enough of a clue that I actually care about her in some fucked up way, I don't know what is.

She presses two fingers under my chin, titling my head up.

"Speak up, sweetheart," she mocks.

"Forget it. Just get in the car," I demand.

Scarlett

TODAY HAS BEEN one clusterfuck of a day and I'm ready for it to be over with. I can deal with a little bit of rain. That's fine. I can deal with Evan seeing me as messy and as gross as ever. Not my favourite thing, but bearable. I can deal with getting a little drunk and Evan being strangely nice enough to offer to take me back home.

What I *can't* deal with is the clamp on my wheel because *somebody* decided to park in the wrong spot. My poor *Bellezza Nera* doesn't deserve this. We're both standing at the curb, staring at it, hoping that blinking will make it disappear. But it doesn't.

"You've got to be fucking kidding me," I groan. I turn to Evan and for whatever reason, he thinks this is the appropriate time to smile at me. His cheeks are flushed from being inside the venue for so long and his hair is a mess. Still, he's fucking *smiling* at me. "You parked us in the wrong spot."

He pulls out his phone, chuckling. "Don't blame me, Angel. You have eyes too." He starts typing for a few seconds, not looking at me.

"Who are you texting?"

"Charles."

"Who the hell is Charles?"

"My driver," he replies flippantly, shoving his phone into his back pocket. "He'll be here in ten."

"Of course," I mutter.

Obviously he has a driver because he's *so* important. I used to have one too during high school, but as I started to grow up, doing things I know my family wouldn't approve of, the stupidest thing would be to have someone driving me around everywhere and reporting back to my parents. Evan is either a secretly good boy or he doesn't give a shit about what his family thinks about what he does.

Exactly ten minutes later, a black Escalade pulls up behind my car. I follow behind Evan as he walks towards it.

He opens the backdoor for me and I slide in there, finally able to take off my shoes. Evan gets in next to me, rattling off my address to the white middle-aged man in the front seat.

Evan must be as exhausted and pissed off as I am because he leans his head against the headrest, manspreading. His shirt sleeves have rolled up a little, exposing his lightly tanned arms and a silver watch on his right wrist which rests between his thighs on the seat. I weirdly get off on the way I can unravel him so easily.

So, I move my sore feet from the floor in front of me to over his lap. I'm messing with him, obviously, but it feels good to know that it wasn't just me who felt that strange pull between us earlier when he was tending to my ankle. We annoy each other. It's our thing. But sometimes, it feels like we're going to burst into flames, and I want to be the one holding the match.

For a second I think he hasn't even noticed my bare legs in his lap until his eyes open. His hot gaze travels from the curve of my foot now resting on the car door, up my legs and then to my face.

I'm watching him, trying to see if his face will crack. It's one thing to look at, but it's another thing to read. He doesn't wear his emotions on his face like many people I know, where you can tell exactly what they're thinking about without asking. His face is blank with a wave of irritation and anger.

"Don't do that, Scar," he breathes.

Scar, that's a new nickname from him. It's either my full name or 'Angel.' I always thought that was out of bounds for him. He rolls his head back onto the seat, closing his eyes again.

"Why not? I've got nowhere else to put them," I joke, scooting closer to him so my knees bend a little and both my thighs and my calves are touching his legs. "It's your fault I twisted my ankle."

"That didn't seem to be a problem twenty minutes ago when you fucked that guy in the bathroom," he relays. I don't respond and I wiggle my legs in his lap. He groans. "Don't do this to me, Angel."

I'm about to make another snarky comment, but the car jolts forward, making me yelp as I almost fall flat on my face. Charles shouts out an apology. I think I mumble something in response, but I can't focus on anything other than Evan's hot and warm hand wrapping around my middle, pulling me back into the seat.

He huffs and I'm smiling, finally having broken him. His woody scent invades my senses as his long arm reaches above me as he pulls the seatbelt down and clips it in.

"I can do that myself," I say.

"Well, clearly you can't," he responds, moving back into his seat with an exaggerated sigh. He runs his hand through his hair, leaving it messier than it was before he touched it. He doesn't even seem to care anymore. In fact, he seems pissed.

"I don't know why you're angry. I didn't ask you to do that for me," I say.

"And I didn't ask you to put your legs on me, and here we are."

So, we're back to this? Perfect.

I avert my gaze from his and turn to look out at the dark night sky. It's hard to see the stars, but if I stare for long enough, I can just about make out tiny silver dots. The smell coming from the crack in the window is one of my favourite smells. It's the deep, humid, and thick smell you get after it's rained, and I love it. It feels like a warm hug or a fresh shower.

When we get to the parking lot of my apartment building, I glance over to him and he's staring out of the window. I hate this uncomfortable feeling like I'm walking on eggshells around him. I want him to joke with me. To fight with me. Anything.

"Thanks for the ride," I say, moving to open my door.

"I'm walking you up," he replies as he opens his door, not giving me a choice. Great. A new way to make this even more unbearable than it already is. I carry my heels in one hand as we walk in silence up to the elevator. When we get to my door, he stands there, hands in his pockets as I lean against the door.

I can't take the silence anymore, so I say, "Why are you being so nice to me today? We're supposed to hate each other."

He shrugs, shifting his weight from one foot to the other. "We can still hate each other. We're just two people who know where the line is. Remember, I need you in one piece so we can finish this project."

"Right." For a second I thought he was going to acknowledge the weird energy that hangs in the air between us. After this mess of a day, I don't know where we stand on the frenemy scale.

"You're not going to throw up or anything, are you?" he asks, nodding to my door.

"Why? So, you can hold my hair back and whisper sweet nothings into my ear?" I tease. His face remains stoic, a look of complete defiance.

"Scarlett," he presses.

"I can handle myself, Branson. I didn't need you to walk me up here. I didn't need you to take me home," I say defensively. Then, for extra emphasis, I add, "I'm fine."

"Yeah, but I did."

"Yeah, but why?"

He scratches the back of his neck, finding the ground more interesting than my face as he mumbles, "Why does anyone do anything, Angel?"

I could say something smart to catch him out. I could sass him in some way and get him to roll his eyes at me. This new dynamic is making me feel uncomfortable. I just want us to go back to our normal before he helped me. Instead, I let out a soft, "Stop calling me that."

He looks at me now, grinning. "I don't think I ever will," he says. He reaches behind me, pushing the door open and urging me to shove me in. "Don't die before morning. We've got a big day ahead of us."

I crinkle my eyebrow. "What's happening tomorrow?"

"Our big plan to find out who that dodgy guy is, remember?"

"Oh."

He tuts, shaking his head. "Don't 'Oh' me. This could be a breakthrough in our case."

"It's not *our* case, it's *my* case. You're just tagging along."

"Fine by me," he says happily, shrugging. "Goodnight, Scarlett."

Standing there dumbfounded for two minutes after Evan descended the stairs out of my apartment helped me come to a startling realisation: I no longer hate Evan Branson, I tolerate him. Maybe even respect him. He's done way more than necessary today while still managing to be a prick. It's weird. I want him to push me around. I want to push *him* around.

Sometimes I feel like I'm desperately waiting to see which one of us breaks first.

16

EVAN

SOMETHING TERRIBLE IS HAPPENING.

Something that should not be happening to a person like me. I'm always in control of my emotions and events. Well, as in control as one can be with a life like mine.

After what went down with Cat and my image for the business, I've been trying to be more cautious about how I present myself. After being humiliated from the whole Oreo situation, not only have I steered clear from those cookie and cream flavoured monsters, but I've also tried to keep a clean record from all things to do with the press.

It's natural to get photographed because of who my family is, but it's worse when you're also out in public with another millionaire. Somehow, while I was helping Scarlett get into the car last night, some dweeb took a picture of us and blew it out of proportion. The picture is low quality, only capturing the back of us, but you can tell it's us by the car and the location.

Everyone and their mothers were at the Greyson Fauvel event last night. I've done my best to get it taken down before more people around NU get a whiff of it, but some accounts are persistent.

After feeling like a fool for crossing line after line with Scarlett last night, I kept my distance in class today. I kept all talk to be strictly academic, planning to talk more about her family situation later. The more I press on about it, the more likely she'll become suspicious.

When classes finished, we agreed to meet at her apartment before heading to the restaurant. Yelsy's is an Arabian restaurant, a good half an hour drive from my house and Scarlett's apartment. According to the reviews on Google, the owner, Gerard Rothschild attends the restaurant every day to help keep it afloat. That is the guy we need.

I'm not exactly sure what it is we're going to do, but we decided that going as undercover as we can is probably the best idea. That's why I'm dressed down today, replacing my usual attire with dark blue baggy jeans and a white hoodie. Miles said I blend more with NU's population looking like this, but I feel like I'm sticking out like a sore thumb.

Just as I walk down the street towards her apartment complex, I send her a text.

> ME: I'm coming up now.

> SCARLETT: Don't bother. Stay downstairs and I'll come down.

I DO AS SHE SAYS, and I stay put, taking a seat in the apartment lobby, lounging in one of the plush black and orange chairs. I flick through a sports magazine for a few seconds, not taking any interest, but trying to make myself seem busy until she finally appears through the elevator doors.

She's dressed differently too, in black jeans and a steel blue crew neck and her brown hair is down instead of tied back with one of those ribbons. I watch her fiddle with the ends of it, slapping it out of her face angrily.

She checks her left and right as if she's crossing a road before speed-walking over to me, a little limp still in her leg. She does the motion for me to get up with her hand, tilting her head towards the exit. I do as I'm told and follow her.

She still hasn't said anything by the time we're crossing the parking lot towards her car and it's then that I put the pieces together. I fall into step beside her, grinning.

"Oh my God. Am I your dirty, little secret?" I gasp dramatically. She turns to me, still walking as she scoffs.

"Yes, you are. I would rather stab myself in the eye than let my friends believe that I'm *willingly* going out in public with you," she says sweetly. We reach her car, and she stands with her arms against her chest, pinning me with one of *those* looks.

"'Going out' is a bit of a stretch, don't you think?" I ask, still smiling. Dropping my voice to a whisper, quickly scanning the parking lot as I add, "We're on our way to assess a possible murder situation. We're undercover spies."

She rolls her eyes. "Just get in the car."

I'm still grinning when we're ten minutes into the ride, and I can tell she's still annoyed about me being here. Some days I'll be the grumpy one and others she will be the grumpy one. On a rare day, we're both grumpy and pissed off, edging each other on. I like getting her riled up. I honestly don't think I've had this much fun since I was a kid.

"We're going to need codenames," I announce. She

glances at me, frowning before turning back to the road as well as turning up the radio.

♫ **TREAD CAREFULLY BY SZA**

"We're not doing that."

I ignore her. "I'm going to call you 'Linda' for the rest of tonight. Is that cool?" She groans in response, although I can't tell if it's from the traffic we merged into or the new name. "Thought so. I'll be Danny."

She nods, a small smile playing on her lips. I knew she'd come around to it soon. Maybe she's into the whole role-playing thing. I wouldn't be surprised.

"Hey, Danny?"

"Yeah?"

"You've got a dumb fucking name," she says. Then she starts laughing. At her own joke. She doesn't need me to laugh. Hell, I don't think she *wants* me to laugh. She just sits there happily, smiling at her own jokes like she's a fucking comedian. I swear she's secretly such a dork. What's worse is the fact that *I* can't stop smiling.

"Well, you got Linda so sucks to suck," I retort, sounding as childish as ever. After the weird conversations we had last night, this is the kind of frenemy territory I want to be in. The kind that we've got used to.

"Everyone knows that Linda's are cool. She's the best character in *Bob's Burgers*," she argues, glancing at me for a split second before turning back to the road. I haven't watched that show since I was a kid.

"Louise is obviously the best character," I say back. "You remind me of her, actually. Instead of her pink hat that she always wears, you have ribbons."

She snorts. "I'm not wearing one today and I'm not having a nervous breakdown." I don't know if she's trying to hide the ribbon I can see tied around her wrist, but I've already seen it.

"Glad to know you have better emotional intelligence than a ten-year-old."

She gives me one of her killer death stares before turning to the road. For a second, I swear I see a small smile on her face.

Maybe I'm imagining it.

THE RESTAURANT IS the perfect place to scope out the current target. It's all brown and woody, giving it an overall cabin vibe with dark orange lights hanging over the table. It has an open kitchen, allowing customers to see straight into the front line of those working the grill, which is also where we're planning to spot Gerard. We took a seat in front of the window, directly across from the kitchen, giving Scarlett the view of the door and both of us a good look at the kitchen.

Since we've sat down and had the waiter take our orders, she's not said anything. I'm still not sure exactly where we stand and how to go about it. I'm used to her talking. I'm used to her shit-talking me and making fun of me.

When I can't take the silence anymore as she fiddles with the napkin, I say, "Hey, look. I didn't want to bring it up, but it feels wrong not to tell you." She looks up at me now, her eyes slightly darkening as her eyebrows furrow. "I've seen a few pictures. Of us. From last night."

She nods once, clearing her throat. "We're both fully clothed, correct?"

I blink at her rapidly. I know she must have dealt with this before, but she seems too calm. "Yes. But-"

"Then what's the problem?" she asks, tilting her head curiously.

"You really want to be seen fraternising with the enemy? You said that you didn't even want your friends to see us together, never mind the whole world," I say.

She chuckles low. "That was a joke, Branson. My friends know we're working on the project together. When a reporter comes up with an interesting story, *then* I'll care. Right now, the best they can probably think of is that we slept together."

She says it so calmly as if it doesn't bother her at all. The waiter arrives with our drinks, placing her Coke in front of her and my lemonade in front of me. She takes a long sip of it.

"And that doesn't worry you?"

"No. Why would it? No one is stupid enough to believe I actually slept with you," she argues.

"Right." I glance over to the kitchen and there's still no sign of him. "What else are we supposed to talk about while we wait?"

She shrugs, pushing her hair out of her face. "I don't know," she says. She drops her eyes to her hands on the table, mumbling, "What are your hobbies?"

She asks the question like it physically pains her for us to talk about something not school or business related. Her whole body practically cringes as the words leave her mouth, ending the sentence with a shudder.

It's good for me though. I'm so desperate to break into her special way of thinking. Sometimes I want to know every thought in her head.

"Seriously, Linda? That's the best you can come up with?"

She rolls her eyes. "Well, I don't want to be here with you to begin with, *Danny.* So, excuse me if-"

"I play piano," I reply, cutting her off. Her eyes widen, mischief and humour dancing within them.

"Oh shit, I forgot. Like, you *actually* play?"

"Yeah. I'm in the band." I regret saying that the second the words leave my mouth.

I love to play. I've had lessons pretty much since the womb since my mom also plays. When I found out North had music rooms available to all students, as well as a grand piano in the Radnor building, I couldn't help myself.

"And you're in the band?" she repeats, smiling. It's not a sweet smile that she gives strangers. It's a wicked one that she reserves only for me when she's trying to piss me off. If her eyes go any wider, I swear they'll of her skull.

"Yes, I'm in the band. Are you going to keep repeating everything I say?"

"You're making this too easy," she says.

"Making what too easy?"

"Being able to make fun of you," she replies, smiling wide. "I'm convinced it's my absolute favourite thing to do in the world."

"You must have a very boring social life," I retort. She shrugs, dismissing me as she moves on to her questioning.

"So, did you, like, go up to them and ask, "Hey, can I join the band," or did they scout you out?"

I'm about to respond seriously, telling her that I was caught playing in the music rooms on campus and they offered me a spot. I haven't shown up to the meetings in a while, but if they ever have a performance, I'll show up.

Then I see the way she's trying her hardest not to laugh at me. I roll my eyes and the sound comes rushing out of her like a wave, crashing against the shore in my brain.

"You're so fucking annoying," I mutter, shaking my head.

She doesn't stop laughing until it smooths out with a long sigh. I wish I knew why making fun of me makes her so happy.

"But you love it," she says when it finally dies down. Her expression borders on sadness instead of joy. Her smile wobbles a little as she says, "I don't have any hobbies. Not really, anyway. I like fashion, music, and Pinterest, but doesn't everybody? I try to make my own designs when I can but... I dunno."

"You don't need to do something extraordinary or special for it to be a hobby, you know?" I say. She holds my gaze for a second, squinting to see if I'm being serious. I am. So serious.

She shrugs. "I guess," she concedes, taking another sip of her drink. "I just don't think I'm that interesting in general. Wren has her writing and skating, Ken paints and swims. I'm just the boring one."

"You're not *that* boring. Your personality can be bearable when you're not being mean to me."

She barks out a laugh. "That's the new way to tell someone that they have a horrible personality, but they're kinda pretty so it's fine."

"I never said you were pretty," I challenge. She is pretty. Anyone with eyes can see that. She's got this regal, old-money look. Like she'll kill you with just a glance. Like she was made specifically to ruin lives.

"You didn't have to," she responds, still smiling.

When our food arrives, we eat in silence. The restaurant isn't as busy as we thought it would be, but there's a low buzz coming from families and tables that are full of students. If the guy who owns it wasn't so shady, it would be a decent place to eat at. The food isn't half bad either.

We're halfway through our meal when Scarlett pauses her fork on the way to her mouth. I'm not stupid enough to turn my head no matter how badly I want to and see what's caught her eye, but that could blow our cover.

"You found our guy, Linda?" I ask, pushing around my food casually. She nods slowly, dropping her gaze, but slightly angling her head right towards the kitchen. I look over slightly, noticing two figures.

One of them is our guy: a tall, tanned, and tattooed man with a deep scar on his cheek that's healed, easily becoming a stereotype for a drug dealer. There's another guy, a little shorter, shoulder-length dark brown hair and an untamed beard.

I accidentally drop my fork the second the overhead music stops playing and they both turn to me.

Shit. Scarlett shoots me a look to ask what I'm doing, and I shrug, picking it back up and continue eating, but their eyes are still on us.

I try to keep my cool, pretending to smile and eat, but I can still feel their hot gaze set entirely on us.

Scarlett sighs, rolling her eyes as she gets out of her chair, tossing her brown hair over one shoulder. I can tell that she doesn't prefer having her hair all down as she's constantly trying to pull it out of her face. I try my best to stay calm, but it's hard to do when she sits in the seat next to me, pulling it closer to me.

"Move over," she demands, her strong perfume hitting me in every place that counts. For a second, it's all I can fucking smell. Just her. I do as she asks and shuffle my chair closer to the window as she moves hers into me, our thighs touching. The heat from her thigh against mine basically burns straight through my clothes, penetrating every muscle that becomes fully aware of her presence.

"What are you doing?" I ask, glancing up at the two people who are *still* watching us and then back at her.

"We need to give them a reason to stop staring," she replies. She places her hand on my thigh, and I swear I almost burst into flames. Her hand looks so fucking tiny against me, and my dick twitches at the sight. That is a No-Go Zone. Especially for her. "Look at me like you love me, Danny."

"Like I- What?" I splutter, trying to search her eyes for something to tell me this is a joke, but there's nothing. All that is in those dark brown eyes is concentration and someone with a plan.

"Just look at me like I'm someone you want to take home tonight. You can do that right?" I just blink at her. She's so close to me now and I'm hyper-aware of every single inch of her.

The soft curve of her nose, covered loosely with freckles that are only visible this close. The golden swirl in her eyes. The fullness of her pink lips as she rolls them in, blinking back at me.

Her right hand is still on my thigh while she uses her other to grab my hand, placing it onto her hot neck, my fingers naturally curling around the back like they just belong there. This is unknown territory.

She releases her hand from mine and places it gently on my shoulder instead. Her face remains unbothered apart from the faint redness of her cheek.

"Just keep your hand there and look at me. Like, *really,* look at me."

"I'm looking," I murmur. I do as she asks and as I stare straight into her eyes. I keep my thumb on the base of her throat, feeling her pulse hammer and my fingers curl to the nape of her neck, and I tug a strand of her hair.

At the contact, her eye twitches slightly as she tilts her head further back, giving my hand more access to her hair. I try to get as much as I can without going too far. Needing her close, but not too close. Everything about her physically is so fucking soft, while on the inside she's as hard as granite. It's like she was made to melt into my hands.

As I keep looking at her, trying to look straight through her, I watch as her breathing starts to quicken, and she grips onto my thigh. Hard. From what was once a gentle touch, her grip suddenly turns lethal as she holds onto it like it's anchoring her.

We're both breathing heavily now, just staring at each other as she holds onto me, and I hold onto her. I don't think she even notices she's doing it.

I notice, though. I notice everything about her.

There's a brief moment that can only be described as peace. Where we're not trying to do anything other than exist in each other's presence. We're not rivals. I'm not the stupid son of a million-dollar company. She's not the only daughter to a CEO of a multi-million-dollar brand.

We're just Scarlett and Evan: two souls who somehow, in some weird way, are looking at each other like they know each other. Like they just understand.

Like I said, the moment is brief.

One second we're staring into each other's eyes – no, each other's *souls* – and the next I'm looking at the back of Scarlett's head as she talks to a man in front of her.

It takes me a few seconds to fully register the bearded man as the guy who was talking to Gerard. Except now, he's got a pleasant smile on his face instead of the scowl he was giving us a few minutes ago.

I didn't even notice that Scarlett wiggled out of my grip,

and my arm moved around her shoulder, pulling her so close to me she might as well be in my lap as her hand rests on my thigh like it belongs there now.

"Scarlett, *tesoro*, what are you doing here?" the man asks, planting his arms across his chest. He has a playful smile on his lips. Scarlett barks out a laugh and it's a little strangled as she squeezes my thigh again.

"Just hanging out with my boyfriend," she says, glancing over to me with 'don't mess this up' eyes. Oh, *I'm* the boyfriend. Fantastic. "Right, boyfriend?"

I press my lips into a line, trying not to laugh at the absurdity. "Of course, girlfriend," I say lovingly. "I'd do anything to make my little sugar-plum Scar-Scar happy."

She nudges me in the ribs, murmuring, "Reign it in, loverboy."

I look back at this dude who somehow knows Scarlett and he looks at me for a second. In fact, he looks at *all* of me. He looks from my blonde hair to the neckline of my shirt, right down to the Rolex on my wrist. He even takes a little step back, no doubt scouting for the kind of shoes I'm wearing.

"Well," he starts, ignoring me and turning back to Scarlett. "I'll let you guys get back to it. Ah, young love."

Scarlett smiles at me, her eyes squinting before turning back to the guy. "Yep. So young and so in love," she says sweetly.

The guy nods and the second he turns back around to stand next to our guy, she practically leaps away from me, grabbing her stuff she left on her side of the table, almost leaving me behind as she rushes out of the door.

I run after her, and I catch her panting behind the building. Her back is pressed against the wall, chest heaving as she clutches her black bag to her chest. I stand in front of her, my arms flapping at my sides, words failing me.

"Jesus. What the hell was all that about?" I ask breathlessly. When my breathing starts to return to normal, I ask, "Who *was* that?"

She gulps, looking down the alleyway we've ended up in and then back at me, her brown eyes wide with concern. "That was Gio. My uncle."

"He knows we were going to check out the guy, right? Maybe he just wanted to make sure we were doing the right thing," I suggest. I mean, why else would he be there? The guy he was talking to is clearly a suspect and her uncle must be looking out for her.

She shakes her head. "I never told him I was coming."

Oh, fuck.

17

SCARLETT

I'VE BEEN TRYING to piece together what we saw at the restaurant for the last four days. Why the hell would Gio be there talking to him? When I asked him about the jewellery store, he seemed a little closed off about it and when I told him that the guy was pretty much unrecognisable other than his posture, he didn't encourage me to go any further.

Gio has already lost so much in his life; his wife and his close friend. I can understand why he wouldn't want to get directly involved in the investigation, but it's his brother, his *family*.

I know he's always wanted to be a more prominent member of the business, but I thought the role he had now was good for him. It's given him the creative freedom he wouldn't get in other jobs. He seemed comfortable with it. It just doesn't make sense to me that he would try and mess this up and lie to me. Especially with how consoling our family has been with everything that went down.

I've thought about calling him, but what could I say? He doesn't know that I'm investigating and if he is working with

Gerard, it's better if I don't know. That could put us all in a terrible position.

I tried rationalising it with Evan, but he was no help. He's such a pessimist sometimes. Or he redirects the ideas I come up with and turns them into something completely different. Even now as we work on the project in the on-campus coffee shop that Kennedy works at, I can literally hear the gears turning in his brain.

Letting him in on this investigation seemed like a good idea. We're both smart, intelligent and have experience as well as inside-access to pretty much anything. I just didn't know how much touching would be involved.

First, the whole bust at the jewellery store where he was breathing down my neck, then the whole 'I'm just going to brush past you while you're semi-naked and touch your waist' debacle, the ankle situation, and the screaming in the woods and then we had to pretend to date each other. That last one was only for a few minutes, but it was still torture. Exciting and weirdly arousing torture.

The thought of being in a relationship with Branson is repulsive, but there is no way I could ignore the way he slipped his hands into my hair so naturally.

Another thing that's driving me insane? Evan taps his pencil on his laptop while bouncing his knee up and down. He does it while we study most of the time, but today it's driving me up the wall.

"God, can you stop doing that?" I finally ask, frustrated.

"Doing what?" He doesn't even look up from his computer, tap, tap, tapping his pencil. I just stare at him until he looks up. "Oh, that?"

"Yes, *that.*"

"Can't." He looks back down at his computer, still tapping.

I groan. "What the hell does that mean?" I ask. *"Can't,"* I scoff, mocking his tone.

"I mean, I can. I just don't want to. It helps me concentrate," he replies, shrugging. He stops bouncing his knee but continues hitting his pencil on the table in a practised motion.

"Tell you what helps me concentrate?" I ask. He looks up at me now, his shoulders relaxing as if he wants me to continue. "Less of the tapping and more weed."

He rolls his eyes. "Weed does nothing for concentration, you idiot."

"It does for me," I retort. "You're telling me you've never completed two weeks' worth of homework in one night when you're high as fuck? It usually ends up as a mess, but it works." I watch as his eyes try to dart away from mine, and he doesn't say no. Sometimes I swear I can see right through him. "I've got a good plug. Obviously, I'm not going to pressure you, but if I'm going to smoke and you don't want to be around me, that's cool."

He thinks on it for a second as he keeps his eyes on the table. When he's made his decision, he looks up at me, sighing loudly. "Fuck it. Let's do it. It's four-twenty somewhere, right?"

I beam, laughing as I say, "That's the spirit, Branson."

LESS THAN AN HOUR LATER, we're sitting on the grey sticky concrete outside my apartment complex and Evan is coughing his lungs up.

We've each had maybe three good hits and I feel chilled out like I always do. Evan, on the other hand, looks like he's been eating spicy noodles, as well as smoking every day for the past two years. I've occasionally seen him smoke cigarettes, so I don't know why he's reacting so badly to this.

Our legs are outstretched in front of us, our heads leaning against the wall as we blow clouds of smoke into the air. When I make a good circle, I giggle a little, thinking about how strange it is that I'm smoking with Evan. I look over to him and he's leaning forwards a little, clutching his chest as he barks out another cough.

"Oh my God!" I exclaim, laughing, a knowing grin creeping up my face. He turns to me now as his coughing fit dies down. "Branson, have you never smoked weed before?"

He leans back against the wall, tilting his head up and I get a very good look at his throat. It's long and thick and wholly masculine, constricting as he swallows. "Of course, I have. I just haven't felt like this... *Fuck,"* he breathes, rubbing at his eyes. He turns to me now, his eyes heavy and red. "Scarlett, I think I'm having a heart attack."

I laugh again. "You're fine."

He shakes his head, scooting further toward me so our thighs are touching. He grabs the hand in my lap, his huge hand basically swallowing mine as he drags it to his chest, placing it right over his heart before dropping his hand.

"Can you feel my heart right now?" he asks.

"You have a heart?" I gasp dramatically.

"Scarlett."

"Evan."

"Can you feel my heart for one fucking second or I'm going to die," he demands. I look for the joke in his face or his voice, but it never arrives. He remains dead serious.

"You're not going to die," I whisper. He doesn't say anything as his eyes suddenly become sad, a little child-like, like he's begging me to do this one thing for him. I brought him into this mess, so it's out of my pure morality that I lay my palm flat against his heart.

Oh my fucking god.

His heart might actually fall out of his chest. With every beat, it feels like my hand lifts up a few inches as I keep my eyes focused on the dark blue button down he's wearing.

Da dum. Da dum. Da dum.

"Oh my god," I whisper. The words barely pass through my mouth before I clamp my mouth shut, not needing to freak him out anymore.

"What is it?" Evan asks, worried. He places his large hand over mine, seamlessly linking his fingers into mine as if it doesn't set every part of my body on fire. He presses my hand - *our* hands - deeper into his chest and I feel like I'm breathing as fast as him. "Can you tell if something is wrong? Because it *feels* like something's wrong."

"Can you breathe for just one fucking second," I seethe. Honestly, I can't tell which one of us needs to breathe more right now because everything about Evan's hand on mine feels so natural. So safe. Just *good*. Then he does the strangest thing. He licks his lips, looks down at our hands and looks back up at me and he nods. I watch him force himself to breathe. Our eyes connect and I whisper, "Your heart is beating really fast, Ev."

"I *know*. I've been trying to tell you," he says back, defensively. I don't know why we're whispering now, but it feels right. His expression changes, the lines in his forehead softening as he realises something. Shit. I realise it too. "You just called me 'Ev.'"

"No, I didn't." *I totally did. It's the weed. It has to be.*

"You did."

"Whatever," I say, rolling my eyes. If I'm going to deny it,

I have to play the part, so I add, "Your name has too many syllables."

"It has *two*," he says back, his voice sounding both shocked and humorous.

"Yeah. Two too many," is the best response I can come up with.

I notice our hands are still connected, my hand pressing against his chest that still hasn't stopped racing. He doesn't make a move to stop the contact and neither do I. I feel like he needs this more than I do. His dark green eyes still haven't left mine as he lets out a forced breath.

"I think it's you," he says.

"What?"

"That's why my heart is racing. It's because of you."

I let out a short laugh. "Really? What could I possibly be doing that's making your heart speed up?"

He shrugs. "I dunno. Just existing."

I must be panting like a dog now because I swear I can't breathe normally. It shouldn't feel like this: electric. He squeezes my hand, his eyes not leaving mine. The motion is so simple and noncommittal, but it sends a strange pang of *something* through me. *What the hell is he doing and why am I letting him?* "Scar?"

Oh, fuck. Not that nickname. Anything but that nickname right now. It's still so new coming from him and now this? *Come on, Branson. You're making things really fucking difficult.*

"Hm," is all I can say.

"I'm scared." I catch the exact moment the vulnerability takes over. I've always known Evan's not an evil person. He's just hard to deal with and annoying. He's stuck up and he can be rude when he doesn't mean to, but he's not evil. How could he be with the way he's looking at me now? All I see is a scared boy with great big green eyes, searching for a harbour.

"Don't be," I say as comfortingly as I can.

"Oh wow. You're being really helpful right now," he argues sarcastically. I knew that it wouldn't last very long.

"And you're being really fucking dramatic," I say.

"No need to shout," he whispers seriously.

"I'm not shouting!"

Okay.

Maybe I am shouting. *Why* am I shouting though? Maybe it's the unnecessary proximity. Maybe it's the way he lasted five minutes without being an asshole. Maybe it's the fact that he used my nickname, and I *accidentally* used his. Maybe it's everything going on with my family and our little moment escaping. Maybe it's just everything.

Breaking my hand away from his, I stand up, brushing myself off as I say, "Get up. We need to go."

EVAN IS in no state to do anything other than eat junk food and sleep. I'm still pissed at him, but I'm enough of a decent human that I walk him to his house only a few blocks away from my apartment. He sulks most of the way and I follow suit, not bothering to have a conversation with him like that.

When we get to his house, Wren and Miles are in the living room, snuggled together watching the end of *Tangled*. Sometimes I question the Gods and how they managed to put two people so perfect for each other in the same place. Wren's in one of Miles' hockey jerseys and leggings, lying on top of him like a koala while he's shirtless like always.

As Evan stumbles in, I shut the door behind us, blocking

out some of the cold. He kicks off his shoes at the door, rounding the sofa to walk into the kitchen.

"Scarlett gave me some dodgy weed, so I'm going to sit in my room and contemplate life," Evan complains from the kitchen.

"I did not," I argue back. I take a seat across from Wren and Miles, laughing as I roll my eyes. Wren climbs off her boyfriend, nodding at me as she sits to the side of him instead, placing her feet in his lap. He immediately wraps his hands around her ankles, massaging them without a word. "Evan just couldn't handle it. I had the same amount as him and I feel *fine.*"

Evan moves into the living room now, a water bottle in his hand as he stands behind them on the sofa. "That's because you're an insane person."

"Wait. Did you guys say weed? I want weed," Miles pipes up, his gaze flicking between us. Wren turns to him, shaking her head.

"Baby, you're a mess on your own. You do *not* need help," she says, patting him on the chest as he sulks back into the couch.

"Don't get any from this one," Evan says, pointing his water bottle towards me. I flip him the double bird. "You're a menace to society, Scarlett."

"Oh, please," I say, waving a hand to dismiss him. "Society loves me."

"Yeah, right. Society loves that your family's business is the only thing keeping it afloat," he argues. The second the words leave his mouth, I'm sure he realises the stupid mistake he just made. It takes a few seconds for Wren and Miles to pick up on what he said before throwing him a puzzled look and I do the same. But because I'm me, I also have the biggest grin on my face.

"That's *not* the insult you thought it was, tough guy," I say, laughing.

"You're right. Actually, no. You're not right. You're never right. About anything," he rambles. I think I have officially broken Evan Branson because I swear he's blushing right now. The way his cheeks turn a slight shade of pink is sort of…cute. Weird and new, but it's cute. He taps the side of his head twice. Three times. "It's the weed."

He finally ends whatever the hell that was with an awkward thumbs up and walks backwards up the stairs, mumbling something about how that's him done speaking for the rest of the day. I'm feeling victorious.

I turn back to Wren and she's smiling like a fool. "You ready to go, Wrenny?" I ask. She nods before turning to Miles and whispering something absolutely filthy. The movie is paused so it's not hard to make out some of the words she's saying. I stand up. "I heard the words 'dick' and 'mouth' and I'm disgusted. Well, slightly impressed, but disgusted," I chide.

When we're linking arms, walking down the block towards our apartment, Wren says, "You know, I was so afraid of talking about sex out loud before I started writing books and well, before you started giving us very explicit rundowns on how your dates ended."

"Yeah, well, I've not been getting any of that recently," I murmur.

"Why not? Is it because of everything going on with your dad?" Wren asks, looking up at me with those green-brown eyes as we continue walking.

How do you begin to explain the situation you're in to your

best friend who has the sweetest relationship with their dad? The easy answer is you don't.

I shake my head. "I'm just having less me-time with the whole project thing," I say.

That is partly true. Working on this project as well as the regular dose of homework is exhausting. I've always prided myself on having a good, strong, and healthy social life. Without it, I feel like I'm drowning.

"You work too hard at school. It's concerning," Wren mumbles. I elbow her in the side, and she giggles. "We should go out tomorrow. Just us girls and maybe you can text Max. He was very cuddly with you the other night. And he's British, so more brownie points for that."

When your best friend of twenty years looks up at you like that, grinning, cheeks red and flushed, you can't say no. Even if it's the last thing you want to do with everything going on. Even if you've hardly slept in four days and you're still a little high from smoking.

That's why I say, "Sounds good. Let's do it."

18

SCARLETT

EVEN AFTER JAMMING out to Gracie Abrams songs while getting ready with Kennedy and Wren, I still can't shake the uncomfortable feeling in my stomach when we get to the bar. I tried not to make it obvious. I don't want to ruin their night. It seems like they both need this night out as much as I do, and I don't want to jeopardise that with my overthinking.

I texted Max on the way here and he agreed to meet me here. I enjoy talking to him for some reason. He makes conversations easy and even though he has this whole bad boy aura around him, I can tell he's a soft and slightly nervous boy on the inside. He's also ridiculously attractive, so that helps. Second dates (if you can even call it that) aren't really my thing, but he intrigues me a little. He tripped me up, he made me blush. That rarely ever happens if I can control it.

After two rounds of shots at the bar, I stay there, watching Kennedy and Wren dance together to whatever pop song is playing. I told them I'll meet them there in a second, but I need to paint on my best 'I'm fine' face before doing so. I can't stop thinking about Gio and what he was doing at the restaurant.

If I think about it theoretically and cynically, he had motives. It could be him. He's lost the most important thing to him. Looking at a darker perspective, it seems clear that he would want to avenge that and become a more prominent member in the family. What I don't understand is that after he lost Sara, our family became the most important thing to him. Why would he try to mess that up?

I'm so deep in thought that I don't recognise the warm body behind me. I flinch at the contact of a strong hand on my shoulder, and I turn around, Max's deep, woody scent clouding my thoughts for a brief moment. He's got that sexy, almost lazy smile on his lips, dressed in a dark blue button down, his sleeves rolled up and black pants. His dark brown hair looks a little shorter than the last time I saw him, and I wonder if he's had a haircut.

"Hi, Scarlett," he greets, sitting in the seat beside me. I angle myself better so we're facing each other, our legs almost tangled together.

"Hello, Maxwell," I coo, smiling at him. He smiles back at me, a dimple popping out as he shakes his head. "How are you?"

"Better now that I'm here." He tilts his head, taking a very deliberate glance at my body and my outfit. Like usual, I'm wearing a black bodycon dress with matching thigh high boots. The dress isn't purposefully 'provocative,' but if you're a person with eyes who's attracted to women, you stare for a bit longer than usual. It hugs my curves in a flattering way, but Max is looking at me like he wants to take it right off me.

"At least buy me a drink before you start eye-fucking me," I say through a laugh. He snaps his gaze from my legs to my face and when he catches me laughing, he lets out a nervous chuckle.

"*SO,* what do you do in your spare time?" Max asks, taking a swig of his beer while I take a sip of my cocktail.

It's really an award-winning question with a million dollar answer. One of these days, I'll have an actual answer. But the truth is, I don't really do anything.

No one wants to hear about the girl who hasn't found anything as interesting as creating outfits or designs and has the opportunity to make them into a reality. The second I tell people I sometimes design clothes for fun and they sell for hundreds through *Voss*, I'm no longer seen as an entrepreneur or a stylist. I'm seen as a spoiled rich girl. But if I was a man, it would be so different. If I were my brothers, I'd be getting patted on the back and praised for my skills. In the words of Taylor Swift, "If I were a man, I'd be *the* man."

"I like to read," I say, which isn't entirely a lie. I do like to read. I just don't do it a lot or in my spare time. I read enough for class as it is. Sometimes just looking at words gives me a headache.

"Oh yeah?" he asks curiously.

Shit.

He's a literature major, I forgot. How is he managing to trip me up already? I shouldn't want to impress him. But, God, having no real hobbies or interests is embarrassing. He seems so put together, educated, and smart. And he's interested in me for whatever reason, and he doesn't even know my last name. I cross my toes, secretly crossing my fingers too, hoping he's not one of those stuck up I'll-judge-you-on-your-favourite-author types.

"Whose work do you like the most?"

"I lied," I admit, the words out of my mouth before I can

stop them. If I want to try this, I'm going to have to be honest, right? His eyebrow quirks. "I do read, though. Just not in my spare time. I didn't want you to think I was boring or uneducated or not interesting. Which is crazy because I don't usually care about what people - especially guys - think about me. I don't know. I think you kind of intimidate me."

He studies me silently for a minute. I didn't have to say *all* that. I'm barely even buzzed, so I can't even blame it on that. It is the truth though. Usually, being with guys like him, it's easy and we sleep together, and it's done. But for some reason, Max is set on making regular appearances in my life and it worries me a little.

"It's okay," he says reassuringly. My shoulders drop. "I get that a lot, actually."

"Really?"

"No." He smirks. "Besides, I didn't want to talk about boring literature stuff. I was only asking follow-up questions to be polite."

"Wow, who knew you were such a gentleman," I say bashfully, pretending to fan myself.

"I can be," he says with a shrug, a dimple popping out. He pulls his chair a little closer to mine, our knees touching. The slight contact sends electric shocks straight to my brain and I shiver, only rubbing against him more. "Let's reverse the questions. You can ask me anything you want to know."

I ask him where he grew up and he tells me about London and how his dad is a fellow American who met his mom there on business. The poor boy is so naive that he thinks Americans are kinder than British people, which is insane. I've been to the UK, and I've spent a week in New York. You can guess where I'd want to go on vacation again.

"I think you Brits are bolder than you give yourself credit for," I laugh.

He nods. "Mostly because we know what we want and we go for it," he whispers, his voice dropping an octave. I swear the heat has climbed up here vociferously. "You Americans bullshit your way through conversations without telling people what they really want."

"Is that so?" I ask, trailing my nail up his forearm. I know it drives men insane. From the way I watch Max's chest rise and fall repeatedly, I know I've hit the target. "Why don't you tell me what it is that you want, Maxwell?"

The end of my sentence ends with a yelp as I stumble off my chair, my back crashing straight into a wall. Max tries to catch me, but his hand only reaches out half-heartedly before he gives up, shaking his head at me or whoever's behind me.

I swear to God, I better not be getting kidnapped right now because even as I kick and stand on whoever's toes are behind me, pulling us to the other side of the room, they're not letting go of me. I look down at the blonde-haired arms wrapped tightly around my front.

No way.

No fucking way.

I tell myself to calm down so I can remove myself from his grip. His claim to my body relaxes when he thinks I'm going to relax and I use the brief moment to leap out of his arms, turning around and facing him.

Evan Branson has a new hobby where he ruins my dates.

I push him in the chest, watching as he stumbles backwards slightly into the chalkboard hung up on the wall. He's not even saying anything, so I push him again. He just blinks at me like I'm the one who crashed *his* date.

"What the fuck, Branson? Can't you see I was talking to

someone or are you not wearing your contacts today?" I quiz. I've stopped pushing him now because that's getting no answers out of him, and I pin my arms across my chest.

"I can see fine, thank you very much," he responds, dusting off his shirt. He looks over to where we left Max. "Why are you even giving him the time of day? I've never seen you talk to a guy longer than two minutes other than him."

"Sorry. Could you remind me why that's any of your business?" I ask.

"If you're secretly planning to murder him and take all of his money, I can keep that a secret. If not, then I want to know why."

"Why is me murdering him your first thought?" I ask, laughing. But he's not laughing. He's being dead serious. *Okay, so we're doing this.* "He's nice and for once, I don't want to chop his head off. He's making me reconsider this whole not-dating-anyone thing."

Is this entirely true? Sort of. If it means getting Branson to back off and stop killing my vibe, I'll say it over and over until it's the only thing he hears when he closes his eyes at night.

"'Nice?" he repeats, exasperated. "You like him because he's *nice?*" I nod. "*Him?* Seriously? The guy looks like he can't even tie his own laces."

I thought I broke him with the weed, but maybe not. Maybe this is his breaking point. God, I want to see him unravel so badly. I just want him to stop trying so hard at showing me up and be real with me. I want to shove him and for him to shove back.

"I don't know why you care so much, Branson," I say humorously.

"I don't," he concedes. He's lying. I don't know how or

why, but he just is. The look on his face is something bordering on disgust and anger. "I just don't understand why *him* of all people. Why now? You could have anyone you want by a tap of your finger and you're considering him. I just don't get it. What made you change your mind?"

Wow. Someone's asking a lot of questions tonight. Usually *I'm* the talkative one. I always have been. There's something slightly unsettling hearing him talk so much in one sitting.

I tilt my head playfully, twirling a strand of my hair around my finger. "You're awfully curious for someone who hated me a few weeks ago. Remember that? The good 'ol days," I point out.

"I don't hate you, Scarlett, and you know I don't." He looks at me with that intensity that I can't place. My heart trips over itself when my name comes out of his mouth in that tone. It's rare that my full name ever leaves his lips. Not like that, anyway. He blinks back at me as if there's something I'm missing. "Just tell me why."

I could lie to him. I could tell him Max is the greatest guy I've ever met and he's just *it* for me. But he's not. Somewhere deep down, I know he's not. There's something about him that is different from most people like us. Sure, he's a little on the nose, but for the most part he's fine.

"He treats me like an equal and I like him for it, okay? It's not like there's anyone else who wants me for me and not to use me for money or sex. And he doesn't want either of those things from me. Well, not now anyway."

Evan looks at me like he's been sucker punched. Jesus, when did he get so pale? It's giving me the heebie jeebies as he sticks his tongue in his cheek and nods slowly as if he's trying to process the information. *What is wrong with him?*

"Good to know, Angel. If he fucks up, just let me know."

I bark out a laugh at the faux protective thing he's got going on right now. "Yeah, like you're going to do anything," I say. He pins me with a look. One of *those* looks and my mouth clamps together before opening. "Fine."

He nods. Once. Twice. And then he's gone.

I stand there for a few seconds, dumbfounded before I collect myself, trying to shake off whatever that was.

I don't like him being protective over me, trying to handle me like I belong to him or like I'm his girlfriend. We're just two people who are working together on a project, sometimes try to solve mysteries together and occasionally smoke weed. That's it. Nothing more, nothing less. And the last time I checked; *bodyguard* does not fit into that description.

When I return to the bar where Max is, he's still waiting for me. His whole face lights up when he sees it's me and I can't hide the blush on my face even if I tried to.

I slide back into the stool. "Miss me?"

"I thought he was trying to take you away from me," he responds.

"Not quite," I say. "Where were we?"

"I was about to tell you how much I want you."

This, I think to myself, *this is exactly what I need.* I need someone who's going to whisper things like that to me over loud music in a bar. Someone who makes me feel weak in the knees by just being in their presence.

Suddenly I'm desperate for him.

For a release.

19

EVAN

I'M NOT A STUPID PERSON. On paper, I get straight A's and I pass every test with flying colours. I have basic road safety knowledge, I know first-aid and I can start and put out a fire. But for some reason, I act like an absolute fool around Scarlett Voss.

Not only did I act like a dick by pulling her away from her date, but her friends also scalded me for it. Which also means if Wren were to complain to Miles, he wouldn't shut up about it. Luckily, after watching Scarlett get into her car with that weird British dude, I got back, and Miles wasn't home yet.

The first thing I did this morning was go for a run. I don't usually run and I'm not the most athletic person, but after having a few days like I've just had, I need to burn off my energy somehow.

Scarlett's being closed off about seeing her uncle at the restaurant, which is not helping because I need to give my dad some answers tonight. I think she's afraid to say what I've been thinking.

From what she tells me, it makes sense that her uncle

would try and attack her dad. He could have used the drugs to blackmail him while continuing to buy faulty diamonds to scare the businesses. It's the perfect motive and the perfect story. Something about it being tied up so neatly with a bow on top doesn't sit right with me. There is something messier, deeper, and darker that we're missing out on.

My run quickly turned into a sprint, so I turned back towards my house, jogging on the cool-down.

When I get home, I shower, clean up the stubble on my chin and try my best to refresh myself. I can't keep getting caught up in whatever green eyed monster that has taken over my brain when it comes to Scarlett. Mostly, it's a primal, protective nature that I have over her. I've always been like this, and she's just been too in her head to notice. I'm mostly at the events she attends, and I covertly protect her. I make sure no creeps or weirdos go near her or when they do, I give them a look to fuck right off. I make sure she gets home alright every night.

Even being in competition, our families have known each other for years which meant I knew Scarlett growing up - sort of. We attended events together when we were in kindergarten and middle school. We never really spoke, but there was always this strange comfortable silence that settled between us whenever we were alone.

She's the youngest of four brothers and I'm the only son of a multi-millionaire who developed anxiety early on and obsessive compulsive disorder not too long after. We were both ignored and belittled. Without knowing, we found a silent solace within each other. It's ironic now because all we do is argue.

Once I've gotten ready, it's well into the second period and I know that I've missed class. The way I lose track of time sometimes worries me. I'll be reading a book, trying to forget for a few minutes and then three hours have passed. I don't know how I managed to do it this morning. I could've sworn my run only lasted twenty minutes. Maybe I shouldn't have skipped breakfast.

I don't bother to give a lame apology to Anderson about missing class and I head towards the music rooms instead.

The rooms are each small soundproof cubicles with a piano on one side of the wall, a mirror above it so when I look in it, I can see the door.

Once I've put my bags to one side in the corner, I stretch out my fingers and I start playing. What comes most naturally is Bach's '*Prelude in C major*', which is the first composition I learned without sheet music. I can play almost anything by ear now, but as a kid, it was one of my great achievements.

Now, I don't even think twice as I let the music carry me to a place beyond this room. To a place where my mom was still living with us and we'd spend the morning waking my dad up by sharing a seat on the bench next to the Steinway, doing a duet. To a place where my anxieties could be soothed by a book and some music. To a place where it's just pure, quiet tranquillity and silence where I'm not obsessing over numbers.

I make a smooth transition into SYML's '*Where's my love,*' closing my eyes as I allow my body and my mind to settle. My hands mostly move on their own accord, playing the song seamlessly. It's a beautiful song. It's one of the few non-classical songs that I take my time to perfect. I had to learn this one to perfection or else it would never do the original justice.

I'm lost somewhere between the chorus and the verse when I open my eyes for a split second and I take a look in the mirror, Scarlett is standing in the doorway, her tote bag on her shoulder, dressed in a two piece black corset top and a black skirt. It gives off the same flair as *Voss* clothing, but I've never seen it on the website. Her eyes are closed and she's *listening* to me play.

I don't get nervous playing around people. Sometimes my dad would make me sit in the living room at soirées just to get the guests to gush over me. But it's judgemental, poised, Scarlett Voss who is listening to me play. I go back to playing, trying not to make it obvious that I know she's there.

I get around to the chorus again and she starts to hum. I don't mean to be dramatic - actually, I don't care how insane this sounds - but the way Scarlett is humming right now is the sound I want to hear when I go to heaven. People can sing, sure. People can play instruments, or they can dance. But the way she's humming is sculptured, crafted, just pure perfection. A lot like her.

Then the worst thing that could possibly happen, happens.

She starts to sing.

It's not loud. She probably doesn't even notice she's doing it. I love that she does that sometimes. She says things, whispers them, or she touches things and I swear she's so in her head sometimes it's like she doesn't realise she's doing it. It's a quiet whisper, but her enunciation of the words seems like she's had real practice or training. It's in a lower key to how the song is originally played, but it contrasts perfectly with the key I'm playing in. After a few seconds, she goes back to humming and I can't help myself.

"Holy shit, you can sing," I say as I stop playing. Her eyes catch mine in the mirror and her expression isn't what I expected. She doesn't look like she's been caught or that she's embarrassed. She just seems at peace.

"I can't," she argues.

"You can."

"Barely."

"Totally," I correct. She drops her gaze from mine in the mirror to my hands on the piano. "Your secret is safe with me."

"It's not a secret," she challenges. I shrug. "Why weren't you in class today?"

"I overslept," I lie. She wouldn't understand if I tried to explain what it's like to be in my head sometimes.

"Bullshit... but I don't care," she says, waving her hand at me. "Look. I've got to cancel the next study session for the project. I've got a date."

Great. She's spending more time with that fuckwad, Max. I don't know him very well, but after a quick google search, I'm fine with keeping my distance. He's got a successful family, but he doesn't act like it. He acts like a regular twenty-something who doesn't feel like he needs to impress anyone. Which is ridiculous if he's dating Scarlett.

The girl has looks to kill. Any man would be stupid not to be on their knees begging her for even a minute of attention from her.

"What? Why do you look like you're going to puke?" she asks, stepping back a little from me. I glance at myself in the mirror, and I look pale.

"I'm not," I say defensively. She doesn't seem too convinced as she raises an eyebrow at me. "I'm just surprised you're dating him because you're..."

"What? Successful, funny, smart, intelligent, interesting, amazing..." she lists. I swear this woman and her ego will be the death of me. She takes a deep breath and continues listing things about herself which are no doubt true.

"Hot," I say, cutting her off. Her surprise is just as good as mine. I rub my hand across my face, defeated, as I see the grin crawling up her face. I can't help but clarify, "You're hot."

"Oh my god," she gasps. "Evan Branson thinks I'm hot."

"You didn't need me to tell you that."

She points at me, making a clicking sound as if she's forgotten something. "Ah, you're right, I didn't. But it still felt good." She smiles at me, but I'm not smiling back, realising what a dumb mistake I made feeding into her ego. She shakes her head as if to get rid of what she was thinking. "Plus, just because we're going on a date doesn't mean we're dating. We're just fooling around...consistently."

"It sounds like you're dating to me," I say. She ends the eye contact in the mirror and instead stands beside the piano, leaning one arm into the top, revealing a sliver of skin on her stomach and hip and I can see the tattoo peeking out again. God, I want to know what it says so badly.

She snorts. "What do you know about relationships? It's weird, actually. You're constantly surrounded by beautiful women, like me as you said, but you never take them home. Why is that?"

I laugh this time. "Okay, calm down. I never called you beautiful. I said you're hot. There's a difference."

There isn't a difference. You couldn't put Scarlett's beauty into words if you tried. Those two words are pathetic excuses of adjectives trying to define the woman in front of me. Nothing could truly do her justice.

"Evan," she presses.

"Scarlett."

"Just answer the question, you idiot," she urges.

I sigh, rolling my head back a little. "I just don't want to. I had a relationship in my first year and it didn't end very nicely. More for me than for her."

She shakes her head at me. "That's why you gotta do what I do."

"And what's that?" I ask. "Just fooling around?" She nods, grinning. "Doesn't everyone's feelings just get hurt?"

"You'd have to have actual feelings for the person for them to get hurt. See, I do this thing where I detach myself from the person I'm sleeping with."

"How the hell do you manage to do that?"

She sighs now, looking around the room, trying to find the words for what she's trying to explain. It already sounds like a dumb idea. And impossible for somebody like me.

"Sex is supposed to be liberating, Evan. A release. It doesn't have to be this magical, slow, candle-lit experience. Sometimes, all I want is a good time and a quick fuck." I just blink at her because holy shit. I had an idea that is how she operates, but hearing her say it aloud is jarring. *A quick fuck.* She narrows her eyes at me as I still stare because...*holy shit.* "Anyway. I don't know why I just told you all that. Erase it from your memory now."

"Done," I whisper.

Only I know I won't be able to. It's hard to forget things when it comes to her. Even when she's gone, I'm still thinking about it.

My mind goes rotten as I think about exactly what she means by a quick fuck. Does she need to be attracted to a person to do that or is she constantly chasing the release of an orgasm? Then my mind goes into an even filthier place, thinking about what she would look like on her knees, desperate, soaking wet and needing for me to touch her. Her hands tied behind her back with that stupid fucking ribbon so she can't touch herself. The power she would lose to stop talking about me while my cock is down her-

Oh, fuck.

I'm attracted to Scarlett Voss, and I want her.

Badly.

WHEN I GET to the Branson estate, I see a black Ferrari in the driveaway. I know my uncle Jack is here. He and my dad are fraternal twins, but as a kid, they'd always manage to trick me into believing Jack was my dad. They don't look much alike now as my dad is desperately still trying to grow out his grey hair while Jack shaved his into a buzzcut. Being around both of them, you'd think they're college students who never grew out of their 'I'm still in competition with my brother' phase.

All in all, it's always fun being around them. Mostly because Jack constantly makes fun of my dad, and my dad lets him.

When I walk through the doors to the living room, they're not in there, only Mila rolling around on the rug. I kneel down next to her, trying not to crease my shoes as I scratch her on the stomach. She's such a good dog. I sometimes wonder if she gets lonely here, though. I know my dad would never admit it, but when I come here early in the morning and my dad's just getting out of bed, I know she sleeps in the bed with him. I guess they keep each other company.

"Junie was too good for you." I hear my uncle's voice booming from the room over. Great. So, we're doing this again. I lean against the swivelling door, trying to get a better listen only to be hit with a strong wave of Deja vu.

"You think I don't know that, Jack?" my dad responds, sounding exhausted.

"You shouldn't have let her go."

"The best thing I could do for all of us was to let her go. You know that."

I accidentally put too much pressure on the door, and it swivels open. I stumble a little, but try and style it out, brushing off my shoulders as if this was meant to happen. My dad and Jack are sitting beside a small table, an unfinished game of Go on it as they both lounge in a plush chair on each side. Jack has the biggest smile on his face while my dad shakes his head at me, picking up his glass.

As he slams it on the table, he says, "Haven't you learned your lesson from last time, boy?"

I shrug, taking a seat across from them. "It's great to see you too, dad. And you, Uncle Jack."

"It would be great to see you too, but your dad is telling me you've not been doing your job," Jack coos, shaking his head. I roll my eyes.

"Which job? The one where I have to lie to someone I actually like so you can try and take her family down?"

"That's the one," Jack says triumphantly. I lounge back in the chair, rolling my head back. I don't want to keep doing this to her. Especially not with the realisation that I might actually, definitely like her more than I would ever admit. "You said you like her."

"Yes, but not like that," I lie. Jack studies me for a minute, nodding.

"I get it. She's pretty and you're distracted. There are millions of beautiful women, Evan," Jack explains. But there's nobody like *her*. No one could even come close to the type of beauty and confidence she exudes.

"That's beside the point," my dad says. "What's new?"

I tell them everything I can. Scarlett isn't giving me much to work with since she hasn't spoken to her uncle since we saw him at the restaurant. I explain to them how it must be him behind all of this and his lack of encouragement for Scarlett continuing the case could be because he was trying to make sure that she didn't find out it was him.

"And.." dad says.

"And something is still missing," I admit. Jack stops looking out of the window, and he turns to me now, silently urging me to continue. "I don't know what it is, but something doesn't feel right. It makes sense that it is him, but we have nothing to pin it on him. Nothing substantial anyway."

"That's what I've been asking you to find out," my dad says. He rubs his hand down his face, sighing. "It's no good hanging out with this girl to not get something concrete. We can't have you wasting your time."

"I'm not wasting my time. You try getting information out of a twenty-year-old girl who wouldn't even look at me a few weeks ago," I challenge. They both snort. "Look, it's not going to be easy. We've known that. But I'm telling you, the second it gets too dangerous, I'm out. For all of our sake."

My dad blinks at me. I had to draw the line somewhere. Each day we're getting closer and closer to something it also means we're getting close to whoever hurt Scarlett's dad. They could hurt us too if we're not careful. I'd easily risk my life for her, but I don't want to be in a position where that would have to be the case.

"Okay, fine," my dad concedes. "Just figure it out quick, boy."

20

SCARLETT

I'VE BEEN TRYING to face my demons. I really have. But it's the actual facing them part that's really fucked me up. What if Gio is actually behind this? What then? Will he try to attack me too?

I should have brought back-up. Maybe Henry or someone. God, even Evan sounds like an option here. I shouldn't be scared to go into the home I've been going into for years, but I'm terrified.

There's a gentle breeze in the mid-November chill, so my legs are absolutely freezing. I can't keep ignoring Gio and I need to talk to him.

The dark brown wooden doors open when I walk up to it, swinging open with a gentle creek. I don't like this. I don't like this at all. As I move further in, the house is eerily silent other than the old Italian music playing from his record player in the kitchen although it sounds distorted. I can't tell if my brain is messing up my senses on purpose.

I called out my uncle's name three times without a

response. I shudder as I pass through the dining area, slowing as I pass a cabinet filled with pictures of him and Sara, as well as family photos from our trips to Italy over the years. I glide silently through the room, reaching the back door which leads to a patio and a huge backyard, expanding into the small woodland that surrounds his home.

I inch toward the open garage door and that's when I see him.

My uncle is hunched over a table that's covered in blood. A bucket lays beside the wooden table, overflowing with a red lumpy liquid. I think I'm going to be sick.

Gio's back is to me, his right arm moving mercilessly over something. His shoulder raises and falls as he continues kneading something, blood splattering from each direction, seeping into the brown wood of the walls. It looks like a crime scene, nothing but the sloshing sounds coming from whatever Gio is doing. I've never seen him like this before.

I take a step back, stumbling. I didn't even realise I was screaming until words started flowing out of my mouth. "Oh my god!"

He turns around now, which only makes me gasp. He's wearing an apron, covered completely in blood, a bloody knife in his hand. I try to settle my heartbeat, but I can hear it roaring in my ears. "Scarlett, *tesoro*! You scared me. What are you doing?"

"What are *you* doing? What is that?" I ask, gesturing towards the bloody board, my voice shaking.

Gio inches closer to me and I step back. He studies me for a second and I blink back at him, words failing me. "Why don't you go inside, and I'll meet you there once I've cleaned up," he says calmly.

I walk backwards from the murder scene and slowly make my way back into the house. Gio would never hurt anybody. Not on purpose, anyway. As much as my dad has always told me that the business is dangerous, I didn't realise just how dangerous.

As he finishes cleaning up, my mind whirs of the hundreds of things he could have been doing.

"What are you doing here, Scarlett?" he asks, his voice pulling me out of my daydream. I turn on the couch, watching as my uncle – now in fresh clothes – sits across from me in the plush leather seat.

"What were you doing?" I gawk, not able to move on as quickly as he seems like he wants to. He runs his hand through his hair, fiddling with the ends before clearing his throat.

"I recently took up butchery," he says plainly. Right. It's just that simple.

"But- In the backyard? Is that even sanitary?" I ask, genuinely concerned. He nods, planning to dismiss me.

"What are you doing here, Scarlett?"

"I'm sorry. I shouldn't have come. I didn't expect to see that and I'm already on edge so I-"

He shakes his head. "You don't need to apologise."

"But I do. I mean, I came looking for answers and now I just saw all of that, so you can imagine what I'm thinking."

"No. I can't. What's going on?"

I snort, a disbelieving chuckle slipping from my lips. "What's not going on, Gio? Dad still hasn't woken up and we're nowhere near finding out about Tinzin and I feel like you're keeping secrets from me!" Hot angry blood surges through me, my cheeks instantly reddening.

Gio's mouth opens and then closes, searching for words. He holds his hands up and then drops them with a sigh.

"Keeping secrets?" he asks, stuttering. "What is there that I haven't told you?"

I roll my eyes, dropping my head back and then facing him again, angry and upset tears brimming in my eyes. "Come *on*, Gio, don't bullshit me. Why were you at Yelsy's?"

"You mean the shop where I've been buying falafel for years?"

My brain short-circuits and I try to get it to start up again. I blink at him, hoping that words will come to me, and I'll have something to say. "Why were you talking to the owner?"

"He's the only reason I got it so cheap. He knew Lucas, so we had a mutual friend. The food they have there is to die for, Scar. You've tried it."

I blink back the tears that have started forming. I hate this side of me. The side of me that's not put together. The side that cries when I'm angry. The side that cries at any given moment when things go sideways. "But- But he's the one I saw outside the jewellery store. I found someone's ID at *Voss* that matches his," I try to explain.

"You said it was dark that night. You shouldn't have gone in the first place. It might not have been him. You probably got them mistaken."

I never get people mistaken. That doesn't happen to me. At first I was confused, but after spending hours looking through security footage and ID's, it made sense that it was him. I recognised his posture and his face shape; I made sure the security footage linked with the time the sign-in cards had his ID. I never get things wrong...I never.... I never do.

"Then why were you talking to him while staring at us?" I ask. I could understand if they knew each other, but having them in the same room, watching us didn't sit right with me.

"I was telling him what a great kid you are," Gio explains,

sighing. I know my uncle loves me. I know that. He always talks highly of me and I appreciate him for that. "Though, I'm not sure about that boyfriend of yours. I don't like the way he was touching you."

My skin instantly gets hot, thinking of the way he was touching me and the way I let him. The second I saw Gerard and my uncle together, I knew something was off, so when they started to stare, I had to think fast.

I didn't anticipate the feel of Evan's heavy hand on my neck, the way his fingers twirled in my hair, the tight tug of it that drove me insane. His huge hand is exactly that...just huge. I don't understand how it can feel so rough but touch me so gently, silently igniting the heavy want in my lower stomach.

The fact that I felt that kind of want – that chase of a release – from Evan Branson is troubling. But strangely exciting. I've been denying the girls' allegations of there being some sort of sexual tension between us, but after having his hands on me like that, I don't know how much longer I can go on denying it.

The last thing I want or need right now are complicated feelings towards Evan. Especially not when my uncle was just...

"He's not my boyfriend," is the lame excuse that comes out of my mouth.

"Are you sure? You made it very clear that he was-"

I cut him off, not wanting to go into that debate as I remember the whole 'so young and in love' conversation. "So, you're telling me that the guy was outside Julia's — most likely smuggling the drugs – was not the same guy owning the restaurant?"

Gio nods rapidly. "*Sì amore mio.*"

"So, my judgement was off?" I ask again, just to make

sure. Gio adjusts in his seat, glancing out the window before looking at me. He holds my stare, swallowing. I stare back at him, waiting for him to prove me wrong. To tell me the truth. Whatever that is.

"It happens to the best of us," he says finally.

But not to me, I think to myself. *Not to me.*

I TRY to keep my cool on the date with Max. It feels like 'trying' is the only thing I've been doing recently. I try to have a fun time. I try to focus on the ridiculously attractive man in front of me who gave me countless orgasms after our last date. I try to enjoy the food at the Michelin star restaurant that only exclusive members are allowed to go into. I try to focus on the heavy hand that's holding mine under the table. I really do.

We booked a seat in the back of the restaurant in a secluded corner with dim lighting. He looks extra good today, his hair is neatly combed back, freshly shaven and unlike Evan, his tie is actually tied.

God, I must really be out of it if I'm comparing my date to Evan as if he's the standard. Not only am I invaded by thoughts of Evan, but Gio too. I can't stop thinking about the noises coming from whatever the hell he was doing. I just wish I could focus on him. He deserves it.

We've been engaging in basic small talk for the last hour over our steak and fries. When the meal is done and we're chatting over an empty table, I slide my card onto the table as the waiter comes to collect it. I return my attention to Max, smiling as he talks about his little sisters.

"How many siblings do you have again?" he asks me.

"Four older brothers."

"Brutal," he says, wincing. "What do they think about us? I'm not in for a major beating, am I?"

"I haven't told them," I say simply. Max is the only guy other than Jake that I can even consider as someone I'm 'dating.'

Telling my brothers would only cause more drama. Plus, my mom would be all over it. It's not that I want to prove her wrong by not being in a relationship. It's the way she views relationships that annoys me. Like she can't fathom the idea of two people coexisting without having to desperately rely on each other and need the other to complete them. I want to be in a relationship with someone that sees me as an equal. Not someone that they see as a threat to their manhood or someone who thinks they can use me and belittles me.

"Why not? I told my sisters about us," he says flippantly.

"Your sisters are five and seven, it's not the same thing," I say, trying to laugh. He just stares at me. "It's just complicated."

He nods and continues talking about London. I've been five times, but he doesn't seem to care as he mansplains how the underground system works. When I've been zoning in and out, I don't realise that he's switched topics.

"You know…" he begins. "Your last name sort of sounds like that clothing brand all the girls at Drayton are obsessed with."

Oh, shit. My card was on the table for everyone to see. When the waiter returns with it, I swipe it off the table, slipping it back into my purse. I've been so out of it today I forgot my one rule. My one stupid and pathetic rule I should have been protecting tonight.

I do what I've been taught to do: deny.

"Yeah? Sounds like it doesn't it," I say, laughing quietly.

He quirks an eyebrow, shaking his head. For a second I think he's going to drop it, but he doesn't.

"Do you like their clothes?" he asks, sipping on the sparkling water he ordered, that I stupidly paid for. I was too tired to put up with the fight of splitting it. I nod at him, not wanting to let this go any further. I'm tired as it is, and I want this date to end. Then we can try again when I'm not feeling like a sack of potatoes. "I heard there's a sale on at the pop up at the mall. Maybe we could go, and I'd get you something you like."

I shake my head at him, almost laughing. "Babe, I don't need you to buy me clothes."

He smiles at me, dimples popping out as if this is a new thing for him. As if he gets off buying things for other people. "They're really expensive. It's just a nice gesture. To say thank you, you know...for...."

I tilt my head. "For what? The sex?" He nods eagerly. God, he's got this puppy-like persona about him. It's honestly adorable. "I'm good."

"I'm just trying to be nice, Scarlett," he concedes, leaning back in his chair as he crosses his arms across his chest.

"I know and I appreciate that, but I don't need you buying clothes for me. Especially not from somewhere where I can get clothes for free," I say, putting an end to it. Maybe if I tell him the truth, he'll still like me. He's been a great guy to hang out with. Maybe he's not like everybody else.

"Oh. Do you have a friend that works for the company or something?" he asks curiously.

"I am the company."

"Really?" I nod, instantly regretting it. He squints his eyes at me, trying to figure me out. I don't like it. I don't like this at all. "But you live in an apartment off campus, and you got the cheapest thing on the menu. If you were actually connected to them, you wouldn't even need school."

Oh my God. He must really think he's hit the nail on the head with that one. This is exactly why I don't tell people anything about me. They either realise that I'm not using the benefits of my family's money to get my way out of school, or they think that I'm a spoiled nepotistic child who gets everything handed to her. Or worse, they realise that I have all these benefits and that they can use me to get what they want.

"Not everyone wants to throw education out the window just because they can. I live in an apartment off campus because I love my friends. I ordered the cheapest thing because it was the best thing to get. I've been here five times and I get it every time, no matter who I'm with. And frankly, I assumed you were paying at first and I didn't want to embarrass you. I also didn't know that you could assess wealth so easily," I get out all at once, finally ripping the Band-Aid off. I want this day to end. I just want to crawl up in my room, pull the covers up to my chin and cry.

"What?" he says, blinking as he shakes his head. He's smiling now, full on grinning. He might as well puff out his chest and bang on it like a gorilla, seeing as he looks like he just won the lottery. "Are you embarrassed by it?" he asks curiously, humour lacing his tone.

"Embarrassed by it?" I repeat, gawking at him. "No. I love my family and I love our company and everything we've done. I'm more embarrassed by the way people act around me when they realise who my family are."

"And how do you think I'm acting around you?"

"Like you want to scream at the top of your lungs that you fucked me last week."

"Can I?" he asks. Is he being serious? There's that slight

smirk on his lips, mixed with a head tilt. He must be joking, right.

"No, you dimwit, you cannot," I say. I might be acting extra defensive, but I can't deal with this right now. My legs shake as I stand up, grabbing my bag from the seat from beside me. "Goodbye!"

21

SCARLETT

THINGS HAVE NOT BEEN GOING my way today. Everything has been just fucking great. First, my uncle completely creeps me out with his casual butcher's shop in his backyard. Then, I can't decide if he was gaslighting me or if I was really that stupid to mix up the person, I saw at the jewellery store and the ID I discovered. Then, my date blew up in our faces. Now I'm stomping out like an overstimulated child.

I shrug my coat on, storming through the door as I zip it up. As I step through the small lobby outside the restaurant, I notice it's raining. Really hard. I stay under the shelter, trying my best to pull out my phone without the wind causing the rain to splash onto the screen.

Of course, it's a Saturday night and most of the cab services are booked and unavailable. I take a look down into the suddenly crowded sidewalk filled with slap happy twenty-somethings all waiting for a cab.

I shove my AirPod's in, blasting *'Space Song'* by Beach House as I start to walk down the sidewalk. Today has already been a shitshow as it is, sad music won't do anything but slightly cure it.

The rain is getting heavier, and I can feel it seeping into my clothes, ruining my hair. My coat feels heavy, my hands no longer feeling comfortable in the pockets.

I think about calling the girls, telling them what an insane day I've had, but I don't want to burden them. They've always got something of their own going on and when they look at my life, it always seems fine and stress free. When I come to them with problems, it usually isn't about a failed date because I never have those. I actually liked Max. For whatever reason, I let my guard down around him and I started to trust him. He became that one good thing in the mess my life has become.

That's how I end up crying as I walk home, the tears disguising themselves in the rain pouring down my face. God, I truly am pathetic.

Part of me blames myself for messing up today's date. If I hadn't been so distant, I wouldn't have messed up the card. If I could chill out for two seconds, I wouldn't have snapped at him and ruined it before having a civilised conversation. Communication has never been my best strength, but I'm trying.

There's that word again.

I'm still a few blocks away from my apartment, convincing myself that if I play this song on repeat twice more, I'll be in the lobby. That logic only works sometimes. My body is too tired to speed up the walk home. I just want the ground to swallow me whole at this point.

I pass the movie theatre and I know I'm not that far from home. It's completely dark outside other than the odd shop light. I try to keep my head high, not wanting to get freaked out by this dark isolation. Then I see a black car slow on the road on my side of the street.

I try to ignore it, not looking directly at it as I speed up my walk but turn down my music. The car's pace matches mine. Shit.

Can today truly get any worse? The last thing I need is some creep following me home. I glance over at the car again as the window rolls down. I turn my head forward, keeping my eyes trained on the bright lights of the pharmacy ahead.

"Scarlett?" someone calls. Okay, now it is time to walk as fast as I can. The rain and these heels are not helping. "Angel?"

Of course, it's him. *Of course,* Evan Branson has to be here when I'm at my worst. Great. He's probably having a field day with this, grinning, and smirking to himself about how much of a mess I look.

"I don't know who you're talking to," I lie, walking as fast as I can now, watching my step so I don't end in a puddle. The car still doesn't leave my side as I cross the street, pushing my hair out of my face.

"Let me take you home," he shouts from the car. I look over at him. His window is fully down, his arm and head hanging out of it, his white shirt sleeve drenched by the rain.

"I can walk," I say back.

"It's going to start thundering soon."

"Perfect. Just what I need to add to this already depressing walk of shame."

"Talk to me, Angel," he presses. "Let me take you home."

"I would rather walk in the rain than talk to you right now." As the words leave my mouth, a loud roar of thunder stops me as I look up at the sky. Of course, he has to be right.

He groans once the thunder stops. "Then let me walk with you in silence. Can I do that?"

I don't respond and I carry on walking. I swear the universe is against me, distorting time, and distance because I swore I was closer to my house before Evan turned up. Maybe I've started going in the wrong direction. I spot his house with Xavier and Miles, and I know I must be close now. Only a few more minutes and I should be home.

I turned my music back up the second he asked that ridiculous question, but I still hear the car door slam. I glance over at the Escalade and Evan's standing outside of it, now walking next to me as he unhooks the large umbrella that has appeared in his hand.

"What are you doing?" I ask, exasperated as the rain seeps into my mouth.

He looks at me, his jaw set, and his stare harsh. He opens the umbrella; his body heat makes me shiver more as his shoulder brushes against mine. He lifts the umbrella above us, shielding me from the rain and I can breathe for a second. He nudges his shoulder into mine. "Walking in silence, remember?"

"Do you ever take no for an answer?"

"I understand what consent means if that's what you're asking. But you're clearly upset, and I was taught better than to leave someone to walk alone when they're upset," he explains simply. I find that slightly hard to believe, but he sounds serious. "If you really wanted me to leave, you would have pushed me into oncoming traffic by now."

He's right, so I don't say anything.

As much as it pains me, we walk the next few blocks in silence. I don't want to tell him about Gio. I don't want to tell him about my date with Max and he doesn't push it or ask me.

It would be too embarrassing and as much as I can usually handle his jokes, right now I just want to sleep and forget today ever happened.

When we get to my apartment, he insists (silently, of course) to walk me up to my floor. I'm a capable woman. I can usually do these things on my own, but he's *helping* me, and I can't figure out why. He's being somewhat bearable and it's messing me up on the inside.

When I get to my door, I stand outside of it, staring back at him.

His white shirt is sticking to him because he's an idiot and he didn't wear a jacket. He's not wearing a tie this time, but his top is slightly unbuttoned, showing off a slice of his tanned chest. His shirt is doing annoyingly wonderful things for his build. It's stuck to him in all the right places, expressing his large chest and the defined muscles of his stomach. If I didn't know what he was really like, I would even find him attractive right now. I'd want to run my nails down the creases in his abs and scrape my nails along his back. Especially with all the nice things he's been doing lately, it's overwhelming.

The filthy thoughts start to bombard me at once. "Stop doing these nice things for me. It's confusing."

He runs his hand through his hair, shaking it off as it drips with water droplets. "What's confusing?"

"I'm supposed to hate you and you're not making it easy anymore. What's your game plan?" I ask. There must be something behind all this. Some grand scheme that I'm not aware of.

"I have no plan," he says simply. He steps closer to me, my back pressing further against the door. This is the kind of proximity I can't deal with right now. Not while he's being so nice to me. He drops his voice lower as he whispers, "As cute as it is watching you try to hate me, just give in. I know you want to."

"That's the thing. I don't want to," I challenge, watching the way his eyes dim as they zone in on me. He's so close to me now, I can see the light shade of blue that swirls within his eyes. So close that I can't tell which of our hearts are beating so fast. I do my best to ignore the strange chill that runs down my spine at his proximity. "You're annoying and rich and blonde and you talk too much shit. Oh, and did I mention that you're blonde? It can't get any worse than that," I say in one go. I take a deep breath. "Actually, it can. You're also really-"

He cuts me off with his hand on my face, covering my mouth. I knew his hands were huge, but Jesus Christ, they're just *massive*. They're still wet from the rain and so is my face, but they still feel warm.

Holy shit.

Evan Branson's hand is covering my mouth and I'm not telling him to move. Something must be seriously wrong with my brain tonight.

"Do you ever know when to shut up?" he growls, those dark green eyes pinning me with a fierce glare. He groans lightly and I shake my head, desperate to smile under his hand. My eyes drop to his hand and then back to his face. "Are you going to stop shit-talking me now or do I have to keep my hand here to keep your little mouth quiet," he rasps.

This guy can have a really filthy mouth when he wants to. On the outside, he's this typical nice guy with a slight bad-boy complex, smiling and smirking at everyone. On the inside, he says things like that, and I wonder for a second – a *second* – if he uses that kind of language elsewhere.

I nod frantically and he drops his hand.

"God, Branson. If you wanted me to be quiet you

could've done that in a million different ways," I sigh, pushing some distance between us as I wipe my mouth. He shrugs.

"Have you got any updates on the situation?" he asks.

"I spoke to Gio, and he says that he doesn't know Gerard in the way we thought. He's an old friend of Lucas' and apparently makes the best falafel in town. He said I was confused," I explain.

He seems to dismiss the first part of what I just said and instead easily asks, "Do *you* think you were confused?"

"I don't know anymore."

"Well, just because *he* said you were, it doesn't mean you actually were. You don't have to listen to him. I know he's your uncle and all, but if *you* know something was off, then go with it."

He's definitely making this whole 'hating him' thing worse when he says things like that. Things that I need to hear that just make sense.

"I know," I say. He nods once. Twice.

"Listen," he begins, shifting his gaze from my eyes to the floor. "I know you don't want to talk about whatever happened tonight, but just so you know-"

The door to my apartment swings open, and I stumble back in my heels, but Evan reaches out and he catches me.

He catches me.

He grips onto my hand, pulling me up into a standing position. I don't even get time to register the sharp electric pang that shoots from my hand to my brain because his hand is shoved in his pocket just as quickly. His eyes roam over my body for a second, possibly checking for injuries, but when he sees I'm fine, he scowls at Kennedy who's standing beside me, smiling ear to ear.

"Maybe check the peephole before opening the door, Ken," Evan says to my best friend in her Christmas pyjamas.

"If I'd known it was you, I wouldn't have opened it at all," Ken says. God, I'm going to kill her. She looks at me, still smiling. "You should have told me you were going on a date with Evan. I wouldn't have burst through the door. Your *Find my iPhone* was still on, but you've been in the building for fifteen minutes. I thought you were getting attacked."

"We didn't go on a date," Evan says sternly. I was going to say it, but the way he seems slightly angry by that pisses me off. Yes, it's true. But the irritation in his eyes and the tick in his jaw makes me queasy. As if just the thought of being on a date with me repulses him.

"Ken, I told you it was with Max," I say to her.

"Could've fooled me. You guys have been sneaking around with this top secret project for class," she retorts, trying to sound casual, but Kennedy does not do casual, so she sounds like she's up to something. "I thought it was about time you two banged out-"

This time I cover her mouth, doing exactly what Evan did to me as he smirks. I swear this girl is a ray of sunshine when she's not trying to meddle.

"*Okay*," I drag out, walking us backwards into the apartment. Evan still stands at the open door, grinning at us.

"I don't think Kennedy finished her sentence," he teases. "You know, if you wanted to tell her to be quiet, you could do that in a million different ways."

"Goodbye, Branson," I say, kicking the door shut with my foot. When he's out of sight, I turn to Ken who's smiling like a clown beneath my hand, so I drop it. "You're so annoying, sometimes, you know that?"

"Ah, but you love me," she says, waving me off.

"You're still annoying."

"No, it means that you love me." She beams at me. "So, I take it the date didn't go to plan if you ended up with Evan."

I sigh, walking into the kitchen. "It's for the better."

"You're just telling yourself that," she says, rolling her eyes. "You don't have to be closed off with me, Scar. I pride myself on being able to read people, but recently, you've been making it difficult. I want to be here for you."

I know I've been off with her and Wren, but sometimes I feel like they won't understand what it's like to be in my position. They always have their own things going on. And though I know they'd never say it, I'm sure they would realise that my problems can't be that big if I have money and a decent family to solve them.

When I look at Ken who has moved away so far from her family and doesn't have her dad anymore after he passed away, I shouldn't be allowed to complain about my dad who is still technically alive. When Wren talks about her parents and their divorce, I can't talk about how sometimes I feel ignored in my own family even when my parents are happily married, which is why I've put off therapy for years. I don't want to take up space in a place where some people have real problems when mine can be fixed temporarily by throwing money at it.

"I know, Ken and I'm sorry," I say truthfully, pulling her into a hug. She somehow always manages to smell like a beach even when she hasn't been to one in a while. She constantly smells like summer despite her last name. I breathe her in. There is nothing quite like a Kennedy Wynter hug.

"I know how you can make it up to me," she muffles into my skin. I hum in response, recognising that slight child-like mischief in her tone. "Miles is doing a Halloween-themed game night at his house next weekend. It'll be a few of the hockey guys and Evan too. You should come."

"I'll be there," I say, squeezing her again. A day not thinking about my dad and the company could be good. I need a few days to recoup and start working on a different theory. Something about what Gio told me is still not making sense to me.

I'm missing something.

22

EVAN

I THINK I almost died walking Scarlett home a few nights ago.

Okay, maybe not, but it felt like it. I was freezing right to the bone, my shirt was stuck to me in every possible place, but for some reason, when I put my hand across her face, flames erupted across my body. I really need to sort whatever the hell that is out, especially when we're getting somewhere with the case.

I miscalculated time for my run again this morning, so I'm sprinting down the hallway, my shirt untucked, tie loose and my hair a mess as I try not to miss the meeting with Anderson and Scarlett about the project. If I'm more than ten minutes late he'll probably lock me out of the room. He's done it before, and he'll do it again.

I somehow messed up my fitness watch and ended up sprinting half a marathon before realising I was late for school. Again. I can't blame anyone for this. I set the time for half an hour, but I set it at nine-thirty-seven, and it messed up my concept of the run. It needed to end at ten-forty or else it would irritate me that it's not landed on an even number.

Still, Anderson wouldn't care for my excuses, so I picked up the pace again, finally in the same building as his office. It's the last one on the corridor, tucked between the business library and a lecture theatre. I get to the brown door a few seconds before I would have been ten minutes late, and I open it.

Scarlett's back is to me at first, sitting in front of Mr Anderson's desk. She looks a lot more put together than she did the other night. Which is a little insane considering the rain and the dim glow of the moonlight only made her features more striking. Now, she's wearing a black dress, half her hair tied back with the ribbon into a bow, while the rest falls onto her shoulders and down her back. She turns around, her brown eyes taking survey of my messy outfit.

She snorts. "You look like shit." I ignore her when she laughs at me and take the seat next to hers.

"Language, Scarlett," Anderson warns, sounding fed up with her.

"Thank you," I say to him sweetly as she gives me a stern side glance. I smile to myself, knowing that tiny comment got under her skin.

Anderson goes into his usual lecture, explaining how the project works and asking us if we're abiding by the guidelines. His office is cool in the sense that the blinds for his windows can convert into a screen which he can project his PowerPoint on. As he turns around, droning on about the requirements, Scarlett scooches her chair closer to mine, her strong perfume hitting me.

"What's wrong with you?" she asks, not looking at me as

she pretends to watch Anderson's presentation. She lowers her voice lightly, "Do you need some weed?"

I choke on air because the question hangs between us as we're in a room with a *teacher.* He could easily get us expelled for that shit, but he doesn't seem to care much about his job to even bother.

Still, as he changes slides he says, "You cannot talk about drugs in my office. I am a teacher."

Scarlett rolls her eyes, seeming way too comfortable with the idea of us getting kicked out. "Yeah, but are you *really?*" I swear this girl has a death wish. She leans into me again as Anderson groans. She whispers, "I'm being serious."

"I can still hear you even if you whisper, Scarlett. We're not even two feet away from each other," Anderson says. She actually laughs at that and I'm too busy trying not to focus on her proximity to laugh with her. She waves a hand dismissively at his back and then turns to me, a question dancing in her eyes: *Well?*

"I definitely do not need any substances from you, Scarlett," I say to her. She turns back to Anderson, slightly slouching in her chair as she crosses her arms across her chest, sulking.

"Okay, jeez. It was just a question. Quit acting like you've got a cork up your ass," she mutters. I ignore her and turn back to Anderson.

"Can we please stay on topic," I say.

THE REST of the meeting goes smoothly.

We explain to Anderson how we're planning on running the app and when we get in touch with software developers, how we'll turn it into a reality. He said our plan is good and that we could be coming out with a good grade if we stick to it. It's kind of hard to do while we're also solving a mystery alongside it.

After the meeting, we moved into the business library across from his office, finally getting back to work. After such a weird morning, it feels good to submerge myself into work that isn't my brain. I can give myself time to focus on something that isn't going to send me into a spiral or lead to a cold shower.

I thought it was working. Then I remembered that it's Scarlett Voss I'm working alongside.

I notice too many things about her. All the time. I've been picking up on small things that she does, most of which drive me a little crazy. Like the way she taps her pencil on the page three times when she's thinking and four times when she's thinking extra hard. The way she crosses and uncrosses her legs when she's listening to me talk. The way she never looks me in the eye for long enough, but how it also feels like it's for too long. How after four seconds of uninterrupted eye contact, she *always* drops her head down to her work.

And today, even though I can tell it was probably perfect before she left the house this morning, the bow in her hair is slipping out. We're both sitting next to each other at a desk facing the window, tucked into one side of the small library. My chair is a few inches further out than hers as she leans over the table and I lean back in my chair, giving me a fantastic view of her hair and the loose bow.

Usually, I wouldn't care. Okay, I would, but I could suppress my compulsions. Today I'm already on edge with after the run this morning and being late to the meeting. Now seeing that bow, seconds away from falling out, it's driving me up the wall.

Finally, I mutter, "Your ribbon is falling out."

She pauses writing for a second. She's right handed. I like that. It means we can sit on the same side of the table without our elbows rubbing together. It's a stupid thing to pick up on, but it adds to the very long list of things I'm starting to notice about her.

"Gee. Thanks for pointing that out," she mutters angrily.

She drops her pencil, her bare slender arms reaching up to fiddle with it. She messes with it for two seconds before continuing writing. It's even more of a mess now.

"You've made it worse," I say, scratching the back of my neck.

She turns to me now — *finally* — and her brown eyes narrow. "Thanks for the play-by-play, Branson. That's really helping. Do *you* want to sort it out?"

She's willingly asking me to touch her. Well, not her, but her hair. And her hair is fucking gorgeous. It's long — *too fucking long* — dark brown, but not black and always with a ribbon. There's no way. I must have heard her wrong because Scarlett Voss would never invite me to touch her.

"What?" I gawk.

"Did you hear me or what? I don't have a mirror and we're going to waste time if I go to the bathroom to fix it. Can you do it or is it beyond your capabilities?" she asks, tilting her head playfully.

I don't even flinch at the insult and instead ask, "Are you sure?"

She sighs. "You know what, on second thought, that bathroom break is looking really good," she groans, standing up.]

Uh, no. Not happening.

I tug on her elbow, pulling her back down to me. Her eyes widen at the sudden contact of my hand on her skin. I gently nudge her into the desk, and she sits on the table, half of her body hanging off it as she angles herself towards me.

I stand up, moving behind her. "Can you be quiet for two minutes?" I ask, not touching her yet.

She shrugs and I can tell she probably rolled her eyes too. I take a deep breath. It's not a big deal at all. I've tied a hundred bows in my life after my mom left and my dad wanted presents to look authentic. Still, this is different. Because it's *her*.

Seeing her like this, finally quiet, below me, her posture straight, has my thoughts going straight into the gutter. I imagine how she would look on her knees, that ribbon tied around her wrists instead of her hair.

I watch her shudder as I undo the ribbon slowly, letting it fall, while keeping one hand in the half of the silky hair that almost melts in my hands. I should not be allowed to touch her like this. Not when I'm getting hard just by doing it. She takes in a sharp breath and my breathing shallows. I finally do what she asked, gently but firmly tying the bow so it looks good and is secure enough.

"Are you done?" she asks. She thinks I don't notice the subtle way she clears her throat, but I do.

"No," I lie, fiddling with her hair because why is it so fucking soft? It's so tempting, yet it feels so wrong. So dirty. "Why do you always have these in? I can't figure you out."

She ignores me and asks again: "Are you done?"

"Scarlett," I press, urging her to answer my question. I tug on her hair, the same way I did at the restaurant, but this time I angle her towards me, her delicate face tilted up. When she looks at me, her mouth parts in a gasp, her pupils dilated.

Interesting. I release my hold on her hair and her shoulders sag.

"What?" she bites out.

"Can you answer my question?"

She holds my stare. "I don't need to answer anything." She stands up and turns fully until she's right in front of me. I straighten, naturally towering over her, but she doesn't back down. Instead, she raises her chin, triumphant as if she's realised something. "I gave you two chances to tell me the truth, and you lied both times. I'm not an idiot, Branson. I can tell that you just wanted your hands on me."

In a way that she usually does, she doesn't sound like she's complaining. She doesn't sound like she's disgusted by the idea of me wanting to touch her. She just seems like she wants to know. Or she wants her theories to be confirmed more like.

I give her the bait. "Then why did you let me do it?"

"You wanted to touch me," she says again as if that makes this make more sense. "I was going to let it carry on. See how long it would take for you to say something, to make you crack. And then you did. You think I don't know you, Ev, but I do. Especially after the other night. I can see right through you sometimes."

Fuck.

"Really? Then what am I thinking right now, Angel."

"You want me," she says. Of course, I do. I have since freshman year, and I've denied it ever since. How could I not? She's a fucking magnet. "I don't know why. I mean, of course, I do. I'm a catch. But why you? *That's* what I don't get. It makes sense now. All the touches, the glances, the helping. You want me."

I don't believe that she's not affected by me for a second. So, I inch closer to her, leaning down as our fronts are practically touching. She's breathing heavily, her chest rising and falling as she tries to keep eye contact with me. She does for five seconds now before dropping her gaze to my chest.

"I don't want you," I lie. The last thing I need is to complicate this when we've got the project and the mystery to figure out. "You drive me insane, Scarlett."

"Yeah, and you let me."

She trails her long fingernail up my arm, not breaking eye contact with me until she reaches my shoulder. My shirt isn't thin, but it fucking feels like it. Each inch her finger moves sets off small explosive bombs up my arm until she gets to my neck where my pulse is hammering.

She's enjoying this.

In some sadistic way, she's enjoying torturing me.

When she reaches my neck, she curls her hand around the back of my head, twisting her fingers in my hair, tugging gently. I close my eyes, taking a second to breathe before opening them again. She's got that sexy, lazy smile on her lips, her cheeks a little red as she presses herself into me.

"Don't do that, Scar," I mutter, placing my hand on top of hers, practically swallowing it whole as I drag it from my face.

"Tell me I'm lying, Branson," she urges.

I cannot.

So, I divert instead.

"Let's get back to work," I say, stepping away from her. When I get to my seat, I don't look at her. I can play along with whatever game she wants to. I'd do just about anything she wanted me to. If she asked me to jump, I'd ask how high.

God, I'd follow her to the ends of the earth if she asked me.

When we settle into a rhythm of comfortable silence, I try my best to ignore whatever just happened between us.

Something shifted.

Either she's playing hard to get, or she genuinely has no interest in me, and she wants to push me until I break. Unfortunately for her, I don't have much self-control.

If we were ever that close again, there is no telling what I would do.

SCARLETT

After Evan and I leave the library, knowing that I'll see him again at the game night, I realise two things.

1. I am going to need to buy more batteries for my vibrator.
2. I, almost certainly, have some sort of pathetic and emotionally draining crush on Evan Branson.

FUCK. My. Life.

23

SCARLETT

I'VE BEEN in the den of Miles' house for almost an hour, and I already want to leave. There aren't that many people here, but with the amount of noise Miles and Xavier make you could have imagined at least twenty of us here.

Cobwebs decorate the ceilings and huge spiders lurk in the corners. The punch bowls are a strange green and orange colour, and all the snacks are some Halloween version of big brands. Honestly, it came together a lot better than I thought it would.

A few guys from the hockey team are all huddled in one corner of the room near the impromptu karaoke machine making a racket. Miles, Xavier, and Evan are all dressed in suit and ties, deciding to be the Men in Black as well as most of the hockey team. Their outfits are boring, but they're men, so who's surprised.

Wren is wearing a green dress and wings, tying her hair up into a bun so she can look like Tinkerbell whilst Michelle is Iridessa from the Tinkerbell movies. I was going to match with them, but as soon as I heard Kennedy was going rogue, I decided to be a devil instead. It's hot and sexy and completely opposes Evan's stupid nickname for me.

Kennedy helped Miles with planning the quiz section of tonight, so she's off in the dining room meticulously planning about how tonight's going to go. She's dressed up as the mad hatter from Alice in Wonderland, naturally. Despite the gory looking games, all I know is we're going to split into teams and compete with one another in a series of random party games. I'm a competitive person, so this will be fun. Especially if I'm playing against Evan.

"We need to start drafting a team name," Wren says around a mouthful of pizza. She wipes her mouth with the back of her hand, rubbing the grease against her skirt.

"I agree," Michelle says, tucking her box braids that fell out back into her bun. "We might even get points for a good name if Kennedy's judging."

"Wren, you're the writer," I say, nudging her in the shoulder. She blushes a little, sighing. "We need something that will win Ken over."

"What about 'Starbucks Lovers.' It's the name of our group chat," Wren suggests.

Michelle laughs. "You mean the group chat I'm not a part of."

"You're in the better one. Most of our messages consist of asking where each other are. 'Folkwhores' sounds better, anyway."

"I agree," I say, laughing at the ridiculous name Ken came up with for our group chat with Michelle.

We all turn at the same time to the horrendous noise that's coming from their boyfriends.

Miles is supposed to be leading the night with the first game being beer pong, but he seems to be engrossed in terribly singing *'Sign of the Times.'* Wren's watching him adoringly from beside me and Michelle watches Xavier add in his own ad libs, both of the boys standing, swaying with each other. Evan is sitting, shaking his head at them, but I can tell he's laughing.

I love my friends and I love that they are happy, but there might be the tiniest bit of me that's a little jealous. If I could get over the first trials and tribulations of an adult relationship, maybe I'd be just as happy as them. I'm fine on my own most of the time. Solitude has always been my thing. I enjoy being independent and doing things on my own. In fact, I hugely prefer it. Still, there's that tiny part of me that wants what they have. To always have someone in my corner. Someone on my team who's not going to make me feel like less than.

I take the opportunity to slip away to the other side of the huge room towards the pool table. I've always wanted to know how to play, but it's one of the things that my brothers failed to teach me. No matter how many times they explained it, I still couldn't get it.

I settle next to the empty table, my back away from the hysterical screaming that's known as Miles' singing. I pick up the cue, feeling it in my hand before settling it down, aiming it towards the white ball.

My first shot is terrible, and I laugh at myself, feeling pathetic. I'm about to put the cue back down, ready to walk away from something I'm not perfect at the first time, but then I feel a heavy weight behind me, pressing into my back.

Almost instantly I can tell it's him.

My ass is perfectly nestled into his crotch, so I try to ease myself up and stand straighter. His huge hands come around mine, caging me in as he slowly runs them down my arms. The movement is so light, but I'm wearing a red short-sleeved corset top and jeans, so each brush of his hand feels like an inferno against my skin. He clasps his hands over mine on the cue, his breathing steady while I can hear my heart rattling against my ribcage.

"Evan?" My voice no longer sounds like my own. His proximity, his smell, the conversation we had the other day about him wanting me. No answer was an answer enough. I just have no idea how to go about it now.

"Hm?" The noise travels straight from the back of my neck where his mouth is to the space between my legs. I can tell he needs to clear his throat. His voice is slightly raspy and deep and just the sound sends goosebumps across my arms. I shiver under his touch, which only causes me to back up into him more, feeling something very big and hard beneath my ass. I can't tell which one of us gasps.

"What are you doing?" I ask. I could guess, but words and all coherent thoughts are failing me right now.

"Showing you how to play, Angel," he answers simply. Like I guessed, his voice is low and raspy, the sound settling in my stomach. His hands tighten over mine for a split second before relaxing, but still holding them. I swear I can't even see my hands now. It should be humanly impossible for him to be able to play piano with hands that big.

Stop thinking about his hands, you perv, no matter how hot they look.

Think with your head, not your tits.

"I can figure it out on my own," I say, my voice wavering.

He tuts. "You can't be showing the opposition weakness

already. Come on, sweetheart. You know better than that." I'm getting sick of these new nicknames. This one especially. What's worse than that is the way it lights me up inside.

"Why are you helping me?" I ask when he's not even showed me how to play yet, his hot heavy hands just hold onto mine.

"We might be playing against each other, but it would be downright embarrassing watching you struggle for the sake of a silly competition," he answers, laughing a little. He's testing me. It's payback for what I did the other day. It has to be. I knew it was risky touching him like that, hoping that he'd crack. That's the only reason he's touching me so close now.

"For the sake of competition," I mutter back to him, trying to get as comfortable as I can with him this close to me.

"Now," he instructs gently. "Can you let go of the cue for me? You're holding it too tight." I take a deep breath, doing as he asks, and I let go of it, dropping into his hands.

"Good girl," he murmurs.

I don't even have time to process those two words and the cobwebs I get in my stomach before he readjusts the cue in my hand, my grip looser, my right hand closer to the tip while my other rests somewhere closer to the top.

"Okay, now hold it like this."

He takes a step back and I take a step back too, giving myself a second to breathe. It doesn't do anything to relieve the tension because I can still feel his hands *everywhere*. He places his hand on my lower back while nudging me in the back of my knee a little, urging me to lean further forward and I do.

I like being in control. I like being the one who makes the other person unravel, but for some reason there's this struggle between us where, depending on the situation, I end up being subservient to him and I actually listen to him. Like now.

I'm leaning over the table and his body heat is all over me, his front pressed into my back and my ass finding its way nestled into his lap again. His gigantic, veiny hands are covering mine again, adjusting my fingers one by one until they're in a position he's satisfied with.

It shouldn't be that big of a deal. It *isn't* that big of a deal, but his hands look so good. He instructs me to hit the white ball from the position it's in, lined up next to the other balls. I hit it and his hands never leave mine.

I watch the balls rattle against each other, and I can't tell if what I did was good or not. The rules of this really mess me up and he's giving no indication if what I'm doing is even right.

Until his hands leave mine and they suddenly feel empty. The sensation is instantly eased by the weight of his hands on my shoulders instead and I stand up straighter. I'm so caught up with lust and his proximity that I don't even have the energy to tell him to stop. He gently massages my shoulder, not speaking for a few beats until he leans his head closer to my neck, his hot breath setting my body on fire.

"That was a good shot, sweetheart," he whispers into my neck. For a second I thought he was about to kiss me there or something, but he didn't, his lips only a few inches away from my neck. "You're doing such a good job."

I don't say anything. He pushes into me again, slightly urging me to go further so I can aim better, and I do, his bodyweight still behind me and his hands return back to their position over my hands.

I'm sure he's talking to me now, but all I can hear is the steady beat of my heart gradually getting faster. I swear to God, I hope he can't hear my heart beating right now.

EVAN

I want to breathe her in.

No.

I want to only breathe the air that she's breathing. Just be hers and hers only. God, I'd give her all of me if she gave me the chance. I can feel her pulse racing all throughout her body, beating against my hands, against her neck and the way her back arches into mine slightly as she takes in deep breaths.

It can't just be me that wants this. I had to get her back for teasing me the way she did the other day, knowing that it drove me up the wall. Still, I'm trying to see how far it would take her to finally do something to ease the sexual tension between us.

I let my body weight fall onto her slightly, loving the feel of the way her hands flinch beneath mine. God, they're fucking tiny compared to mine. I don't get a second to instruct her further before her friend's voice makes her flinch.

"Hey, Scar," Kennedy calls. "We're getting into teams now."

Scarlett clears her throat. "Okay, I'll be there in a sec," she replies. She turns back to me slowly, trying to twist out my grip but I keep her there. She sits halfway on the end of the pool table as I tower over her, setting my hands on both sides of her. She crosses her arms against her chest. It's the first time I've really seen her face since I came over here and it's redder than I thought it would be. She never blushes and now her face is a deep red. Some girls get embarrassed if they blush a lot, when she does it, I think it's hot.

"Do you always get this close to the girls you teach pool?"

I know this is a trap, but I don't care anymore. "No," I say. "Just you."

She smiles, holding her hand to her chest, feigning surprise. "Awh. Am I that special, Branson?"

"You'd be extraordinary, Scarlett," I admit, leaning further into her. She leans back a little, her eyes flickering to my lips and then back to my eyes. "If your ego wasn't so big."

She snorts. "I *am* extraordinary, Branson. Hearing you say that shit only makes me realise that I'm even *more* amazing."

I shake my head at her. "Only you would take an insult as a compliment."

"Because it's not an insult," she says, pouting slightly. She's cockier than half the guys I know. I just wish it wasn't so fucking attractive.

I take a step back from her. "You're ridiculous."

"No," she says, sighing as she jumps off the pool table, the horns on her head bobbing. "*You're* ridiculous."

Then she walks past me, shoving her shoulder into mine on purpose. I turn and watch her walk away, her ass swaying side to side as she greets Wren, Kennedy, and Michelle in one corner.

She's going to ruin my life. And I think I'm going to let her.

WE PLAY BEER PONG FIRST. I'm on a team with Miles and Xavier against Wren, Kennedy, and Scarlett. We've been drawing up until this point. I'm competitive at any game. If it involves Scarlett, I want to win. I don't go easy on her just because she's got a pretty face. I play to win, no matter what.

The last shot is down to Miles.

If he gets it in, we win and if he misses we lose. Xavier stands behind him, rubbing on his shoulders as if he's about to run a marathon. I give the basic advice, telling him to focus and stay calm so we can win this round. The cups are covered in fake cobwebs, the ball with tiny black spiders' hand-drawn across it.

It doesn't help that he's a lovesick puppy and his girlfriend is on the other side of the table, purposefully stretching her hands above her head so she can distract him.

Miles is an idiot, so he gets distracted easily.

"Wren's cheating!" he shouts at his girlfriend. She laughs, dropping her arms. Scarlett watches Miles carefully, probably trying to psych him out with her intense staring.

"I'm not," she replies defensively. "You're just a sore loser, baby."

"You're trying to trick me by calling me 'baby,'" he shouts back, sulking. "You know it's my weakness."

I groan at their constant bickering and all the girls laugh. Wren says, "I'm not doing anything," while slowly shimmying off the wings to her costume, dropping it to the ground.

"Look at me like that one more time and I swear to god-"

"Just throw the damn ball, Davis," I say, nudging him.

He throws it finally. It's like watching it in slow motion. The split second before the ball leaves his hand, Wren winks at him. From that, I can tell the shot is going to be a miss. Still, I watch it play out. The ball bounces on the table once. Then twice. Then again and it rolls right off the table. The second it drops to the ground the girls all jump in unison, cheering loudly.

I watch the sly smirk on Scarlett's lips, and she turns to me. As they're laughing, they make their way over to our side of the table. Wren goes up to Miles, laughing hysterically in his face and he takes it, letting her make fun of him.

"Are you done?" he asks her. She shakes her head, still

laughing before he grabs her face and kisses her deeply, silencing her laughter.

"Very weird reaction for someone who just lost," I mutter. Scarlett's beside me now, leaning against the wall as she watches them make out before diverting her eyes to the ground.

"I don't think he could ever lose if it came to her. Losing a game against Wren is just like winning to him," she replies, a short laugh escaping her mouth.

"Doesn't it get sickening?" I ask. She looks up at me, not understanding. "I mean being around them all the time, they're constantly making out. Doesn't it annoy you?"

She shrugs and then sighs deeply. "No," she says simply. I hum in response. "I'd much prefer this…" She gestures to the Wren who is now sitting on the table, her legs wrapped around Miles' waist as they make out. "Than pure silence."

I laugh at that. "You'd prefer anything over silence. You talk too much."

"I know." She smiles at me for a second before dropping it and walking away.

WE STAY in the same teams for most of the night. I play against Scarlett at pool, and I actually go easy on her. She was struggling and after our impromptu lesson, she's not exactly an expert.

I sit out on playing charades because it's always such an awkward game when your teammates are shouting at you, so I don't participate. The only time I play on her team is when we play a very butchered game of True American, which just ends with us getting buzzed from shot gunning too many beers.

Now, we're ready for the final game of the night; trivia. Kennedy is the host for this one, leaving me on a team with Xavier and Miles against Scarlett, Wren, and Michelle. We beat the two other teams, so we're in the final heat.

Our team won the sports round and the horror movie round while the girl's team won the true crime knowledge and the song round. I think it's rigged because most of the questions were relating to pop culture or inside jokes, which gave them an unfair advantage. There's one round left and it's a history round about NU.

Kennedy is standing on a makeshift podium (it's a cardboard box with two bricks beneath it and an easel stand she stole from school) shuffling the index cards in her hand. It's mostly quiet in here now as the teams that lost have now branched off into other parts of the house. To her left, me and the boys are sitting on plastic chairs while on the right the girls are sitting, each of them glaring at us.

"Can each team please select a candidate to represent your team in the final round," she instructs. "In the meantime, I'll play some elevator music." She turns on her phone and instead of playing elevator music, she plays *'High Enough'* by K.Flay adding to the already tense atmosphere.

I turn to my team and they're already staring at me. I roll my eyes. "You can't be serious," I mutter.

"Come on. It's history stuff. Miles and I won't be any good," Xavier says.

"He's right," Miles adds. "If we know anything we'll give you a hint. It'll be subtle. If you're smart enough, you'll figure it out."

"Fine. You owe me for this," I say, brushing off my jeans as I stand up.

"You've got to be kidding me," Scarlett mutters and that's

when I see that she's standing too, the nominee from her team. I beam at her, not giving her the satisfaction of thinking she'll throw off my game just because I'm going against her.

Kennedy turns down her music. "Perfect," she says, looking at the two of us. "So, I just decided on a new prize for the team captains. The loser has to ask the winner out on a date."

Both of our teams laugh at us, and I just blink back at Ken, hoping she's going to take back what she just said. She doesn't. Scarlett rubs at her temples.

"That makes no sense," she retorts.

"It's my quiz night and my rules," Kennedy argues.

"So, it's a lose-lose situation. Regardless of who wins, I'll have to go on a date with *him.*" Wren giggles from the other side of her. Scarlett shoots her a look and she tries to tamp down her smile.

I lean into Scar and whisper, "Don't think of it as a date, sweetheart. We can do our casual detective stuff."

She pulls away from me, turning so we're facing each other. "I'm not going anywhere else with you."

"You won't be saying that when I'm done with you," I murmur, intent on changing the way she feels about me. She's got to give up this 'I hate Evan' game at some point. Her nostrils flare as she crosses her arms akimbo.

"What the fuck does that mean?"

I don't say anything because Kennedy has stepped down from her little podium as she gently pushes us apart to our respective sides of the easel. She writes our team names on each side of the sheet; the Folkwhores and Nacho Average Team. Guess who came up with our team's name.

And why did you guess Miles?

The rules are simple: Kennedy will ask a question, you

have five seconds to answer, the first one to write it down on the board wins and if you don't write anything in five seconds, the other team gets the point.

"Folkwhores, are you ready?" Kennedy asks Scarlett. She pins me with a glare, opening her pen with a pop, not letting her eyes leave mine. Kennedy turns to me. "Nacho Average Team, are *you* ready?"

I nod and the game begins. The first two rounds are easy. The first question is about how many sports NU covers and the closest answer wins. I guess eight and Scarlett guessed seven. I got the point.

The second question is about who the Dean before Ms Hackerly was, Wren's mom, took over. Scarlett had an advantage on that one, so she won, leaving us to draw.

"How many years has Ryan Redmond been at NU?" she asks, and I smirk. I went to the same middle school as Ryan, and he was a few grades older. I was confused as to how he was still at NU by the time I started. Hell, he's still here now.

I write down my answer quickly, my handwriting barely eligible as Scarlett pauses. "Seven and a half," I say for extra emphasis.

"A point to N.A.T. Well done, Branson," Kennedy coos and I smile. Scarlett sticks her tongue out at me. "Okay. We only have two more questions left. If Scarlett gets this one right, you'll be in for a draw, making the last question the tiebreaker. If Evan wins this question, there will be no chance at victory for the Folkwhores."

We both nod, getting ready in game position. She licks her lips, and it distracts me for a second. I need to win this round. I want her to be the one who has to ask me out. Not the other way around.

"Taylor Swift released a new album a few days ago. How many songs are on the track list?" Kennedy asks.

"That's an unfair question. It's not even related to NU," I blurt out as Scarlett starts writing. I give up. There's no way I'd be able to get that quick enough without thinking about it for a minute.

"Thirteen!" Scarlett screams and her team cheer for her, including Kennedy. I knew having her as the judge would be a conflict of interest. Scarlett holds up two of her fingers in an L shape. "How does it feel to lose, loser?"

"We're drawing, dumbass," I retort. Still, she's smiling, waiting for Kennedy to ask the tie-breaking question. She did that on purpose. She wanted Scarlett to win, and she knew I would never get the answer. The rules for this game are very loose.

"The million-dollar question," Kennedy begins dramatically. If I win, she'll have to ask me on a date. If she wins, I'll have to ask her on a date. "Now, the mascot for North is a bear. What was it before?"

Everything happens in slow motion again.

As the words leave Kennedy's mouth, I hear the faint sound of meowing coming from the boys. Then I remember what they said about helping me out discreetly if the question came up. They must be doing it on purpose to trip Scarlett up. She looks over at them, forgetting the strict time limit, smirking as she thinks she's got the right answer and I use the opportunity to write 'dog' on the sheet.

"And time!" Kennedy shouts. "Please step away from your board." We do as she asks, each of us taking a step back. I can't help but grin at the proud look on Scarlett's face, the way she's standing tall, her head held high. "So, we have opposing answers here. Folkwhores believe it was a cat while the Nacho

Averagers believe it's a dog. I'm delighted to announce that the correct answer is…" There's a dramatic pause of silence. Scarlett's eyes zone in on me and she still wears that victorious smirk on her face. God, I can't wait for it to wipe right off. "A dog. Congratulations, Nacho Average Team. You have won tonight's trivia."

The boys get up from their seats cheering as the girl's sulk in their seats. I'm about to step down to join them, but Scarlett barrels past Kennedy and straight into me. She almost trips in the process, her foot getting caught on the cardboard. I grab onto her arm.

"Careful, sweetheart," I whisper, laughing. She drags her arm away from mine and instead jabs her index finger in my chest.

"You're such a…fuckwaffle!" She digs her finger into my chest harder, her chest rising and falling. Seeing her pissed off is my absolute favourite thing.

"What the hell is a fuckwaffle?" I ask, laughing. She stands there, opening and closing her mouth and fucking hell, watching those round pink lips open and close like that is driving me crazy.

She blinks at me. "I- You- That's what you are."

"A fuckwaffle?" I ask curiously. She nods. "You think I'm a waffle you want to fuck?"

"That is not what I said," she challenges. Her face is almost entirely red now.

I tilt my head, grinning as I ask, "But it's what you meant, no?"

"Shut your pie hole," is all she can come up with.

"Make me."

She steps closer to me, and everyone is still watching. She takes me by my loose tie, tightening it before pulling it until my face is right in front of her. Her breathing pattern changes, as she wets her bottom lip before looking at me. She pushes herself against my chest, stepping between my feet. She's basically strangling me with this tie, but if she's going to kiss me right now, it'll be worth it.

What would she do if I leaned down and pressed my lips to hers? If I kissed that smug smirk right off her face. If pressed myself closer to her and she could feel how fucking hard I am by just being near her. What would she do then?

She tugs on my tie again. "If you think I'm about to kiss you right now, Branson, you've got another thing coming. Because what I *really* want to do is rip your balls from your body, shove them in a blender and make you drink it."

I swallow. Hard.

"Stop thinking about my balls, you perv," I say.

She doesn't laugh and my joke was pretty funny. Instead, she tugs onto my tie harder, almost causing me to choke.

"Brilliant but scary," I mutter. I think she catches the Harry Potter reference because she *almost* smiles. She lets go of my tie, but she tries to turn away from me, so I grab her elbow, pulling her right back into me where she belongs. "Hey, loser. I think you're forgetting something."

She crosses her arms against her chest. "I'm not asking you out."

"Don't worry," Kennedy says, reaching into her back pocket as she pulls out a handwritten note, handing it to Scarlett. She winks at me. "I've got you covered."

Scarlett scans the sheet, frowning. "Ken. You pre-wrote this? You knew he was going to win, didn't you?"

She shrugs innocently. "I had a feeling." Kennedy is such a meddler. I guess that's why they love her so much unless she's meddling in their business.

"Our names are literally written on the sheet," Scarlett groans, flapping the white paper around. She looks up to me as she scoffs, "Can you believe this?"

"No, Angel, I can't. You're going to have to read it out to me," I say, trying to hide my laugh.

"Read it," Kennedy urges. It takes three seconds before the room all erupt in chants, telling Scar to read it out loud. I'm standing, waiting for her with the biggest smile on my face. "Okay! Quiet, everyone."

Scarlett looks at me now, sighing as she pushes her hair behind her shoulder. She starts to read. "'I, Scarlett Evangeline Voss, have the absolute pleasure of asking you, Evan No-Middle-Name Branson, out on a date." She continues reading before glancing at Kennedy who's beaming like a proud parent. "I'm not doing that."

"You've got to do what it says," Kennedy explains. I try to take a peek at the sheet, but she holds it away from me.

"I'm not holding his hand," she murmurs.

"You're holding my hand," I correct for her, prying her steel fingers off the sheet. She's absolutely hating this, and I love it. My cheeks hurt from smiling too much.

She groans. "I promise to not complain and be a good date," she reads before adding, "I'm not making that promise, but fine." Kennedy frowns. Scarlett rolls her eyes before she continues reading. "I solemnly swear that I will go on this date within the next two to five business days and will not bail unless there are unforeseen circumstances that will result in my failure to attend." She rushes the last bit of the sentence before looking back up at me. "So, will you, Evan Branson, the winner of this quiz, go on a date with me?"

"I thought you'd never ask," I coo.

"You're ridiculous."

"No," I say, shaking my head, ready to repeat her words back to her. I reach out and flick her headband with the horns on it. "*You're* ridiculous."

I don't think either of us even realise we're still holding hands.

"WE REALLY DON'T HAVE to do this," she says, turning to me in the back of my Escalade.

"Oh, but we do," I tease. I open my door as she sulks, rounding the car to open the door for her. "You promised me a date so that's exactly what we're doing, sweetheart."

She steps out, her Louboutin heels tapping out onto the pavement. I reach my hand out to her, but she ignores it. She's going to make today hell and I can't wait until she gives in. I'm bringing her to a new art showing at Origin Hall in Colorado. I've never been, and I've seen the art pieces around her apartment that aren't Kennedy's. I noticed the way she paused for a second when we were walking from the business building to the parking lot and there was a painting from one of the first students at NU in the art department.

I know she's going to enjoy it. She might have insisted on going on different flights to get here (I took my private plane, and she took hers), but I'm determined to make her smile.

"Couldn't we have just lied to them? We didn't have to *actually* go on a date," she whines as we walk up the stone steps to the museum entrance. It's a large grey building that resembles a huge brick with small cut out windows. It's supposed to be one of the best up and coming museums in Denver.

"What would be the fun in that?" I ask. She looks up at me, pinning with me with a look as if to say *'Are you serious'* and I grin back at her. "Come on. The contract said you had to be a good date and you're not being a very good one right now."

"I'm being as pleasant as I can be considering you're my date," she mutters as she pushes open the large door.

Immediately, we're met with silence. I've come to enough museums and galleries to know that they're sacred places for collectors and people who love art. People in uniforms work silently, cleaning down surfaces. The only noise I can hear is my heavy breathing and the click of Scarlett's heels.

She's wearing a striped navy pantsuit with a *very* short crop white top underneath as she leaves her blazer open, allowing me to see lots of her exposed, smooth, tanned skin. Her hair isn't tied up today, instead it falls halfway down her back, but I can still spot the blue ribbon tied to her wrist. I think she keeps it there in case of emergencies. The same way I spontaneously bought a back of hair ties because I know it irritates her to have her hair down from the way she was fighting herself with it in the restaurant.

Maybe I didn't think this one through because I am also here with the most talkative person on the planet. I don't know how she's planning to deal with the silence in here. It's like taking a kid to a library.

As if she's reading my mind she murmurs, "I don't think I can do this."

I turn to her. She's pulled her lips between her teeth, her cheeks a faint glow of red. She's not wearing any makeup today, she usually doesn't, but today her freckles are even more prominent on the bridge of her nose. Fuck, she looks cute. The way she's trying to stop herself from talking or laughing – or both – is just fucking adorable.

"You can do it, Scar. I believe in you," I whisper, winking.

"No. I don't think I can," she says, shaking her head. Hard. "I'm good at a lot of things, Branson, but not talking isn't one of them."

"Come on," I say, urging her to walk further in since we're still in the lobby. "The art's going to be so fantastic that you won't even need to talk."

"I doubt it," she mutters, dragging her feet as we walk down into a large room. This space is dedicated to all oil paintings made by an artist called Arnold Luc. Most of them are captivating pieces of boats and scenes at sea. It's pretty, but not my kind of thing.

My kind of art is the woman standing in front of the painting.

I knew she would shut up as soon as we got to some of the paintings. Her head is tilted slightly as she bends down to read the plaque beneath the painting. The one she's looking at is a scene of viscous waves, looking like a scene from the movie 'The Little Mermaid.' She shoves her hands into her pockets, taking her time to read and appreciate. She's not saying anything and there's one else in here, so she could.

Even I can't take the quiet, so I say the first thing that comes to mind.

"I've never been on a proper date before," I admit. As embarrassing as it is to admit, it's true. I've never had to plan anything to take another girl out. Even though Cat and I dated for a few years, we never went anywhere romantic or planned things to class as a date. Most of the times we hung out was spontaneous and we didn't do much talking. Towards the end of our relationship, it was filled with a lot more uncomfortable silences than anything else.

Scarlett turns around slowly, her hands still in her pocket. I get a very good view of her tanned and toned stomach. No sign of the tattoo though. She has a smirk on her lips, ready to torment me.

"You're telling me you and your rich girlfriend never went on dates?" she asks. I can't tell if she's trying to make fun of me or if she's genuinely curious. I shrug.

"We did. Just not like this," I reply.

"Is that why you wanted to come here?"

"That's one of the reasons," I say, shrugging again. "She wasn't really the going out type or the kind to like PDA. We were public but private."

She nods, stepping in closer to me, studying me. Her gaze could come off to others as scrutinising, but I can tell that the bolts in her head are working overtime trying to figure me out, so I let her. "Do *you* like PDA?" she asks.

"I don't hate it," I say truthfully. She nods, smiling slightly, and then walks past me. Of course, I follow her into the next room.

This one not only has large paintings on the walls, cased in gold frames, but it also has small sculptures inside glass boxes. Most of the paintings are abstract, unable to tell whether they're people, places, or objects. They just exist on the page and they're magnificent. The small sculptures are mostly nude crafts of torsos and breasts.

She's quiet again as we walk around the room slowly. She's capable of more than she lets on. As much as she likes to brag about how amazing she is, she *is* extraordinary. She told me she wouldn't be able to be quiet and she's managing it perfectly. For once, we're not arguing. We're not giving each other dirty looks. We're just existing, enjoying art and each other's company. Well, I hope she's enjoying my company. It's hard to tell if she's in her own world or not.

She stops still in front of a painting towards the end of the room near the door. It's a painting clearly with many layers, shades of orange, brown, blue, purple, and black lathered over each other in no particular fashion. She stands, hands in her pockets again, her ankles crossed as she reads the plaque over and over.

'Germiane Eckbert b. 1803. You are home, 1829. Acrylic on canvas.'

"It's beautiful," she whispers.

"It is," I say, staring at her and only her.

The paintings in here are gorgeous, sure. They took years of perfecting. Months of making sure each stroke was made to perfection. Weeks of staring at a blank canvas to create something so beautiful. With her, she only gets more and more beautiful over time. God only had one try and she made her perfect in every way that counts.

She stares at the painting while I look at her side profile, watching her truly take it in. She's still staring, so I don't even realise that she's moved her hand, settling it right into mine.

Her small hand clasps over mine, squeezing it gently, not looking at me. Her warmth and her touch are like something I've never experienced before. It's so soft yet anchoring, like it could keep me alive. It has that underlying strength like it could move mountains while also bringing about a strong sense of calm and tranquillity. It just feels safe.

When I'm with her, I'm not worrying about what could happen tomorrow. I'm not thinking about stupid compulsions that tell me if I don't do something by a certain time I'm going to die. I just exist. And she exists with me. Together but separate.

"What are you doing?" I choke out, hoping she can't feel how hard my pulse is hammering.

She sighs. "Don't make this weird."

I ignore her. "Why are you holding my hand, sweetheart?"

"Because it's upsetting that you've never been on a date before. You might piss me off, *but* you've been more bearable than usual and the fact that you've never been able to experience the fine art of handholding is just downright sad," she explains smoothly.

"Since when do my feelings matter to you?"

"They don't."

I groan, throwing my head back. "This thing that you're doing, Scarlett, it isn't cute anymore. Cut it out. We're *not* doing this. Got it?"

The second things start going somewhere, she says shit like that. It doesn't usually piss me off. Most of the time I hope she's joking, but it gets to a point where I can't tell anymore. She can tease me all she wants. She can tell me how much I annoy her just by breathing and I'll take it. But I thought that something shifted the other day when we spoke. When she told me that she knew I wanted her.

She turns to me now, her eyebrows scrunched together. She seems a little taken aback from my sudden seriousness. "Doing what?"

"*This*," I say, gesturing between us. I try to keep my cool. We're in a goddamn museum for God's sake. "You hating me. Pretending you don't care about my feelings. What is so bad about me, Scarlett, huh? Tell me. Tell me what you don't like about me because I'm going insane trying to figure it – you – out."

She drops her hand from mine now and it feels empty, like a piece of my heart has been ripped out. "Stop acting like you don't know, Branson."

"Scarlett, sweetheart. Tell. Me," I warn, needing an answer.

She scoffs. "Why are you getting so serious about this?"

"Because it *is* serious," I retort, my voice slightly climbing up. I sigh, walking to the other side of the room where a white bench rests against a wall. I sit down, running my hands through my hair as I hear her heels click until she's sitting beside me. "Angel, I can't do this. I really can't. I can't have you hating me every day. I can't have you looking at me like I disgust you."

"You don't disgust me," she whispers. I take my hands out of my face and turn to her.

"Then tell me. Tell me what I've done wrong so I can *fix* it," I press, rubbing at my temples. She blinks at me. "I don't want to keep going on like this. Jesus, I just want to be your friend."

"You want us to be friends?"

"Hasn't that been obvious?" I ask exasperatedly. She shakes her head a little, pulling her bottom lip between her teeth. "At the very least I want us to have a conversation where we're not screaming at each other. It's exhausting."

"It is?"

"Yes. Now tell me what I've done wrong."

Scarlett sighs, pushing her back against the wall, tilting her head up to the ceiling. I can't tell if she's trying to blink back tears or if she's trying to compose herself. She opens her mouth multiple times before closing it again. I could wait for her all day if she's finally going to tell me what I did so we can move on from this weird stage in our lives.

"You said that I would never amount to anything," she says finally. Her words sound like a punch to the stomach. I'd much prefer that than the words that come out of her mouth, knowing that it was me who said them. "That I'd never be more than a stupid girl in her brother's shadow." She turns to me now, her eyes filled with angry and upset tears. "And I already knew that, Evan. I've known that since the day I opened my eyes. I thought starting NU would be a fresh start and it wasn't. What you said to me felt worse than all the years at high school. So, I resented you for it and it led me to trying to one-up you in every class game and you played right along. I thought you hated me too and kept going. I know, it's stupid and pathetic, but at first, it felt better than letting you get under my skin, so I made it a mission to get under yours."

This is definitely worse than a punch to the gut. Hell, it's worse than a punch to my crotch. What hurts more than hearing the strangled sob in the back of her throat is that what she's saying is what I said to her.

Those first few days at NU were hell for me. I was bitter and miserable because my dad had cut me off. I had to move in with the boys. I had lost my girlfriend, and I was embarrassed for embarrassing my family and myself in the process. I should never have said those things to her. I knew that I remembered her from our childhood, but she didn't seem to recognise me. I forced myself to erase it from my memory as soon as I started to get better, and I must have forgotten about it. But she didn't.

"I'm so sorry, Scarlett," I say. "I'm so fucking sorry. I was in a bad place, and I was just projecting it onto you. I know that's not an excuse, but Jesus…I'm sorry."

I lean my head back against the wall, scrubbing my hands across my face.

"It's fine. It was stupid. I don't let those things get to me, so I don't know why I kept it up for so long," she replies, and I turn my head back down to look at her. Tears are rolling down her face now, slowly. I don't think she even notices. "I should have let it go."

"No," I say, shaking my head. I don't want her to cry. Jesus. I've hurt this girl too much already. If she cries right now, I won't be able to handle it. If it was someone else making her cry like the day I walked her home, I'd want to beat them up. I'd beat them bloody until they apologised to her. But it was me. *I* did this to her. "I was cruel to you. You're allowed to feel things. It doesn't mean you have to downplay your feelings because it took time to get over it."

A sharp sob rips through her and she shoves her face into her hands. I don't know what to do. She wouldn't want me to see her cry. *I* don't want to see her cry.

I inch closer to her, trying my best to comfort her by my proximity.

"Shit. Uh...Don't- Don't cry, Scar. I really can't have you crying on me right now."

She pulls her hands from her face, slamming her small fists into her lap. How in the world is she able to look so pretty when she cries? I almost want to smile at her for it, but she doesn't need my teasing right now.

"Then don't say those things!"

"Say what things?"

"That I'm allowed to feel things because then I just feel more...things," she sobs again as she desperately tries to push her hair out of her face, but it continues to stick to her forehead. Why the fuck is her hair so long?

"Come here," I mutter. Another sob rips out of her in response. Before she can say anything with actual words, I turn her around, scoop her closer to me and pull her hair out of her face, tying it back with the hair tie on my wrist. I secure it tightly in a low ponytail and she doesn't put up a fight. "Better?"

She sniffles, moving out of my grip to sit beside me. I still keep my arm around her shoulder, trying to comfort her. "You just *happen* to have hair ties on you now, Branson?"

I swallow. "You hate it when your hair is down."

"That didn't answer my question," she replies. I shrug. She relaxes after a few seconds, settling into my chest. "Why can't you just be mean to me like you were at that time?"

I laugh quietly. "I don't want to be mean to you. I never meant to be cruel. But as you started to play those games with me, I played along. I'd do anything you asked me to, you know that?"

"Why?" she asks, almost frustrated. She's not crying as hard now, thank God.

"Because I don't hate you. I'd never want to make you feel like I did that time. If you want to hate me and make fun of me, I can play along with you, but none of it is real."

"Then what's real?"

"What you said the other day," I admit, swallowing. Her eyes widen. "I do want you, but you don't. You're not going to forgive me overnight and I can live like that. Like you said, you prefer sleeping with nameless dudes and a quick fuck. We'd probably kill each other."

"Evan," she presses, blinking up at me.

"Scar, spare me," I say, laughing. "It's fine. I should be the one comforting you even though your snot is covering my shirt."

She punches me in the stomach, trying to move out of my grip, but I keep my arm around her shoulder, needing her close. "It is not! I'm not asking you to do any of this."

"That's the whole point," I say, chuckling. She shakes her head at me but she's smiling, her face still red. God, I want to kiss her so bad right now. What would she do if I did? She'd probably punch me in the stomach. She knows that I like her, and she can do with that information whatever she wants. When she's ready to have that conversation, I'll be here.

I'll wait.

Honestly, I'd probably wait forever for her.

25

SCARLETT

I DID NOT HAVE 'Crying in front of Evan Branson' written on my 2022 bingo card and I'm a little terrified. Not only did I hold his hand because I felt bad for him, I cried in front of him, he held me and he told me what I had been expecting. What's worse is that I enjoyed having him hold me. His weight is new and comforting and those hands…

I never would have been vulnerable with him like that, but I was emotional as it was, I was trying my best to ignore what's been going on with my family and he was there with his kind words and less dickish personality. I'm a simple girl, I cry when people say nice things to me.

Knowing that he might have actual feelings for me worries me a little. Relationships aren't my thing. They never have been, and they never will be. I'm still navigating my feelings towards him, just as a human, let alone romantically.

He's a good-looking guy.

Okay. He's more than good looking. He's fucking gorgeous. He's been on the cover of B&Co website and magazine for God's sake. His jawline is sharp, he has a dimple that appears every once and a while, his eyes are so fucking green it's scary. But what's more attractive is his vulnerability and his honesty. I've never met a guy as in tune with their emotions as him. If he's upset, you know. If he's angry, you know. If he's uncomfortable or needs something to squash his compulsions, you know. He doesn't hide things from me, and I appreciate that.

After our new truce was established, I even took his plane back to Salt Lake with him. We didn't speak for much of the plane journey. It was still a bit awkward. There was only one large TV on his plane so we ended up arguing over who could choose the movie. We landed on *'Dunkirk.'* I only wanted to watch it for Harry Styles, and he was obsessed with the Second World War when he was in high school. Weirdly enough, I didn't make fun of him for it. We just sat and watched the movie in silence. He did glance over at me every time Harry appeared on the screen though.

The new friendship thing we've established is the *only* reason I'm calling him right now. My mom suggested an impromptu dinner at home with all my siblings, excluding Alexander. She made it very clear that I needed a date. She even added in some very Oscar-worthy sniffles and insisted that it is 'what my dad would have wanted' as if he's gone already. After visiting him this morning, confirming that he's still stable, I'm getting ready in my room, waiting for Evan to pick up the call.

"Hello?" he asks when it finally connects.

"You took your time," I mumble.

"I was busy."

"Well, I was hoping you weren't. I need a date to come with me to my family dinner. My mom made it very clear that she wanted to meet someone I'm seeing, and I don't have the energy to scour through dating apps to find someone not serial killery to bring. So, I was thinking you could come, but if you're busy, it's fine," I say in one go, rambling like a fool.

"Oh, so you cry to me one time and now you think you're entitled to favours?"

"Fine, I'll call someone else," I drawl.

"What time do you want me there?"

"I thought you were busy?"

"I'm not anymore," he says easily. "What time, Scar?"

"I'll send you the address. Meet me outside the estate in an hour. Don't knock and wait till I get there," I instruct. "And wear something appropriate."

"Obviously. I'm not an idiot, Angel. I'm about to have dinner with five millionaires."

"*Four* millionaires," I correct. "My mom just hit a billion, so you better tell her that and you'll be on her good side." I'm only bending the truth a little, so he'll be on his best behaviour. Not much would take my mom to like someone. Especially since she thinks it's someone I'm 'dating.' She'd be thrilled whoever it is.

"Yes, boss," he replies. "I'll see you there."

EXACTLY AN HOUR LATER, I'm standing outside the huge doors watching Evan's escalade pull up into the driveway. I don't know why I'm nervous. Maybe it's because I don't usually bring my dates here and my mom is expecting some respected gentleman who will sweep me off my feet and help me settle down. Evan is not that person. Still, I know he can put on a good show when necessary.

I adjust my black dress for the hundredth time, trying to

pull it down my thighs as I watch him climb out of the car. It's not as tight as the ones I usually wear, but it shows off a little cleavage and cuts off halfway down my thighs. My hair is tied into a low ponytail, a few flyaways at the front and my black bow in the back.

I look and I feel hot as fuck.

Evan smiles at me when he sees me, holding a bouquet of roses in his hand. God, he's such a cliche. Luckily, my mom loves roses. He's wearing a tailored navy suit and a white shirt. He's also wearing a tie to match, but it's not tied properly. He looks annoyingly good.

"You look lovely, Miss Voss," he drawls when he gets to me, even bowing for extra effect. He holds the roses in one hand, his other shoved inside his pocket, standing tall.

"And you look like you're trying too hard," I say, grabbing onto his lapels to pull him into me. He stumbles a little but manages to regain his balance as he opens his arms a little to give me better access to his tie. My hands are shaking, but I do my best to fiddle with it, tightening it so it looks presentable. I can feel his eyes on me as I keep mine strained on his tie and chest. I can tell that he's not looking at my face. When I'm done, I tap the space between my eyes and say, "My eyes are up here, you perv."

He snaps his eyes to me, and I swear he blushes. It's hard to tell. It's freezing outside, so it could be because of the cold. Still, I smile to myself, knowing that in one way or another, my proximity affects him; possibly as much as his affects me.

He plucks a flower from the bouquet and hands it to me. "Uh, thanks."

"I asked for a dozen, and they gave me thirteen. I think they wanted it to be an extra one, but it just pissed me off. Uneven numbers and all," he explains, avoiding my eyes.

"Thirteen is supposed to be a lucky number," I say, retrieving the flower. He shoves his hand back in his pocket, fidgeting with the seam of his trousers.

"Says who?"

"Taylor Swift," I respond, grinning. He rolls his eyes, shaking his head. I turn around to open the door and he follows behind me.

I stop for a second, taking a moment to breathe and Evan holds onto my elbow. His touch is featherlight. I almost miss it, but then he tugs on it harder, making me turn towards him.

"Are we supposed to hold hands and kiss and all that?" he asks, his voice quiet as he subtly scans the foyer.

"You're my date, not my boyfriend. There's a difference."

"So, I can't hold your hand?"

I roll my eyes. "If you want to so badly," I say, holding out my palm to him. He looks at it and shakes his head. He's nervous. That's fine, but I don't like the way it's making me feel like I should be nervous too. I can handle my brothers and my mom. They're nice people when you get to know them. I haven't told Evan anything about them so he's just going to have to find out.

"What?" I ask, shaking my hand at him.

"No. I don't want to do it if you don't want to," he whispers almost angrily.

"Ev," I warn, watching the way his face softens and his shoulders sag at the use of the nickname. "Stop making this weird."

"I'm not."

"You are."

"I'm not. I'm just-" I cut him off by dragging his hand that isn't holding the flowers, slipping it around my waist. His heavy hand rests on my hip and he grips it tight. I gasp at the force of him. He releases his grip gently, tugging me into his side a little.

"Better?" I ask, looking up at him as he stares down the hallway.

He clears his throat. "I guess."

It takes us a few seconds to get comfortable with his hand on me like that as we walk down the hallway. By the time I've finally settled into his touch, I'm pulled out of it. My brother pulls on the back of my ponytail, and I yelp as he drags me out of Evan's arms, and I turn to face him.

"You're such a dick," I say when he faces me. Leo's got his signature Voss smile on, grinning at me. He's not dressed appropriately for dinner, but he doesn't seem to care. He's wearing sweats and an old grey shirt, his dark brown hair a mess like always. "You could at least get dressed. We have a guest."

He shrugs, turning to Evan. "How much did she pay you to come here?"

"Oh my god, shut up," I say, groaning as I link my arm through Evan's. He seems a little starstruck. Still nervous. "This is Leo. One of the twins. He and Arthur are identical, but you won't get them mixed up, trust me. Their personalities are a dead giveaway."

Evan nods, holding out his hand to my brother. "I'm Evan. It's nice to meet you."

Leo smirks before grabbing his hand. He glances at me as if this is the most unnatural meeting in the world and I give him a tight smile. "Pleasure," Leo says before turning to me. "Everyone's ready to eat and Hen's looking for you."

"Great," I say, holding tighter onto Evan's gigantic bicep and twisting us around to walk towards the dining room. "And

Leo, please take a shower before sitting at the table. You smell like weed."

Evan snorts and Leo laughs from behind me. "So, that isn't your youngest brother?" Evan asks. I shake my head, chuckling.

"Where would you get that idea from?" I ask sarcastically just as we stop outside the door that leads into the dining hall. Henry is sitting on the floor, his back pressed against the wall, his legs spread open in front of him, a pack of Swedish Fish resting between them. He's wearing a black tux, but he still looks put together. "*That's* my youngest older brother."

Henry's head pops up now and he smiles wide. "*Mia sorella Scarlatta*," he gets out between a mouthful of sweets. I can't help but smile back at him. "I've been looking for you."

"I'm here now," I say, detangling my arm from Evan's so I can help my brother up. He leaves the packet on the ground, wobbling as he stands, brushing off his trousers. "This is my date." I turn and gesture to Evan and he holds out his hand to Hen.

"Evan," he introduces. Henry takes his hand and shakes it. "It's nice to meet you. Henry, right?"

Henry nods. "Evan?" He turns to me, his eyes narrowing. "Don't we hate him?"

"*I* used to hate him," I say, chuckling. Henry's about to get me into some real trouble tonight. "It turns out he's not that bad."

"*L'hai scopato*? Is that why we're suddenly best friends with someone we didn't like two days ago?" Henry asks. I know he's trying to be protective but it's not helping. The last thing we need is my brother suggesting that we're sleeping together right in front of him. Good job he doesn't speak Italian.

"*No, non l'ho scopato io, stronzo. Non ancora,*" I reply, muttering the last part as I paint my face into a smile to not arouse suspicion. Henry shrugs, not believing me. "You ready to go in?" I ask Evan.

Henry interrupts, whispering, "That's why I was trying to find you. Arthur's giving mom a lecture about dad's care. He thinks that they should stop life support."

My stomach bottoms out. Evan catches me as I stumble back a little at his words. It's been months now since my dad's been in the coma and we've still not figured out how or why. He's going to pull through. He has to. Arthur's been a dick since Alex left for London and he's been trying to fill in this pathetic role as the CEO of *Voss* even though he'll never be.

"That's bullshit," I mutter, brushing past both of the boys to storm into the large dining hall. A long, oversized mahogany table sits in the middle, ten chairs spread around it. On one side, a large window opens into the backyard: a large field containing a miniature golf course. "What the fuck is wrong with you? Do you not care about our dad?"

My mom and Arthur are sitting at opposite ends of the large table. I'm looking directly at my older brother, his brown hair tied back in a short ponytail. His face is hard and focused, his mouth pressed into a straight line. My mom stands up out of her chair, her arms wide as she tries to trap me in a hug, but I dodge her.

"Have you not got anything to say?" I ask Arthur.

"Scarlett," he chides before adding calmly, "Don't cause a scene." He's not even looking at me anymore. His eyes are focused on the black placemats, his hand clasped around a cold glass of wine. "We'll talk about this another time. Preferably when guests aren't present."

Evan shifts beside me, still holding the flowers. For a

second, I forgot that he was there. That I invited him. I hate that he had to see me like that. What I hate more is the way my mom's face lights up when she sees him. I don't know how I'm going to let her down easily when I tell her we're not actually dating.

"Oh, Scarlett," my mom exclaims dreamily. "You really brought someone."

I sigh, trying to push back all my feelings and anger towards Arthur. I link my arm into Evan's again. "These are for you, Mrs. Voss," he says, handing her the flowers. I don't know where mine went. I think I lost it on the way from the door to here. I'd be a terrible girlfriend. He places his hand over mine. It calms me for a second, remembering that when this is over, I can relax. "I heard the big news. Congratulations on your new milestone."

"Oh, you are lovely. And *these* are lovely," my mom says, fussing over the flowers. Evan smiles proudly, puffing his chest out. Of course, he'd be perfect at the boyfriend thing because I'm terrible at it. "And thank you. I'll put these in water. You two can take a seat." She walks off through the swinging door into the kitchen, shouting Leo to come back down.

As we make our way over to the table, ignoring eye contact with Arthur, Evan tugs on my arm. Luckily, there's faint jazz music playing in the room so no one can hear him as he whispers, "What did your brother say before?"

"Oh, nothing. He was just asking when we started dating. Don't worry. I made a believable lie," I say, lying straight through my teeth. He hums in response, pulling out a chair for me. He takes the seat closest to Arthur and I take the one next to him. Henry comes stumbling into the room, sitting across from me.

I try to tell myself to breathe. To remember that everything is fine. To stay in the present moment and remember that whatever happens, I'm going to get through this alive. Even if I want to commit murder just by looking at my brother.

Evan's hand on my thigh is not helping this either. I don't know when he put it there, but it feels comfortable. Everything about him just feels too damn comfortable. Too safe. I try not to look at his hand, but it's so veiny, huge, and just *right*. Why do his hands have to be so fucking attractive?

He leans into me as he squeezes my thigh. My skin is already sensitive there, but coming from him, my whole body feels slightly overstimulated. "Hey, can you relax for me? You're making me sweat and no one's even talking to me," he whispers.

"This is worse for me than it is for you. Trust me," I mutter. I shift slightly in my chair, slouching a little as I lean my head back, allowing myself to breathe properly. Evan's hand starts to rub circles on my inner thigh and my breathing picks up again. Great. "Can you stop doing that?" I breathe.

"Doing what?" he asks innocently. He even leans his other hand on the table, staring at the jug of water, all while *still* rubbing his thumb over the sensitive spot on my thigh. "It's helping, no?"

"No, you're making it worse, and you know you are so cut it out," I warn. He stops, finally and places both of his hands in his lap. I sigh, pulling my dress further down. Arthur scrutinises me from beside Evan and I roll my eyes. "What?"

"Why are you wearing that?" he asks, looking at my outfit.

"Wearing what? A dress?"

"It's too short."

I bark out a laugh. "Do you think I would wear this if I cared what you thought?" I turn away from him and I can see

Evan sticking his tongue in his mouth, trying not to laugh. Arthur ignores and sticks a thumb at Evan.

"Who's this?"

Evan clears his throat. He doesn't seem intimidated. Good because he shouldn't be. Arthur is not scary at all. *Alexander* is scary. Arthur's just trying to fill in that role since he left and he's doing a fucking terrible job at it. "Evan Branson. It's a pleasure to meet you."

I may have left out his last name for several reasons. One reason being the reactions I get from everyone at the table. Henry snorts. Leo smiles, nodding as if he somehow knew all along. My mom grins, a little confused, but prouder. Arthur... looks like he's about to set the world on fire and is deciding where to start first.

I sit up straighter, matching Evan's confident stance.

"You brought a fucking Branson here? What are you *doing,* Scarlett?"

"I'm doing what I want," I say, picking up a napkin from the table, trying my best for my hands not to tremble as I lay it on my lap. "Now, he's my date, so can everyone play nice for one night?"

26

EVAN

I KNEW family dinners were tense, but Jesus. The Voss' are full of emotional outbursts and petty comments. I tried to help her relax by keeping my hand on her thigh. I've watched enough movies and read enough books to know that pulling that kind of stunt is either supposed to turn a girl on or drive her insane. Or, in Scarlett's case, both.

The small glances she gives me each time I squeeze her thigh make my chest bloom with pride. The way she stands up for herself against her brother is probably the hottest thing I've ever seen. I'm fully convinced that pretending to date Scarlett for one night might be the best thing to ever happen to me.

We eat the lasagne Scarlett's mom made mostly in silence as small talk gets dragged out by long chews or generous gulps. I don't usually enjoy talking about myself, especially when I'm nervous, but I can't mess this up for her. So, when her mom asks me what I study at NU, I feel like I can't stop talking.

Scarlett cuts off my rambling, finally. "Loves to talk, this one," she says, laughing lightly. Everyone on the table laughs too. Apart from Arthur – he just glares at me.

"Ah, not as much as you," I say back, and she gives me a fake smile.

"So, Evan," Henry starts whilst he's in the middle of eating some garlic bread. His mom swats him at the back of his head for talking with his mouth full. He swallows before speaking next. "Do you speak any languages?"

"Uh, French and a little Italian," I lie. I had a tutor growing up who taught me how to speak fluent Italian. I only picked up a little French after countless trips there. Henry's eyes light up.

"Only a little, huh?" Henry asks and I know he's got me figured out. This must be where Scarlett gets it from. She looks at me curiously, probably not realising what she's about to find out. "*Come va?*"

"*Bene e te?*" I reply. Henry replies back in Italian, telling me that he's doing okay. Scarlett rests her head in her hand now, looking at me seriously. I smirk at her and she shakes her head a little, as if silently asking me what I'm doing.

"*Cosa ne pensi dei cavoletti di Bruxelles?*" her mom asks me, wanting to know how her brussel sprouts tasted. "*Erano a norma per te?*"

"*Sì, erano perfetti,*" I say. Smiling as I whisper, "*Proprio come tua figlia.*"

Scarlett's mom claps her hands together happily. "Ah, I see you learnt all the good stuff."

I nod, grinning. I turn to Scarlett. Her cheeks are a little pink now, which is hard to tell if it was from the wine she's had or if she's blushing.

I know what her brother asked her earlier and I know what she said. I just wanted her to admit that she said what she did.

"*Did you fuck him?*" he had asked earlier. "*No, I didn't*

fuck him, asshole. Not yet, anyway," she replied. She can't hide from this as much as she tries to.

"Sei fluente, vero?" she asks me.

"Sì, tesoro, lo sono," I admit, unable to stop the smile exploding across my face as her mouth hangs open.

"You little shit. You knew what Henry said earlier, didn't you?"

I lean into her and whisper, "Every word."

SCARLETT

The rest of the meal went smoothly. Well, as smoothly as it could with my brothers there. We even make it to dessert. Until Leo asks Evan about how B&Co is doing, no doubt to cause drama. Evan answers the questions with ease, telling my brothers exactly what they want to hear. Their sales are doing fine and they're picking up more now as it's getting closer to the holidays. My mom eats it all up, but Arthur can't stop himself.

"Your little rebellious phase isn't cute anymore," he spits at me.

"Who said I'm trying to rebel or act cute?" I ask confidently, keeping my posture straight, looking and acting picture-perfect as I take a sip of my wine. He's trying to get to me, and I won't let him.

"What are you trying to prove?" he asks, sounding genuinely concerned.

"God, give it a rest," Henry mutters. Evan's trying to act like he can't hear, probably not wanting to get involved in a sibling argument. I would be surprised if he had even a molecule of understanding what it's like to grow up with four older brothers, him being an only child and all.

"No, because she's acting out like a desperate whore who could have a decent man in her life, but instead chooses him," he argues. My mom gasps, but she doesn't say anything.

I don't even flinch.

Evan does. He bangs his hand on the table. Everyone turns to look at him. I've never seen him look this upset before. No. Not upset. This is pure rage.

I watch as he forces his breathing to settle – a technique I've noticed too many times not to pick up on it.

"I know I'm a guest here and I knew you were not going to be happy with my presence. By all means, call me every name under the sun because of who my family are, but do *not* talk to her like that. Indirectly or not, you should never call your sister what you just did. You're a fucking animal. Pardon my language, but it's true. You're supposed to be protecting her from guys like yourself. Scarlett can date who she wants to, and it really shouldn't matter who their family is, especially when your family isn't perfect either," he shouts. I blink up at him, but he's not looking at me. He's looking at my mom, his eyes stormy. "I'm sorry for raising my voice, Mrs Voss. *La cena è stata deliziosa.*"

His hands are balled into fists on the table. I place my hand gently over his and they are fucking scorching. I push out my chair, trying to pry open his fist so I can slip my hand into it. He finally lets me and I squeeze his hand.

"Evan and I would like to be excused."

I drag us from the table and he almost trips over his chair. I don't know what I'm doing, but I can't sit at that table with them for any longer. He follows behind me and I take him into my old bedroom to cool off.

My room is one of the biggest in the house; one of the limited perks for being the only girl beside my mom. It's still painted the same pale blue colour I asked for when I was younger, a beige canopy bed pushed against one wall, huge pillars surrounding it.

Evan has been awfully quiet since his outburst at the table, and I don't know what to say. He's subtly looking around the room and when his eyes find mine, he drops them to his shoes. I turn away from him, walking towards the pillar of my bed, playing with the tassels. For the millionth time today, I contemplate why I'm nervous.

"You didn't need to do that," I whisper quietly. "But thank you." *Am I really thanking Evan Branson right now? Apparently.* I turn around, trying to lean causally on the pillar. His hands are in his pockets, his chest heaving.

Is he mad at me?

"Do they talk to you like that all the time?" he asks, grinding his jaw together.

I shrug. "Sometimes. It's only Arthur since Alex left. He's just trying to play the role of the big older brother, but it's really just annoying as fuck," I say with a weak chuckle.

"God, Scarlett," he mutters angrily. He runs his hand down his face, sighing. "And what do you say back?"

"Nothing."

"So, you don't talk back to them, but you want to argue with me any chance you get?" he asks, his eyes squinting.

"It's different with you. You're an only child, so you don't get it. You can act how you want around me, and I can't hold that against you because you don't owe me anything," I explain.

He nods. "And how do I act around you?" he asks, slowly walking towards me. His chest is so close to mine now, I have to tilt my head up slightly to look at him, those piercing green eyes staring straight into mine.

"I don't know," I whisper. "You hate me most of the time or you act like you hate everyone else *but* me other times. I thought I had you figured out, but now… It's confusing."

His face is so close to mine. A breath away. He gently angles his head down, so it moves to the side of my face, his breath hot on my neck. What the hell is happening and why don't I want it to stop?

His hand drops onto the pillar behind me, just above my head and he places his other hand on my hip, squeezing me gently. I try to swallow, but my mouth goes dry. It feels like his heavy hand could burn straight through my clothes.

"Is this confusing you?"

"Yes."

"And this?" he rasps. My body registers it before my brain does as he presses a hot, open-mouthed kiss onto my neck where my pulse beats rapidly. His mouth barely grazes the surface and I still get chills everywhere.

Evan's touch is like something I've never experienced before. It's not like anyone else's. It's overwhelming, calming, yet powerfully seductive. It's just *his*.

♫ **CALL OUT MY NAME BY THE WEEKND**

"Ev," I plead breathlessly, not sure what for. My voice catches as his breath hovers over my exposed neck, my stomach somersaulting.

"Yes, sweetheart?"

"What are you doing?"

He inhales, his nose brushing against my neck as he murmurs, "You smell so fucking good, and I want it all over me."

I try to relax, but it's really fucking difficult. My chest is rising and falling rapidly, the space between us no longer existing as our bodies press together. His hand is still on my hip, his thumb slowly caressing my hip bone.

"I can, um, find the perfume I'm wearing if you don't mind smelling like a Voss," I joke.

"That's not what I mean, and you know it," he says into my skin.

"Then what do you mean?"

He brings both of his hands to each side of my face. His grip is firm as his long fingers snake into the back of my hair, pulling it tightly to turn my head up to him as he crowds over me. He runs his thumb under each side of my face, slowly caressing my cheeks. He runs his thumb across my lip and my knees go weak. Immediately, my mouth parts in a desperate gasp.

"Don't play coy with me, Angel," he warns.

"Me? Playing coy? How dare you assume that I-"

He slips his pad of his thumb into my talking mouth, and I almost fall apart as he tips my head back, looking down at me. I've never enjoyed this kind of intimacy before – the way he looks at me with fire in his eyes, the power he has over my body. I should not be enjoying it, especially because it's *Evan's* hands that are invading my face. He pins me against the pillar with his hips and I can feel him through his trousers.

"See how much I like it when you're quiet?" he rasps. "Can't talk now, can you, Scar?"

A strange whimper comes from the back of my throat, and I disguise it by biting on his thumb. A wicked grin spreads across his face as he withdraws his finger and strokes it under my eye. My chest is heaving now, my eyes silently begging him for *something*. He's tripped me up and I need to regain control, but I just *can't.*

"So pretty," he murmurs, almost to himself. His strong

hands pull my head forward and he leans down so we're eye level, our noses basically touching. I'm frozen with lust as his breath moves over the base of my throat and he actually kisses me there.

Once.

Twice.

I've broken him.

Officially.

This is it. This is what I wanted right? I just didn't expect to enjoy it either.

"Pretty, sweet, Scarlett."

"I'm not," I seethe, instantly getting defensive.

"Not what, pretty girl?"

"Sweet."

"You are on the inside," he says, still kissing my neck. I can't ask him to stop. Hell, I don't think I want to. My hands fumble for something to hold onto and I settle on holding onto his lapels, keeping him close to me. My neck is so sensitive to his touch, and it feels like my whole body lights up at the sensation.

"And what about on the outside," I ask breathlessly.

"Fucking lethal."

I've never cared much for words of affirmation, but there's something about the way Evan says it that turns me inside out. He says it like it's true.

I try to turn my head to catch his lips but he's just a breath away, not touching me just yet. He's teasing me. Making me work for it. It was even up until now. Until one of us makes the final move.

"Are you going to kiss me?" I ask out of impatience, my voice sounding old and scratchy.

"Maybe," he whispers, brushing his cheek against mine and inhaling my scent. "I haven't decided yet."

"What do you mean 'maybe?' It's either yes or no, Branson. Because I can find someone else to do it if you're going to keep-"

He stops my rambling with a firm grip on both sides of my face, forcing me to look directly into his green eyes. We're both staring at each other, breathing heavily, the energy between us crackling like fireworks.

There's something about him that lights me up on the inside, making me feel like I'm somehow refracting light through every opening of my body.

"Fuck it," he mutters.

My mouth parts in exasperation before he captures my lips with his in a strong battle of dominance. My eyes widen in surprise as I register that *his* lips are on mine. Evan Branson's perfect, hot, wet lips are on mine, and I don't care. In fact, I encourage it.

He tips my head back to deepen the kiss as his tongue runs across the entrance of my mouth, teasing and retreating while I melt into his touch. It's a frustrating feeling, but it makes me want it even more. I pull on the hair at the back of his head and he groans happily in response. So, he likes it when I touch his hair. Good to know. Because this definitely won't be happening again.

Kissing Evan is like seeing the end, but being happy that you spent this moment with him. There is no easy way to say this - kissing Evan feels like fucking. Kissing Evan might be the only thing keeping me sane right now.

My back is probably going to be bruised from pressing into the pillar as his hips pin me to it I'm desperate for him. Desperate for more. All I want is him. His mouth. His hands.

Is this a selfish and greedy thing to want? His hands are strong and certain, like he knows what he wants. Which is a good thing because I fucking don't.

The kiss is all tongue, whimpers, and strangled moans. It's *everything.*

"Scarlett," he whispers against my mouth. For a second, I don't think he's going to follow it up with anything as he keeps his lips pressed against mine. He's just saying my name as if he needs to believe it. As if he's trying to convince himself that it's me that he's kissing. "I can't- It's just...*You.*"

My thoughts come to a stop when his hand drops from my face, stretches across my chest before dipping down over the material of my dress where my nipples are hard. He pinches me and I moan into his mouth. *I fucking moan.* And because my bedroom is huge, it echoes on the walls.

It snaps us both back to reality as he sighs while he breaks away from me, leaving my chest heaving as I blink up at him. I open my mouth to speak, hoping to say something – anything – as I take in his smug face, but no words come. I press my fingers to my swollen lips, my hands practically shaking.

"Desserts ready," Henry calls with a flourish as he raps on the open bedroom door.

I would smile at him and thank him, but he saunters off while I stare at Evan. His pupils are dilated, and his eyes search my face, watching the arousal and heat across my face and neck.

"What was that?" I ask when I can remember to form coherent sentences.

"Nothing," he replies, fixing the cuffs of his shirt.

"What the fuck does that mean? Your tongue was just inside my mouth," I say, searching his face for something, but coming up empty. He chuckles again, running his hands over my shoulders as if he's trying to straighten me out.

"I mean that was nothing compared to what I would do if your family wasn't one floor below us," he whispers as if that makes more sense.

"What? That doesn't even-"

"I do have a thought though," he says, cutting me off, looking at me thoughtfully as if he didn't just try and fuck me with his tongue. He brushes a strand of hair out of my face and tucks it behind my ear. He tilts my chin up and I swallow as he turns my face towards the large mirror on the wall across from us. "Look at you. So undone. So messy. I want to know if you look exactly like this after you come."

He doesn't wait for an answer. Instead, he looks at me for a second as my face floods with heat for the millionth time and he smirks to himself, knowing what his proximity does to me. He steps back. He takes another step. Then another, still staring at me before turning on his heels and walking out of my room.

27

SCARLETT

EVAN'S ACTING WEIRD. Okay, maybe I'm acting weird too. I could deal if one of us was freaking out, but now both of us are, it's driving me mad. I'm trying to keep calm. I kiss dudes all the time. It's what I do. But with Evan... That's something different. The way he made me feel was not what I'm used to.

Kennedy is in her meddling era, meaning that she's doing just about anything to make me spend more time with Evan than necessary. She doesn't know about the kiss, but for some reason I'm convinced she's telepathically been able to figure me out. After our very awkward goodbye after the kiss, he practically bolted out of my house, and I haven't seen him since then.

That was three days ago.

Now, I'm sitting on an air mattress between Wren, Miles, and Kennedy on top of a tarp outside while we watch a show on the makeshift projector Miles bought for their backyard.

Kennedy planned yet another hang out session and Miles has been dying to try out the projector that Wren got him for his birthday. Xavier is sitting in front of us, lying on his stomach and Evan is next to him, off in the corner like a little hermit.

Why is he avoiding me like a fucking disease as if he isn't the one that kissed me? Okay, maybe I had sort-of, kinda, definitely asked for it, but *still*. He shouldn't be the one who's embarrassed. It was a moment of weakness. We were in my room, he was wearing that fucking suit, looking angry and sexy at the same time, while I just looked like my usual gorgeous self. The amount of angry and sexual tension running through us finally burst into flames. It was bound to happen.

It was the best kiss of my life. That is what pisses me off the most. He shouldn't be allowed to make me feel like that. He shouldn't make me feel like I want more of him. So much fucking more.

I can still taste him. I can still *feel* him.

I should be the one that's embarrassed. Especially after the dirty dream I had about him last night. That kiss has been all I've thought about for the last three nights. All I could imagine was him on top of me, his weight pressing into me, calling me a good girl, his face buried between my legs as I panted his name. I had to fuck myself with a toy to relieve the tension. I hate that I did that. Especially while thinking about him.

"How was your date?" Kennedy asks as the last episode of Brooklyn Nine-Nine transitions into a new one. She's at it again. Great. The date. Right. I almost forgot. It feels like everything that happened before that kiss doesn't even exist anymore. As if he completely brought me alive from just one touch.

"Great," I say.

"Terrible," he says. He turns around then, and I glare at him. "I thought we were-"

"It was *fine*," I amend, cutting him off. Kennedy nods,

throwing popcorn into her mouth. I know she's not going to let me live it down. Telling either of them about the kiss would only prove their points and I am still so unsure as to what I want. All I know for certain is that I want to touch him again, in whatever way.

I need to feel him, and I need him to feel me.

EVAN

I've not slept in three days.

Kissing Scarlett was a bad fucking idea. Not because it was a bad kiss. Not because of everything that's going on with her family and my family's pressure, but the fact that I enjoyed it so much that I want more. And more. And more.

My dad has been texting me non-stop, and calling me since then, asking for more updates. I don't know what I'm supposed to tell him. I've started to get real feelings for this girl and she's still unsure whether or not to trust her uncle or the Gerard dude. My money is still on her dad and Gio being involved in it. Sure, Gerard is sketchy, but what real motives would he have to want to take down *Voss*?

I couldn't focus on that anyway. Not after feeling her body pressed against mine. The noises she made when I touched her. How responsive she was to every light brush of my mouth on her neck, my fingers in her hair, my hand over her breast, pinching her nipple, the way my cock swelled at the moan that left her mouth.

I've spent the last few days thinking about her and only her and it's been absolute torture. It's a problem, I know. But it's not like my other obsessions or compulsions. This is something more.

She could have regretted it. She could have run to the bathroom, scrubbed her mouth clean to get rid of the taste of me. For someone who likes to run her mouth all the time, she doesn't exactly talk much about her feelings and it's driving me fucking crazy.

I try not to look at her while we watch the show, but it's hard not to. Everyone's wearing comfortable clothes today and seeing her in those baggy sweatpants, a crop top, her hair tied into a messy bun is not helping the thousands of thoughts running through my brain.

I steal glances at her while she watches the sitcom, snuggled between her friends. Her face is a little red and I can tell she's forcing herself not to look at me. She's twisting the ribbon around her wrists. Maybe she's nervous too.

God, I hope she's nervous too. It'll make me feel better about this.

I'M ACTUALLY SO ENGROSSED in the show that I don't notice that it starts to rain. Hard. We're covered by a plastic sheet on top of the waterproof gazebo, but the rain picks up and the roof starts to dip.

Miles jumps out of his seat, screaming expletives and Wren laughs at him as we all stand up, starting to pack things away. Most of the food was finished anyway, so I shove it into a plastic bag.

"Shit," Miles groans. "I only planned on getting one thing wet tonight and it wasn't my PlayStation."

Everyone laughs at his joke as he rushes to get his wires and other equipment that we weaved through the kitchen window. Kennedy and Xavier rush out after him, their hands full of whatever they could pick up. A roar of thunder and another downpour of rain shakes the gazebo as Wren picks up the blankets, almost tripping over as she runs inside.

"Everyone with devices, go in first," Miles shouts, his voice almost drowning out in the rain. "Can you guys take down the gazebo? My mom will kill me if it gets ruined and beat down by the rain."

"Sure," Scarlett grumbles. I turn and it's just us two now, staring at each other. She rolls her eyes at me before walking through the gazebo. "You do that one. I'll do this one."

I move to the outside of it, instantly getting drenched with rain as I fumble to unpeg it. Why are we constantly getting caught in storms? The universe must be playing tricks on us. It's hard to sort out the gazebo when the rain is making everything slippery and I'm already on edge as it is.

I'm still detangling the first peg when Scarlett comes around to my side. "You're doing it wrong," she chides.

"Do *you* want to do it, Angel?" I ask, looking up at her while the rain streams down my face like tears.

She rolls her eyes before bending down, slightly pushing me to the side as she unhooks it with ease. As she moves to the other one, I start packing up the other sticks into the bag they came in. She finishes it in a few seconds, and we silently work together to fold it up and shove it back into the bag.

sling the bag over my shoulder, running across the grass to the backdoor. I'm careful up the steps, glancing back at Scarlett making sure she doesn't fall. I sigh when she gets to me unscathed, and I jiggle the handle. It's locked. Of course, it's locked because God likes to test us more and more every day.

I turn to her and she's staring up at me, her eyes wide from a step below me. "It's locked," I tell her.

"This is your house too. Don't you have a key?" she asks. I check my pockets and come up empty. I never use the backdoor anyways. She sighs, turning her back to me as she sits down on the step. "Of course, you don't have a key."

"Of course, it's *your* friend that's probably behind the reason we're locked out here," I say. Kennedy is sneaky. She has been since the day I met her, subtly trying to push me and Scarlett together. I pull out my phone to call Miles and it goes straight to voicemail. The same with Xavier.

"She becomes a Swiftie and suddenly she thinks she's a mastermind," she mutters. I have no idea what that means.

She looks up at me then, the rain soaking her face as she pulls her knees to her chest. I take a seat next to her, throwing the bag onto the ground. She rests her head on her arms across the top of her knees. She whispers, "We're messing everything up, Branson."

♫ THE BEAUTIFUL DREAM - GEORGE EZRA

Apart from when she cried in the museum, this is the most vulnerable I've ever seen her since then. She looks tired. Exhausted, actually. As if keeping this game is as tiring as it is for me.

"What do you mean?"

She groans. "I mean you're distracting me. You're making me forget about what's important. My *family*. I don't want this to complicate things."

I can't help the smile that spreads across my face. Scarlett has always held her cards close to her chest. She's never tried to let me in, but something has shifted between us. I want us to have better communication. To actually tell each other how we feel. We wasted so many days denying and ignoring it. I want it to keep going. To see how this plays out. I want her to fight me. To fight with me. I want anything she's willing to give me at this point.

"So, you're admitting there's a *'this'*?" She turns to me.

"I'm admitting there's a *something,*" she replies, rolling her eyes as if the thought is stupid. I'm full-on grinning now. God only knows how badly I want this girl. "Neither of us are stupid. There's been sexual tension between us for years. We tried to ignore it, but…God, you've been making it really fucking difficult recently."

I watch her take a survey of my outfit. My white cotton shirt is sticking to my chest. My hair is flopping in my forehead, heavy and wet with rain.

"Only you would try and blame *me* for finding me attractive," I say, pushing a hand through my hair for extra emphasis. She groans, flickering her eyes to mine, studying me.

She barks out a disbelieving laugh. "You're ridiculous, Branson. That's why I don't get it."

"Get what?" I ask, tilting my head.

"That I want to slap you as much as I want to make out with you," she admits. Her admission shocks me a little and I blink at her. She doesn't seem embarrassed about what she wants. Sometimes, when we're alone I think she puts all of her trust right into the palm of my hand, silently begging me to believe her.

"You can do whatever you want to me, Scarlett."

"That's a little terrifying," she laughs.

"*You're* a little terrifying," I mutter.

She fists my shirt, pulling me into her and she crashes her mouth to mine. Is this a dream? I'm kissing Scarlett Voss in the rain and she's kissing me back.

Her lips are so soft and careful at first, as if she's testing how it feels. I let her take her time, waiting until she's comfortable until she gives me *everything.*

Her tongue slips into my warm mouth and I groan happily, loving the taste of her. She tastes like that feeling you get when you *just* fall asleep. Just peace. Only she's not peace. She's a fucking hurricane and she knows it.

I need more of her, and I don't know how to get it. My hands find their way in her hair, pulling and twisting as most of her hair falls out of her bun. As I do, she smiles against my mouth.

She fucking smiles.

I try to get closer to her, try to get anything she'll give me, but it's hard to do. Her hands have now found their way in my hair as she tugs onto it greedily. I let her. It's hard to move when we're just angrily, hornily, sweetly kissing each other. It's a confusing combination. Everything about her feels so soft, she looks like a fucking daydream, but she makes me feel like I'm on fire.

"Jesus," she mutters into my mouth. "It shouldn't feel this good."

"But it does," I reply, kissing her deeply until all my thoughts become her.

Her.

Her.

Her.

Finally, I push back slightly onto the step, my back digging into the stone and she uses the opportunity to climb into my lap. She sits on me perfectly, our bodies practically moulding together.

I run my hands up and down her back, loving the way her body sags against mine, her tits pressing into my chest. My head lolls back as she kisses and sucks on my neck. I've not been this close to another girl in months and it's fucking up my insides. She bites me softly and when I groan with pleasure, she bites me again. Harder.

"*Fuck*, Angel," I say, basically whimpering. Then she bites me again as she starts to kiss across the base of my throat.

"You good? Sounds like you want me to stop," she murmurs, her voice low and so insanely sexy.

"No," I breathe out and she rolls her hips against me again. "Don't fucking stop."

Then I realise it.

As I'm hard as a fucking rock in my jeans when her lips start to travel down my neck and my hands move down to her ass, I realise that I don't just want her sometimes. I want her all the time.

I want her to angrily kiss me like this whenever she wants. I don't want to keep lying to her about why we became closer. Why I wanted to help her. Even if it started to become more than just helping my family, I want her to know the truth.

"Listen," I say. Instantly groaning as she grinds herself against my crotch. That feels too good. Too much. If I'm not careful, I could finish like this. She starts to move across my jaw, one of her hands holding the other side of my face, carefully like she's trying not to break me. "I have something I need to tell you."

"Right now?" she asks, rolling over me again and I hiss. "I'm kinda busy."

"Yeah, but-"

I'm interrupted by the loud buzzing of her phone against my hand in her back pocket. I pull it out for her, and it's covered in rain splashes. I hand it to her, and she rolls her eyes at the contact.

"It's Gio," she explains. She tries to climb off me, but I wrap my arms around her back, keeping her close to me. Needing her close. She swipes the call button and answers it, holding it against her ear. "Gio. *Cosa sta succedendo?*"

She asks him what's going on, but it's hard to hear what he's saying over the sound of the rain. She mumbles something back to him, her eyes widening with terror. My grip tightens on her back, trying to comfort her although I'm not sure what for. After a few seconds, she ends the call, standing up off me and heads towards the door banging on it.

"Kennedy, I swear to God, you better open this fucking door right now," she shouts. I flinch at her biting tone. I stand up, turning to her, I place my hand on the small of her back. "We need to go," she whispers. "Like, now."

"Hey, what's going on?" I ask.

"Gio said we need to meet him downtown. He thinks he's got something tying someone to Tinzin," she explains.

"Shouldn't we go to the police? What if it's dangerous?"

"Evan, he's my uncle. If he says he needs me, I'm going to be there," she challenges.

"Okay," I say, nodding. She looks at me curiously, trying to make sure I'm okay with this. If anything happened to her, I'd never forgive myself. "Okay," I say again.

28

EVAN

WE RUSHED FROM MILES' house to Scarlett's apartment, the rain still crashing down onto the asphalt. When we get to her Bellezza Nera, she fumbles for her car keys, and I rush over to her side of the car. Her hands are shaking, her outfit is completely soaked, and her hair has fallen out completely of the bun it was in a few hours ago.

♫ CALIFORNIA - LANA DEL REY

I place my hand over her shaking hands. "Scar," I press, and she looks up at me. God, I want to kiss her again. Her eyes are huge, a little frightened, but there's still that look of — as she describes it — *something*. "I'm going to drive, okay?"

She nods once. Twice. She swallows before opening her hand and letting me retrieve the key. "Just don't crash my car."

"I'm going to keep you safe, Angel. Don't worry," I say, trying to be comforting, but she throws her hands up, exasperated.

"Of course, I'm going to worry, Branson. My uncle is a possible attempted murderer. I still don't know how much I can trust him right now. He might be leading us into a trap," she rambles. "Just get us there so I can talk to him. Got it?"

I nod and she turns around, walking to the other side of the car as she slips into her seat. When I'm settled behind the steering wheel, I want to tell her that it's going to be okay. I want to promise her that we're going to be fine. But the words don't come. Because how can I promise something I'm not sure is true?

She doesn't speak the whole drive down to Provo, which is a long fucking time. She taps her nails anxiously onto the window. Gio has some information, we're going to meet him to get it. It should be that simple. But for whatever reason, we're both running on fumes, scared and a little terrified. I want – no, I *need* – to be brave for her.

We ended up in an alleyway similar to the one we were hiding in when we staked out the jewellery store. God, how different things are now. Then, she couldn't even look at me without seeming like she was about to throw up. Now, she's fucking moaned into my mouth multiple times.

"Did he say where to meet him?" I ask when I've parked. She turns to me, her face drier than it was before, but her hair still sticks to her forehead. It's still raining outside, so she's bound to get it messed up again. I want to brush it out of her face, cradle her head in my hands and kiss her on the forehead. But I don't do any of that. Instead, I tilt my head a little, noticing she's probably in her own world. "Scarlett?"

"Hm?" She looks me in the eye then before shaking her head a little. "Yes. He said that we should wait in the car, and he'll call us over. He thinks someone is following him."

"Shit," I mutter. "Should I have been checking while we drove? I'm so out of it, Scar. Everything's a fucking mess right now."

"Hey," she says, cutting me off. "It's fine. I wasn't just looking out the window lifelessly. I checked. We're okay."

I turn my head back in front of me and lean my head onto the headrest. So much for being the brave one because I'm freaking out. I still need to speak to her about the real reason behind why I wanted to help her with the project as an opportunity to find out more about her family. As much as I'm going to regret it afterwards, I'd much rather keep her safe and have her hate me later than let her do this on her own.

I open my eyes, tilting my head towards my window and across the street from where we're parked, a man with long-ish hair and a messy beard stands with his hood up. This street is dodgy as it is and I don't like the idea of us, especially at this time of day.

The sun has only just set, so the sky is painted a deep blue, littered with rain clouds. I'm sure that guy is her uncle, but I nudge Scarlett, urging her to look in my direction, just to make sure.

"That's him," she says, unclipping her seatbelt. I start to unclip mine. "You stay here. He probably wants to talk in the restaurant."

"Scarlett, if *anything* happens - and I mean, *anything* - let me know, okay?"

She rolls her eyes. "How? Do you want me to scream or tell you telepathically?"

"Scarlett," I press. "This isn't a joke."

"I can handle myself, Branson."

"I know. Just...Just be safe."

She nods and with that, she slips out of the car, rounding it to my side where she stands, giving me a thumbs up. She's suddenly too relaxed. I don't like it. She grins at me like this is such a normal thing. Unless she knows deep down that her uncle is a safe person to be around.

The thought of anything happening to her is too terrifying to risk not being protective right now. I know she's strong. I know she's resilient. I know she's brave, but there's a part of me that feels the need to be near her all the time, making sure she doesn't get hurt.

That's why my heart almost falls out my chest as she walks towards the sidewalk, and she trips over her shoelaces.

Immediately, I open the door, my heart pounding as I try to get to her. She didn't fall into the road, thank goodness. But it was close. Too close. Cars still whizz past, no one stopping to check if she's okay.

"You okay?" I pant when I get to her, clasping my hand over her elbow. She turns to me, and I can tell she's pissed at me for not staying put.

"I'm fine, Branson. Jesus. Do you listen to anything I tell you?" She argues, bending down to tie her shoes. I sigh, knowing that she's fine and I look back up across the road to where her uncle was standing.

Everything happens too fast.

Gio must have had the same thought to help Scarlett as she tripped over. A black car with frosted windows speeds down the street and I hear a crunch. A snap. I flinch.

It takes me a few seconds to register the screech of tires, the gasp that escapes my throat and the body on the floor. My heartbeat is all I hear as the rest of the world goes quiet.

Scarlett starts to stand, and my first instinct is to turn her around to face me, so her back is to the scene. I swear I throw up in my mouth a little, but I force myself to swallow. I'm being the brave one.

It's still raining – a little lighter now – but there's so much blood. Too much blood. It's pooling out of his head, but I have to keep Scarlett as calm as possible. I have to keep her safe. She can't see that. I tighten my grip on her shoulder, my nails digging into her.

It's only been a matter of seconds, but it feels like it's been hours.

"What the hell is going on, Branson?" she asks, oblivious. I swallow, looking down at her. I try to get the words out, but they don't come. How are you supposed to tell someone that their uncle just got brutally hit by a car and is not standing up? Scarlett could easily turn her head to see, but I think she knows. "Did you hear that car? I swear some people don't know how to drive. Nobody got hit, did they?" She rambles and I nod.

She nods back, her eyes twitching. Her mouth forms into a slight frown at my silence and her eyebrows soften a little. "It was Gio, wasn't it?"

I nod.

That's all I can do.

I watch the exact moment she tries to turn around, but I tighten my grip on her shoulders and crash her into my chest, holding her there. She doesn't need to see it. She can hear the gasps of onlookers, yet no one is fucking doing anything. I feel her starting to cry against my chest as I keep my eyes on the top of her head, unable to look at the scene.

It feels like a part of me is being ripped out of me as she cries. The sound comes straight from the back of her throat. Not like the way she cried at the museum. This is the sound of pure agony.

"I need to see him," she sobs, trying to turn around again.

"Hey, look at me," I demand, gripping onto her shoulders, my hands finding their way back to her face, holding tight. She blinks up at me, more and more tears streaming down her face. "Angel, I promise you, you don't want to see him yet."

She's crying harder now. "He's my family," she cries, trying to turn *again* but I grip onto her face, firmly urging her not to turn her head. She's sobbing, holding onto my forearms, trying to get me to pull them away from her, but I don't. She's strong, but I'm stronger. "Let go of me," she groans.

"Listen to me," I say, my voice wavering. "Go to the car. Stand outside the passenger side and sit on the floor. Don't turn around until I've got him out of the road, and I'll bring him to you. Use my phone and call nine-one-one and ask for an ambulance. Tell them there's been a hit and run. Can you do that for me?"

She nods her head so hard I'm sure she almost goes dizzy. She's still trying to pry my hands from her face, but she has no luck. This is not the time for her to be stubborn. Can she not see that I'm trying to protect her? That I don't want her to see what I can.

"Scarlett, you need to talk to me," I urge. She's practically gasping for air now, her chest heaving. "Tell me that you can do that."

"I can do that," she says through a cry. I pull my phone from my back pocket and put it into her hands, clasping my hand around it to make sure she's got a hold of it. Her hands are shaking too much. I wipe the tears that have fallen down her face only for more to fall. I can't help it, so I press her to my chest again and kiss her on the forehead as she stands lifelessly in my arms. She pulls away from me and she walks back towards the car.

I hope for both of our sakes she doesn't turn back.

A few cars have started diverting his body, yet no one tries to get out and help him. I walk over to him, my shoes squelching in the rain. I'm not good with blood. Not at all. But Scarlett would not be able to handle this. Not when he's this hurt and in the middle of the road. When I get closer, I notice the huge gash at the side of his face as his whole body trembles. I shudder.

"Can somebody help me get him out of the road!?" I shout to anyone. For anyone to help. Nobody responds. It's even quieter now. Only the sound of the rain and the gurgling coming from Gio. How could someone do this? Just hit someone and speed off. And more importantly, why?

I hold my breath as I slip my hand under his neck, feeling the soft flesh there. The whole right side of his face is covered in blood from where he landed. His leg is twisted outwards, and his mouth is full of blood, his eyes rolling back in his head.

"Gio? It's Evan. Can you feel anything?" I ask, patting down his arms and across his torso. It's faint and weak, but he shakes his head. I take off my shirt with one hand. It's already soaked through but, I need to do something to stop the blood coming out of his head. I wring it out, folding it over four times before pressing it to his head. I ease him off my lap to undo my belt, wrapping around the side of his face. I know it looks painful, but it's the best I can do.

"I'm going to take you out of the road and get an ambulance so stay with me, okay?"

His mouth opens and closes like he's trying to speak but nothing comes out. He coughs, tilting his head away from me as he spits blood onto the street. I close my eyes for a second, trying my best to be brave.

"*Sca*," he garbles.

"She's behind the car. She's safe. We're going to get you help, okay?" I try my best to seem convincing as I try to stand.

I try to look around the empty street, hoping someone will appear. I see a middle-aged man closing down a florist and I sigh. "Hey! I need some help over here!"

He turns around and his face drops. We don't have time for this. I know how bad this looks. I can *smell* how bad this is. I don't need someone who's going to throw up or scream. If Scarlett hears anyone else's reaction, she's going to freak out even more. We need to get Gio somewhere that isn't in the middle of the road, and he needs medical attention as soon as possible.

"Jesus, what happened?" the guy asks, rushing over. He's dressed in a puffer jacket, and he immediately zips it down, pulling it off. He stops still, looking down at us and I glare. Now is not the time for questions, bud. "Nevermind. Where are you trying to go?"

I tilt my head towards the alleyway where Scarlett's parked. Jheez, I hope she's okay. "You see that car there?" I ask. The guy nods. "Just help me get him there and then stay on lookout for an ambulance. One should be coming soon."

The guy doesn't say anything as he helps me get Gio to his feet. He's not really walking as much, as he's hovering as we use our strength to keep him up. I feel bad that I've dragged him into the middle of this, but there was no way I'd be able to drag him across the street on my own. Gio's head lolls to the side as we take each of his arms over our shoulders. This is bad. Like really *really* bad.

We manage to get him to the side of the car that Scarlett isn't on and he's groaning now. At least there's a sign he's still with us. What the fuck do I do now? The guy drops his coat over Gio, trying his best to keep him warm. I would thank him if I could think properly, but I can't. The guy kneels beside me, trying to look at Gio's face, but there's not much to look at anymore. It's covered in blood.

Just so much blood.

"You're doing everything you can, kid," the guy says, patting me on the shoulder. If I had the energy in me, I'd tell him to do something more. Say something other than that. Gio's head wobbles in my lap and I pull my knees in, trying to elevate his head. The guy points down to the end of the alleyway where the rain is slowing. "I'll wait there for the ambulance."

I close my eyes for a second, leaning my head against the brick wall, trying to breathe. Trying to be strong. This is exactly what I didn't want to happen. I told my dad the minute something puts us in danger, I'm out.

"Ev... Your shirt..." I hear her mumble. I look up and Scarlett's standing over us, staring right at her uncle's weak body. She's not sobbing anymore, which is good. She's had time to calm herself down. She's gasping, though, holding her hand to her chest. My once white shirt is still wrapped around his head, soaked through with blood. I ignore her, pressing my shirt onto the side of his head.

I don't think I'm doing enough.

I need to do more.

"Didn't I tell you to wait by the side of the car?" I ask, frustrated. She gulps, not responding. "How long until the ambulance comes?"

"Any minute now," she whispers. She kneels down, trying to look at him, but I can tell it's paining her. Fuck, she's going to have nightmares about this for weeks. I know I will. I tried to protect her from that as much as I could. She presses her hands to the side of his neck. "Have you checked his pulse? My hands are still shaking."

I gently move her hands away from him, placing them in her lap. Instead, I press two fingers onto his wrist, and it takes a while for me to feel something. "It's weak, Scar."

"Are you sure you're doing it right?" she asks, gently pulling his arm into her lap and she tries to feel for it. She probably comes to the same realisation that I do. "No. No. No. He's not gone yet. He can't be."

"Scarlett," I say quietly. That's all I can say. I gently try to pry her hands off of him, but she won't budge. She must have realised what I did. He's not got long left.

"No, Evan," she shouts at me. "No," she says again, quieter. She pulls Gio's face into her hands and I have to look away, not able to stomach the large gash at the side of his head, but I still press my shirt to it. "Come on, G. Stay with me, okay? I can't lose you too. Stay with me. Please."

She tries to wipe the blood out of his face, but I can tell that part of it disgusts her. I silently tell her to stop. I clasp both of her hands in mine, holding them tight as she cries hard on my shoulder. I press a kiss to the top of her head.

"I'm here, Angel. I'm here," I whisper over and over again until three heartbeats slowly fade to two.

29

EVAN

MOST OF WHAT happened next is hard to remember.

I stayed next to Scarlett when they took her uncle's body into the ambulance. I sat by her next to the stretcher as she held onto his hand, whispering prayers, and begging him to stay with her. I stayed with her when we waited outside the operating room. She paced the hallway and ignored me when I asked her to sit down. I think halfway through she realised that he wasn't coming out of the operating room alive. I stayed with her when the doctors came out and told us they were sorry for our loss.

She didn't cry. She didn't run into the room like I expected, demanding they do more. She just stood there, staring at the doctor until I clasped my hand around her elbow and led her to a seat. When the doctors changed our clothes, giving us scrubs that weren't covered in blood, a nurse had to dress her because she didn't want to move. Even when her mom and brothers came, she sat there, staring at the blank wall, the smell of chlorine and chemicals invading our senses. They didn't know what to do or say, so they left me with her, and I promised them I'd get her home safe.

I sat with her for hours. I brought food to her, but she didn't eat. She didn't speak. She didn't even look at me. I tried to comfort her. I never left her side. I couldn't. And I didn't want to. I need to be close to her, at all times and even with her in a state of grief, I still want to be with her.

Now, I'm driving her back home in her car and she's still silent. It's stopped raining, but her body temperature keeps fluctuating. At the moment, her face looks pale, but she feels warm. I can tell she's going to fall asleep. She's still in shock and her head keeps lolling forward. I slow down the car so I can use my right hand to lift her head up. Her head is so hot it almost scalds me.

"Hey, Scar?" I ask, tilting her head to lift back on the head-rest. I glance at her, trying my best to keep my eyes on the road at the same time. Her dark hair is covering most of her face.

"Hm?" she mumbles. It's the most I've heard her speak in the last six hours, so I hold onto the moment and urge her not to fall asleep.

"Stay with me, okay?" I let go of my hand for a second, seeing if she'll keep her head up, but she can't do it on her own. Maybe we shouldn't have left the hospital. "I've got you."

"I'm literally fine," she groans. Of course, she has the energy to give me sass right now.

"You're not," I say, still holding her head up. She turns her head into my hand, gently nuzzling her cheek into my palm like a kitten. I lower my hand, so it rests in my lap, and she sets her head in it. I continue driving with one hand, stroking her hair out of her face with the other.

"I'm trying," she groans, and it sounds like she's crying again. Her voice sounds so filled with pain that it tears my heart in two. "I'm just so tired...so tired of everything. Everything hurts so badly."

"What hurts, Angel?" I ask, moving my hand from her face down her spine, running my fingers up and down. She relaxes into me for a second and I can tell she's forcing herself to breathe calmly. I don't want her to sleep yet. Not when she hasn't eaten all day.

"Everything hurts," she says again. "My head. My back. My heart. My chest. My hands. I feel like I can't breathe anymore, Ev."

"I've got you, Scar. What do you need?"

"I don't know," she groans, pressing her hand to her temples.

"Can I take you back to the hospital?" I ask.

She shakes her head. "No. No hospitals."

"Okay, then what can I do for you, Scarlett? I need to help you," I say quietly, still running my finger up and down her back.

"Just take me home. Please," she whispers. She turns in my lap so she's looking up at me. Her face is paler than usual, but her cheeks are a little red. She grabs my hand, pressing it to her heart. "I feel like my chest is on fire."

"I know, sweetheart, I know," I whisper back to her, massaging the top of her chest gently and she lets me. She lets me be there for her.

SCARLETT

Have you ever had that feeling after you've felt things so intensely, where you feel it right to your core, it sits in your stomach, it stays there and then it's just...gone?

I get that feeling after being so high on energy at a concert and I have to go back home, where I have to pretend, I didn't have the best time of my life. I got that feeling after I finished high school. Everyone was sad about leaving their friends and moving away, but what stuck with me was that I was leaving a place and it felt like losing a person. It felt like losing a part of myself since it was somewhere I spent so many years creating memories with my best friends.

That's what it felt like when the doctors told me my uncle had died. I already knew from the moment in the alley that he wouldn't make it, but the doctors made it official.

He was just *gone*. There was nothing left of him. That's the hardest part about someone dying is knowing that it's just...it. Their memories cease to exist. Their thoughts, their feelings, everything that made them *them* doesn't even mean anything anymore. You don't get to ever speak to them again. You won't ever know what they would have thought about something new happening. You'd never know if their voice would change with age or if it would stay the same. Their mind, their soul, their body...everything is just gone.

I'm still trying to process it when Evan takes me back to my apartment. The girls' cars aren't in the driveway, and I don't know when or if I'll tell them. I'm not planning on talking to anyone right now. I don't want to wallow and sit in silence, but I don't want to talk either. I just want to stop feeling. To stop the noise in my head that keeps replaying the same thoughts over and over.

He's gone.

He's gone.

*He's just **gone**.*

When I open the door, I switch on the lights and Evan follows behind me. I know this is the last thing he wants to do right now. I've shown too much to him recently. I've basically laid my soul bare in front of this man more than once. But he never makes me feel like I shouldn't. He just lets me feel things.

I tell him I'm going to take a shower and he nods. I leave him in the kitchen, needing a minute. I've had hours to get my shit together. I've had too long to stop acting like my life has ended. It hasn't. I know it hasn't. But for some reason my whole body feels like it's being weighed down, like somebody is standing on my chest, telling me not to get up. But I need to. I need to push that demon off me and get my act together.

I take a long shower, needing the space and the time. I end up staring at the white tiles of the bathroom for half an hour, naked, the hot water pummelling on my back that I don't even end up using any soap until almost an hour goes by. I always take hot showers, but right now, I need it to scold me. I need it to make me feel more than this heavy, numb feeling that I can't escape.

I hate feeling like this. It's not that I'm sad. I mean, that's what I'm supposed to feel, right? Pure and utter sadness? So, I probably am deep down. But on the surface, I can't even put it into words how it feels. It's like trying to remember the last time you saw someone who you don't talk to anymore. Where you try so hard it just hurts at the thought of it.

There's just nothing other than a dark nothingness that rests on my chest. I can't even conjure in my head most of what happened on that street.

I try my best to feel as normal as I can when I get ready, so I can go into my room and wait until my body decides to fall asleep. I shove on a pair of pyjama shorts and a tank top, throwing a sweater on top. When I wander back into the kitchen, Evan is still here.

I think it's the first time I've really looked at him since we got into the ambulance. He had to change his clothes into a pair of scrubs, the same as I did and he's still wearing them. His hair is a lot messier than usual, and his face just looks worn out. It's way into the morning now, probably around two or three. I haven't checked my phone, but Evan must have if he's sorting out takeout food onto a plate.

I inch further into the kitchen and his head shoots up, his eyes softening on me. I still don't know what's going on with us. Part of me wants to see what happens, let it spiral out of control, but the other part of me needs to know what's going to happen. Now is not the time for that. All I know as of right now is that I want to be close to him and I don't want to be alone for once.

"You should have gone home. It's late," I whisper, making my way to the kitchen counter.

"I didn't want to," he explains, closing the lids to the plastic containers. "You need to eat."

I'm not hungry, but I don't tell him that. I take the plate of Chinese takeout and make my way over into the living room, settling between the soft plush blankets we often leave lying around. Evan follows me, sitting beside me with a sigh, manspreading like always. The TV is in front of us but neither of us make a move to turn it on.

"Why are you being so nice to me?" I ask once I've eaten a forkful of noodles. The food makes me feel sick, but it was a nice gesture, so I force myself to eat some of it. I push the plate aside, pulling my knees up to my chest as I lean my head on them.

"Because I want to," he says quietly. I don't look at him. I don't know if I want to. I just keep my head buried in my knees.

"Why?" I ask quietly.

"Scar," he murmurs. I feel the soft brush of his fingers on my shoulder, and I flinch. "Scarlett, sweetheart, look at me, please."

I slowly move my head, turning towards him, still resting on my knees. He looks so tired and sad. I feel terrible that he's had to lose out on sleep because of me. I don't know how bad Gio looked before I saw him in Evan's lap but I'm sure it scarred him. His eyes usually have this ocean-like glow in them, but now, they just seem dim - almost like the deep noth-ingness that lurks at the bottom of the ocean. Completely empty.

"We're not doing that, okay? I know things are hard right now, but I'm going to be nice to you and you're going to let me. Deal?"

I nod. He keeps his hand on my shoulder, gently rubbing it. I don't tell him to stop. I don't think I want him to. "Are you not going to eat?"

"I already did when you were in the shower," he says. I nod again. He sighs as if he's been holding his breath and I think at that moment, we both realise the severity of today. He watched somebody die. My uncle died. In my arms. He's gone forever. I feel the dryness at the back of my throat, and I start blinking rapidly.

Evan doesn't say anything other than, "Come here."

I don't climb into his lap, so much as he pulls me into him. I allow myself to release all the resentment I held towards him, and I let myself wrap my arms around his neck as he snakes his hands around my shoulders, holding me tightly just the way I need. I'm hugging him and I'm letting him anchor me because I need it. And I think he needs it too. I don't care about that one thing he said to me years ago. I don't care about the stupid games we've been playing since then.

I just want him to hold me, and he does.

"You know that I've got you, Scar, don't you?" he asks thickly. I nod into his neck, inhaling him. "I'd never let anything happen to you. Ever."

"I know," I choke out. He's not a monster. He's not evil. He's just Evan Branson who *cares* about me. He cares about me enough to sit with me in silence when I can't find the words. He cares about me enough to buy me food and make sure I eat it. He cares about me enough to sit with me in front of a blank TV and hold me when he knows I need it. When he tells me he's got me, I believe him.

Even when I slip out of his lap, settling beside him, he keeps his arm around me as I rest my head on his shoulder. I pull my knees up and he grabs one of the blankets, laying it over our legs. After he's smoothed it out, he slips his hand under the covers and his hand finds mine. And I hold it.

EVAN

She's doing it again. Well, I think she is. She's doing that thing where she does something without realising that she's doing them. She's stroking her thumb against my hand, and I want to crawl up into her lap even though she's the one that's hurting.

I wish she could be like this all the time. As much as I love her screaming at me, I like the quiet moments too. The moments where we share a blanket in her living room, not talking and staring at the blank TV. We don't say anything to each other, but we don't need to because each stroke of her thumb against my hand is telling me enough.

I'm glad you're here.

Thank you for taking care of me.

I needed this.

*I need **you.***

I don't even realise that we fell asleep until the sun starts to peek through the blinds of the living room and the front door opens. Neither of us have spoken to the rest of the group since we left suddenly. They must have heard about it from the morning news and came straight here.

We fell asleep sitting up, so when the girls came rushing into the room, I gently pushed apart from her making my way to the pillar between the open living room and kitchen. No matter how upset she is, I want her to tell her friends whatever is going on between us on her terms. I don't want them to assume anything that she's not comfortable with.

"Scarlett," Kennedy coos quietly, climbing onto the couch next to a sleepy Scarlett. She smiles weakly before she wraps her in a hug. "We heard. We're so sorry."

I watch as Kennedy fusses over her that I don't realise Wren's hand on my back. I turn to her and she's a lot shorter than me, so she blinks up at me, her green eyes filled with concern.

"Is she okay?" she asks me quietly. I shrug, nodding gently.

"She will be. I think she's still in shock," I explain. Wren pulls her bottom lip between her teeth in worry as she turns back to Kennedy and Scarlett.

"Thank you. You know, for taking care of her. She's our girl and she pretends to be tough, but sometimes she needs someone to look after her. We try when we can, but she's not easy to deal with, but you calm her. I think you make her feel safe and she needs that."

"I do?" I ask, shocked.

What me and Scarlett have done up until now has been anything but calm. I've always wanted that peace that we once had when we were kids, but I thought it never came back. Unless things look differently to her, I wouldn't know what Wren's talking about.

"Yeah. She would never admit it, but I've seen you guys sneaking around and I assume you're enabling her compulsions for finding out what happened to her dad. If she was doing this on her own, she'd be freaking out. But she hasn't been. I think you're good for her. In whatever way you want to take that," she says, turning to look up at me. "You should get some sleep too. You look exhausted."

I smile at her and when she walks over to fuss over Scarlett on the couch, I turn around and slip out of the door, finally sighing a breath of relief. Today has been one long fucking day and I can't wait to get back into my bed.

I make it about five steps out of the building before I hear Scarlett running and shouting after me. I turn around and there she is, a blanket wrapped around her shoulder, her hair a mess, her face still tired, but she smiles at me weakly.

"You were going to leave without saying bye?" she pants, tilting her head to the side.

"Well, your friends came back, and it seemed like you

needed some time alone," I explain, instantly moving my hand to the back of my neck nervously. She studies me for a few seconds, not sure what to say. I just stand there until she jumps into my arms, her arms around the blanket wrapping around me, covering us both in the warmth.

She tightens her arms around my neck, and I feel every single part of me come alive. I wrap my arms around her small waist, pulling her as close to me as I can. I should not be getting hard right now. Especially after everything that has happened in the last few hours, but she just smells so fucking good all the time.

"Thank you, Evan," she whispers, her mouth and her hot breath against the rapid pulse on my neck. I finally believe I can breathe again. "For everything."

"You're welcome," I say back. "For everything."

30

EVAN

"SO, that's it? He's just gone. Dead."

After not sleeping properly for four nights, the last thing I want or need to deal with is my dad and my uncle. I've been sitting in my dad's office for almost an hour, and he keeps asking me questions about Gio. I answer them and then he asks more, usually the same question. Something is not adding up to him, which is the last thing I can focus on right now. My priority is being there for Scarlett.

Since Gio's death, reporters have decided to keep quiet about it, claiming that the only thing that has happened is *Voss* has lost a vital member to their team.

What they don't say is how B&Co believe that Gio was the one smuggling the drugs into the business, and he died in an accident, tying up the story neatly. Motives are still loose, but they could make sense. He wasn't a leader like Mateo was. He wasn't in the spotlight. He lost his wife and his close friend the same night. Maybe he wanted more, and he wasn't getting it. It just doesn't make sense that he would try and put Scarlett in danger, enabling her on his concerns and worries about the business, knowing that she would try to figure it out on her own. I've had days to get my head around, but it still seems so foggy.

"I just don't believe you're telling me that our lead suspect has just died. It would have been one hell of a story," my dad says, sighing as he looks through the window into the frosty forest of the backyard. "Do you know who killed him?"

I shake my head. I've been trying not to relive that night. The last thing I want to remember is all that blood, her screams…. "No, it seemed like a freak accident."

"Seemed?" He quirks an eyebrow as he turns to me. I rub my sweaty palms against my trousers.

"Well, I don't know for sure, obviously. Everything happened so fast. It makes sense that it was an accident. The only person who would want him dead is Mateo and he's not even alive fully himself," I say, voicing my theories aloud. My dad nods slowly before recounting the story I've told him three times.

"So, he never got to tell you what he was going to say?" he asks.

"No. I'm assuming it was some fucked up confession or something," I say, shrugging.

"Right. Well, keep an eye out," he says, getting up out of the seat to walk me out. He pushes the door open, but I don't walk through.

"Yeah. About that…" I start and he tilts his head at me. I rub the back of my neck anxiously before shaking out my hand. "Look, I'm out. I'm done. Whatever it is that you want to keep digging for, you do it on your own. We could have also been killed if we weren't careful and God, if *anything* happened to Scarlett, I would have personally murdered whoever hurt her."

My dad nods at first. He understands what it's like in this industry. He tries to protect me, and he tried to protect my mom. I know he would do anything to make sure we're safe and he has to understand that I would do the same thing for Scarlett.

"You're starting to sound like you love her, boy," my dad says playfully, smirking. Weirdly enough, I don't want to punch him in the throat for suggesting that. I stand my ground.

"She's my partner in everything, in every way. She can give me a hard time, but that doesn't mean I don't want to protect her. She's not done anything wrong to deserve any of that," I say. He studies me for a moment, and he doesn't say anything. For a second, I think he's proud of me in some way. I glance down at my watch. "Speaking of her, I'm meant to meet her now, so we don't fail our class. And I meant what I said. Anything I find out; I'm not doing it for you."

He holds out his hand to me and I look at it for a second before shaking it. "Weirdly, I respect that," he says with a low chuckle. I give him one of my best smiles, finally feeling like a weight has lifted off my shoulders.

"Good."

MOST OF SCARLETT and I's conversations over the last few days have been a lot of one-worded ones. I'm fine with it. This is her process and I'm going to be with her throughout all of it. I just wish I could do something to ease her pain.

She came straight back to school on Monday like nothing happened. She came in, attended every lecture, completed her homework, and gave nobody any reason to suspect that she just lost a family member. She still dressed the same. She still let out her snarky comments while we studied. She's good at pretending everything's fine. Too good.

"How are you feeling?" I ask when I return from the bathroom. We've not said much to each other today, but we're getting closer to finishing our app. We need to work on a colour scheme and more finer details, but it's coming together perfectly. She looks up at me, her eyes still a little heavy and dull.

"Not great," she mutters before dropping her eyes to her laptop.

"Do you want to talk about it?" I suggest quietly, shifting in my seat.

"Not really."

"Want to sit in silence and read?"

She nods and we do.

She finishes up her final research for getting the app together, emailing back and forth with the software developer, while I stare at colours, so I don't stare at her.

Don't get me wrong, I love it when she shouts me and tells me I'm doing something wrong, but there is something incredibly special about these quiet moments where she lets me help her and be there for her.

There is nothing more that I want or need more than Scarlett Voss. She's just *everything*.

"Hey," she says quietly, snapping me out of my daydream.

I look up at her. I was doing the thing that she does – where she does things without realising them. Maybe that's what happens to her. Maybe she gets too stuck in her head that she doesn't know what her body is doing. I don't know why I'm doing it. I shouldn't be stressed, but I am. We've still got to finish the project. I don't know where we stand or how to help her. The thought of the mystery still not being solved is making me worry more than usual.

"You're tapping the table again. Can you chill for two seconds?"

"I can't," I whisper.

"What's the matter with you?" she asks quietly, glancing around the empty library. I've stopped tapping as fast as it was before, and it's now slowed down to a rhythmic tap.

"I don't know. I just...I just need to do something," I say, running my hands through my hair as I lean back in the chair. When I look at her, her eyes have softened, and her mouth is pulled into a small smile.

"What do you need?"

You, I almost say like a fucking lunatic.

The last thing I want to do is confuse her having a hard time with actually liking me beyond the new friendship we discovered. I'm losing my shit here. Why is this coming to such a surprise for me? It shouldn't be, right? She's been right in front of me for years and I've been aware of her before that. I can't get awkward now. Not when she's already going through so much.

"Ev," she presses. *That nickname*, I think to myself. It makes my heart almost fall out of my chest. "Why don't you go to the music rooms or something? I'll finish up here. Your stress is going to rub off on me."

"Are you sure?" I choke out.

"I'm going to be nice to you and you're going to let me. Deal?" she says, repeating my words back to me. She tilts her head when I don't say anything, silently trying to figure me out.

"Okay," I say, packing up my sheets and my laptop to put

into my backpack. She smiles weakly before dropping her eyes back down to her work.

When I get to the music rooms, I have a moment to think, to stop the constant worrying about what could happen or what has already happened. I know I need to live in the moment and God knows that I try, it's just hard sometimes.

It's so easy to tell yourself that living while you can is the best option, but there is always going to be that fear about tomorrow or yesterday. The worst part is, when you spend the whole day ignoring your worries and compulsions, the second your brain is not focused on something else, everything comes rushing back to you like a tidal wave and you feel like you can't breathe anymore.

I get through almost an hour of playing intense dark melodies until I decide to slow it down and choose something more light-hearted. I'm not playing for an audience, but I'm sure people are walking past and assuming I'm having some sort of breakdown, which I kind of am.

I got an email from Diane Scavo, the teacher of musical arts at NU about a showcase coming up. She wants me to perform an original piece, but I haven't composed my own music in a while. I try to give it a go, seeing if the melodies will come naturally to me, but they don't.

My old piano teacher told me that the best way to create your own music is to relieve your greatest memories. Recently, it's been harder to dig back into those joyful times with all the doom and gloom happening around me. Still, I try my hardest and think of a time when I was truly happy.

The first thing that comes to mind is Scarlett teasing me in that dodgy restaurant about how I was in the band and when we smoked weed and she pressed her hand to my heart or at the museum when she held my hand. All my best memories are with her, and they've only occurred in the last few weeks.

My all-time favourite was last Christmas when she shoved bacon in my face because I joked about her eating the last piece. I thought she felt it too – that slight spark of connection – when she locked eyes with me and I smiled with bacon falling out of my mouth as she continued to shove more in my face.

I sigh after stringing together a decent three-minute piece. It's not perfect, but it's something.

When I open my eyes, she's there, standing like an angel, watching me play. If I didn't know any better, she's probably been hiding, listening to me all this time. But I don't know any better, so I smile at her in the mirror.

She takes a seat across from me, still watching me in the mirror as she asks, "Is it going to distract you if I watch?"

I shake my head. "It's better, actually," I say, although I don't know if it's entirely true. "Can you sing for me?"

She laughs and the sound runs right through me like water. It's the first time I've heard her laugh in a few days. God, I missed that sound so much.

"I told you I can't sing," she concedes.

"Fine," I say, moving to leave space on the bench as I gesture to it. "Let me teach you something then."

She sighs a little, but she accepts my proposal, sliding next to me on the bench. Our thighs are touching, our elbows brushing against each other, and it feels like my whole body is being dunked inside a volcano. Everything about her just lights me up: her wit, her charm, her intelligence, her beauty, her smile, her eyes, her *everything.*

Jeez, this is starting to get pathetic.

"You gonna teach me or what, Branson?" she asks sarcastically, watching me watch her in the mirror. I nod and I place my right hand on the keys, playing A to G slowly. "I know where the notes are. Just teach me something good."

"I'm the teacher, remember?" I say, nudging her with my shoulder.

"Yeah, a pretty shit one," she mumbles.

"Okay, I'll show you *Moonlight Sonata*," I say, and she nods. "I'll play the right hand and you can do the left since it's more repetitive."

I play the first few lines of the song with both hands at a faster tempo than usual, so she gets the gist. She watches my hands carefully, twisting hers in her lap. When I'm done, I replay the part I'm going to teach her.

"I can *not* do that," she says quietly.

"Oh my god, are you a quitter, Angel?" I hold a dramatised hand to my chest, gasping and she kicks me under the seat, and I wince. "Come on. I'll show you it one more time and you can do it. I believe in you."

"Your belief in me is doing nothing for me right now," she mutters.

"Well, it better," I say back before playing it again.

I watch her as she tries to do it on her own. She does it slowly, but she messes up a few times, so I encourage her to continue. I have sheet music on my phone, but that would only confuse her, so she's mostly doing it by ear. Honestly, she's not half bad. She messes it up again and she hits the keys, so they make an ugly sound.

I place my hands over hers and she gasps quietly, looking up at me. I keep my eyes on her brown ones as I squeeze her hands softly. Her mouth parts as her gaze drops to my lips for only a second and then back up to my eyes.

"You're getting too worked up," I tell her. "You don't have

to be perfect at it on the first try. I would teach you every day if you wanted me to."

She laughs a little. "You would really do that?"

"Of course, I would," I say, staring at her until she accepts it. Until she accepts that I'm always here for her. Finally, she nods, and I drop my hands from hers. "Now play it again."

AFTER WE BOTH had enough of playing, she went to meet Kennedy and I walked home. I needed the time alone. I feel guilty, though. I didn't know Gio, but for some reason I feel like I'm sharing Scarlett's pain with her.

When I get home, I pull out my phone to text her.

ME: Thank you. I needed that.

SCARLETT: I know.

THE THREE DOTS appear and then disappear again. She's thinking about what to say to me and I let her take her time while I pace my room.

SCARLETT: Me too.

31

SCARLETT

I'VE PUT off going to therapy for so many reasons.

I always thought that my problems were never big enough to receive professional help. There are people with real struggles and I'm just a girl with a slightly dysfunctional family and a need to always do her best. Voicing my fears out loud as well as someone trying to help me navigate it just felt like I was burdening them with my issues. I know it's their job, but I can't help but think I'm taking away space from people who truly need it.

Since Gio's death, I've been trying my best to be strong. I need to move on and continue with my life. I know what grief does to people. I know how it holds people back from their potential and I don't want that to happen to me. I already showed too much weakness towards Evan, so I cleaned up my act, put on a decent outfit and I went back to school. People talk. They always have. Before, the looks I got were either disgust or jealousy and now its pity.

My family is also trying to move on. When I went to visit them, no one spoke about it and they put their best faces on, acting as if nothing happened. I don't know which is worse: talking about it or ignoring it. The latter makes me feel less lonely though.

My mom forwarded us all an email of a list of therapists in and around the area. The twins aren't bothered about going, Hen says he's considering it, but I actually took the leap. If I'm not going to talk to my friends, the least I can do is talk to a professional. What I wasn't expecting was for her to see right through me.

I've been sitting in Dr. Nelson's minimalist office for almost half an hour, and she's already managed to figure me out. Sometimes, I feel like I don't even know myself and the perception I have is simply based on how other people think of me. It's fucked up and it doesn't even make sense because I do know myself. I have to, right? I know how I present myself, but what I can't figure out for the life of me is why. Which is one of the first questions Dr. Nelson asks me.

"Why do you think nobody likes you?" she asks. She reminds me of one of my old high school teachers. She has short light brown hair, owl-framed glasses and is wearing a grey romper. She seemed like the best choice because she's young and doesn't make me feel like I'm talking to a professional even though she is one.

I shift in the extremely comfortable seat across from her. "I never said that."

She shakes her head lightly, glancing down to the notebook in her hand. I had to fill out a questionnaire before arriving, so she already knows what happened and how I'm feeling on a scale of 'not great' to 'fantastic.' I noted down somewhere closer to 'not great.'

"No, but you're thinking about it, right?"

I chuckle a little, brushing my hair that has fallen in front of my eyes out of my face. "I don't see what that has to do with anything. I'm here for grief counselling."

"Yes, but that also requires me to get to know you, too," she explains. I resist the urge to roll my eyes. She's just doing her job. "Can you talk to me about why you feel like you don't have many friends other than the ones you live with? You wrote down that high school was particularly difficult. Do you think you could reflect on that time?"

I take a deep breath, trying my best to go back to that time. That part of my life stays with the other suppressed memories of my childhood, locked away in the deepest corners of my brain in a chest labelled 'Do not open.' I try not to think about it most of the time because I know that I've grown since then.

"I've always been confident. Well, I thought I was. I mean, I had to be. I had an image to uphold. I couldn't embarrass my family and even though my parents dismissed my achievements, it only made me want to work harder. It paid off. I passed every test with flying colours, and I even became valedictorian by the end of high school, but still, nobody wanted to be my friend other than Wren and Kennedy. My brothers teased me about it, saying that it's because I tried too hard at school and people thought I was stuck-up. But I just didn't get it. There were so many people who could be pretty, smart, and popular, but just not me.

"Everyone would make groups that I wouldn't be a part of. They'd plan times to hang out in the bathrooms and no one would invite me. They'd have parties and I would never go. I tried to rationalise it, believing that people were just jealous. It wasn't until junior year until I finally plucked up the courage to ask someone in my Spanish class what was so wrong with me. *'We just don't like you. Your vibe is just off,"* she said. They just didn't like me. What the fuck does that even mean?

They just had one look at me and decided they didn't want to get to know me. And because it was high school, word got around fast, and everyone collectively decided they didn't want me."

I take a deep breath, my hands shaking.

"I thought things started to turn around senior year. Everyone wanted to party, and no one was taking anything seriously. I made the stupid decision to host a party, hoping people would come and when they heard how big my house was and the amount of food I was bringing, they did. Suddenly everyone was interested in me and because I was stupid and I got high off being needed and somebody choosing me, I made friends with the wrong people. I got used for my car, my house, my money, my fame. People would make up any excuse to hang out with me and I let them. For a few months, it was bliss. I was trying hard to fit in and it paid off. Then, when one of the biggest parties of that year got busted by the cops for underage drinking at a party I didn't host, I got blamed for it. Still, that short period where we hung out, I sort of miss it."

Dr. Nelson watches me for a second, processing the word vomit. She writes something down in her notebook before looking back up at me. "Do you miss it because they chose you?" I nod, tears fighting my eyes not to fall. "Why do you think that's so important to you?"

"Because no one has chosen me just for me before," I admit. Oh, shit. I'm going to cry right now. It's my first session and I'm already about to bawl like a baby. Yet, I don't want to stop talking. It feels too freeing. As if talking about it will take the pain away. "At the time, it felt like people were starting to really like me. Before I could even understand it, people have always taken one look at my family and *their* achievements and based me off that. I never got the chance to show my true talents or figure things out on my own. I thought that they started to realise I wasn't as bad as everyone made me out to be and that they wanted me. Looking back, I know it was stupid because they didn't want me. They just wanted what I could give them."

"Do you think you still do that now – allowing people in because you'd prefer that they want something from you than nothing at all?"

I shake my head, wiping the tears with the back of my sweatshirt. "No, I've stopped doing that. I realised that what I need is people to like me for who I am and if they don't – if they want more – then I don't need them."

"How do you manage relationships and friendships with this fear?"

"I don't think it's a fear. I'm not scared of it happening again because I won't let it."

"How do you ensure that doesn't happen? I'm curious about your process, Scarlett."

"I just don't let people get too close romantically. That's where it hurts the most," I say easily. It's the most natural response and the one that's the truest. This isn't an interrogation, but for some reason, it feels like it. She's just trying to get to know me, but it's so hard to explain that to her when I don't even know who that is sometimes.

"Do you not think that limits you from gaining something possibly great?"

I shrug. "Maybe. I'd rather have nobody and deal with solitude than have people who are destined to break my heart."

She nods, writing down in her notebook. I take the opportunity to take a real deep breath and allow the weight of the world to be off my shoulders for one minute.

"And now, as you deal with losing your uncle, are you still

shutting people out or are you allowing anyone in?" she asks. "You said you weren't alone when he passed. I'm assuming you still talk to that person."

Just the mention of that day, the way Evan held me and cared for me makes me cry even more. He was just *there*. She holds the box of tissues towards me, and I grab them.

"God, I'm so fucking embarrassed," I mutter, wiping my eyes and my face. She doesn't say anything, but she smiles softly. "Yes, I still talk to him, but not about what happened. It's hard to talk about it."

"That's understandable. It's not something you exactly want to remember and that's okay. Dealing with it and moving on is just as important," she says gently. "Do you mind me asking what you talk about instead?"

I shrug, tilting my head up to the ceiling so I can stop the tears from falling. "He helps me forget. He distracts me and I don't know if he's doing it on purpose, but he doesn't push me to talk about it," I say, remembering the way he taught me how to play piano. How he let us sit in silence when I didn't want to talk.

"And does that help?"

"With Evan it's just…He listens to me. Even if we have a complicated relationship right now, he still manages to care and it's beyond me why. I haven't given him any reason to. We weren't the kindest to each other for a while and then we talked, and I don't know…I misjudged him. I think we're similar in that way," I explain. "Maybe if people got to know me more, they'd actually like me despite my money and my family. But I'm constantly putting up this barrier, terrified of rejection."

"And you think Evan likes you for more than that?"

"I mean, he has to, right? I've put him through some real

shit for the last few years and I know he's probably scarred from witnessing what happened to Gio. And God, I feel like such a hypocrite," I say when the realisation hits me, and I bark out a disbelieving laugh. "I just said that whole thing about people judging me and deciding they don't like me, and I did the same thing to him. I've got to know him over the last few weeks and he's...He's probably one of the kindest people I know. He listens to me, he takes care of me, even when I don't want him to. It's not about him choosing me for me because in some way, I don't think that would matter with him. Even if we had a rocky start, all he's done since then is make me feel like I'm capable of more than I give myself credit for. He's gotten to know me, and he hasn't run away yet."

Dr. Nelson smiles as more tears run down my face. I rub at my cheeks, sighing as the realisation that I might, actually, definitely like Evan Branson washes over me. "He seems like a good friend. Why do you think you care so much about being liked, Scarlett?"

I laugh. "I don't care."

"You do care, Scarlett and that's okay," she presses. She's not going to let this go.

"It's so easy to say that you don't care about what people think of you, but the truth of the matter is, you do. Everybody does. Because people's perception is what makes you, *you.* You can try to be a good person, and someone will think you're trying too hard or you're not trying hard enough. You can try and showcase your intelligence and you'll get put down for it. So, really, even when I try to be my authentic self, I can't ever find it because I'm still, subconsciously, trying to please others."

"Don't you think it would be freeing if you let go of that?" she asks curiously.

"People don't need a reason not to like me and they just don't and that sucks, okay? Even before everything that happened with the party, people had one look at me, and they realised they don't like me. One person I could deal with. Maybe I'm just not their vibe, but when it's *everybody,* I'm starting to wonder if maybe *I'm* the problem. Maybe *I* need to be the one to change because nobody else will. I thought I was just a hard person to love. I tried to change, and it didn't get me anywhere. But I don't want to do that anymore because I love myself and I just...I just..."

"Want to fit in and be accepted," Dr Nelson says, finishing my train of thought. I nod. "It's all anybody wants."

"I want to stop feeling this way. I really do. I never used to think about what happened or what people think of me until Gio died and suddenly I'm questioning everything, my loneliness included. I just want to be happy again, but it's only been two weeks," I say.

I want to move on. Not because I'm cruel and that I didn't care about my uncle, but because I have so many goals and aspirations that I can't achieve if I'm stuck in my head. I don't enjoy being down and feeling helpless. I like being a fun friend. I like laughing and having a good time, but I feel so guilty about doing that when I've just lost one of my closest family members.

"Grief and happiness can coexist. You don't have to feel guilty for wanting to be happy right now. Nobody chooses to sit in grief, it just happens and that's okay," she says gently, as if reading my mind. The way she talks to me makes me believe her. She tells me things and for some reason, I believe they're true. "You can be more than one thing, Scarlett. You can be brave as well as being scared. You can be confident and have insecurities. You can be rude or mean, but you can also be kind and selfless and loving. Really, you can be anything you want."

I laugh a little. "Are you sure you're not just saying that because it's your job to talk me out of jumping off a cliff?"

Dr. Nelson laughs too, nudging her glasses further up her nose. "No, I'm not just saying that. You're a smart girl, Scarlett and you're feeling a lot of things right now. The best advice I can give you until our next session is to *feel* those feelings. Don't push them away because they'll creep up on you and come crashing down when you least expect it."

I do my best to take in what she says, to let it truly settle with me. It turns out that I've had this warped perception of therapy for so many years. I knew I had shit to figure out but saying it aloud really showcased just how deep those worries go.

As I leave the office, I make a promise to myself, the same thing I've been trying to tell my friends for years, but never thought of applying to myself.

I'm not going to downplay my feelings. If I feel something, I'm going to do just that; feel it. Ignoring it just leads to breakdowns in therapist's offices on your first sessions and I really don't want to do that again.

32

EVAN

"YOU'RE DOING IT WRONG," Scarlett warns.

We've been walking around the library at school for almost an hour, picking up books to use for references in our final report. Not only do we have to craft the app, but we also have to create a written report, outlining how we came up with the idea and how it would work, as well as another essay about the project as a whole and how it would function as a marketing device.

Scarlett came up with the idea of scouring through the business library and taking pictures of pages of books we'll read later. She's convinced this is the most foolproof way to find resources efficiently. Still, each time I pick up a book she has a problem with whichever I choose.

Each time she brushes past me, her soft silk shirt smooths against my skin, I feel her touch like electricity. We haven't touched each other since that kiss in the rain outside of my house four weeks ago and I'm still confused as to where we stand.

Every time I look at her, I just want to catch her lips with mine, slip my tongue into her mouth while my hands do whatever they can to make her feel good. I just wish I could see into her brain if she's feeling it too.

She leans against the bookshelf, looking all innocent again with that black shirt and matching skirt, her blouse unbuttoned enough for me to see the slight swell of her breasts. Her ankles are crossed, looking at me accusingly, her fuck-me eyes staring right into mine that I almost forget how to speak.

"What am I doing wrong?" I ask playfully, looking at the hardback book in my hand.

"Everything," she says, stalking towards me and she pulls it out of my hand. "Move."

And I do.

I step out of the way so she can look at the shelf I was scanning. She runs her slender fingers across the dusty books, the white ribbon in her hair bobbing as she pulls out a book to read the back. She slides it back into place, sighing.

♫ Love Is A Bitch - Two Feet

"When will you stop telling me what to do?"

"When you stop letting me," she mutters. She moves down the aisle and I follow behind her. "Maybe learn how to read first and I'll consider it."

"I can read perfectly fine," I retort, and she chuckles. I bet if I could see her face, she'd be rolling her eyes at me. "You're just a perfectionist."

She turns to me now, stopping, pressing her back to the bookshelf. She lifts her chin up. "Oh, *I'm* the perfectionist?"

I step in closer to her and I watch the way her breathing goes shallow. The closer I walk into her; she backs up further into the shelf and it wobbles slightly with her weight.

"Yes," I say, my voice still low. There's basically no one here. The only people I've seen have noise cancelling headphones on, tucked into a darker corner of the library. More privacy for us. For what? I don't know. But I'm dying to find out.

"You took two weeks to decide between crocodile green and pickle green even though they're the same fucking colour," she says, holding her gaze with mine, but I don't miss the slight tremor in her voice. She's trying not to be affected by my proximity, but I want to see her unravel.

"They're not and you know they're not," I say sternly.

"They are."

"They're not."

"They are."

"They're not."

"They-

I cut her off by swiftly snaking my hands around her hot neck, feeling her pulse hammering, pulling at her hair, tilting her head further up to mine. She's shorter than me as it is, but this is taking it to another level. She blinks up at me and she licks her pink lips, making my dick twitch. I try my best to suppress a groan.

"Say it one more time and I'm going to drop you to your knees, work you up just right until you're begging for me and see how much you'll like to argue then," I whisper, bringing my face closer to hers. Those brown eyes never leave mine and I can see the arousal on her face, those perfect cheeks turning the cutest shade of pink.

She swallows. "Don't threaten me with a good time, Branson," she chokes out.

I wouldn't be able to help it anymore if I tried, so I press my mouth to hers, stealing the gasp that left her lips as I gripped onto her hair. Her body instantly responds to mine as my tongue finds a home in her mouth, feeling the warmth right down to every pressure point in my body. I hear the greedy hum in the back of her throat at the same time her hands find their way into my hair, pulling and yanking as if I'm the only thing keeping her alive.

That first kiss we had was insane. The second one? Even better. But *this?* This is like fucking outer space. I'm a cynic when it comes to astrology but fuck me if it doesn't feel like the stars aligned just for me and Scarlett at this moment.

I need more of her.

I use both of my hands to firmly grip the side of her face, feeling how small it is in my hands as I tilt her head back, deepening the kiss. I try to get more of her, and she lets me, each touch of mine gaining a spark reaction from her. Her hands loop around my neck, pulling me closer into her and I let her as she presses her chest against mine. Fuck. Our shirts are both so thin that I can feel the tips of her nipples pressing against my shirt.

Each time I try to press her further into the bookshelf, she pushes back, her back arching straight into mine. She's fighting me for it. Good. I'm starting to get dizzy just by kissing her. Is it hot in here or is that just us? Her angry, hard, and wet kisses light a fire within me, and I can't stop wanting more of her. I open my eyes for a second.

Big mistake.

Her eyes are closed, and her cheeks are completely red, her soft eyelashes resting against them. I've never seen her so caught up, messy and just turned on. She can't deny the pull between us as much as I've tried to. I lean down so I'm able to kiss along her throat, feeling her heart fluttering against my mouth.

"Is this what you want me to do, Angel? Do you want me to keep touching you, teasing you, feeling every inch of your skin until one of us can't take it anymore and give in? Because if you want to play that game, you'll be the first to lose."

"No, I wouldn't," she pants.

"No?" I repeat, biting the soft flesh on her neck before smoothing it out with a kiss. Her grip on my hair tightens. "Tell me stop, Scarlett."

"I- I can't," she stutters.

"Exactly," I murmur. "Are you ready to play this game?"

She nods enthusiastically. "Get on your knees," I say into her skin, and she moans quietly. My determined hands roam across the curves of her waist, down to her hips and back up again until I reach the underside of her breasts.

"I'm good from here," she whispers. Of course, she has to make this difficult.

"Scarlett," I warn.

"Evan."

"I said get on your knees," I say again, tilting my head until I'm face-to-face with her. She looks confident – proud of herself even. She's going to make me work for it, but I'm not a stranger to competition.

"I heard you," she replies, almost laughing. She leans up off the shelf as she steps closer into me, while I stand frozen. She tugs on my loose tie, pulling my face into hers. I brace my hand on the shelf behind her to keep me from falling into her. "Tell you an even better punishment?" Her voice is low, but thick and heavy with lust. "You on your knees for *me*. Because the way I see it – if you do your job right, you'll be the one begging me to stop moaning your name before we get kicked out of here. Would you like that? Does the thought of us getting caught excite you, Ev?"

This woman is going to kill me, and I think I'm going to let her.

I don't say anything other than trailing my hand up her bare thigh as she slowly releases the grip on my tie, a satisfied grin across her face as she relaxes back into the shelf. She wants me to make her feel good and that's exactly what I'm going to do.

She's a fucking dream.

Every inch of her feels perfect. Like it was designed specifically for me. Her body is so smooth that I ache just by touching her. She feels like she could just melt into my hands.

I grip onto her inner thigh, knowing it will drive her crazy before skimming the outside until I reach her round ass. I knead her ass with my palm as I press a kiss to the side of her neck and she sighs, finally relaxing more. She needs this just as much as I do.

"God, you're fucking perfect," I whisper.

"I know," she replies, laughing.

I love that she's confident. She doesn't *need* me to tell her she's pretty or that she's doing a good job because she knows it. But I know it turns her on to be praised, to feel like she's doing something right. I could tell from the second I helped her play pool.

"You're going to have to be quiet, Scar. Do you think you can do that for me?" I ask as both of my hands search around her ass, her arms resting on my shoulders.

"I'm starting to think I won't have a problem keeping quiet at this-" Her words cut off when I slipped my hand around from her ass to her panties where she's already wet and waiting for me. I've dreamt about this for fucking years, but nothing is compared to the real thing. "Oh my *god,*" she whines, her voice trembling.

"What was that, pretty girl?" I murmur into the side of her neck, my fingers light against the fabric of her panties. "It's funny, actually. You were about to shit talk me, but you're the one who is this wet and I've not even done anything yet."

"On. Your. Knees. *Now*," she demands, her breathing choppy. I tease her again and she gasps, tilting her head back and it gives me the perfect view of her pretty throat, all flushed and hot that I can't help but kiss her there.

"You know what? I think my view from here is pretty good," I say, repeating her words back to her.

"I'd prefer my view to be of your face between my thighs with your mouth glistening. How about that?" she argues, urging my shoulders down as I slowly sink to the floor. I run my hands down her thighs as I go down until I'm kneeling in front of her.

I want to die in this position.

"You really have a way with words, Angel," I murmur, stroking my thumb on the inside of her thigh. "You're a smart girl, Scarlett. Very smart, in fact. But you've got to promise me you'll be good and keep quiet, so we don't get kicked out."

I lift her skirt up, using her panties to rub against her pretty pussy as I swallow, trying to keep my composure.

"Ev," she whimpers. Not the answer I was looking for, but the sound sends waves pulsing straight down to my dick. We could get caught any minute, but for some reason that thought only makes me want this more because I'll be the one pushing her over the edge, and I want to see how far she'll go.

"Scarlett," I press, my tone light and teasing as I look up at her. She's not looking at me, though. Her head is tilted up, her hands gripping onto the lower bookshelves behind her as her ass presses into it. I rub the fabric against her again, urging her to look at me. She sighs, shuddering, finally looking down Her tongue darts out, running against her bottom lip, her chest heaving.

She's a fucking sight.

"I'll be good," she pants. "I promise."

"That's what I like to hear," I reply. I tug on the waistband of her panties. "Can I take these off now?" She nods eagerly and I take my time easing the material off her until it falls to her ankles.

I've not fooled around with many girls and Scarlett has a lot more experience than me, so I try not to let my anxieties show as I swipe my thumb over her swollen clit. Her thighs shake at the sensation, her whole body being completely responsive to me. So sensitive. I run two fingers over her flesh again, loving the soft, needy, and sweet sounds coming out of her mouth.

She needs me to do more and I'm sure as hell going to give it to her.

I tap on my shoulder. "Put your leg up here, sweetheart."

"No," she pants. "I can't."

"Why not?" I ask, still teasing her while goosebumps spread across her legs.

"Because it'll feel too good," she admits. Pride warms my chest. I'm hardly doing anything to her. Fuck. It turns me on just how easily she can come undone. "I don't know what the fuck you're doing, Evan, but…Oh my *God.*"

I laugh a little. "It's because you've been dreaming about this, Angel. I can tell. You've wanted me as much as I want you and now, you're finally having it," I explain. She doesn't argue. She does hook her leg over my shoulder though, her underwear hanging on the foot on the ground, giving me the perfect angle and view of her bare pussy.

I can't help myself anymore, so I collect her arousal with my finger, circling her clit before slowly pushing one of my fingers inside of her.

We both freeze.

This is it. We've officially crossed that line and I couldn't be happier about finally doing what I've been thinking about for years.

I know how big my fingers are and I can tell just how much I fill her by the way she clenches around me, her body lurching forward a little. I pump my finger in and out of her in a practised motion, watching the way her body reacts to mine.

Her leg trembles on my shoulder and I use it as ammunition to press my mouth to her.

Our reactions are both the same.

Pure and utter pleasure.

Everything about her tastes so good to me. So fucking sweet. I lay my tongue flat against her, her whole body trembles as she grips onto the shelf, causing it to shake. She's doing as I told, keeping quiet, but what's worse is that she's letting out these soft, half-moans, whimpering and gasping, which only spurs me on more.

I continue pumping in and out of her, hitting the spots that I know will tip her over, dying to find out how her body will react when she finally does. My tongue moves seamlessly with my fingers, sucking and licking like I'm starved. For her, I have been. Wanting someone – no, *needing* them – and then finally having them is a different kind of euphoria.

And she gives everything to me. Every moan. Every whimper. Every tremble of her body. Every shake of the bookshelf because she's gripping it too hard. Every fucking thing. And I take it all happily.

"Evan, I don't think I can…'" she cries as I push in and out of her mercifully, her body arching forward. She's not being vocal, which is good, but she keeps shaking the shelves which is just as bad, if not, worse.

"You can, baby. Just relax," I whisper into her flesh, the sound vibrating against her. As the words leave my mouth, I hear her slap her hand across her mouth, her other hand gripping onto my hair as she climaxes with a groan into her hand.

Her body shakes as she comes down from the high and I gingerly pull my fingers out of her as she moans softly. Jesus, she's a masterpiece. She slowly lowers her leg from my shoulder, and I help her slip her panties back on as I stand to my feet.

She avoids eye contact with me as she straightens out her blouse as if I didn't just wreck her and give her the best orgasm of her life. Her face is sweaty, hairs sticking to her forehead and her cheeks are the reddest I've ever seen. I can't help myself, so I stroke her cheek, her face resting in my hand. She melts into it for a second, her chest still heaving as she lets me hold her.

"That was just…" She sighs, her eyes closing slightly. She doesn't need to finish her sentence because I know exactly what she means.

"Yeah. It was," I reply. She tilts her head out of my hands, and I smooth her sweaty hair out of her face. "I knew you'd be a good girl for me."

She rolls her eyes, but I catch the satisfied smile on her face. She swats my hand from her face, turning away from me. "Let's just pick out a book and get out of here."

33

SCARLETT

I'VE NOT BEEN to many funerals in my life.

As a kid I went to my mom's parents' joint funeral, but I don't remember it. I remember the bleak colours and the crying, but that's about it. I remember that I had to stay by my family the whole day and there was a party after.

I went to two in the same week for Lucas and Sara, even though there were no bodies to be buried. I felt like I dissociated throughout most of the service anyway. It's not that I didn't care, but more that it was hard to feel. With my grandparents, I felt something so painful for them and I remember crying because everybody else was. But for Lucas and Sara, mostly because they were extended family, I didn't feel much. Or anything, really.

I either feel things at full volume or I feel nothing at all. For Gio, I'm in the middle of those two extremities. He meant so much to me, but hearing the way everybody is talking about him like he tried to murder my dad, it's hard not to feel a bit of anger towards him. All I can think is that he manipulated me into believing he is in danger, but he really was behind it the whole time. It explains his sketchy behaviour at the restaurant and at his house.

The service was nice, though. Quiet. Even though we held the service in LA because of the company and where other family members were buried, tons of people showed up. So much so that there were people standing outside the church waiting until we went to the cemetery. Both girls came with me for support and Evan did too, sitting with his dad in one of the far corners of the church.

It's good he didn't sit anywhere near me because of what happened in the library. I don't think I'm ready to look at him without my thoughts turning filthy and now is really, not the time. I still have no fucking clue how he managed to make me feel so good. Everything he did was so overwhelming, and it felt so... right. Which is fucking terrifying.

Evan and his dad are both wearing blacked out shades. His dad, Sam, is the exact double of Evan. I don't know what his mom looks like, but I doubt he has any of her features because of how alike he and his dad look. They've both got that sly smirk, blonde hair, sharp jaws, and a glare to kill. Sam's a handsome man and he doesn't look all that old. He could even pass for Evan's brother. I let myself wonder if Evan will look that good when he's older.

As we gathered around the burial spot in the cemetery amongst other Voss family members, Wren, and Kennedy by my side, each of them linked their arms in mine, I knew something was wrong before it happened.

The pastor was still reading his 'There is a time for everything' bible verse, Gio was already lowered in the ground, but not covered, when I locked my eyes with him. I saw the realisation that he'd been caught dawn on him the exact same time I put the pieces together.

"I'll be back in a minute," I told the girls.

"Okay, we'll be by the car when you're ready," Kennedy said, squeezing my hand before I slipped away from her.

So that's how I ended up following a guy who looked suspiciously familiar in the middle of my uncle's burial.

The second I laid eyes on him; he dropped his gaze to the ground and bolted. If he is who I think he is, why is running from me? I mean, people don't usually come back from the dead, but if it's not him then he doesn't need to be running.

It rained yesterday so my heels are getting stuck in the mud as I try to keep up with him. There are not many places to hide in a cemetery when the graves aren't big enough to hide a six-four man in a black hoodie and jeans.

"Listen," I shout. I'm only a few paces behind him now, far away from the burial. "Can you stop running? I can only go so far in heels."

Obviously, that doesn't stop him. Why would it? He's only come back from the dead. I try to keep up with him again, but he's picked up the pace, now darting along the path. Only it's cobblestones and my shoe keep getting stuck in the stone.

"Shit," I groan when I trip over, falling to my knees. The stones hit my knees and my hands graze the concrete, stinging both my knees and palms. As I go to stand, brushing off my skirt, he's turned back around now, standing right in front of me. He looks exactly the same; a full head of hair, messy and untamed beard, looking the same as the picture they used at his funeral service.

"Lucas?"

I knew saying his name out loud would make this all so real. For a second, I thought maybe I was going crazy. That I had made it all up in my head. I didn't expect the sick feeling I have in my stomach as he looked at me. He reaches out, to steady me maybe, but I take a step back.

"Did anyone follow you out here?" he asks. I look back and we're a good five minute walk away from the burial. I turn back to him, swallowing as I shake my head.

"What- What are you doing?" I ask. I try closing my eyes and opening them again, hoping that will make him disappear. This isn't happening. There is no way this is happening.

"Listen, Scarlett, I know you're probably confused, but you have to understand that-"

"You're alive, Lucas. Like, you're living and breathing right in front of me, of course I'm confused," I say, tripping over my words as I take another scan of his body. Yep. He's right in front of me. Alive. Not a corpse the police couldn't find. He's a real person with a beating heart and he's talking to me.

"As long as no one sees you, you need to go back. I've been trying to keep a low profile," he explains, glancing behind me. I just stare up at him, words failing me. He sighs, rolling his eyes. I need an explanation, but my brain still hasn't fully processed what I'm seeing, so words are the last thing that can come out of my mouth right now. "Look, only certain people know that I'm alive and I shouldn't be here, but I had to see Gio. I can't believe what happened to him. In hiding or not, he's still my best friend."

I nod, trying to understand him, but I'm still stuck on the part that he's *alive.* I went to his funeral. My dad cleared out his office. My mom lights a candle for him on every anniversary and his birthday. He was *gone.*

But he's not.

"Scarlett?"

"Yes," I say, shaking my head a little to look at him better. "Yes. Okay. I'll go back."

He nods at me, and I turn back around, mumbling to myself because...What the fuck? There are so many people here, all of us packed in like sardines.

I doubt anyone saw him, but I did. Sometimes I notice the most peculiar of things and that just happened to be one of them. I get why he would run away, but I need to know who the few people are that know he's alive and why they've been hiding it from the rest of the company.

When I get back to the burial area, I walk behind the girls, heading straight towards Evan, who's standing with his dad behind a huge group of people. They've both got their hands in their pockets, staring at the ground, looking identical. I'm panting by the time I'm in front of them.

"Ev," I say, gripping onto his arm so I don't fall into him. He looks down to me, his eyes a little sad and tired.

"Yes, Angel?" he asks. His dad raises his eyebrows at the nickname and my gaze snags on him for a second. What is in the Branson genes? They both look so picture perfect. *Not the time, Scarlett.*

"Can I talk to you for a minute?" I whisper, glancing back at his dad nervously. He smiles that Branson smirk and I do a double take before looking over at Evan. He must notice the weirdness of me sort-of meeting his dad for the first time because he also looks at him.

"Go talk to your girlfriend, boy. Seems like it's important," his dad says, still smiling.

Evan rolls his eyes as he smoothly removes my hand from his arm only to thread his fingers through mine as we walk in the opposite direction. His touch is so firm, yet everything about him is so sweet. He squeezes my hand as we walk through the crowd of people.

"Why does your dad think I'm your girlfriend?" I ask curiously, looking up at him. But he's not looking at me. He just starts to walk faster, tugging me along with him.

"Don't mind him," he says easily. When we're further away from the crowd, we stop at a large tree, and he pulls me behind it so we're out of view. "What did you want to talk about?"

I'm suddenly so hyper-aware of his presence that I almost forget what I was meant to say. His black suit is doing nothing but aid these filthy thoughts I've had since he went down on me in the library. Neither is the slightly angry look on his face. I shake my head as if it will get rid of the thoughts. I only realise we're still holding hands when he brushes his thumb against mine and it brings me back down to earth.

"Do you remember when I told you that Gio hasn't been feeling himself since his wife died in a plane crash along with his friend?" He nods. "Well, he's here." I wait for his reaction. For what? I don't know. He doesn't say anything, but he swallows. Hard. "Did you hear what I said, Branson? My family friend just came back from the *dead* and you've got nothing to say to that? Do you realise how fucking insane that is? And he's just here...At my uncle's funeral."

My mini ramble consists of more hand gestures than it does actual words. Evan just blinks at me. He slips his hand from mine, and I try to reach for it again, needing his warmth, but he doesn't let me take it.

"Scarlett," he says quietly. Once. He places his hands on my shoulders, his eyes dropping to the floor. I narrow my eyes, trying to figure out what's going on. The tone of his voice feels like a weight has dropped onto my stomach.

"Why are you talking to me like that?" I ask, worry coating my tone. My heartbeat starts to pick up, but I don't know why. He keeps his eyes on the ground, and I kneel down slightly, urging his head up. Even when he's looking at me, he's not really *there*.

"I already knew, Scar," he says. I don't understand the severity of his words, but I feel it in my stomach. It's that feeling you get where you don't know what's wrong, but your body already knows. It's like I just stepped off a rollercoaster. He swallows thickly, blinking up to the sky, his hands still gripping onto my shoulders. "My dad just told me and pointed him out to me. I was going to tell you after the funeral, but you saw him already."

"Ev, what aren't you telling me?" I ask. He finally looks at me, sighing. Those green eyes shimmer with something I can't quite place. It's something so far, yet so close that I don't think I even want to go.

"My dad asked me to get involved with you to find out what was really happening. They wanted to be the first to find out before the scandal went public, but then Gio died and they realised that it wasn't a good enough story to tell, so we ended up with nothing," he explains. His face has gone pale, as if he's forcing himself to tell me. Today has been weird enough. Each one of his words feel like daggers straight to my heart, but I tell myself to be strong.

"So, you used me?" I ask, my voice sounding foreign.

"You need to know that I didn't want to hurt you, Angel. I would never let anything happen to you or let my dad say anything harmful about you or your family, no matter how bad it got."

"That's not what I asked," I whisper, my chest heaving. I let out a shuddery exhale, trying to regulate my breathing. I need to stay calm. I can't spiral out. I just need to understand.

"Yes, it looks like I used you to get what my dad wanted, but everything that happened with the project was pure coincidence. I didn't plan that, I swear. As things started to get too real, I stopped doing it for them. I did it for us. Because I wanted to help *you* find closure. Everything you told me was because you trusted me, and I kept it to myself."

"You really expect me to trust you, right now?" He doesn't respond because that's when I start to feel the hot, angry tears running down my face. I can't cry right now. He can't see how badly this hurts. I wipe my tears quickly, stepping away from him so he can't hold onto my shoulder anymore. "Did you kiss me just to get closer to me? Was all that fake? You, saying those things, touching me like that... Did you not mean any of it? I had a feeling it was weird how you were being so nice to me, and I was stupid enough to believe you."

He steps closer to me. I take a step back. "I didn't kiss you for any other reason that I wanted to, that I've been *dying* to do since I met you. I care about you, Scarlett, more than I have ever cared about anyone. I respect you and I'm sorry. I'm so fucking sorry."

"You don't do things like that to the people you care about, Evan," I say through a sob, shoving at his chest as he tries to close the distance between us again. He looks more upset now, his face suddenly red. "I asked for one thing from you. I forgave you for what you said. I wanted to be your friend, for God's sake and you ruined that."

He runs his hand through his hair. "You're right. I fucked up and I'm sorry. I don't want to argue with you, but I don't want to make you upset, and I can't bear to look at you cry," he says thickly. He turns to walk away, but I go after him, pulling on his arm, turning him back to me.

"No," I warn. He heaves out a breath, looking around. "No," I say again, quieter. "You're going to argue with me, Evan, because that's what we do. You fight with me and you're going to fight *for* me. So, explain yourself. Now. Because I *really* don't want to think I was stupid enough to have trusted you, so you better give me a good enough reason or – so help me God – I will make your life a living hell and I will never speak to you again."

I want to have a conversation. I don't want whatever we built to dissipate just because he did something stupid. I've done countless stupid, manipulative, and ridiculous things in my life. I wasted so much time hating him without hearing him out that first week at NU. I'm not about to do it again. Not after the way he's held me, taken care of me and spoken to me in the last few weeks. This isn't like the other guys I've hooked up with. This is him. I refuse to believe that was all for nothing.

He runs both of his hands down his face. "Scar."

"Explain yourself. Now," I say, rubbing the last of the tears from my face. I take a deep breath because I need to be strong. I can't keep missing out on possibly great things because I'm scared of people hurting me. If he hurts me, he's going to fix it.

"I was desperate, Scarlett, you've got to understand that. I was cut off from my family after what happened with Cat, and this was the only way my dad said he would let me back in. You probably won't get it because your family is different. You might not get along, but you love each other, and you show it. I've always wanted that - a family, a relationship where love and intimacy wasn't so unheard of. I thought, maybe if I get back in, I could try and get that for my family, too. But it got to a point where I didn't even realise that I was doing it for them because I wanted to help *you*. I gave him half-assed explanations because I wanted us to figure it out because..." He lets out a shaky breath, his green eyes looking directly into mine. "Because we're a team, Scar. Me and you. We do things together. We might fight and argue, but at the end of the day, it's just me and you. It always has been."

I flicker my gaze to the ground for a second, needing the short time to collect myself before I get completely lost and transfixed in his eyes again. His words mean more to me than anyone else's. His words, his actions, are what are going to keep us together in whatever way that is.

"You could have told me, and we could have figured it out, you know?"

"I tried to tell you, but then Gio-"

I cut him off. "You had so many chances, Ev. So many. When we were smoking, you could have mentioned it. The countless times when we worked in silence could have made a perfect opportunity. When we kissed... There's been so many opportunities."

"I was scared, Scar. I was fucking terrified. You already hated me, and we were starting to get somewhere, and I didn't want to push you away again. I know that's exactly what I've done, but you've got to see that I didn't want to do that," he says, his voice thick with emotion. "I just want to be close to you. All the time."

I believe him. From the way he's treated me, regardless of his initial intentions, I know he would never try to hurt me. I know that he's been trying to prove himself to me, to show me who he really is. I didn't believe him the first time and it gives me all the reasons to want to trust him now. People have used me before for their own personal gain, but from the look in his eyes, the pain in his voice, I can tell that all he wanted was his family back and a chance at a real one. He doesn't need my money. He doesn't need my fame. From the way I've treated him, he's had limited options to get me to like him.

That's the reason why I walk closer to him and as his hands fall from his neck, I wrap my arms around his middle, resting my head on his chest. I feel the exact moment he relaxes, where his heartbeat steadies and his arms wrap around me.

Sometimes, no matter how much he makes me want to rip out my hair, I want to be close to him. It feels like no matter how far apart we can try to get from each other, how much we can piss each other off, there's always this string tugging us closer together. Needing each other. Even if that was just to argue or shout, we've always needed this. Each other.

"Are we going to be okay?" he asks into my hair.

"I still think I'm going to need some time to really mull it over, but... I don't know," I say truthfully. I want, more than anything, to give him the second chance he deserves from the hell I've put him through. But I also need to get my emotions and feelings in check. Weirdly enough, therapy has been helping with that and I want it to continue.

"Are you angry with me?" he asks, and his strangled voice breaks my heart. I look up at him, resting my chin on his chest. I watch his throat contract as he swallows before looking down at me.

"I don't think I could give you a proper answer to that right now," I admit. He nods, finally looking down at me. He's going to have to understand that and be patient with me while I figure this out. He presses the softest kiss to my forehead, and I melt into his touch, sighing a true breath of relief.

"Is that- Can I still- Was that..." he mutters.

"It's okay," I say, resting my head on his chest again,

turning my face away from him. "I want us to be mature about this, Evan. I don't want to spiral. I'm so sick of doing that. You did something bad, you apologised, but I'm going to need to take a step back for a bit to figure my shit out."

"Okay," he says, softly, holding onto me tighter. "That's okay. Anything you want."

34

SCARLETT

SOMETIMES, your best friends can help you so much. They can give you insane advice and make you realise you've done something stupid. They can tell you over and over, potentially lying to you to convince you you're a fantastic person. Or they're like my friends, who go back on their word every two seconds as well as changing the topic.

I came to them for advice on the Evan situation. They don't know that we kissed. *Three times.* They also don't know that I let him eat me out in the library and how much I fucking loved it. Those are the kind of memories I like to keep to myself for a late night and a battery-powered friend. If I told them, their advice would definitely change, and they'd be gloating about how right they were. They said that breaching that sexual barrier would smooth things out, but it hasn't. It only makes me want him more. I itch to be near him again. To touch him again. To have him whisper dirty things in my hair. To tell me I'm his good girl. It wasn't like kicking a habit. It's just like starting one.

I explained to them how we got closer and how he was in it

for his family. Still, saying those words aloud did not make me feel any more resentment towards him. In fact, it helped me understand him.

His family is a mess and he wanted to fix it. Was the way he did it unconventional? Yes. But it also brought us together in a new way. Sometimes I could see right through him, and I never saw an evil bone in his body, and I just have to trust that. I just have to trust him.

As soon as I started crying when I went back to them at the burial, Wren called her dad and booked us a flight to Vegas so we could spend a week away escaping. Since Wren's dad is a hotelier, he would take me and Wren on trips to his new hotels across the country where we'd spend the whole time at spas and feeling older than we actually were. As soon as Kennedy joined the group, she came along too and then we started to get into cheesy rom-coms, eating room service and staying up past our bedtime, talking about everything and nothing.

That's why it feels so natural to be sitting in a California king sized bed, all in our robes, our hair tied into a towel, *The Proposal* playing on the flatscreen while we eat a pizza. We've been going in circles for the last hour and I'm not sure we're getting anywhere with my current situation.

"I mean, it's not like you guys made out or anything. That would be a *lot* worse. The physical stuff is always harder," Kennedy says through a mouthful, wiping the grease away with her palm.

"Yeah, that would be insane," I say, trying to laugh a little. Wren studies me curiously, but I drop my gaze from her, not letting her figure it out. I take another bite of the pizza. "But," I add, before swallowing. "I can see where he's coming from and why he did what he did, but I also know that he would never want to intentionally hurt me. He's proved that to me more than once."

I think back to the number of times he's helped me without asking. How he doesn't complain. How he does things willingly. *Just because.* He's never asked anything of me. He doesn't invalidate my feelings when I feel like doing it. He encourages me and makes me feel capable even when sometimes I don't.

"You like him, don't you?" Ken says, easily as if she's got me all figured out. Maybe she has. When I don't respond as I feel my face crowd with heat, she starts giggling. "Oh my god. You *liiikkeee hiiimm.*"

I push her playfully in the shoulder and she breaks our little circle by toppling over onto the bed. She's been rooting for us to sort out our frenemy relationship and now she's getting what she wanted. She's still laughing like an evil genius as she leans up on her elbows.

"So what?" I try to say it casually, but it's hard to do when it feels like my whole body is on fire. Every time I think about him, everything he's done for me, everything he's said to me, it's impossible to feel cool, calm, and collected. I feel the opposite. I most certainly have the hots for Evan Branson.

What is life?

"So what?!" Wren repeats, basically shrieking. She holds my stare. "I'm not saying to over analyse it. But babe... You always tell us not to invalidate our feelings, but you're about to do that, so don't."

I sigh, knowing she's right. When she tried to deny her feelings for Miles, I told her not to. I didn't tell her to confess her love for him, but to let herself feel how she's feeling. Maybe I need to do that too. But God, that's terrifying. Being attracted to someone is one thing. But caring about them, wanting to see them happy, wanting them all the time... That's a new one for me and weirdly exactly how I feel about Evan.

"Okay," I say, sighing and they both smile wide, grinning ear-to-ear so I continue. "He's kind to me, he listens, he brings me food, he's not bad looking, he-"

"How long is this list?" Kennedy asks, cutting me off as she narrows her eyes at me, smirking. I twist my lips, pulling them into my mouth as I shake my head.

I shrug. "I don't know."

"There's your answer," she says with finality, her elbows buckling as she lies back down, her towel coming undone, unleashing her wild hair.

Wren twists the belt loop of her robe between her fingers as she says quietly, "What he did was messed up, Scar. We know that. I'm trying to be optimistic here and isn't it kind of a blessing in disguise? If he never approached you for the project, you wouldn't have come up with such a cool idea. The app is amazing so far and it could honestly make you famous if you two continued it. You wouldn't have been able to find out what happened to your dad, and you wouldn't have broken that barrier that was keeping you two apart. You just needed a shove."

She ends her explanation with a shrug, almost scared of what I'm going to say next. I tilt my head back, taking in a breath to mull over her idea.

"I don't like the way he did it. Out of every way he could have made a move to be my friend, to let him in, he chose the one that hurt the most," I reply.

Technically, nobody got hurt as bad as it could've been, but it still stings. His family has nothing on mine, so it's not like we'll go down for anything. Reporters are taking the situation with Gio into their own hands, but since he's gone it's easy for them to dismiss him as a traitor. Weighing the pros and cons like I've been taught, only puts him more and more in a better position, making me want to give him a chance.

"You don't have to like the process to enjoy the outcome. If you like him now, if you want him, in whatever way, lead with that. What happened is in the past. Believe me, I could have prevented mine and Miles's break up if I just spoke to him. If I trusted him."

I nod, remembering how hard her breakup with Miles was. Their communication wasn't the greatest, but as they started to figure it out, they came back stronger than ever. Now they're basically attached at the hip. Sometimes I think Miles doesn't breathe when she's not around him. They're always holding hands, he's always touching her waist, her hair, basically anything he can get his hands on when she's next to him.

"Do you trust Evan?" Kennedy asks, leaning back up now.

"I did. I was learning to and then this happened," I respond.

"He's telling you the truth now, though, isn't he?" I nod. He has to be. He knows how badly this has affected me and I could see in his eyes, in his voice, that he wants me to trust him for real. But sometimes those things take time. "Is that not enough?"

"It can be," I whisper. "I don't want to be in my head all the time. It's fucking exhausting. I know that everything that happened in high school made that hard, but I don't want to go back to that place. I know deep down that Evan's a good person."

Wren's face lights up as if I've told her the greatest news ever. Another *Scarevan* supporter as she likes to call us. She pokes me in the leg.

"He always has been. You've just been too stubborn to notice it."

"I know," I sigh, feeling ridiculous and hopeful at the same time.

"Okay," Kennedy exclaims, standing up from the bed. "Pool time!"

♫ WHAT WAS **I Made For? By Billie Eilish**

WE GET DOWN to the infinity pool and it's empty for once. It's pretty late into the night and the glow coming from the lights in the pool is the only thing keeping it bright. Bright stars shine in the sky, making everything that has happened feel so small and insignificant.

After timing Kennedy's laps in the pool, we all sit in the jacuzzi.

Timing her laps has been a requirement for our friendship. If there's a body of water she can swim in, we have to see if she can beat her personal record that she had back home.

We all lean our heads against the sides, breathing in the chilly air whilst also feeling the warmth of the tub. We're well into the middle of December now and it's freezing, but there's still that warmth coming from the jacuzzi that I hardly notice.

"Can I ask you guys something? And you've got to be honest with me," Kennedy whispers. I keep my head back, not wanting to break the spell of this moment, here with my girls.

"Always," Wren says. I hear Ken take in a deep breath, the exhale sort of shaky.

"In five years from now, when we're done with school,

we'll hopefully all have a job, do you think we'll still be friends? And I mean friends like this. Friends who complain about my stress induced pee breaks, friends who cry over edits together, friends who take last minute trips to Las Vegas because one of us is going through a hard time. Friends like *that*."

The weight of her words hit me like a punch to the stomach. I try not to think about the *after* period of our lives. Living together has brought us closer in so many ways and I always wonder what's going to happen after. Miles and Wren will most likely move in together and maybe me and Ken will be left on our own.

What then? Will we still use The Whiteboard for emergency meetings? Will I still pick her up from Florentino's, even though it's only a fifteen minute walk from our apartment. Will it even still be our apartment? Will Kennedy move out and go back home to South Carolina? Will I be on my own?

There's a time, like now, where our bond feels like it transcends above space and time. As if we would exist even if we weren't the entities we are now. Even if we were rocks, or stars, or pieces of dirt, it would always be us three. Wren Hackerly, Kennedy Wynter and Scarlett Voss. My girls. My sisters.

"Of course, we will, Ken," I say, needing so desperately to believe it. As the words leave my mouth, I cling onto it, knowing that we all need it. "Why would you ask that?"

She sighs. "I don't know. Sometimes when we have these great moments, I can't help but think they won't last. Like we'll burn each other out."

"I could never get sick of you guys," Wren says, laughing a little. "I'll be honest. I thought I would want to kill you all by the second week of living together, but I didn't. I think it's because I know that even when things get hard, these are the kind of moments I'm going to cherish forever. No matter what happens."

"See," Kennedy says, almost angrily. "*That*. The '*no matter what happens*' bullshit. We can't do that. We can't accept the idea that we'll eventually drift apart. I need you girls. If you're going through it, we're all going to go through it. Together. I want *us* to grow old together, and have our kids grow old together."

"I want that too," I say.

"Me too," Wren adds. I lean my head up, looking between them both and my heart just feels so…full. So complete. "You guys are my forever friends."

"Forever friends?" Ken asks.

"Until my teeth rot and my boobs sag," I say in a grandma voice.

"Until my backs crackin' and my toenails are scraping against the floor," Kennedy adds, making it seem like she's gonna be a hobo when she's older. Odd, but great.

"Until I'm dead and gone and buried," Wren says.

"You just had to bring Taylor into it, didn't you?" Kennedy says laughing.

"It was instinct. She'll never go out of style."

Then we're all laughing again at the reference. Kennedy's gripping onto the tub, laughing hysterically. Wrens wheezing and I'm just grinning ear to ear because I know what they mean. We will always have each other. I had always wanted a sister growing up, someone I could turn to for advice, but I know I don't need one. I've always had two of them.

Forever friends.

35

EVAN

LEAVING Scarlett that day was the hardest thing I've ever done, but I had to do it. No matter how shitty these past few weeks have been without seeing her, only exchanging texts about the project, I know it's for the better. She needs time and I'm sure as hell going to give it to her.

She's right. I did a stupid thing. So, I'm facing the consequences, which means fucking my fist to the images of what we did in the library and having my dad berate me over the phone. The latter, happening more frequently than I'd like to admit. I can't even go into the kitchen to get a drink without my phone ringing. I know better to answer it, or he will drive here himself to talk to me.

"We've got nothing now, Evan. Do you hear me? *Nothing. Nada,*" my dad shouts. I hear the glass he's most likely got in his hand slamming against the table, and I flinch.

"Jesus, stop shouting," I say, resting my phone on my shoulder wedging it with my ear so I can open the fridge. I filled it the other day, but Xavier and Miles eat like animals, so we're already in need of a refill. I pluck out a protein shake and shut it.

"Was it worth it?" my dad asks. I sigh, moving to look out the window, only to look into the backyard, remembering the day we watched Brooklyn Nine-Nine episodes in the gazebo and everything that happened after. I shake my head, desperate to get rid of the longing feeling in my chest.

"Was what worth it?" I ask.

He groans. "Dropping us for her. Because I sure as hell can't see any benefits when this story is tied up too neatly and we've got nothing out of it. The only upside is that Mateo is still comatose."

I don't see how that's an upside, but I think better than to argue.

"Yes, I think it was worth it, dad. She's an amazing girl and she doesn't deserve to be treated the way I treated her. I've spent so long trying to get her to notice me and I fucked up and I want to fix it. Even if that means you're still cutting me off."

"Are you sure you want to do this? You could keep digging without her knowing," he suggests. Just the thought of it makes my stomach turn. I don't want to ever be the reason she's crying again. Ever. And I'm going to make that promise to her over and over because I don't want her to hurt because of me.

"And lie to her again? I'm good," I mutter, turning away from the bleak backyard to lean against the sink. "Look, I'm not expecting you to understand it, but dad, she is quite literally the perfect person. *My* perfect person. I hate what I did, and I want to make it up to her. The mystery is solved, and I've got a grade to get. So, I'm going to drop it and I'm going to try and get the girl. Is that cool?" He doesn't say anything other than a groan. Jesus, I sound like a lovesick puppy now. "Good. Now stop calling me, you freak."

I close my eyes for a second, finally being able to breathe. I still have no idea how *exactly* I'm going to get the girl, but saying it aloud has helped. There's nothing I want more than to get her to notice me again. To get her to let me be there for her, be good for her, all the time. Not just sometimes when she's feeling vulnerable, but every day.

"Who are you calling a freak?" Miles asks, walking into the kitchen. He's topless, of course.

"My dad," I say, rubbing at my temples.

"Oh," he replies. He opens the fridge, only to stare at it as he says, "Hey, I'm actually kinda bummed about what happened with you and Scarlett."

"What are you talking about? Nothing happened."

I'm in denial, clearly. She said she's going to take time and we're gonna go back to talking — or arguing — again. That's all he needs to know. He doesn't know about what our relationship was like before and he doesn't need to either. He's a loyal friend, but he also talks too much. If he knew we were fooling around, he'd most definitely tell his girlfriend.

"Right…" he says, clearly unconvinced. He pulls out a can of soda, shutting the fridge door before leaning against it, staring at his shoes as he twists the can in his hand. "Well, Wren said you've not been speaking, which is saying something considering you used to argue all the time. I don't know the full details, but sort it out, okay? You guys might not always get on, but you're like my family and I don't want to lose that because of a stupid fall out."

As much as I give him a hard time, living here isn't so bad. The nights when we're all home and their girlfriends aren't over, we tolerate each other. We can put on a good movie and just hang out. Or we play a game of pool in the den or a stupid drinking game. I act like I hate it, but secretly, I've always wanted brothers.

"I know," I sigh. "I'm trying here, Davis."

He nods thoughtfully before that mischievous smirk takes over his face. "You know… I could teach you a few things. You can learn how to grovel."

I close my eyes for a second at his stupidity. "And how do I do that?"

He cracks open the soda and my eyes pop open. "So, say Wrenny's mad at me because I turned up late to dinner or I forgot her sister's birthday. What do you think I should do?"

"Apologise and wear a watch?" I say. It's the most natural thing to do. How else are you supposed to be forgiven?

"Right, but you've also got to factor in a few other things," he explains, going full-on teacher mode. He stands up straighter, talking with his hands. "Firstly, I'd apologise, give her a mind-shattering orgasm, apologise again and maybe do something that she likes. Like reading a book she likes. You know, showing her that I'm interested in what she likes."

I snort. "You think the best way to get Scarlett to forgive me is to give her a mind shattering orgasm?" I mean, I've done it before, but he doesn't know that.

"Well, I guess it's different for you. you guys hate each other," he mutters before sipping his soda innocently.

"Can you stop saying that? I don't hate her, and I never have," I snap, sick of these accusations. I get it. It seems that way because of the way she's treated me and the way I've played along, but for once, I'd like somebody to see that I've liked her for as long as I can remember.

"Well, you act like it," he murmurs, looking to the ground again.

"Because she hates me, and I want her. I've wanted her since the first time I saw her with that stupid fucking ribbon in her hair. I've wanted her since she shouted at me for the first time in class. I wanted her when she shoved bacon in my face at Christmas. I finally got her to trust me and now she hates me again. Is that so hard to understand?"

Miles gulps. "No."

"Okay, look, I'm sorry for shouting, but it's really hard not to get angry right now, especially when I shouldn't be because this is my fault. I'm the one that messed up," I say, running my hand through my hair.

I probably shouldn't have told him that I want her but fuck it. It's obvious at this point or I wouldn't care. I wouldn't have cried like a fucking baby when I got home after the funeral. I wouldn't feel this heavy, dirty weight on my chest for making her cry.

"Admitting that you both hurt each other doesn't make you a bad person, you know?" Miles says. When did it get hard to breathe again? And why is what he's saying making sense to me? I hate it. "You can be angry at her for how she treated you, the same way she's angry at you for how you treated her. It's okay, Branson."

That is when I start to feel it; the tightening of my chest and nothing but the sound of my own blood sloshing through my body.

I feel the hot flushes on my neck and my back, making it feel like my shirt is suffocating me. I grip onto the countertop, my other hand over my chest, smoothing it out

God, does this have to happen right now? In front of him?

I've been trying to keep cool about this whole thing since it happened. I know what I did was stupid and reckless, but I didn't want to be angry at her. I can't be angry at her. I'm the one who hurt her, but I still can't help but think about all the time we wasted when I could have had her from the beginning. If she didn't immediately cast me as the villain without hearing me out.

"You good?" Miles asks, coming behind me. I try to speak, but words fail me as I attempt to regulate my breathing. The more I tell myself I'm okay, the faster my heart races and the more it hurts. "Panic attack?" I nod, taking a deep breath. I glance at him as he stands beside me now, crossing his arms against his chest. I can't tell if hearing him talking is making it better or worse. "Yeah, I used to get those, too. Not that much anymore."

"Thanks for that, Davis. You're really helping," I get out, still clutching my chest. I rub my palm against my heart, trying my best to relax but it's really fucking difficult.

"Do you remember the first day you moved in here? Me, Carter, and Xavier were trying out our first keg and it exploded all over you and your prissy suit," Miles says, laughing at the memory. I remember that day. I remember it being one of the worst days of my life.

"What are you doing?" I choke out, basically panting.

He ignores me and continues talking. "After you got changed, we went to apologise, and you told us we'd never get on. You said we were too much for you and the only reason you were here is because your dad was being a dick. When Carter died, you fed me, and Xavier and you watched stupid cartoons with us that first night and every night after that for weeks. We never said anything because we thought we were too cool for it, and you didn't either. When we started to get on our feet again, we still didn't say anything. But you helped us even though you swore you wouldn't. Because that's what family does, Branson. We can hold grudges, but we can also be there for each other when we need it. And you're that person. You're always there. No matter what."

When his rant ends, I realise I've been breathing normally again. He was distracting me. My hands still tremble, but I can feel my body slowly settling back to normal. I take in a deep breath, my chest shaking on the exhale.

"Thanks for that," I say. He smiles wide, dimples popping out and all.

He shrugs as if it's no big deal. "It's fine. I never really thanked you for that, but you should know how grateful we are. We seriously would've died without you."

"I know you would have," I say, chuckling.

"In fact, to make it up to you…" Miles starts, sounding as cheery as ever. He opens the fridge again, scanning its contents. "How about I cook tonight? I make a mean chicken salad."

"For both of our sakes, I'll stick to cooking. You stick to doing the dishes."

He turns back around, grinning. "Good idea"

That's when I realised that these guys have my back. They always have.

36

SCARLETT

HAVE you ever tried to find the contact information for a guy that was pronounced dead three years ago? Because I have. And it wasn't an easy feat.

After scouring through records at Voss HQ, I couldn't find anything on Lucas. I know I should stop digging, but I'm still confused as fuck as to how he's just alive and breathing like nothing happened and why nobody told me about it.

I even considered asking Arthur what was going on, but we've hardly spoken since he called me a whore in front of everyone at dinner. Even if I pestered him enough, I knew he wouldn't tell me anything, so I had to take matters into my own hands. Again.

Things have been tense in my family during the holiday period. Christmas was a shitshow. I spent Christmas Eve at my parents' house like always and we ate dinner in near silence. I spent Christmas day with the girls, but it didn't feel anywhere near as good as it usually does.

Because Evan wasn't there, and I didn't have a tray full of bacon to shove into his mouth like I did last year. Instead, I spent the day curled up in bed, watching *The Grinch* while I ate my body's weight in chocolate.

For the first time in years, I stayed home on New Years Eve as I encouraged the rest of the girls to go out without me. Instead, I stayed in bed, alternating between texting my therapist or Evan. In the end I settled for neither, preferring the comfort of popcorn and a cheesy sitcom. Dr. Nelson is concerned, but I promised I'd call her back eventually.

It took days, hours, and hours of staring at a screen and flicking through books and calling random people until I finally found Lucas's number. I used my burner phone to call him so he would actually answer. Still, I have no idea what I'm planning on saying until the phone connects.

"Hey, it's Scarlett. I know we got off on the wrong foot, but I just wanted to speak to you. You know, about you being alive and all that," I say, trying to make light of the situation as I ramble on. I watch the black and white clock on my bedroom wall tick as he doesn't say anything. I double check that he hasn't ended the call on me, lifting my feet up to rest on my desk. "Hello?"

"I already told you what you want you need to know, Scarlett," he says finally. Good. At least he's talking. Sort of. I'm not a fan of his tone, though. He sounds annoyed – pissed, even.

"Yeah, I know, but I just don't fully understand," I say, trying to keep calm. "Why would you come to the funeral? Risk being seen?"

"Giovanni was my best friend. In hiding or not, I was going to show up for him. He showed up for me. As soon as I heard what had happened, I had to go," he explains. That makes sense. If I was undercover and my best friend died, I wouldn't care. But *why* is he undercover? What is he running from? I'm sure people would be delighted to know he made it out alive. "And I'm sorry for that. For you having to see what you did."

It takes me a few seconds to realise what he's talking about. Even though Dr. Nelson tells me it's okay to be shutting out the memories of what happened, a part of me still feels guilty. I don't want to remember it because of how much it hurt seeing him like that, in so much pain. But those are also the last memories I have with him and the one I had before that — thinking he was covering up a crime scene in his backyard — is not any more pleasant. Blocking it out feels right for now.

"I never told you I was there," I whisper. Our conversation was short at the funeral. There's no way I would have dumped that on him. I was already in too much shock.

"Reports," he replies, "they talk." Of course, they do because I can't get one minute of privacy apparently, even after people walked past the scene, leaving us to clean it up. I tried to have the bad stories scrubbed clean, getting the best bits of Gios personality, but they've not made any changes, still casting him as the villain. "Listen, I'm glad you called, Scarlett, but I don't have time."

I snort. "You don't have the time? You're a dead man walking. What could you possibly have to do that's more important than answering a few questions from your best friend's niece."

"I can think of a few things."

"Yeah? Name one," I challenge.

"Bills," he replies gruffly. Bills my ass.

"You're full of shit," I argue, my temper rising.

"Look, I know you're upset about your uncle, and you're

shocked. It's understandable. Right now, all you should focus on is school and your dad getting better if he wakes up."

"*When*," I correct, my throat goes dry.

"What?"

"*When* he wakes up. Not if."

"Right. I'm sorry," he says. I don't respond to that. Just the thought of my dad not waking up makes my stomach swarm with angry butterflies. "I really do have to go. Take care."

THE GIRLS HAVE NOT LEFT my side since the trip to Las Vegas. I thought we were attached at the hip in middle school and high school, but now it's even worse. I can't decide if it's a good thing or not. I meant it when I said they are my forever friends. But that also means they're up my ass twenty-four-seven as if they're talking me out of jumping off a cliff. No matter how many times I tell them I'm fine, they can't help double and triple checking.

"Do you want some ice cream, Scar?" Wren calls from the kitchen.

"No, I'm good," I reply.

"Baby, I want some," Miles chimes up from his spot across from me on the sofa. Kennedy rolls her eyes and I scoff.

"I wasn't asking you," Wren retorts. Miles sulks in his seat, pouting his lip and crossing his arms. God, he's such a baby. *How does Wren cope?* She also can't resist him sometimes, so she asks, "What flavour do you want?"

"Chocolate, please," he replies happily, grinning at me like he won the lottery. I stick my tongue out at him, and he sticks his out at me. See? He's such a baby.

"Do you want a croissant, Scarlett?" Wren asks again.

"My answer is the same as before, Wrenny," I say, trying not to laugh at her protective tendencies.

"You've got to eat something. I'm worried about you," she says, and I don't have to look behind me to tell she's frowning. She's like a full-time mom right now. Each week, we switch who gets to play the mother and clearly this week it's Wren's turn.

"Well, don't be," I say. "We just had pizza." I turn to Miles, narrowing my eyes at him as he eats the chips on the table. "Your boyfriend is the one with a vacuum for a mouth."

Miles flips me off as Wren laughs, padding into the room with two bowls of ice cream. She hands one to Kennedy in her bean bag as she retrieves it happily and gives the other to Miles before she slides into his lap. I hit play on the episode of *New Girl* we're watching, and we all fall into a comfortable silence.

Even with Wren and Kennedy up my ass every two minutes making sure I'm okay, I'm getting used to preferring this over solitude. They make everything feel better. It helps me feel like everything is going to be okay. If I want to ignore something, they'll pretend it never happened. If I want to shit-talk somebody, they'll do it happily. They just get me and allow me to exist without feeling like a burden.

🎵 **It'll Be Okay by Shawn Mendes**

When the episode transitions into a new one, I use the opportunity to sneak into the kitchen for a drink. We've been stocked on — *what Kennedy calls* — 'Sad Snacks' for the last few days, the girls insisting that I need them.

As I reach for the shelf where the glasses are, I'm hit with strong déjà vu, remembering Evan towering over me, touching my waist, his breath hot on my neck. The way I could feel his eyes lingering on my almost naked body. His strong, hot hand holding me, steadying me.

"Do you want me to get that for you?"

I turn around and Miles is behind me, placing the bowls into the sink. I realise that I must have been frozen on my way up to get the glass and he tilts his head to the side curiously. I blink at him a few times, trying to get the image of Evan out of my head.

"I'm okay," I say, jumping slightly to reach it. I almost miss it, but I end up getting it anyway, triumphant as I move to the fridge to fill up the glass with the water dispenser. I'm ready to make my escape back to my seat, but Miles grips onto my elbow, pulling me back into the kitchen. "Can I help you, Davis?"

"Actually, you can," he says cheerfully. "Do you think you could possibly, maybe, definitely be friends with Evan again?"

"What?" I almost laugh.

Miles and I's relationship isn't as close as it could be, so I don't know why he's asking me. He's dating my best friend. I hear him fucking her more often than I'd like and he's annoyingly good to her. He likes to irritate me and call everyone stupid nicknames. And he talks too much, too. I guess we're alike in that department.

"I know what he did was fucked up, but he cares about you, Scarlett. I've never seen him cry the way he did when he came back that night," he says thickly, and it feels like a punch to the stomach.

"Are you trying to make me feel even worse than I do, Davis?" I ask, looking to the ground and then back up at him. He's watching me, trying to figure me out.

"You feel bad?" he asks, genuinely shocked.

"Of course, I do. I know I shouldn't because he's the one

that hurt me, but I know that he's never had a malicious bone in his body. I know he's been waiting for *me* to look up and notice him, but I've been too stubborn and scared to admit that he's not actually a bad person. He's done countless nice things for me to make up for it and I was too frightened to let him."

Miles' mouth hangs open in an 'O' shape as if I just told him Victoria's secret. I don't know what he and Evan have been talking about, but he looks like he's seen a ghost.

"Then tell him that," he says, exasperated.

"What?" I laugh.

"Go and tell him that. He's been making himself sick over you, Scar, and his bad mood is bringing down the vibes. Go and tell him that you're sorry, that you love him so we can all move on with our lives already."

"I never said I love him," I say defensively.

"You didn't have to," Miles mutters. *What the hell....* Wren better gets her man in check because he's seriously confusing me right now. "I'm not trying to force you, obviously. That will come on your own time, but it sounds to me that you understand each other more than you realise, and I can't take him looking like a sad puppy all day. Honestly, I think he'd prefer you to scream at him rather than this silence."

"Do you really think so?" I ask quietly.

"Oh, I know so, Scarely," he replies, grinning. He really surprised me with that analysis of our relationship. I don't know when he started to sound so wise. I knew him back when I dated Jake, and I've never heard him talk like this. But he's back to being annoying. Great.

"Stop calling me that, you dork," I say, laughing.

"Not until you and Evan become frenemies again," he challenges.

"Since when were you two besties?" I ask, genuinely curious. "Last I heard, he said you guys weren't even friends."

Miles clutches his chest dramatically. "Okay, ouch. He was in denial. We've come to a truce."

"Right…" I drag out, eying him suspiciously.

"All I'm saying is, when you're ready, put him out of his misery. His bad vibes make me queasy." He shudders for extra effect.

"You make me queasy," I mutter as I walk past him, back into the living room.

Maybe I do need to talk to him. I've had time to reflect, and I don't want a good thing to go to waste because I'm scared. Watching Wren and Miles cuddle while we watch the show, they make it seem so easy. Almost dangerously easy.

SHE'S WEARING THE DRESS.

She hasn't seen me yet, but she's wearing it. The same dress she wore the first time she came to my house, only to tell me she's wearing it for someone else. The same one she wore when I carried her through the muddy forest. The same dress she wore when she put her legs in my lap in the car ride home.

The fucking dress.

We've hardly seen each other in the last few weeks, and it's been harder and harder to resist her. I don't want to approach her first and I don't want to scare her off. Since winter break, most classes have gone by in a blur. We listen to whatever Anderson has to say, she texts me what I should do for the project, and I do it. We're going to have to get together soon to work on our presentation, but I was planning on waiting until then to see if we could talk.

What I wasn't planning was seeing her tonight. Especially not dressed like that.

The Bailey Foundation is one of the most prestigious and popular nights for businessmen and their families. It's a night filled with good food, expensive drinks, decent music, and obnoxious men hoping to expand their businesses or create greater trading links. My dad told me to stay by his side tonight, but it's hard to do when I can see Scarlett, Wren and Kennedy walking around and I'm itching to be near her again.

My dad has kept us busy, talking with boring businessmen about stocks and shit I couldn't give a damn about. Maybe another time, but not when she's here. Especially not when she's looking like *that*. She's not got a ribbon in tonight, so her hair rests angelically on her shoulders, her natural wavy style, not straightened.

I realise I've been looking at her for too long when my dad elbows me in the ribs. Hard. "Isn't that Catherine?"

The words take a while for my brain to process. Catherine Fables, my ex-girlfriend, and the reason I was banished from the company. Okay, that wasn't her fault. We weren't addressing the unhappiness in our relationship for a long time, so it was my fault too. When she called it quits, it felt like a piece of me had been torn out. It was bound to happen, yet I was so stupidly confident that it wouldn't.

We were friends before we got together and good ones at that. But after her mom passed away, we started to drift, and I realised that I couldn't be what she needed, and she needed to take a step back. I was fighting for something I knew I'd never get back. Both of us being in the public eye just made that harder.

Still, it feels like the wind is knocked out of me when I see her after following my dad's line of vision. She's just as gorgeous as she was the last time I saw her. Her dark brown skin glows in the lighting of the venue, her curly hair flowing down her back against the midnight blue dress she's wearing as she smiles at the tall brunette who is talking to her.

She must have felt my eyes on her because she turns around and her smile falters a little. She whispers something to the boy who nods and kisses her on the cheek before she makes her way over to me.

"Evan," she says simply as her mouth twitches into a small smile. "It's nice to see you."

I clear my throat, trying to smooth out my voice as I say, "You too."

She nods a little before turning over to the corner where Scarlett stands. I haven't been able to take my eyes off her all night. "Is that your girlfriend?" she asks.

"No, uh.. Not yet, anyway," I reply. One way or another, I'm going to get her to come back to me and saying it out loud only solidifies that fact. I redirect. "Is that your boyfriend?"

I nod over to where the brunette is standing as he watches our conversation. "Connor?" she laughs. I shrug, not remembering much from my time at Drayton Hills. He looks oddly familiar, though. "He's Nora's brother, remember? My friends who are twins?"

"Oh, yeah," I say, trying to put my finger on the twins she used to hang out with. "He's a football player, right?"

"That's the one," she says, looking back at him and only him.

He's got a medal around his neck, the ones they give out to the kids at these events, so they don't feel left out. He gives her a double thumbs up and she snorts, turning back to me, that knowing grin on her face. Weird.

"Anyway, good luck getting the girl. You really deserve it, Evan. I know things were hard between us, but I think it was for the better. You're happy now, right?"

I look back to Scarlett as she laughs, throwing her head

back as Kennedy and Wren's faces turn red with laughter. "The happiest."

Cat turns to me, resting her hand on my shoulder. "Perfect. I'll see you around, Evan. It was really nice to see you, seriously."

"You too, Catherine," I reply.

And then she's gone. I feel all the tension evaporate from my body as she walks over to the guy she still didn't confirm if he was her boyfriend or not - not that it's any of my business anymore. But she seems happy, that's all that matters.

My dad appears back at my side after a few minutes as my gaze settles on Scarlett once again, sudden nerves running through my body.

"Are you going to *try* to look happy, son?" he asks once one of the most boring people I've ever met leaves the conversation. "You're scaring people off."

"This *is* me trying," I say, painting my face into a fake smile, baring my teeth and everything. I really couldn't care less about tonight if I tried. He glares at me. "What do you want me to do?"

"I want you to act like you're happy to be a part of B&Co," he replies.

I scoff. "Am I happy, though? I'm hardly a part of it anymore, remember?

"Maybe if you clean up this 'woe is me' act, I'll reconsider it"

"Seriously?"

"Yes," he replies. He nods towards the bar where Scarlett is standing, wedged between a married couple and an older man. "Now go talk to that girl before you lose your mind." This time I glare at him. "Sorry, Scarlett's her name, right?"

"Yes," I reply, basically beaming. "That is her name."

I rub my sweaty hands against my trousers as I make my way over to her.

Fuck. I shouldn't be this nervous.

Maybe I should have taken Miles' advice, but Scarlett doesn't seem like the type to appreciate me pestering her, so I left her alone and we worked on our project through emails and text messages. Grovelling didn't seem like her vibe. I gave her the space she needed to figure things out, even if that meant making me overthink every single decision I've made up until now.

The second I'm within her proximity again, I feel my whole body come alive. Just the smell of her drives me crazy — fresh, clean, and just *rich*. Everything about her screams 'I have money' and I love it. But not as much as I love her mind and the way she sees the world. The way she managed to constantly keep up with competing with me in classes, shoving her intelligence down my throat.

"I was wondering how long it would take you to come over," is the first thing she says to me. She turns around at the bar.

God, she looks so pretty. It's hard to even look at her. Yet it's all I want to do. I want to memorise her, burn it into my memory for days to come. She looks like she's wearing a little bit of makeup because her cheeks are a new shade of red and her lips are glossier than usual.

"So, you knew I was here the whole time?" I ask playfully.

"Come on, Branson. You and your dad have been brooding in the corner the whole night. It's kinda hard to ignore you two," she says, rolling her eyes lightly. I look over to where my dad stood and she's right. He's brooding.

"I'm guessing you want to talk?" I say, shifting my weight on my feet. I shove my hands in my pockets.

"I do," she says, holding her chin up to me, showing me that beautiful confidence that I love. "You lied to me, Evan."

Jesus. I knew this was coming, but…I didn't see it coming. I didn't predict the way the words would roll out of her mouth so easily. The fresh glint of betrayal in her eyes as she tells me exactly what I did.

"I know and I'm sorry and I don't deserve you to forgive me, but you have to understand the position I was in. It was my *family*. We didn't find out anything anyway. Even if we did, I'd never let them do anything to purposefully harm your family," I explain.

The words come out of my mouth in a rush, as if they're competing with my brain. I probably sound stupid. She looks at me curiously, trying to understand me and I let her. I'd lay my soul bare to her if it would get her to trust me again.

"My dad is fighting for his life in the hospital right now, so don't bullshit me about how important family is. I know you don't have the greatest one, but you could have tried to get that back in any other way. If you wanted to tell me the truth, you could have. If you knew more than you were letting on, you could've told me before it got too far, but you didn't," she says, her voice levelled and calm. Her voice cracks a little as she says, "I would have listened to you. I would have understood you if you just told me."

"I'm sorry, Scar. I'm so fucking sorry," I say again, really meaning it. If I was smart enough, I would have told her from the beginning. I would have told her the truth and we wouldn't be caught in shit shitstorm.

"I don't want you to be sorry, Evan. I want you to stay, to listen, to do this fucking project so we can get on with our lives." She steps in closer to me now, still holding her head high.

"So, that's what we're gonna do?" I ask. I need something more than that. I need *her* more than that. More than just existing in each other's presence. "We're just going to get on with our lives? I know you don't do serious and I'm not asking for that, but we…You know…"

She knows exactly what I'm talking about because her face flushes as she remembers the series of hot, angry kisses and everything that led up to her whimpering my name inside the library.

"This is such a fucking mess right now," she says, running her hands through the ends of hair, quickly. "Usually, I go with the flow. But with you, I need to know what we're doing. This isn't like what I usually do. You know that."

I swallow, trying to think. I don't want to scare her off, but I don't want to lose her either. "I don't know what this is either, Scarlett. If I did, you'd be the first to know. I just want to be close to you. I don't want to lose you after all this."

"So what? We're dating now?" she asks. Her face scrunches up at the idea and she looks adorable. She's pretending again. I thought I knew it before, but I now know for sure that she's forcing herself to act like I repulse her, which only makes me smile harder.

"Do *you* want to date me?"

"I don't know," she says through a sigh, shrugging. "I hardly like you, Ev."

That fucking nickname is going to kill me, I swear.

"Yeah, sure you don't," I say laughing. "Look. If you want to date me, you tell me that, Scarlett, and I'll be the best boyfriend you've ever had. If you want to fool around, pretend you hate me, I'm cool with that too. You like me. I *really* like you. It's that simple."

"Is it?" she asks, tilting her head to the side playfully, pushing her hair behind her ears.

"It can be if you let it," I whisper. She smiles then. A real smile. I lean forward to tug on the strand of her hair that I realise is not as long as it used to be. "You cut your hair."

"Took you a while to figure that one out, genius," she says, rolling her eyes.

"I like it. A lot," I reply through a smile, unable to stop myself.

"Okay. But like it from a distance," she says seriously, swatting my hand away from her.

"Why would I do that, Angel? I just said I want you close to me," I murmur, slowly wrapping my hands around her waist as I pull her against me.

"I can do that," she whispers, smiling up at me. Her smile is small; her lips rolled in slightly, but I can see the faint glow of red on her cheeks like she's happy to be here with me. Finally.

"Yeah?"

"Yeah, it's no big deal." She shrugs again as if she's too cool for this. Well, she's already way cooler than me, so maybe she is.

"Dance with me, then."

"Don't push it," she warns, squinting her eyes.

"Come on, Scar. Please?"

As if with perfect timing, the song changes to *Turning Page* by Sleeping At Last, the perfect song to dance to. I step back from her, letting her come to me. I hold out my hand, still walking backwards. She shakes her head at me, dropping that beautiful smile to the ground before she walks to me, clasping her hand with mine.

I pull her into me, our hands linking as I wrap one arm

around her waist, her head resting on my chest. I don't dance. Neither does she. But this right here, is probably the thing that solidifies how I feel about her. Everything about her fits so perfectly with me. Like no matter how many times we argued or pushed each other away, we were always destined to find our way back to each other.

We sway to the music, and I close my eyes, letting the moment take us away. I've needed to be this close to her for weeks. Now that I have her, I'm never letting her go again.

"I want to move on," she whispers into my shirt. "I want to see wherever this goes, but you hurt me, Evan. What you did really fucking hurt."

"I know."

"You can't keep getting involved with my family anymore, it's too much. If we're doing whatever the fuck this is, that doesn't mean you need to know everything about what's going on. So, drop it, okay?"

"Already did," I say thickly. When the words leave my mouth they sound like a lie, because the second I say it, I look up and my dad is staring right at me. I mean it when I say I'm not going to get involved. I don't want to do anything to hurt her again. I can try to protect her the best I can, lay down my life for her, but that doesn't mean my dad won't try.

38

SCARLETT

"TWO UPDATES. GO!" Kennedy screams. We're sitting in Florentino's, but she's clearly not afraid of getting fired, even though she's the loudest person in here during her break. She basically runs the shop, doing everyone's job for them.

"I'll go first," Wren suggests. "Number one; Marley finally started calling me by my name and it's the cutest thing I've ever heard. Number two; Miles taught him how to call me 'Wrenny.'"

She sulks at her boyfriend's insistent use of the nickname she hates. It's a little sickly, but mostly it's adorable.

"I was rooting for this update," Kennedy says, shaking her head. "Miles is so cute with Marley. Do you think you're ready for kids?"

"Kennedy!" I scream, looking between them.

"It's just a question. I love kids. If I had a man who loved me the way he loves you, I'd be begging for a child," Kennedy says, her eyes lighting up at the idea.

"No, I don't want children right now, Kennedy," Wren

argues, a little confused. "If Miles ever put a baby in me, I'd never speak to him again. My body would be ruined."

"But isn't it worth it? You'd get to see a baby you or a baby him," Kennedy coos.

"Trust me, nothing turns me on more than seeing him fall asleep with my nephew on his chest, but I do *not* want any children right now. It's way too early to think about," she says with finality. If Kennedy doesn't stop, she's going to end up manifesting it. "Anyway, enough talk about children. Scar, what are your updates?"

I think for a second, picking apart the banana bread I ordered. I shove a piece in my mouth, needing the time to think.

I still haven't told them about me and Evan becoming whatever we are again. And they still don't know about the kiss, which I'm never planning on telling them about. If they know we kissed multiple times and that he finger fucked me into next week in the library, they'd never let me live it down. It's too difficult to put into words the way he makes me feel and I don't know if they would fully understand it yet.

"Okay, update one; I've got through the final chapters of the sequel to Stolen Kingdom. And no, Wren, before you ask, I'm not okay. That ending was brutal," I say, and she grins, knowing that her book is full of emotional turmoil. "Oh, and second; Evan has got this nerdy band recital thingy at school, and he wants us to come. Xavier, Michelle, and Miles are going too."

"Huh," Wren says.

"What?" I ask, narrowing my eyes.

"Nothing," she chirps, shoving her milkshake straw into her mouth. I raise an eyebrow. "It's just the first time you've mentioned him since the event."

"Yeah, well, we're back on good terms now," I say, shrugging noncommittally.

"By good terms, you mean you confessed your undying love for each other, right?" Kennedy says.

"I don't love him for God's sake. Why does everyone keep saying that?" I mutter angrily. I deflect. "Ken, what are your updates?"

She narrows her eyes at my very obvious change in subject. "Uh, I don't have anything this week. Sorry."

"What do you mean? Something is always going on with you."

"Okay, jeez, you don't have to make it sound like a bad thing. I'm not a complete disaster, you know," she says, trying to laugh, but it comes out strange. She's clearly upset about something, and I want to figure it out before Wren says something back.

"What's going on, Ken," I press gently. She sighs, playing with her plastic coffee cup.

"I'm just struggling a bit with classes. Inspiration isn't an easy thing to find these days," she admits, her shoulders slumping. "I'm trying to be positive about it, but the truth is, it sucks."

"I get that, Kenny," Wren says, placing her hand over Kennedy's so she stops fidgeting. "I wasn't trying to sound rude earlier. I just mean you usually have something fun to talk about. I was just surprised, that's all."

"I know. It's okay. It's just me. I don't know... I just can't be happy all the time and it's exhausting," she replies. "And I *want* to be happy for you guys. You guys need me to be the happy one. It's how we work, isn't it?"

"You don't have to be '*the happy one,*' Ken and that's okay. I mean look at us," I say, gesturing between Wren and me. "We're grumps most of the time. It's okay not to be happy, you know?"

"I know. I just really, really like being happy and positive for you guys," she replies quietly.

"Then let us be happy and positive for you. We'll be your cheerleaders, Ken," I say, smiling up at her.

"Yeah?" she asks hopefully, those brown eyes lighting up.

"Of course," Wren says, waving imaginary pom-poms.

And we do. We tell her our full-proof tactics to give your brain a rest and allow it time to breathe and settle. We eat, talk, laugh, and cry over the table, even facetiming Gigi while we're at it. When Ken returns back to behind the counter, finishing the shift I'm unsure how she gets paid for, it's just me and Wren at the table.

She talks to me about how she and Miles are thinking of doing skating classes at the local rink this summer. There's something so magical about the way Wren talks about him. As much as she rolls her eyes and calls him an idiot, there's also that unwavering sense of appreciation and love in her eyes. Honestly, it makes me a little bit queasy.

As we walk back to our apartment, my phone buzzes in my pocket and I pull it out.

MOM: Come over to the hospital as soon as you can. Some updates on dad. The plane is ready.

MY MOM IS a sucker for a cryptic message. I stop walking towards the apartment as I laugh a little at her weird trait and type out a reply.

Me: I'm on my way.

"HEY, I'm going to go to the hospital to see my dad," I tell Wren when we get to the doors of our building. Wren turns around, her brown-green eyes instantly fill with worry.

"Is everything okay?" she asks.

"Yeah, probably. My mom's just being her usual cryptic self," I explain with a shrug.

"Okay. Let me know when you land," she replies before slipping into the building.

I'M STRAPPED SAFELY into the cream leather seats of my family's plane when my phone lights up with a call. Since the event, Evan and I haven't been able to talk or meet up much, but apparently he thinks now is the appropriate time to call me.

Since Gio died, I've tried to be more accepting towards everything in life, realising how fleeting life is and to actually embrace the smallest of things. Well, I don't have that tattoo on my hip for no reason.

Still, I like to mess with Evan as much as he likes to mess with me.

"What do you want, Branson?" I ask when the call connects, talking through a grin.

"Miss Voss, you're going to have to put the phone down. We're preparing to take off," the pilot on the intercom calls.

"Yes, one second," I shout, covering the end of my phone.

"Where are you?" Evan asks when I press the phone to my ear again.

"On the plane to Denver. My mom told me to go to the hospital. Why?"

"Have you taken off?" he asks.

"Just about to," I reply, looking at the runway as the plane starts to move slightly. I've always enjoyed flying, but I like watching the take off the most and Evan is ruining my ritual.

"Miss Voss," the guy over the intercom calls, warning me again.

"Your mom did?" Evan asks, stuttering slightly. I wish he could see me rolling my eyes right now.

"Yes, Branson, my mother who gave birth to me. Now, I've got to go. I'm turning my phone off so I can try and catch up on some sleep," I explain. It's been a tiring day with exam stress, as well as the project almost being completed, and this random phone call is not helping.

"No, Scarlett-"

I cut him off. "You're awfully clingy for someone I've just forgiven. Remember your place, Ev," I say as I end the call. Can I not get one moment of peace? I shut off my phone, sinking further into the leather seat and close my eyes.

THE HOSPITAL IS MORE eerie than I remember. It's usually pretty quiet in my dad's ward because most people are in the same situation as him. I walk down the abhorrent, nauseating, yet once again irresistible hospital hallways that are as narrow as closest as the bacteria flies in the air. My dad's room is the last in this corridor and I try to pick up my pace to get out of the unsettling chill, safe within the comfort of his presence.

I reach his door and the curtains are drawn shut, no doubt trying to shield him from the fluorescent lights. My mom read somewhere that the lighting can affect even comatose people, so she often tries to be extra careful even though I'm not sure if it's really that big of a deal.

"Look, Mom, if this is just another one of your games…" I say, laughing as I open the door.

"Hi, Scarlett."

The voice doesn't belong to my mother.

Sweat instantly begins to gather on my neck and chest as I look at the sight before me. Lucas is standing beside my dad's bed as he sleeps peacefully. He's not an intimidating guy. Well, he shouldn't be since he's supposed to be dead and all. I've never had a reason not to like him, but after that weird phone call the other day, he's been freaking me out more than usual.

"What are you doing here? Where's my mom?" I quiz, shutting the door behind me.

"Why don't you take a seat?" he says, chillingly calm.

"I'm good," I say, holding my chin high. I refuse to be afraid of him. He looks sick. Like he hasn't eaten in weeks. "Where's my mom?" I ask again.

He swallows. "She's fine. She's safe."

I step closer in the room, trying to keep calm and levelled while my heartbeat starts to pick up. I can hear it everywhere, beating rapidly in my ears. "Why wouldn't she be safe?"

"Your boyfriend just couldn't stop digging." His voice is rough like sandpaper, the sound scratching against my scalp. He's not looking at me. He's staring right at my dad.

"What are you talking about?" I whisper softly.

"She wasn't supposed to be on the plane," he says, rubbing

his hands on his temples as if he's trying to erase a memory. He turns to me now and I blink rapidly, my throat suddenly dry. I don't reply. I don't know if I'm supposed to. "It was supposed to be Gio, but he messed up the plan. He was the one that was supposed to die that night. Not Sara. She was innocent."

"What- What are you talking about?" I ask, my voice shaking. His eyes are disturbingly blue as he stares right at me, scratching his chin. I stumble a little, holding tightly onto the medicine cart near the door when I notice the thick black object in his hand, tapping against his thigh.

He has a gun.

"You know that I was Mateo's friend first, right? He and Gio could be tied together by blood, but they didn't even like each other until *I* pushed them together. It was me. *I* did that. It was mine and Mateo's idea to take over the business, to change it, make it our own. But Giovanni just *had* to get in the way, didn't he?" Lucas groans, shaking his head again. I gulp, trying to find some words, but they don't come to me. He continues talking. "The plan was so perfect. Gio was going to take that flight, Marcus would fly it, crash it and he'd be gone. But he had to send Sara alone. That wasn't going to stop me. I managed to think of a second plan. Mateo was too smart. He'd figure it out too easily, so I had to eliminate him first. I'd secretly insert myself into the business, plant Tinzin within the imports, tie people to it without knowing and I'd pin it all on him. It was going to work. I could see it happening, *tesoro*."

His eyes gleam with pure mischief. He just confessed a crime to me. Multiple. Why is he telling me this? I hold onto the cart tighter, needing stability. The disgusting look on his face makes my stomach turn. I force myself to swallow the bile in my throat, feeling the liquid go straight down to my stomach.

"Then *you* had to get involved and it became too easy. He was working on finding out what happened, and you were asking too many questions. He was too sensitive. Too protective, so he didn't tell the whole truth. His trip to the restaurant colliding with your stakeout was pure coincidence, I'll give him that. He was making it almost too easy. Gerard and I went way back, and he was the one to reach out to Gio. He talked him into taking up butchery and it was only a matter of time until your young, naive brain would see him slicing some meat and it would turn your thoughts rabid. We thought you would figure it was him, report him and he'd go down. Then some idiot had to hit him with his car, making his death and the story too easy to clean up, not the way I wanted."

"Why are you telling me this?" I ask, my voice wavering, sounding completely foreign to me. I have to be stronger. Braver. He stalks closer to me, only a few feet away now as I back further up, aimlessly reaching for something to defend myself.

"Because your boyfriend was getting too close. He was starting to figure me out and the only way I can blackmail him into staying quiet is if you're gone and he thinks he's next."

I swallow, my chin wobbling. Evan wouldn't lie to me again. He wouldn't. "You're lying. He said he dropped it," I argue.

"Sure, he might have dropped it, but it doesn't mean his family has. They're a smart bunch, the Branson's. Too smart for their own good. But I'm smarter. I know the second his dad thinks I'm the villain, he'll tell his love-sick son and he'll come rushing here. I'm giving him five minutes before he bursts down the door."

He glances towards the door, but the curtains are still drawn shut, blocking out any passers-by. Do they not have any cameras in here?

"What are you going to do to me?"

He chuckles lightly, sounding like pure and utter evil. "Oh, nothing yet. I want him to watch me kill you. It's the only way he'll take it seriously."

I don't let myself flinch at the threat. *Be strong, Scarlett. You have to. You **need** to.* "What are you getting out of this? You wanted Gio gone and now he is. What is killing me going to do?"

"Ah, I forgot to mention that your dad is going to be gone too. Meaning, I'll probably have a few more weeks to resurface, play the whole 'I survived a plane crash' charade and the world will be at my fingertips. No one will be running Voss anymore with Mateo gone and you and your meddling boyfriend's family out of the way. They'll be feeling sorry for me, practically begging me to take over."

He's a narcissist. I can deal with that. I can manipulate that. I must be able to or else I won't make it out of here alive. I *need* to make it out of here alive. There are so many things waiting for me on the other side of this door. So many wonderful things that I've just grasped, and I can't afford to let them slip through my fingers. Not again.

"How are you so sure they'll want you to take over?" I ask, playing into the idea.

"Why wouldn't they?" he says triumphantly.

Once I get him talking, I start to tune him out. I need a plan. I need an escape from him. If he's not bluffing, he really could kill me. If Evan is really on his way, I would never forgive myself for having him traumatised again for watching someone die. I couldn't do that to him.

That's when I saw it.

I've seen my dad's hand twitch before. He's done it count-less times, but the nurses always say it's reflexes. But this time, his whole hand lifts from the bed and happy, angry, and confused tears start to spring to my eyes. Lucas probably thinks I'm backing down, that I'm terrified but the thought of my dad waking up has given me the push I need.

I try to keep my eyes on Lucas even though just looking at him disgusts me and starts to make me a little dizzy. As he rambles on, I subtly flick my gaze to my dad as his eyes are now open. He's awake. He's back. He's *here*.

I'm suddenly grateful that I was an annoying child who begged my brothers to teach me everything. I begged them to teach me how to play soccer, how to change a tire, and how to complete basic first aid. I asked them for anything to give me a head start in the real world. Including sign language.

I ask more fabricated questions to Lucas about his ridicu-lous plan to kill me, frighten Evan into keeping quiet and taking over the company. He's so invested in what he's saying he doesn't even notice the beeping increasing on my dad's machine as his heartbeat picks up. My dad lifts his hands up, signing three simple words: *keep him talking*.

So, I do. But as he continues talking, I slowly try to move towards the door, angling Lucas away from my dad's bed so he can't see him. He tracks my movements, watching me try and get away from him.

"Where are you going?" he asks, squinting at me as he taps the gun against his thigh. I flick my eyes towards it and then back up at him before saying probably the most stupid thing I've ever said in my life.

"Just shoot me."

"What?" He blinks at me.

"You heard me. If you're going to do it, you might as well do it now," I say. Jesus. I don't even know what I'm saying. If this guy is as stupid as he sounds, he won't aim for any vital organs and I'm in a hospital for god's sake.

"I'm doing this on my terms. I want your boyfriend to see," he growls.

"For the thousandth time, he's not my boyfriend," I groan. I've been pivoting so long; he hasn't caught up on the fact that I'm now next to the table at the end of my dad's bed. I might be about to get shot right now, but I don't want to die with people knowing me as Evan Branson's girlfriend.

Lucas tilts his head curiously. "No? Then what is he?" Now he wants to chit chat. Perfect.

"Behind you," I say quickly, and he takes the bait, giving me enough time to whack the gun out of his hand and it slides under the bed. When he turns back to me, realising he fell for my stupid trick, he doesn't notice the lamp I picked up before I hit it as hard as I can against his head and watch his body fall to the ground.

39

EVAN

IF SOMEONE WOULD HAVE TOLD me I'd be sitting in a police station with my sort-of-girlfriend as she grins at me after being stuck in a room with a murderer, I would have laughed in their face.

But that's my reality.

Since we talked to the police, explaining everything we know, as well as my dad being brought in for questioning for meddling in something he shouldn't have, Scarlett hasn't been able to stop beaming. She's lucky that dude didn't attack her. But even as my heart is still racing, she's basically bouncing off the plastic chairs as I try to make sure she's not in a state of shock right now and that she hasn't been injured.

"You told him to shoot you?" I gawk, staring at her, still checking her face for any bruises or injuries. Her whole face lights up again, those deep brown eyes shimmering.

"Yeah," she says, smiling wide, bearing all of her teeth. I shake my head at her but then I notice the cut on her lip. I run my finger across it, the finest bit of blood coating the pad of my finger.

"Did he do this to you?" I ask, gruffly.

"No. I bit it when I was hitting him across the head. You should've seen the way I-" When she sees I'm not smiling with her she stops, her shoulders sagging slightly as she pouts at me. As much as I'm proud of her, she gave me the fright of my life when I got the call from her mom telling me that Lucas had taken her phone. She was already on her way down to Denver when she called me, so I had to get here as soon as I could. "What's wrong? Were you worried about me, Branson?" she coos.

"Of course, I was worried about you, you idiot. You could've gotten seriously hurt or worse. He's a *murderer*." I punch out those last few syllables with a poke to her cheek, but she swats my hand away.

"Yeah, but I'm fine now. See," she says, standing up, wiggling her whole body for extra emphasis. A few people in the station turn around to us, shaking their heads. I grip on her arm, pulling her back down to her seat, resting my hand on her thigh as she looks up at me, a little confused.

I keep my eyes on her thigh, stroking my thumb on the fabric of her leggings. She places her hand on top of mine, squeezing it gently.

"When I put the pieces together, I was so scared, Scarlett. I thought this was going to be the day that I lose you and that thought fucking terrified me. I should've got to you sooner," I say, looking back up at her. Her mouth opens, but I cut her off. "And don't you dare tell me that you can handle yourself because that guy was, like, twice the size of you."

She squeezes my hand again, smiling softly. "But I *can* handle myself. You saw it with your own eyes."

"That doesn't mean I wouldn't want to protect you anyway."

She leans forward. Even though we've been in the hospital and in the police station for hours, she still smells like herself. She presses a kiss to my cheek and when she pulls back she's smiling, her cheekbones high and her eyes squinting.

I knew it already. Of course, I did. But after being so incredibly proud of her, watching her handle the questions from the police with ease, the pure joy on her face as she recited the story, I realise now more than ever, that I'm in love her.

"SO, it was true? Your family is still looking into it?" she asks me when we finally get back to Salt Lake, driving back to my house after a longer than necessary plane journey.

All we've done since we got back is retell our stories to each other. She tells me about how she ended up in the hospital room with a murderer and I tell her about how my dad went behind my back to continue digging into Scarlett's family and how he found out about Lucas. Part of me is grateful that he did so I could get to her, but I didn't want her to think that I was trying to do it behind her back.

As much as she wanted to talk with her dad, the doctors thought it was best for his recovery if she went home since she is still in some state of shock over what happened. It's going to take a few weeks for Mateo to get back on his feet again. I promised her dinner so I'm going to give it to her.

"Yes and I didn't know, I swear. If I did, I would've told you. They said they dropped it, but I think my dad must have kept digging from the funeral," I explain to her, glancing over as I drive. I swear I've started to become her personal chauffeur no matter how protective she is about this car.

"Thank you," she says.

"For what?" I look back at her and she's watching me drive. Well, she's watching my hands on the steering wheel.

She shrugs. "I was so scared, Evan. Deep down I was petrified, but I was trying to be strong. To be strong for my dad, for my mom, for you. For everyone. And if I didn't…"

"But you did," I say with certainty. I take one of my hands off the steering wheel and rest it on her thigh instead, squeezing it gently. "Scarlett, you're a lot stronger and tougher than you think. You always put on this confident persona, this armour, but it's okay to be scared sometimes, you know. If you ever forget that I'm here to tell you. Every day."

"Every day?" she asks, laughing a little.

"Every day," I repeat.

Even after all that, she's still acting awkward around me. As soon as we got into the empty house, she kept her distance. Even when the food came, she stayed in the living room, her knees pulled up to her chest. She's either plotting to kill me or overthinking. I know better than to disturb her, so I start to dish out the food in the kitchen.

"It's just food, Scarlett," I call through the hatch in the kitchen. I hear her bark out a laugh over the sound of the TV.

"Yeah, it's just food," she says back to me, but her pitch is higher than usual. I knew the initial adrenaline would wear off at some point.

I go to the opposite end of the kitchen, retrieving the rest of the Thai food to dish onto the plates. "Do you want any crackers or are you one of those weird people who-"

I turn around and Scarlett's body is pressed up against mine, her lips inches away from my mouth. She's standing on her tiptoes a little, trying to reach my face.

Wait. What?

I pull back from her, slightly. "Uh, hi?"

"Hi," she whispers back, pulling her pink lips between her teeth before rolling them back out. I place the bag of food in my hand onto one of the counters. Her voice is still low and quiet as she says, "I don't know what I'm doing."

"That's okay," I whisper gently, pushing her hair behind her ear, loving the way she blushes ever so slightly. I can't help the grin that spreads across my face as she continues pressing herself to me, holding her head higher. "It seems like you want to kiss me, Angel."

"Seems like I'm not the only one," she says, pressing herself into me and I can feel the way my dick presses against her stomach. I don't know when I got so fucking hard, but it's just her.

She wraps her arms around my neck, pulling at the hair at the back of my neck that's wrapped around her finger.

"This doesn't mean that I like you or anything, by the way."

"Shut up," I murmur against her mouth.

My lips connect with hers and I instantly feel at home. I don't know how I've managed to deal without this for weeks. Without her. Because when Scarlett kisses me, she doesn't just give me five percent, she gives me everything.

I crush her body closer to mine so she can feel everything. She can feel how badly I want her. Her hands play with my hair, pulling and yanking greedily and I let her. When her tongue sneaks into my mouth, I swear I die and come back to life. The kiss becomes frantic. Needy. Just fucking desperate. I curl my hands tighter around her waist, pulling her up until her legs cross against my waist, walking her over to the counter.

Her face is practically glowing red, her lips already a little swollen. She keeps her legs wrapped around mine as I go back in, tilting her head back to get more, as she moans happily into my mouth. I tug tighter on her hair, loving the way her legs tighten around me when I do.

I press rapid kisses across her face and her neck, watching her whole body flash with redness. She stripped down to only the thin top she was wearing under her cardigan so I can get a better access to her chest and the swell of her breasts. I bite and suck and kiss until she's writhing beneath me.

I capture her lips again, needing to taste her. And God, she tastes so fucking good. It's all sweetness and pure bliss.

"You shouldn't feel this good," she whispers into my mouth.

"But I do," I say back, biting on her bottom lip and she groans. The sound goes straight to my dick.

"But you do," she repeats back to me.

She kisses me deeply then, letting me push my tongue into her mouth and she sighs. As she relaxes, my hands start to make a journey up her shirt, feeling her bare skin against my hand. I know I've touched her like this before, but I don't know what I was expecting.

"You feel so fucking *soft*," I groan, kissing along her neck until I get to her ear.

"What does that even mean?" she says, laughing when I bite the smooth flesh just under her ear.

"I don't know, but it's driving me insane," I say. I trail my hands further up her shirt until I get to the underside of her breast, but she reaches a hand down to stop me. My hand pauses as she holds onto my wrist. I pull back a little. We're both panting, her lips swollen as her chest rises.

"I don't think I want to do anything more, just yet," she says nervously. "I mean- Of course I do. I enjoyed it last time, but not right now. I just- I just want to kiss you, Ev."

"Then kiss me, woman," I demand, and she does.

She kisses me so hard I almost pass out. I can't help my bands roaming all over her body, silently claiming them. Every inch of her just makes me want more, but I tell myself to stop, only going as far as she lets me.

"Is this okay?" I ask into her neck while my hands reach around her back, trailing up her spine. My movements are soft and gentle against the warmth of her skin, taking my time to feel the beautiful inches of her body. She lets out a shuddery exhale as I run a finger down her back again. "Do you want me to stop?"

"It's okay," she pants, pulling me closer. "It's good."

"Are you sure?" I ask again, double checking. She pushes apart from me slightly, both of her soft hands holding onto my face in front of her. She tilts her head in that playful, sweet, and just fucking adorable way that I like.

"Hey, Ev?"

"Yeah?"

"Just relax," she whispers, pressing her mouth to mine, smiling against it.

"I don't think I've ever been able to relax when it comes to you," I say back.

"Can you try for me? I'll tell you if it gets too much, okay?"

"Okay."

We start to find our rhythm. She tells me what she enjoys, and I give it to her. Anything she does makes me feel good, so I don't even have to tell her. But my hand is wrapped around her waist, my other holding her neck when the front door opens. Both of our eyes shoot open, her hands pause on my chest, and I step back from her as I help her down from the counter.

As much as she tries to smooth out her outfit and her hair, her face is a dead giveaway. Her eyes dilated, her cheeks are deep red, and you can see where I've kissed across her chest. Just looking at her like this makes my dick ache. I turn my back to her as Xavier and Miles' loud voices boom through the house.

"That was the worst game I've watched in my life," Xavier says, walking into the connecting living room and kitchen. He looks up at Scarlett and then at me. "Oh, hey, Scarlett."

"Scarley's here?" Miles asks before coming into view. When he sees her, his eyes flicker between the two of us, his whole face lighting up. "Thank fuck for this."

"Hi," she says quietly, twisting her fingers together. God, she's so cute when she's nervous. "Evan was just-"

"Getting her and the girls some food," I say, saving her. She sighs and I hand her the bag of food. We were meant to share it, but I'll just make something of my own later.

"Okay, well I guess I'll go. Thanks for dinner and... Everything."

"You're welcome and.... Everything," I say back.

She walks backwards until she's back in the living room as she picks up her cardigan and stumbles through the door. When she's gone Miles and Xavier look at me accusingly.

"*Okay*. What the hell was that?" Miles asks, narrowing his eyes at me.

"Nothing. They were screaming about not having any takeout this late, so I got them something. It's no biggie," I lie, shrugging.

"You're a shit liar, Branson," Xavier says.

40

SCARLETT

"WHAT THE HELL IS THIS?"

Evan looks down at the ribbon I dropped in his hands. He has five minutes before his performance in the hall and his nerves have been rubbing off on me, so I'm offering him something to keep him settled.

"Are you dumb, or are you dumb?" I mutter, pulling the blue silk out of his hand.

He smirks. "Are you giving me a gift, Angel?"

I roll my eyes, fiddling with the material to tie it around his right wrist. "Yeah, well, I missed Christmas and your birthday, and you're just *so* obsessed with me, keeping hair ties on your wrist and all that, so I thought I might as well just-"

He cuts me off with a kiss, wrapping his now free hand around my neck, pulling my closer to his bare chest. I feel like I'm drowning in his touch. In his presence.

"You don't ever know when to shut up, do you?" he whispers against my mouth.

"It's your fault," I mutter, trying to regain my composure. "You do this thing where you look at me like-"

That bastard. He's shirtless, his shirt hanging over the back of a chair in the music room, his face is freshly shaven, and he looks so fucking sexy, and he expects me to form coherent sentences while he gives me *the* smile. What a fool.

"You can't look at me like that, Branson. It's ridiculous," I say, pushing away from him, but he catches his arm around my waist, pulling me right back to him.

"I thought we established this already, sweetheart. *You're* ridiculous."

THIS IS GOING to be torture.

I've been to the grand hall at North University twice in my life. The first was on the first day of school, where we had an induction assembly where they told us that futures were made here. The second time, I was sitting in a row with Wren, Miles, Xavier, and Michelle all sitting next to me as we watched Evan Fucking Branson perform a piano piece on the stage in front of us.

He walked onto that stage with all the confidence in the world, his head held high, a huge smile on his face, dressed in black pants and a white shirt. No tie. It honestly might be the hottest look I've seen him in and that's saying something. Even hotter? The fact that we're only a few rows from the front where he can see us and he's sitting in front of a grand piano, his sleeves rolled up, and I can see *my* ribbon on his wrist.

I swear I'm getting flustered just looking at him. I hope the rest of them don't notice. We almost got caught by Miles and Xavier the other day and even Anderson picked up on the subtle kiss he gave me as we stood outside of his office, waiting for our final check in for the project. It's getting harder and harder not to show people how much I'm drawn to him, but hiding it only makes the pulsing tension between us burn more.

Kennedy and Wren are giddy beside me, never having seen him play before. But I have. I've seen him play just for me. I've seen him teach me. I've seen the way he gets lost between the notes and the melodies, his whole body moving with the song.

He pulls the microphone to him even though he's not singing. "Hi, everyone. I'm Evan Branson," he introduces. Miles lets out a loud whoop and Wren elbows him to keep quiet as everyone's head turns towards our row. Evan laughs a little into the mic, the sound rushing straight towards me. "This piece is called 'Linda's Song,' and it's dedicated to someone special I know. Her name is Linda if that wasn't already obvious. Anyway, she's going to hate that I'm doing this, but she's the best Linda to my Danny a person could ask for. My partner in crime, as they say."

I don't get time to process what he just said because the second his fingers press down on the keys; I swear my soul leaves my body.

I love music. I always have. But the way Evan is playing right now is something I've never experienced before. It starts off slowly, dramatic, and sensitive, immediately bringing tears to my eyes, before building into a symphony made specifically for me.

Or, well, Linda.

"Who the hell is Linda?" Kennedy asks quietly, leaning into me, her mouth practically hanging open.

"And who's Danny?" Wren asks from the other side of me.

"I don't know," I say but I can tell the smile on my face is a dead giveaway. Miles leans forward, across Wren as he tries to keep his obnoxiously loud volume to a minimum.

"Awh, this sucks for you, Scarlett," Miles whispers.

"Why does this suck for me?"

"Because he's clearly into that Linda girl and last I checked, your name isn't Linda," he says, sounding genuinely upset for me. Wren elbows him for the second time tonight and he slouches back in his chair, locking his gaze back on Evan.

"He must really like this Linda girl, huh?" he mutters.

"Yeah," I whisper, "he really does."

Then it gets worse.

Not only is he completely transfixed by the music and the melody, three people enter the stage with horns and flutes. *Fucking horns and flutes.* Everything sounds so beautiful together. Nothing is too loud. Nothing is too quiet. Everything is just perfect. Pure and utter bliss. I swear I start to tear up. Nearly everyone in the crowd does. When he turns to me, still playing, everyone in the crowd in awe, he smiles faintly, and I smile back.

Because no matter what, Evan Branson is going to continue to surprise me for the rest of my life.

The song goes on for a while, but no one gets bored. How could you? Every note is part of this beautifully crafted piece that tugs directly on your heartstrings. I even rest my head on Kennedy's shoulder, closing my eyes while I listen, goosebumps rising up my arms.

"It's just so…" Kennedy says, clearly lost within it too.

"I know," I reply. "I know."

AS HE PROMISED, we all walked out of Evan's escalade into a Michelin star restaurant downtown for a celebratory meal after his performance. Really we should be celebrating him, but he insisted on booking us all a table, pre-paying for our meal so we could eat together.

We haven't been able to have a moment alone since that moving piece, but he's been standing behind me the whole time. I said congratulations but that's about it. I don't know how to put into words the amount of emotions I'm feeling right now.

As we get through the doors, I pull onto Wren's arm, so she turns around to me. "I'm just going to use the bathroom. Text me where you get seated."

"Okay," she replies, happily, linking her arms within Miles's waiting one.

I stumble over to the bathroom, needing a moment to collect myself. Unlike most restaurants, this one holds a corridor of single unisex bathrooms instead of huge ones with multiple stalls. Still, they're large enough to fit at least three people in, with huge mirrors surrounding the whole room. Of course, it does because Evan had to pick the fanciest restaurant for tonight.

When I get into the bathroom, I lock the door, looking at myself in the golden-rimmed mirrors. My face is still a little red from his performance, so I quickly splash some water on it, letting it cool me down. My phone buzzes on the counter.

EVAN: Where are you?

EVAN: Do you want me to order you a drink?

> ME: I'm in the bathroom. Last one in the row. Come here.

> EVAN: So, no drink....?

> ME: Just come to the bathroom.

AS I EXPECTED, a few seconds later I hear a faint knock on the door and I open it, all six feet and three inches of him filling the large space.

"Hey, what the hell was that?" I ask, going to lock the door. When I turn back to him, I see him watching me in all the mirrors. My back is completely exposed by my black dress, so that's probably what he's looking at, his eyes roaming all over my body. I suddenly feel so exposed to him with the mirrors reflecting my every angle.

"What was what?" he asks innocently, leaning against the wall with his arms crossed. I copy his position, my back against the sink.

"Evan," I warn.

"Scarlett," he purrs, the sound creating a pool of heat in my lower stomach.

"Drop the act for one fucking second and be real with me," I say, waving my hand between us.

"What do you want me to say, Scar?" I groan, knowing that he's playing coy with me which is the last thing I want or need.

"Why would you write a song for me and not tell me and play it in front of everyone?" I say. He chuckles lightly, rubbing the back of his neck.

"No one knows it was about you," he replies.

"You were staring *right* at me while you were playing," I accuse and then mumble, "Which is insane because I don't understand how you can play without looking."

He steps closer to me, my ass already digging into the countertop. "Are you trying to compliment me, sweetheart?"

I gulp. "I would never," I say, holding my chin up to him. He doesn't buy it, clearly, because he still stalks closer to me until he's a breath away, his whole body covering mine. "You're the most arrogant person I've ever met."

I shove him in the chest, seeing if he'll back down, but he doesn't even stumble. Instead, he unties the ribbon on his hand and grips both of my hands together, pinning them above my head. I gasp, tilting my head up to him.

"Really? That's not what you were saying the other week when my fingers were deep inside your pussy *or* the other day when you were kissing me senseless," he murmurs, seamlessly tying the ribbon over my wrists. "Tell me if it's too tight, okay?"

"It's not," I gasp, needing him to give me something. Something more.

"Good," he rasps.

The way he can switch from innocent, golden retriever to this burly, almost animalistic man, baffles me. My chest is heaving now, desperate for a taste of him, as he stares down at me while I look up, wiggling my hands in his grip. He holds on tighter to them, pushing them higher until my whole chest is stretched for him. He kisses along my neck, causing me to shudder and shift under his touch. In one swift motion, he bunches up the skirt of my dress, palming my thighs near my underwear, his huge hand wrapped around them.

"I want to know something, Scar," he breathes into my ear, his hot breath bringing me one step closer to unravelling. I'm panting now and he's not finishing his sentence. He's teasing me, edging me, with the slight stroke of his thumb on my thigh. "If I were to slip my hand into your panties right now, will you be as wet as I'm imagining?"

Just the sound of those filthy words on his mouth sends a rush of want straight down to where I'm waiting for him. Everything in my body lights up from the way he touches me, teases me, and mixed in with his words makes my whole body spread with goosebumps, desperate and aching with need.

"No," I lie. I can feel it coating my thighs, begging for a release. Just being this close to him gets me hot and bothered. The silk around my wrist, knowing that I gave it to him just for him to use it to tease me.

"Don't lie to me, Angel," he warns, pressing a kiss to my neck as his fingers dance across the thin fabric of my panties.

"I'm not ly-" My words turn into a guttural moan as he slips his hand into my panties. My mouth hangs open instantly, but he nudges it closed with his nose, his thumb paying very close attention to my clit as it responds needily to him.

"Fuck, Scarlett," he breathes into the crook of my neck, causing me to turn away from him. I can see myself in the mirror and the image is obscene. I'm pressed against the sink, my hands above my head, Evan's strong hands wrapped around my wrist as he kisses my neck with his other hand inside my panties. He presses his cheek to mine, watching me watch us. "Look at you. You're a fucking mess and I'm hardly doing anything."

"Ev," I pant. "Don't stop."

"Angel, I've not even started," he whispers. I don't know how his touch unravels me so easily. Maybe it's because it's been on my mind for weeks now. But actually, having it suddenly makes every nerve so sensitive to his touch. And I just want more. "Do you want me to put a finger in that sweet pussy of yours or will this do?"

Will this do? He's got to be fucking kidding me. I try to move against his hand, needing more friction. He's being too soft, toying with my wetness against my clit, not giving me what I want just because I haven't asked.

"Two," I say roughly. "Two fingers. I want to feel you everywhere."

The sentence is barely out of my mouth before he penetrates me with his middle finger and his index finger, filling me with his large hand. It's exactly what I wanted. Exactly what I needed, but...

"Ev, your fingers- They're so...big," I moan, my hands struggling against his grip. I can't help but roll my hips against his hand, still needing that bit more.

"I'm just doing what you asked." he rasps, biting and nipping at my neck. The stimulation I'm getting from his mouth on my neck and his fingers deep in my pussy, driving me insane. His pace increases slightly as I rock my body into his.

"Does it feel good, hm?" His voice is low and raspy, so the only thing that comes out of my mouth is a moan as I clench around him. "As good as that feels and sounds, that isn't an answer, pretty girl."

"*Evan*," I moan, sounding pathetic and needy. That's exactly what I am now; a moaning, shaking, desperate and needy mess. All for him. Every touch from him feels like an inferno and I can't get enough. "It feels good. Too good."

"Do you want your friends to hear you moaning my name?" he asks, and I shake my head, still trying to move against him. I don't know why I do it, only knowing it's going to push me over the edge, but I want this to last forever. "Good. Now let me cover your mouth."

He drops his hand from holding mine above my head and plants it across my mouth instead. Now my hands are flailing, trying to grip onto something for stability as he continues pushing his fingers in and out of me, the slick wet noises filling the room.

He teases my clit with his thumb, still pumping in and out of me with long strokes. Jesus, Christ. I've never felt this good before. He pulls his fingers out of me only to pinch my clit and I shudder, moaning into his hand while he stares right at me, his face painted in a satisfied, evil grin. I'm sure my saliva is completely covering his hand, but he doesn't seem to mind. In fact, it seems like he's enjoying it. My body is trembling now, my hips unable to keep up with the brutal thrust of his fingers, needing to finally be pushed over the edge.

"Are you going to come for me, Angel?" he asks. I nod my head, my eyes watering as he pulls out of me. *Again.* He's trying to destroy me. He slaps my pussy and I moan again. "Good girl."

He sinks two fingers back inside me, keeping his eyes locked with mine, but they keep rolling back in my head, overcome with pleasure. Needing more. But needing less.

When he picks up his pace, his thumb still circling my clit, I feel the orgasm about to hit me and I roll my head back, still moaning into his hand. My back arches, my legs writhing as he mercilessly pushes his fingers in and out of me, the whole experience feeling like stars are bursting.

"*Evan,*" I cry.

"Yes, sweetheart?"

"I need-" He increases his pace again before slowing it down. My hips aren't able to move anymore, my body hot and confused with the game that he's playing. *Is he trying to kill me?*

He ignores my needy whimpers, instead saying, "What do you need?"

"Stop teasing me. I need to come," I moan.

"Good, because I'm fucking starving," he groans as he slowly sinks to his knees.

My head tilts back, unable to look at him even after he releases my hands and ties the ribbon around just one of my wrists instead. He presses his tongue flat against me and my legs shake as I hold on tight to my dress. He's eating me out so good like he's been paid to do it. He pushes his tongue into me, and I feel my whole body flush again.

When the pleasure takes over again, my head instantly falls back, moans falling out of my mouth that I forget to keep quiet, but I don't care. I don't care how loud I sound with how good this feels. When he looks back at me, watching me on the brink of falling apart, he squeezes my ass.

I twist my head to the side again, not able to look at him as he continues sucking my clit, lightly grazing his teeth against me. I turn to the mirror, watching as his head bobs up and down, my skirt only covering half of his face. I don't know how much I can take of this. He's too fucking good at everything.

"Don't do that," he warns, his voice thick and heavy, "I want you to look at me when you come for me, Scarlett."

That's what does it. The way my name sounds on his lips – desperate and fucking needy. The way those green eyes are staring into mine as I try to speak, and nothing comes out. The orgasm rips through me and pulls through every nerve in my body in waves, as he holds me on the come down, gently massaging my clit as it passes through me.

I want him.

I want all of him.

"I need you to fuck me," I say when I catch my breath.

"Right now? When your friends are on the other side of this door?" I nod. He stands up to his full height. He pushes the sweaty hair on my forehead out of my face. "Scar, I've been dreaming about fucking you since the first day at North. I've fucked my fist imagining doing it raw, hard, and fast. I've imagined doing it slowly, taking my time, easing my cock into you until you can't take anymore. I've imagined fucking you so hard in that tight pussy of yours until it's the only thing you remember, and you can't walk straight, which means it's not going to be a quick fuck in a bathroom of a restaurant. I'm going to want the whole day having my way with you. I'm going to look after you afterwards, clean you up and tuck you into bed with me. Because that's what it's going to be like when I finally have you all to myself. But today isn't that day. When I do, I'm going to fuck you like your mine."

I swallow at the images he's just painted. I want all of what he just said. Every single fucking thing and more. Does he really expect me to have dinner with everyone after all that? *Apparently*.

"Okay," I breathe out. He tilts his head to the side.

"*Okay* is all you have to say?"

"Yes, *okay* is all I have to say because I want you so badly – now – and you're telling me to wait. I'm an impatient person, Branson, so your golden dick better be good."

"Trust me, sweetheart, it will be."

MOST OF THE meal goes by in a blur. After timing our exits from the bathroom to perfection, nobody asks us any questions while everyone gushes over Evan's performance. I sat across from him, needing the distance.

Still, he managed to convince Michelle to switch places, so he ended up next to me the second half of the night. I had to pretend his large hand resting casually on my thigh wasn't making me go crazy like his fingers weren't inside me only minutes ago.

"What's everyone's food like?" Kennedy asks innocently as she pokes around her food. "Is anyone else's lasagne…"

"So wet?" Evan says, his voice low, but no one picks up on the way he squeezes my thigh, inching his hand further and further up so my pussy aches.

"Yeah," Kennedy says, sulking as she refuses to take a bite of the food. She looks like a little baby, and I laugh, pushing my hair out of my face. When her eyes widen, I immediately notice the mistake I've made. "Oh my god! Did you two get matching friendship bracelets?"

"What are you talking about?" Evan asks, his eyebrows knitting in confusion. Oh, that poor, sweet, not-so-innocent boy.

Kennedy points at my wrist. "That ribbon. You were wearing it at your performance. I thought I recognised it," she says, tutting.

"Oh, yeah, I remember too," Wren says, looking between the two of us. "Go on, Evan. Show us yours."

"I don't have one," he says, glancing over at me and then back to Kennedy who is not buying it.

"Then why do you both have the same one?" she asks, titling her head.

"Yeah, and come to think of it, your wrists are looking a

little red, Scarley," Miles chimes in. I swear he just wants me to murder him.

"Oh my god," I groan. "I always wear a ribbon my wrist, you guys know that. Evan must have *stolen* one of mine for good luck in his performance. He probably took it off between then and now. My wrists are red because I keep switching them around. End of fucking story."

Everyone falls silent before Kennedy nods, a little frightened at my outburst until they all eventually fall back into a quiet conversation. Evan doesn't say anything other than moving his hands further up my thigh, knowing that I'm still drenched for him. He hisses when he feels my arousal, his knuckles brushing against my clit.

"That's my smart girl," he murmurs, only for us to hear.

How much longer am I going to have to wait for him and that golden dick?

41

EVAN

THIS IS our last time having a chance to run through our presentation before we have to hand in our final report. We've managed to keep up with the progress of the app. Watching it come to life has been incredible. The last thing we need to do is perfect our presentation before we have to present it in front of the class.

Scarlett came over to my house this morning to start working on it. My dad isn't home — thank God — so I haven't had to worry about speaking to him. Since Lucas's arrest, we've hardly spoken about him going behind my back and betraying me when I told him to stop digging. He could have got us all killed if he didn't stop. I'm not ready to hear him out yet and I don't know when I will be. Still, having Scarlett here, safe, seemingly happy, is enough for me right now.

"Are you listening to anything I'm saying?" she asks, turning towards me. We set up a projector onto a huge whiteboard so we could go through the presentation in my office. She's standing in front of it in a pencil skirt and a blouse, giving a hot teacher look as she flicks through the cue cards. After hearing those delicious moans come out of her mouth in the bathroom and she asked me to fuck her, it's all I've been thinking about.

"I'm looking," I say.

She smirks. "I said 'Listening' not looking, you perv. We don't have a lot of time left and we need to make this as close to perfect as possible."

"Okay, run through it one more time."

And she does. She explains to me how we're going to start giving a pitch about *Hard to Tell* and how we would advertise it. She goes on to vaguely explain the details of the app with notes from the software developer before handing it over to me.

Whilst I'm doing my run through, flicking through the slides, she stands next to the window, staring out into my bleak backyard. I try to continue talking, to keep practising, but she's distracting me without even doing anything.

"Are *you* even listening?" I ask playfully, stopping my rant. She doesn't respond or move to suggest she's even heard me. I stalk closer to her. She has one of her arms wrapped around her middle, the other resting next to her mouth, biting her nails. I place a hand on her waist, coming behind her. "Scarlett?"

"Hm?"

"Did you listen to anything I just said?" I ask. I rest my chin on her shoulder, tightening my hand on her waist. She nods. I kiss her neck lightly, inhaling her perfume and she hums. "What are you thinking about?"

She swallows, dropping her hands from her mouth. "Is this where you used to play as a kid?" she asks and it's the last thing I was expecting.

The field that we call our backyard goes on for miles, eventually leading into a forest containing a small pond and deck. It was every little boy's dream. It was *my* dream. For a while anyway.

"Yeah," I say. I twist us slightly, pointing east towards where my old tree house used to be. "I used to have a tree-house there. I called it the EvCave."

She laughs a little. "That's cute."

I wrap both of my arms around her waist now and her hands rest on mine on top of her stomach, her head resting against mine on her shoulder. Holding her like this, where we're not arguing, where we're both watching the same thing, makes me feel like we're more than what we really are. That we're capable of more than we give ourselves credit for.

"What's the matter, Angel?"

"Didn't you ever get lonely?" she asks. "I mean, I had a yard as big as this and even with four brothers, I still felt alone. I couldn't imagine what you must have felt like. Didn't you get lost?"

"I got lost all the time, but it didn't mean anything. My mom was the greatest until she left. She and my dad tried to make me feel special and loved, even though they swore off having any more kids," I admit, thinking about all the days it was just the three of us.

"Do you think you would want siblings?" she asks quietly.

"Not if it would have changed who I am. People around you shape you, they make you who you are without knowing. I like who I am now. Who I am now brought me to you and I would hate to have that ruined because of the way I was brought up," I say. She twists in my arms, turning to me as her eyes search my face. "What?" I ask, feeling suddenly nervous under her gaze.

"Nothing," she replies, shaking her head as she looks up to me. "That was just a perfect answer."

Some of the things that come out of this girl's mouth completely messes up my insides. As much as she can tell me how much she hates me, she can also say sickly sweet things like that or hold my hand when I don't ask her.

Completely overcome with the joy of being in her presence, I press my mouth to hers, letting her soften into my touch before going in harder. More frantic. Her body moves with mine, her hands curling in my hair as I take a strong hold of her delicate face, slipping my tongue into her mouth. When the warmth hits her, she moans before smiling against my mouth and I almost die. I want more of her. I need more of her all of the time. And she lets me have her.

She lets me run my hands over the curves of her waist around her back, until I can press her body flush to mine, until it feels like we've become one. She lets my hands search across her soft thighs, squeezing and kneading. She lets me swallow every whimper and soft moan that leaves her mouth. I pick her up as she wraps her legs around mine and I place her on the windowsill, my hips grinding into her.

"How do you make everything feel so good?" she murmurs angrily when I kiss across her neck, biting her there softly. When she's caught up like this, she compliments me more and I love it.

"Because I know you," I say. Her head tilts to the side, allowing me to kiss across the base of her throat while my hands inch further and further up her skirt. Her fingers curl in my hair, grabbing and pulling tightly, pressing my head further into her.

"Listen," she pants, gasping as she pulls my head slightly

to face hers. Those pretty lips are glowing pink, swollen from kissing me too hard. "I'm still learning to trust you."

"I know," I sigh, letting my shoulders relax. I knew this was going to come at some point. "What else is it going to take for you to trust me? Do you want me to get on my knees and beg you? Because I'll fucking beg, Scarlett. I'd do just about anything."

She drops her arms from my face, her hands resting on the windowsill as she studies me. She holds her chin up in challenge. "Crawl to me."

"What?" I choke out.

"If you're going to get on your knees and beg, you might as well do it the right way," she says, gulping. This girl is full of surprises. "I want you to take off your shirt too." She rubs her hands over my shoulders before dropping her gaze to where I'm hard and waiting for her. "And your pants."

I do as she asks, stepping back from her and she drops from the windowsill, standing straight. She keeps her wild eyes trained on my chest as I shove off my white shirt, throwing it onto the floor to the side of the room. She swallows as I start to unbutton my trousers, but I pause before zipping my fly down.

"Are you sure you want this, Angel?" I ask, double checking because once we cross that line, it's over.

"Positive," she says, watching my hand and I zip down my trousers, my dick already hard and waiting for her as it's finally able to breathe from the restraints of my pants. I shove them to the floor, kicking them off to the side, my socks and shoes following them until I'm in nothing but my boxers. She swallows audibly.

I walk backwards until I'm closer to the door and I get

down on my hands and knees, the carpeted floor rubbing against my bare skin, and I start to crawl to her.

She watches me intently as if I'm the best fucking film she's seen in her life. She's smirking, clearly enjoying this, but she's shifting too, her thighs obviously rubbing together in that skirt. Just the thought of her already wet for me makes my dick ache.

When I get to her, she watches me as I lift her heel up, undoing the straps before setting her foot down and she loses a few inches. I do the same to the other one before kissing her there and she sighs happily. She stumbles against the radiator a little as I sit back on my heels, holding her leg to kiss along her calf and up her thigh.

I continue my journey up, getting soft and sweet whimpers of my name in return. Her thighs are already sweaty and slick with her arousal and I lick every last drop that she gives me, until I get to her panties where she's glistening for me.

"Let me show you how good it would be if you let me be nice to you. How good it would be if you stopped calling me every awful name you could think of. Let me be good to you. Let me be good *for* you," I whisper as I press a kiss to her heat above her panties where she's soaking.

"Okay," she breathes. I lay my tongue flat against the fabric, tasting her and she shudders. "Fucking hell, Ev. I said 'Okay.'"

"Okay?"

"Yes. I just want you so badly," she whines as I suck on her clit gently.

SCARLETT

When I've stripped down to nothing but my panties and a bra, I'm standing in front of Evan, wet and needy while he just... watches me. I can't stop staring at him. His chest is sculpted perfectly, his hair already messy and his face is red. It confuses me how he can look so adorable and hot at the same time, while saying the filthiest things.

I need him.

Desperately.

He wraps his huge hands around my waist, his fingers dancing up my spine as he pushes my chest closer to his bare skin against mine. I need to taste him, but he doesn't let me have him.

Instead, he unclips my bra, my chest still against his as I lean up slightly to let the material fall to the ground. When my tits press against his chest, my nipples hard peaks, he groans.

"Jesus, Scarlett," he mutters, looking at the space between us and I feel him growing in his boxers, pressing against me. He swallows. "Everything about you is just so... Perfect."

My whole body flushes at his words, feeling the praise right down to my fingertips as his hands roam around my waist. Only he can make me feel like this. Each touch is absolutely maddening. When my eyes connect with his, his hands shoot to my face, holding me tightly as he presses his mouth to mine.

It's not like the other angry kisses we've had. This one is soft. Sweet. Timid, almost – a stark contrast to what we're about to do. He's being soft with me again and I want to melt in a puddle at his feet.

He pulls back from me, his cheeks glowing the most adorable shade of red before diving into my neck, sucking, nipping. His quick kisses become long, hard sucks when he reaches the swell of my breast as he holds onto my waist, my back arching.

His hot mouth covers my nipple and I moan, loving the way he's taking care of my body like he knows it. I know he wants me to watch – and God I want to – but it feels too good, and I know that looking at him, watching him devour me, will make me crave more.

He's like an animal.

His lips touch every sensitive part of my breasts as he swirls his tongue around it, making me call out his name. He starts to make his journey down my chest, kissing and touching me like I'll break.

"Tell me what it says," he murmurs into my skin at my navel, and I know he's talking about my tattoo on my hip. It's a small butterfly next to a couple of words.

"Can't you read, dumbass?" I ask playfully, putting him out of his misery as I take off my panties. Maybe I didn't realise the severity of being absolutely naked in front of him until he fell to his knees again, his green eyes full of wonder.

I feel like a God.

"I want you to tell me," he says, his thumb rubbing circles on the inside of my thigh. He collects my arousal with one of his fingers, teasing it against my clit and I have to clamp my mouth shut, so a moan doesn't slip out. "What's wrong? Can't talk, Scarlett?"

He pushes one finger inside of me and it feels like my whole world is falling apart. I hold onto his shoulder for stability, needing something to make sure I don't fall over or explode into a thousand pieces.

"Talk," he urges again, looking up at me, those green eyes not leaving mine. He picks up the pace of his fingers, so that I have to try to focus on something else before I can talk without whimpering.

"It's four words," I say finally, panting to stop myself from crying out. "It's the title of my favourite poem. Let it enfold you."

"What does it mean?" he asks calmly, as if he isn't pumping in and out of me. This man is going to absolutely wreck my life.

"It means finding the simplest moments in life. The first line is, 'Either peace or happiness, let it enfold you,'" I get out, most of it sounding like one word.

"That's beautiful," he whispers, pressing a kiss to the tattoo. "Just like you."

He spins me around, so my naked body is pressing against the windowsill, my ass in his face, as his fingers leave me empty. He roams his hands over my back, kneading his palms into my ass and I gasp, loving the way it feels.

"I want to explore your body and see if every inch of you tastes as good as I imagined," he murmurs into my skin.

"You dream about me, Branson?" I croak out.

"Every night."

"You're so obsessed with me," I say, laughing.

"Don't act like you haven't been dying for this too."

"Dying for it is a bit dramatic, don't you think? Have I wanted this? Yes. Have I been *dying* for it? Not so much," I say easily. I'm teasing him, edging him on, seeing how far he will go until he finally cracks and gives me what I want.

"Ah," he tuts, "you shouldn't have said that, Angel."

"Why not?"

"Because I'm about to prove you very wrong. When I'm done with you, you're going to dream about the way I touch you every night," he says through a groan. I go to stand, but he still keeps his hands on me, dancing across my stomach, his mouth on my neck.

"Prove me wrong, then," I challenge, twisting around in his grip to grab onto his neck, pulling him into me so I can crush my mouth to his. His body is surprised by my sudden roughness, and he stumbles backwards slightly. I want him inside me. I want to feel him fucking everywhere. "Do you have a condom?"

"Yes," he says into my mouth, smiling against it. He pulls me with him as he reaches into a drawer, retrieving the packet.

My eyes can't leave his body as he shucks off his boxers in one motion, his huge erection making me gulp. I knew he was going to be big, but…Jesus. He strokes the head of his cock, leaking with pre-cum and I snap my eyes up to his, unable to look at it. He pumps his shaft a few times while keeping his eyes trained on me and it takes all that I am not to touch myself too with the way he's looking at me – his gaze is hungry, dirty, and insatiable. He rolls on the condom, and I sit back up on the windowsill.

He braces one hand under my thigh, lifting it up as he positions his cock with my needy, wet pussy. "Tell me when you want to stop, okay?" I nod, needing him now more than ever. He gently eases the tip into me, and I gasp. Not much is inside me, but it's already filling me up. He adjusts my thigh, opening my legs wider so he can push into me again, giving me more of him.

"*Fuck*," I moan when more of him slips deeper inside me. I loll my head back, unable to look at where we're connecting, knowing it will take me over the edge. Once he's pushed in as much as he can and I've adjusted to his length, he braces both of his hands on my hips as I try to keep my legs as high as possible, wrapping them around him.

"Jesus, you're so tight," he groans into the skin on my collarbone.

"I'm not, you're just fucking huge," I say back.

"You trying to compliment me, sweetheart?"

"No," I bite out, moaning again. I look down to where we're connected – my pussy stretched perfectly for him. I bite back the moan in my throat as he drives into me. "You're going to ruin me."

"Good. I was planning on it," he says. He pushes just in and then just out again, each stroke slower than the last. He's trying to punish me. He has to be. This is torture. Each time he pumps into me, another desperate moan leaves my mouth, reverberating through the room.

He breaks the hold on my hip, only to use one hand to gently play with my clit, rubbing at the same slow pace he's using to fuck me. We're both nothing but frantic moans and pants, gasping each time he hits me in the right spot.

The pain mixed with the pleasure drives me over the edge multiple times without fully getting there because he changes his pace. Again.

I've had enough.

"Stop treating me like a porcelain doll and just fuck me like you mean it, Branson."

"You have a really dirty mouth. You know that, Angel?" he murmurs, pressing a kiss to the space behind my ear. I tilt my head away from him, needing to catch my breath.

"What do you expect? You're the one who insists on calling me 'Angel' when you know I'm not," I choke out after another slow stroke.

"Over the desk. Now."

EVAN

She scrambles to her feet, her perfect ass and tits bouncing as she does what I ask. Still, she wants me to work for it, so she sits at the edge of the desk, not where I told her, crossing her ankles, her chest heaving.

"Do you not like to listen or do you just like being punished?" I ask gruffly.

"Both," she replies, grinning. I grip her waist, turning her around, gently easing her down until her chest is flat against the desk. I pull her up lightly by her ponytail, curling it in my fist.

"I told you I was going to fuck you exactly like this, Angel. But you've got to tell me if it gets too much for you. Okay?"

"Okay," she breathes as I rub my cock between her ass.

I nudge the head of my cock into her slowly at first, seeing how much she can take and when a whimper leaves her mouth, I push in harder on instinct. This angle gives me the opportunity to hit every spot inside her until all she sees is fucking stars and all she feels is me.

Once I've filled her up and she situates, I start to pump in and out of her, slowly at first as she gets used to my size again. I pull her head up, wanting to see those tits bounce for me as I push into her, her ass bouncing against my lap. The wet, sloppy noises we're making, mixed in with the sounds coming out of our mouths is obscenely glorious. As I try to tilt her head towards me, so I can capture her lips, she keeps her eyes closed, completely consumed with pleasure.

"Don't get shy for me now, Angel. You're perfect," I murmur. All that comes out is a soft whimper at the praise. I drive my cock into her again, making the desk shake. "Does this feel good?"

"Mm hmm," is the only thing that comes out of her mouth, and I tilt her head towards me, stealing the sound from her lips, kissing her senseless.

"Use your words, pretty girl," I whisper against her mouth. Her eyes roll back in her head, her face twisting with pleasure as I continue my merciless strokes, giving her everything.

"I- I can't," she stutters.

"You can," I encourage, wiping the hair from her forehead before grabbing her ponytail again. "Try for me."

"It feels so good. Too good," she moans. That's exactly what I want to hear because this feels like fucking heaven to me. Her warm pussy is so tight around me, and she won't stop clenching, milking me, pushing me closer to the edge. I slip out of her, leaving her panting on the table. "What are you doing?"

"I think it'll feel better if you come all over my mouth. Don't you think?"

I flip her around with one hand under her waist until she's on her back. Her whole body is red now, full of pleasure. Her sex is already soaked, every inch of her upper thighs covered with her arousal. I lower myself to position my mouth with her desperate pussy and she leans up on her elbows, watching me.

I keep my eyes locked with hers as I press my mouth to her extremely sensitive clit, my tongue circling it as she cries out, her legs instantly closing on my face.

She needs to get used to my touch. She needs to get used to the way I make her feel. Every time I touch her, her body becomes so sensitive to me.

"Spread your legs for me, sweetheart," I murmur, pressing her thighs apart. She rolls her head back and she does what I tell her to. I suck harder on her clit then, rewarding her for listening to me.

"*Evan*," she whines. I can't help but fist my dick as I eat her out, needing to come with her.

"I've got you, baby, don't worry," I say into her skin. She tries to roll her hips against me, but her body gets taken over with pleasure that she doesn't get very far. "You've got to keep your fucking legs apart," I demand when she tries to clench them across my face again.

"Evan, I can't..."

"Do you want to come or not, pretty girl?"

"Yes," she cries. "*Yes*."

"Great, then act like it."

When she finally listens to me, opening her legs just right, I suck and lick over her flesh, driving her to the edge while pumping my dick in my hand. It's a fucking mess when she finally comes, her whole body trembling and shaking beneath me as white streaks burst behind my eyes, the cum spilling out of me onto the desk.

After we both get over the initial shock and the after-sex bliss, I take her into my shower, cleaning up every part of her body and she lets me, trapped in some sort of haze. I hold her close to me as I wash the soap suds across her body, finally being able to have her in my arms. I can't stop touching her, holding her.

It feels like, for so long, I've been searching for this *thing* – not necessarily a person, but more of a feeling – to finally complete me. To quieten the noise in my head and the tremble in my hands. And slowly, easily, Scarlett has become that for me – my absolute everything.

In realising that, I've also realised that I just need her close to me.

Always.

When we get to my bedroom, she doesn't freak out like I

expected. Instead, she shrugs off the towel I wrapped her in, shoving me on the bed before straddling my lap and riding me like a fucking goddess, while I worship her like one.

"That was really good, Ev," she whispers against my chest when we've both come down from the high. "Like, I'm *surprised* at how good that was."

I laugh a little, running my hand down her spine. "I told you it would be worth it."

42

SCARLETT

AS 1 OPEN MY EYES, I feel like my whole body is being weighed down by a bulldozer. I can't tell if it's because my body aches so much, or from Evan's larger-than-life chest, pressing into mine. His weight calms me somehow, makes me feel like everything is going to be okay.

We slept together. Evan Branson basically fucked my brains out and now he's sleeping on my chest, naked. I think — no, I *know* — that was the best sex of my life. From the touching, the whispers, the edging, the teasing to the cleanup; everything was fantastic. I'm still in shock about it. I knew when he promised me his dick would be worth the wait, I just didn't know how much.

Just thinking about it — and feeling him against my leg now — makes me extra giddy. I muster up the strength to push his body off mine as he stirs, falling onto his back. He looks like a God, and he fucks like one too. His face is perfectly relaxed, his jawline still sharp as hell as his chest rises and falls, the sun peeking into his room, giving his blonde waves a gentle glow.

I can't help myself anymore, so I climb onto him, straddling his abdomen as I press my hands to his chest, feeling his heartbeat steady beneath my palms. I press a kiss to his forehead. He still doesn't wake. I press another kiss to his cheek. I'm smiling so hard my mouth hurts when I start to slide down him, kissing across his toned chest, until he starts to stir more, opening his eyes a little, blinking rapidly.

"Good morning, sunshine," I say, kissing along his face again. He doesn't say anything other than that boyish, I-just-woke-up groan that leaves his mouth. "What's the matter with you?"

"What's wrong with *you*?" he asks, his voice heavy with sleep that it sounds so low and sexy. For someone who has a naked girl on top of him, he doesn't seem too thrilled. He rubs his eye with one hand, the other finding my hip as he runs his thumb across the bone. It feels like he's been tethered to me. As if he just *has* to touch me. That's more like it. "It's, like, six am."

He's not a morning person. I love it. I'm not a particularly a morning person either, but I think I've turned into an Evan person. If being a morning person means I get to wake up to this sight beneath me, I'll get up at six every day for the rest of my life.

"So?" I ask, cheerfully. He looks up at me now. Well, he looks at my bare chest first before his eyes wander to mine. His cheeks turn a pretty shade of pink that I can't help but stroke my thumb against it. He's like a damn puppy – all sweet and soft.

"So…Why do you have so much energy?" he asks, but he's grinning now, his thumb still circling my hip and I notice the ribbon he's still wearing. I lean forward and press a soft kiss to his lips, loving the fresh taste of him. He tastes faintly like toothpaste, but mostly like me.

"I always have energy. There's never a dull moment with me, Branson," I say.

"Yeah, I realised," he replies, laughing. He leans up in the bed, rests his back against the headboard as he wraps his hands around my waist, shoving me closer to him. I can feel his already hard dick pressing against me and my heartbeat starts to pick up as I look down at him, matching the smile on his face. He does the stupidest thing he can do and rolls my hips against him.

"Ev," I warn, narrowing my eyes at him. He ignores me.

"You just woke up and you're already this wet for me?" he whispers, pressing a kiss to the top of my chest. I would be embarrassed, but I always feel everything so deeply when it comes to him. Even if that means being so incredibly turned on just by waking up on top of him. He rolls me over him again and I can feel my arousal coating his dick. I brace my hands on his shoulders, leaning further into him.

"Don't start things you don't have time to finish," I say into his neck.

"I could go on like this all day with you, Scarlett, you know that," he says, diving into a messy kiss that's all teeth, skin, and lips. A huge part of me hates feeling like I'm no longer in control, but another part of me, buried deep down, secretly loves it. I've not felt this happy in a long time and God, I deserve it.

I hear the sound of scratching against the door. I ignore it, kissing him back before it gets louder.

"What the hell is that?" I ask, breaking away from the kiss, narrowing my eyes at him.

"It's just our dog. Come closer to me," he replies, pushing my chest closer to his, but I resist when the scratching intensifies.

"Let that poor dog in here right now, Branson," I demand. He scoffs, not taking me seriously. When I don't laugh or smile at him, he huffs, sliding out from underneath me.

All six-foot and three inches of him slides off the bed as he pulls on his boxers. He's got a nice, firm ass that sways slightly as he walks over to the door. I pull a soft cotton shirt from his bedside drawer, slipping it on.

Before I get time to process it, a huge golden Labrador jumps right onto the bed, trapping me down.

EVAN

I might pass out.

I might die.

Or I might throw up. I don't know.

All I know is that Scarlett Voss is playing with my dog in my bed, giggling and my heartbeat won't stop beating a million miles an hour.

"You like dogs?" I ask when the words come. Mila has basically squashed her, but she doesn't seem to mind. Scarlett's red face pops up under Mila's tummy.

"I *love* them! I didn't get a proper look at her last time," she replies, gasping as Mila pins her down again. "My dad never let us get one because Henry gets too irritable with fur." She manages to sit up next to me, and Mila lies across both of our legs, her head in Scarlett's lap.

"You're such a good dog, aren't you?" she coos in a sweet baby voice. "What's your name, sweet girl?"

"Mila," I say through a grin. She looks up at me and I swear I see tears in her eyes.

"*Mila*," she repeats, cooing again as she scratches her on the head. "You're just so cute. I want to take you home."

"Like she would ever let you," I scoff. Scarlett frowns and Mila looks up at me with those doe eyes. "She's too loyal for he own good, aren't you girl?"

I look over at Scarlett as we both fuss over the excited puppy as she rolls over my bed, and I swear I get a glimpse into our future. Mornings like this. Both of us snuggled up in bed. *Our* bed. A huge Labrador rolling around us as we treat her like a baby. That's what I want my future to look like. There's no future I want to be a part of where Scarlett isn't with me.

When she's still giggling, running her hands over Mila's fur, I grasp her chin in my hand, turning her towards me. "Scar?"

"Hm?"

"You're it for me."

"I know," she mutters, pressing a soft kiss to my lips. "No one would be willing to put up with your shit other than me."

"Guess you're stuck with me, then."

She shrugs. "Guess so."

SCARLETT

"Fun night?"

I'm startled by the sound of Kennedy's voice as I lock the door behind me. It was already a struggle trying to sneak into the building without people from school seeing me, especially not Miles since his house is so close by and he often practices early. I usually see him when I'm doing my weekly walk of shame, and I did not want him to catch me this morning. Instead, I'm caught by Kennedy. She's sitting in the dark, the blinds in the living room closed as she eats some cereal on the kitchen island.

"Jesus, Ken, you need to start wearing a bell," I say, sighing against the door before walking over to her.

"How would that work if I'm sitting down?" she asks curiously, tilting her head to the side. Some of the milk dribbles down her chin and she wipes it away with the sleeve of her dressing gown. "Good night?" she asks again.

"Yeah, it was okay," I reply, moving towards the fridge, opening it so the cool air can hit me. I'm lying to both of us here. 'Okay,' doesn't mean shit compared to what happened last night. It was more than *okay.*

"These came for you this morning," she says. I close the fridge, turning towards her and then I notice the black box and bouquet of flowers. The box is covered in tissue paper with an envelope on top. The bouquet is a mix of orange and pink tulips. "Who are they from?" she sing-songs, peaking over at me as I pick up the envelope. We both know who they're from. Still, I open the envelope and read the note.

I got you these in hopes of doing them together. Then, I figured it would turn into a screaming match where you'd tell me I'm doing it wrong, and I'd let you. Let me know when you want to start, and we'll see who finishes

first. Spoiler Alert: I'm not going to let you win at everything.
  Yours, Evan Branson.

I LAUGH to myself as I re-read the note. I did not peg him for the romantic type at all. Still, it fills my chest with warmth and my smile doubles. Kennedy watches me like a movie as I open the box to find Lego flowers, matching the ones that are sitting on the island, as well as a Bonsai tree made of Lego.

Evan Branson bought me Lego flowers.

I THOUGHT the weirdest part of this whole thing was the fact that I actually like Evan, but it's not. The weirdest part of it all is that I feel totally and completely safe with him and I don't worry about him doing something that can hurt me. Everything about him just feels right. Beneath all the arguments and petty comments, I feel like I just know him as much as he knows me. We spent so long picking at each other's weaknesses, knowing where to hurt each other, but it really just allowed me to know him.

That's why I know that when he's not in the library, he's in the music rooms. As I make my way over, I try to think of a way to thank him for the gift. I've not received any gifts before from people I've slept with, but the fact he got me something makes me feel like it's much more than that. That it's bigger than the both of us.

When I get to the room, I stand outside it for a minute,

transfixed by the piece he's playing. It sounds like '*Linda's song*'. The one he wrote for me. It's going to take me a while to get used to the fact that he wrote something and dedicated it to me *just because*. That's the thing about Evan, he doesn't do things because I ask him, he does it *just because*.

"Are you going to come in or keep staring some more?"

I didn't even notice that he had stopped playing until his eyes connected with mine in the mirror. I push open the door slightly, slipping into the room. It's hard to look at him without thinking of everything he did to me last night. About every dirty word, every touch...

"I just wanted to say thank you for the flowers and for the Lego ones," I say, twisting my fingers in the sleeve of my shirt. He angles his body towards mine, swinging his legs over the bench.

He shrugs. "You make me want to do cute shit like that for you."

"I suck at giving gifts," I admit. This is why I've been so nervous. I don't want him to buy me things because I know there's nothing I can give him in return. He could try to ease my guilt, telling me that all he needs is me, but sometimes that can't be enough. I can't be enough to satisfy him. There's no way.

"You probably don't," he says easily.

"See you said 'probably.' Which means a part of you knows that what I'm saying is true," I challenge.

He frowns. "Scarlett," he says gently.

"No, like, I'm actually terrible. Unless someone tells me exactly what they want, I get awful gifts," I argue, cutting him off. He studies me for a minute before pinning his hands across his chest. I notice the ribbon he's still wearing on his wrist, and

I tug it. "See, that's the best you're going to get from me, Branson."

He laughs quietly. "So, if it was my birthday next week, what would you get me?" he asks. I think about it for a minute. It's not that I don't know him. I could get him a hundred things I know he likes, but I don't know how to get someone something so meaningful that it makes them cry. Something abstract and just *different*.

"A tie," I say finally.

He tilts his head as he repeats, "A tie?" I nod, pulling my lip between my teeth. "That's pathetic, Scarlett. Come on, you can do better than that."

His encouragement makes me think harder. Dig deeper. "Okay, maybe a plushie in the shape of a music note because I know you like music."

"Now that's better," he praises. He tilts his head towards me. "Keep going."

"Maybe I'd make you a playlist."

"You'd do that?"

"I love music and you love music. It's one of the things we have in common, but our tastes are different. I could find something that's a bit of both of us."

"I like that idea."

"Yeah?" He nods. I shift uncomfortably, trying to think of something else to say. This shouldn't be so hard. I've spent so long arguing with him, now I don't know what to say, or how to act. I've never been a relationship kind of person, but he makes it seem easy.

"Hey, Scar?" My stomach responds first with butterflies at the stupid nickname. "Stop worrying. You're fine. I'm fine. *We're* fine. Just let yourself have this, okay?"

"I'm trying."

"Good."

"Great."

"Perfect."

"Amazing."

"Fan-fucking-tastic," he says, punching out each syllable with extra force. I lean forward, grab his shirt, and pull him into me, kissing him so hard that I lose my balance.

43

EVAN

"WHAT HAVE YOU DONE TO HER?" Miles asks, storming into the kitchen as I sit by the breakfast bar, eating my cereal. Last time I checked, I was on my best behaviour. My grades have gone up. I've felt more relaxed than usual. I might not have got what I wanted by being back in the business, but I'm starting to like this new life a lot more because I get to share it with my favourite person.

"Done to who?" I say through a mouthful of Cheerio's.

"Scarlett, you idiot."

"Oh," I say. I try to think of something that we've left unresolved, but I come up empty. All I've done recently is whisper filthy things in her ear while we prepare for our last report, eat her out until she's a whimpering mess, and hold her hand. That's it. I end up shrugging in response.

"*Oh*?" he repeats, throwing an empty can at me, hitting me in the arm.

"Okay, ouch?" I say, rubbing the sore spot of my shoulder as he walks further to me.

"Wren is freaking out. Scarlett hasn't left her room all day because of something that got delivered." He leans forward and pokes me in the arm. "From." Another poke. "You. Did you send her a dead body to her room or something?"

"No, you sicko. I just sent her a gift," I say truthfully, picking up my bowl to put it into the sink. Miles follows me, watching me intently. "Why are you breathing down my neck?"

"Because my girlfriend is worried about her friend because of you. So, you better-"

I cut him off with a condescending hand to his chest, pushing him away from me. "Careful who you're talking to, Davis, or I'll personally deliver a dead man into your room."

He sighs, rolling his eyes. "Just fix it, please,"

"She's just being dramatic. I'll go over when she's cooled down."

Except when I get to her apartment an hour later, Wren and Kennedy are standing by their kitchen island, arms across their chest, expecting me. It's like walking into the Lion's den. I didn't know two girls could be so fucking terrifying, but they are. They both glared at me, their faces red with anger.

"What did you do, Branson?" Kennedy asks.

"You guys need to chill. She's just being dramatic. I promise you when I speak to her, she'll calm down," I say, doing my best to convince them, but they don't seem to take it well. I step further into the room, but they make me back up, their protective presence deterring me a little.

"She better. Or so help me God, you will not live to see another day on this earth," Wren warns. She's a lot scarier than Miles's empty threats.

I hold my hands up in surrender, side stepping down the corridor until I reach her room. I knock on the door twice, calling out her name, but she doesn't respond. I hear the faint footsteps as she unlocks the door. I wait a few seconds before opening it.

As I expected, she's standing with her back to me, staring at the painting I bought her. Her room must be the biggest one in the apartment because she somehow manages to fit a queen sized bed, a desk, a walk-in closet, and en suite. Her walls are painted a light grey colour with black and white movie posters covering the walls. It's just so *her*.

I knew the second she stared at it in the gallery on our fake date as she held my hand, I had to get it for her. It took me longer than I needed to, but I wanted her to have it. For it to be just hers. There's already so much art in this apartment - courtesy of Kennedy — but I wanted her to have something of her own and the painting makes so much sense for her. '*You Are Home*' because that's what my brain tells me whenever I'm around her. She is what home feels like.

"You got this for me?" she whispers. I can't tell if she's angry at me for doing this or if she's that emotional that she can't look at me. I take a step towards her.

"It was supposed to come tomorrow. I was meant to take you out for dinner first," I say, admitting the truth. I wanted to show her how good I would be for her and to her before giving her a gift as expensive as this one, but the universe had other plans, apparently.

"How did you even get it?" she asks, slowly turning around to me, her arms still against her chest. My breath nearly gets knocked out of me as she blinks up at me, her brown eyes full of innocence, but I know she's all sin. Her hair is down again, those deep brown waves bouncing off her shoulders. "It wasn't for sale."

"I have my ways," I say, shrugging, shoving my hands into my pockets. She steps closer to me as she narrows her eyes.

"How much did it cost you?"

"Two hundred thousand." Her eyes basically bulge out of her head. I rest my hand on her shoulder, steadying her as she sways a little. I had enough savings and I wanted to do something nice for her. I know she's not a stranger to money, so I'm confused as to why she's so shocked. "What? Are you mad at me?"

"Evan," she whispers. "Don't tell me you used all your savings to buy me this. I don't even spend that much money on myself. I- I'm going to pay you back."

I silence her ridiculous rambling with a kiss and she's still in shock before she melts into me. She kisses me back, but she pushes off my chest as she looks up at me, her eyes filled with worry. "I'm serious. I'm going to pay you back every penny."

"Stop saying that, Scar. Let me be nice to you," I say before kissing her again. I hold her face to mine as I kiss the side of her mouth. "Plus, I know a better way you can pay me back. Without money."

"Yeah?"

"Come to dinner with me tonight. I'll pick you up at eight." She thinks about it for a second, twisting her lip between her teeth before smiling wide. I want to take her on a real date. One where we're doing it because we want to.

"Okay, but I'm paying."

"If you pay, you've got to wear the red dress."

"This deal seems like you're getting the better end of it," she challenges, holding her chin high.

"Just wear it. I'm begging you."

"You know I love it when you beg for me, Branson," she purrs, trailing her hand up my arm. She's going to have to wait for tonight. Her friends still don't know what we're doing and I sure as hell know she wouldn't keep quiet if I touched her now. "You won't be able to keep your hands off me if I do."

"That's the whole point," I whisper back.

SHE WAS RIGHT. Of course, she was right. I told her to wear the dress and she did. And she looks fucking stunning. She looks like she's mine and I can't stop touching her.

On the car ride here, I kept my hand on her thigh, needing the warmth beneath my fingertips. When I stepped out of the car, I held my hand out for her to clasp her palm into mine. When the wind swayed in her face, I brushed her hair out of her eyes and kept my hand linked with hers until we reached the restaurant.

I took her to one of the fanciest restaurants in the city, everyone's heads turning when we walked in like fucking royalty. She held onto my arm, letting me guide her until we got up the stairs to a balcony seat, overlooking the rivers and the mountains.

I said I would be the best boyfriend she ever had and that's exactly what I'm trying to do. To show her how in awe I am of everything she does. How I'm so incredibly proud of her. How every single thing she does lights me up inside.

As the sun starts to fade, I can't stop looking at her. Her face is flushed like it always is whenever I'm around. She is practically glowing as she talks animatedly with her hands, while I watch her. She still drops her eyes after four seconds of uninterrupted eye contact, glancing to either the plate in front of us or to the scenery.

All I can think about is how full my heart feels to finally

have her. How badly I'm in love with her smart, brilliant, and beautiful mind.

"Stop staring at me," she mutters, pushing her hair behind her ear, showing off her silver earrings. "You're making me nervous."

"Angel, you've been making me nervous all my life. How do you think I feel?" I say back, chuckling. She shakes her head at me as she tries to hide her giddy smile.

"Can I ask you something?" she says as she picks at the garlic dough balls in the middle of the table. She shoves a piece in her mouth.

"Anything."

She swallows. "What do you fear the most?"

"Getting all existential on me before the main course, sweetheart?"

She laughs a little. "I'm being serious. We have these great moments — moments where we argue, and you look right through me, and I don't know…I feel like I want to know everything about you."

"I'm scared of a lot of things, Angel," I say truthfully. She leans back in her chair a little, listening to me intently. I want her to know everything about me. *Everything*. "Growing up, I was always anxious, always waiting for the other ball to drop. I thought that things would happen to me — bad things — if I didn't do a certain thing. I always had to count to a specific number before falling asleep and if I didn't, my brain would trick me into believing that I was going to get killed. And that was just at the beginning." She leans forward now, reaching out to hold onto my hand. "Then when my mom left, I thought *that* was the other shoe. That it needed to happen to stop the compulsive thoughts, but it didn't. I just got worse until one day I wouldn't leave the car because it didn't feel right. Something in me was telling me that if I left, something bad would happen. So, my dad finally took me to see a doctor and I got diagnosed with OCD and then a few months later, I realised I had anxiety."

"Why do you think you were anxious all the time?" she asks quietly.

"I guess I just couldn't believe the life I was living. It felt like I was trapped in someone else's body. Nothing truly felt like it was mine. Everything felt so fleeting, like it could just disappear at any moment, and I was just constantly in anticipation, waiting for it to happen."

She nods before dropping her gaze to the table again. "Do you still feel like that now? With me?"

I shake my head. "Not anymore. Not when I know I've got your back and you've got mine, no matter what." She squeezes my hand again, rubbing her thumb against it and it makes me relax, feeling that much lighter. "What about you? What's your biggest fear."

"Being forgotten," she replies instantly. "I know it's stupid because there's going to be a day where that last person who remembers you disappears, and you just become nothing. That's what I don't want to happen. I want my name to mean something when I'm gone."

It feels like she's speaking right into my soul. There's always been that looming fear that no matter how hard I can try to make something of myself, to make myself seen, it's not going to last forever. Day by day, people are forgetting you. Whether that be strangers or people you once knew. Then one day, there's going to be that last person who remembers you and they're going to go too. The worst part is, you'll never know when it's going to happen. It just will.

"It already does. You and your name mean so much to me.

And it's going to continue to mean so much to me until I can give you my last name," I say easily. She narrows her eyes at me, sizing me up.

"First of all, what makes you think we're going to get married? And second of all, what makes you think I want your last name?" she quizzes, sounding and looking genuinely taken aback. I know dropping the marriage hint is way too early, but I know what I want. There's not going to be anyone else but her. She's it for me.

"Because I know you. I understand you more than I understand myself, sometimes. We're not just a one-time thing, anymore, Angel," I say. Her lips part slightly, her brown eyes huge and wild. "But you're right. You'd only take my last name to combine it with yours."

She nods at that, her face breaking into a smile so beautiful it almost hurts. "Exactly. Because we're equals."

"Exactly," I say back.

"Which means no more trying to save me when I'm a damsel in distress. Or buying me expensive things *just because*." She says the last two words with an eye roll, including sarcastic air quotes. "I'm perfectly capable of doing things on my own, Branson."

"I know. I just-" I sigh, shaking my head a little. "There's nothing I wouldn't do to make you happy, Scar."

She snorts. "How many women have you said that to?"

"None."

"I don't believe you."

"Well, you should because I mean it."

We spend the rest of the meal talking about everything and nothing. She tells me about her dreams about having her own clothing line for Voss and I tell her that I know she can do it.

She tells me about everything she wishes to do when she

finishes NU as we walk back to her apartment. It's a long walk, but she doesn't stop talking. She tells me about how she's excited to see her dad again when he's home and I tell her that I'd want to meet him too at some point.

She tells me how she wants to get cats when she has her own place, and we argue over her being a cat person and me preferring dogs. Really, I could be convinced into being a cat person if she wants one so badly. After seeing her with Mila, I'm sure I could convince her too.

Even when our throats dry, my feet are aching and she's laughing at her own jokes, I wouldn't change it for the world.

As I stand with her outside her apartment door, she shoves her hands into her coat pockets, neither of us wanting the night to end.

"You know what you said earlier?" she asks. I hum in response. "Would you really do anything for me, or were you just saying that?"

"Anything," I say.

She laughs quietly, her hair brushing in front of her face a little. "You'd even steal a whiteboard for me?"

I groan, throwing my head back. "How many times are we going to have this conversation, Angel? I didn't steal your damn whiteboard."

"Oh, so you'd do *anything* for me, but stealing is where you draw the line?" she retorts, her cheeks flaming as her hands fall to her side. "What if I was being attacked, or stalked, and my stalker had a collection of whiteboards, a fetish of some sorts. You'd have to steal one to prove to the police that your girlfriend isn't crazy. What then, Branson, huh? *What.*" She pushes me in the chest. "*Then.*"

Girlfriend. That word does something insane to my insides.

It sits on my chest nicely, like a warm fuzzy cat making itself at home. *My girlfriend, Scarlett.* I love the sound of that.

"So, you're my girlfriend, now, huh?" I mock.

She rolls her eyes. "That's beside the point. I want to know if what you said was actually true."

I grip her chin in my hand, watching the surprise wash across her face as her eyes search mine. I bring my face closer to hers, nudging our noses together as she takes in a deep breath.

"Yeah," I murmur against her lips, "I'd steal it for you, *tesoro*."

Her eyes widen in surprise. "Did you just call me-"

I silence her with a kiss. "Just shut up."

44

SCARLETT

I DON'T THINK I've ever felt this light and freeing in my life. The doctors have finally cleared my dad to go back home, and I haven't been able to see him since he woke up. According to my mom, he's been begging for us all to get together again and I want to be back at home.

Arthur gave me a dirty look when I walked through the doors, but I held my ground and my head high. He's always been protective over me, but he's started to just become an annoying leech. Even after all that went down, he's not bothered to ask if I'm okay even if I was trapped in a room with a murderer. I know we're never going to have a perfect relationship and I can live like that. I've got Henry and Leo when I need them, knowing they'll always have my back. And Alex too, when he's available to talk given the time difference.

Seeing my dad here, walking around, smiling is something I didn't think I would see. As much as I tried to be optimistic, the possible reality was terrifying. I never thought I'd see him work a barbecue again. I never thought I'd see him smile as I surprised him at work. I never thought I'd hear him sing while spinning my mom around in the kitchen.

No matter how tense our relationship gets or how many times I've felt ignored by him, I've always known his intentions were good. All he's wanted is to keep me safe which is why I was surprised he didn't scream at me for putting myself in danger multiple times just to find out what happened to him. It's all been worth it though. To be in my dad's arms right now, neither of us saying anything as we hold on tight to each other, all of the pain has been worth it.

"Where's your boyfriend? I thought he was coming," my dad says when he pulls out of the hug, looking around the room as if Evan was just going to turn up out of thin air. That lasted longer than I thought. After keeping small talk just that — *small* — I knew my nosy family would be wondering about me finally finding my person.

"Word gets around here fast, doesn't it," I mutter, shooting Henry a look as I move out of my dad's arms. He shrugs, innocently, downing a glass of orange juice.

"Not really. It was kind of obvious after the way he came rushing after you at the hospital," Leo says, puffing a cloud of smoke into the air.

My mom walks behind him, pulling the joint from his lips and he frowns.

Everyone's in here now: my dad sitting on the stool next to the island, my mom behind him rubbing his shoulders, Leo by the counter with a fresh joint in his hand and Henry by the fridge, eating as much as he can. There has nothing I've missed quite as much as I've missed this chaotic, brilliant, and wonderful family. They're just *my* family. My perfectly imperfect family who are surprisingly okay with me dating someone they would have despised months ago, no matter how desperate my mom was to get me into a relationship.

"Why are you guys so chill about it?" I ask, looking between my brothers and my parents. Arthur is off brooding in the corner, being a complete baby about this. "You do know he's a Branson, right?"

"We know, but I know he likes you. A lot. He always has," my mom says, beaming at me dreamily. It's been her dream for years for me to get into a stable relationship and now that I'm finally in one, she can't stop smiling like a Cheshire cat.

"What do you mean, *always*?" I ask, confused. They must have been able to pick up on the fact we were faking it last time. It doesn't take a genius. My mom's smile is so wide I don't know how her face doesn't crack.

"You probably don't remember when you went to your first event with us as a family and Evan was there. You two were the youngest at the kids table and you were crying because your brothers were leaving you out. He helped you stop crying and held your hand and walked you to us and told us to take care of you so you wouldn't be alone."

The flashbacks come back to me in a blur. I hardly remember many events from when I was a kid, but I knew I wasn't the only child at them other than my brothers. There were always little kids running around, their parents scolding them for getting their Sunday best dirty. I do remember feeling lonely most of the time while my brothers purposefully left me out.

"That was him? I always thought it was some random boy, but it was... him."

"Yes, my love. And he sent me a home cooked meal while I was in hospital after I woke up with a note and everything."

"You're lying," I gasp.

"Nope. I was there when he came. I thought he already told you," Henry says. He pulls his phone out of his back pocket, swiping until he pulls up a picture he took of a handwritten note. In Evan's handwriting.

Hi Mateo,

You don't know me, but I wanted to tell you a few things. Firstly, I'm sorry you have to wake up to the news of your brother passing. From the very short conversation we had, he seemed like a kind person, and I know Scarlett cared for him a lot. You should know how highly your daughter talks of you. At first it was kind of annoying, knowing my dad isn't exactly a saint but then I realised it's because no matter how hard of a time you give each other you're always there. She's been working hard on trying to find out what happened to you and now that she has, she's turned into an even more confident and brave woman. She makes me work for every smile she gives me. She frightens me by doing reckless things and grinning as if she didn't try to give me a heart attack. Anyway, what I'm trying to say is that all she really wants for you is to be seen, appreciated and respected. I know how important it is for her to be treated that way and I'll try my best to do it too, but I *ask one thing of you: look at Scarlett. Like, really, *look* at her. Because if you look long enough, you'll see exactly what I see: an absolute angel.*

"HOLY SHIT," I whisper, blinking at the phone like it's going to disintegrate. "Holy, holy shit."

"Are you done?" my mom murmurs. I nod, my mouth still wide open. "We've seen your designs, Scarlett."

My heartbeat starts to pick up. I only showed Gio my designs because I know they're not perfect. He managed to change a few and get them into the clothing discreetly, another designer taking credit so my dad wouldn't know.

"You have? Did- Did you like them?" I ask nervously.

"They're beautiful, *tesoro*," my dad says, smiling wide.

"You think so?"

He nods before sighing, dropping his shoulders. "I think I was so afraid of seeing what would happen if you became like us. If you were dragged into something as messy as it was these last few months, but you've proven to me that you can handle it. And with a little work with an expert, I'd want you to be our fashion designer for the new collection of Voss."

Am I dreaming? I *must* be dreaming right? This is not supposed to happen to me. In my dream, I was meant to create a portfolio, present it to my dad and the board and then they'd accept me. Not this.

"Holy shit. Are you serious?" I exclaim, basically jumping with joy. God, my mouth is starting to hurt from smiling so much. My mom glares at me. "Sorry," I mutter.

"Yes, my love, I'm serious," my dad says, and he barely gets the words out before I trap him into another huge hug, his large arms wrapping around me tightly, tugging me closer to him.

I THOUGHT I was on cloud nine this morning, but now I've reached a new high. One I don't ever want to come down from. When I get to Florentino's there's no queue and I get my coffee within two minutes. As I walk home in the dark, I don't feel worried or unsafe near campus. It's quiet out and my music shuffles to all the perfect songs. It's a good day. It's been a good day.

For once, I don't feel like the feeling won't last. I don't worry that I'm going to run out of this insanely positive energy. I just want to bathe in it, soak it all up until it's all I become. Just pure bliss.

Even when I get into bed later that night and I check my phone, I'm smiling at the screen so hard it almost cracks because Evan texted me. He sent me a picture of an adorable black kitten, smushed against his face. His cheeks are a little red in the photo, his smile contagious as this random kitten claws at his shirt. God, he looks so handsome like that and so cute at the same time. I immediately save the picture, adding it to an album I hope to keep adding to.

EVAN: Saw this kitten and thought of you. Tiny but viscous.

ME: Ew stop!!!

EVAN: Stop what?

ME: Thinking about me. You're like obsessed or something.

EVAN: Or something.

EVAN: Do you ever think about me?

ME: Not on purpose...

EVAN: Sounds like a win to me.

ME: This oddly feels like that one episode of New Girl.

EVAN: GAVE ME COOKIE GOT YOU COOKIE!!!!

ME: You're getting blocked.

EVAN: You'd never do that. I can see that you saved it to your camera roll, Angel.

FUCK. I've been caught.

ME: Only so I can print it out and frame it.

I REALISE how that sounds and quickly send out another response.

> ME: NOT IN A WEIRD WAY, YOU WEIRDO.

EVAN: Sure.

EVAN: Send me a pic of you. It's only fair.

I SIT up further in the bed. I look like a certified mess right now; my hair is unruly; I'm wearing one of Henry's old shirts and sleep shorts. I'm not my usual put-together self. But with him, I don't seem to care anymore. It's hard to be concerned with how he sees me when he's seen *all* of me – the good, the bad, and the ugly.

So, I send him a selfie, flipping him off.

> ME: Saw this and thought of you. Hot, but still pisses me off.

EVAN: Very funny.

EVAN: Are you calling me hot or yourself?

> ME: Both?

EVAN: Right answer.

> ME: Thank you, btw.

EVAN: What for???

> ME: My dad. The letter. The food. Holding my hand.

ME: I got a job, too.

EVAN: I hope you know how proud I am of you. Like, so, fucking, sickeningly proud of you. You could do anything you wanted to. I'm in your corner, Scar. Always.

THIS IS a new low for me because I'm sitting in my bed, staring at my phone screen as I start to cry over a text Evan has sent me. I might just be hormonal and overwhelmed with the amount of shit that has gone down these last few weeks. I try to compose a reply, but my eyes can't help but snag on those words.

I hope you know how proud I am of you.

45

SCARLETT

IF THERE'S one thing us Voss' like, it's a big party. But not just any party. It needs to be a blowout party with a DJ, a buffet, and a dance floor, or nothing at all. We always hold our best parties out of state, usually in L.A, where most of our family live as well as where our headquarters is located. The second my dad got back on his feet, he put together one of the best 'Welcome Back' parties he could.

With Lucas put away and the people infiltrating the committee out, I've felt so much better. It also helps that Evan and I have submitted our final report and we're due to hear our grade within the next few weeks. I thought we could all use the getaway and celebration, so I brought Wren, Miles, Evan, and Kennedy with me on the flight to LA.

Only problem? Having to explain the room situation. I booked three rooms and I've been trying to tell Kennedy that I'm not sharing a room with her since we got to the runway, but she's not been making it easy.

"This is going to be exactly like the good old days," Kennedy says, clutching her iPad to her chest like a kid. We've been waiting on the runway for almost half an hour. Wren and Miles are standing in front of us, Evan beside them. He keeps turning back, glancing at me and it's making me blush. I hate it.

"Yeah, Ken-"

"Oh my God," she exclaims. "Did you pack the face masks? Because I didn't get any. I mean, it's LA, we can find some anywhere but still. Do you think the room will-"

I cut her off with my hand on her shoulder. "Actually, I'm sharing a room with Evan." He turns around now, the satisfied smirk on his face. Wren and Miles are caught up in their own world as she lists things to him, making sure he packed them while he kisses all of her face, leaving her in giggles.

"What?" she screeches. "Did he bribe you?"

"No, Kennedy. We've been, sort of, definitely dating."

Wren and Miles still don't turn around to that. I was sure it would set off some trigger in her brain, but she's too caught up. He's still kissing all over her face and she's letting him.

Yep.

It's their world and we're just living in it.

"It's about time that you two broke," Kennedy says, beaming. "It was getting sickening watching you guys pretend to compete with each other."

"Oh, we still do," Evan says.

"Yeah," I add. "The sex is better that way."

When the plane finally arrives, I take my seat next to Evan as everyone else gets comfortable to sleep for the two hour flight. I don't think I could sleep if I tried. I'm constantly hyper-aware of him. Our seats are the normal distance apart, but with his heavy hand on my thigh, it feels like every part of us is touching.

"You know what, Branson?" I ask into the comfortable

silence, the second the thought pops into my head. "I think you're good for me."

"Finally," he groans. "I've been telling you that for ages."

"I know," I giggle. *I giggle?* What the fuck is wrong with me? I shrug, trying to play it off. "I don't know. I think you challenge me, push me to go that extra mile and I do. The same way I challenge you, but not in a way that means you're trying to do or be better than me. I like that about us."

"Yeah?" I nod, looking up at him. He places his arm around my shoulder, pulling me closer to him. "I'm on your team, Scar. I always have been. I always play by your rules. If you want to hate me, fine. If you want to hate-kiss me or beat me up, fine. I'd give you the world if you let me. God, I'd give you anything you want."

"I don't want the world, Ev."

"Tell me what you want, Angel, and I'll give it to you."

"Right now? I think I just want you," I admit. "Just you."

"I'm yours."

BY THE TIME we get down to the lobby, the party is raging outside while people dance around with champagne flutes, the music carrying from the lobby right outside. I hold onto Evan's arm as we walk through the crowd, feeling claustrophobic and at home all at the same time. I've been to parties before. I've been to millions of them over the last few years but for some reason, this feels special. Different. A *good* different.

Because I have a job in the company that I've been dying to get for years. My friends are here, enjoying themselves and best of all, I have Evan Branson on my arm. Just thinking about that sentence makes me want to throw up a little. I never thought I'd end up here, actually enjoying his presence, it being the thing that comforts me. In a way, part of me knows that it was inevitable.

"Do you think they've seen us yet?" I whisper to him, glancing down towards the pool where my parents stand. My dad's being greeted by one of our partners, while my mom links her arm in his, most likely drowning out their boring conversation.

"We just walked out the door, so probably not," he whispers back, leaning down to me. I twist us in the opposite direction, finding a corner to the side of the building to hide behind. When we're out of view, I push his back up against the wall. "We've been here two minutes and you already want to rip my clothes off. This is new, even for you."

"Oh, shut up," I murmur angrily, but he grins. I start to smooth out his tuxedo. It looks perfect. He looks perfect. His bow tie is actually tied, but I'm just nervous. "Do you know what you're going to say?"

He shrugs. "Talk about how amazing I am?" I frown. He places his hands over mine, my blue ribbon still tied around his wrist. I take in a breath. "Just relax, sweetheart. I've already met your mom and I've halfway won your dad over."

"I *can't* relax," I say back. "My mom is easy to please, but my dad...I've never had a boyfriend before. Not a real one, anyway. He's either going to hate you or love you. There'll be no in between."

"Do I make you happy?"

"What?"

"Do I make you happy? Do I constantly try to make sure you're comfortable, happy, safe, and satisfied?" I nod. He said he would be the best boyfriend I ever had if I let him, and he is. "That's all a dad would want for their daughter. I'd want the same thing for my kid if I had one."

The thought of Evan having a kid makes the butterflies in my stomach go feral. From the way he takes care of me, looks after me, I can tell he would be perfect at it. Even with all of his anxieties, he would be the best parent ever. Especially to little girls. Holy shit, I'm getting flustered just thinking about it.

"You want kids in the future?" I ask.

"Of course, I do. I'd need something to break the cycle and give someone more than I had," he admits easily. He holds my hands to his lips, kissing them. It's cheesy, but I let him do it. "Come on. We're going to be fine."

And of course, because Evan says we're going to be alright, I believe him.

When we make our way over, I keep my cool and hold my head high. He's right. My dad would want nothing other than my happiness. My dad's tanned face breaks out into a huge smile as he looks at me and Evan. I swear my mom is already on the brink of tears.

"Scarlett," my dad greets, nodding at me. Everything feels too emotional already and nothing has even happened yet. He flicks his gaze to Evan who is still holding my hand.

"Dad, this is Evan," I say, turning to Ev, who has the sweetest smile on his face as he extends his hand to my dad. "My boyfriend."

Those words are seriously coming out of my mouth right now. This feels like some sort of alternate reality. It feels so right, yet so unreal. Being with Evan is like seeing all the good and the bad things with the world and still loving them effort-lessly. Nobody makes me feel more cared for or as beautiful as I do when I'm with him. And now he's shaking my dad's hand.

"It's nice to finally put a face to the name," my dad says through a smile before dropping his hand.

"Likewise," Evan says. "It's nice to meet you." He grins down at me and then back to my dad. "I hope you know what an amazing daughter you have, Mr. Voss."

I elbow him in his rib at his comment as he looks at me adoringly. That's just the thing about Evan; he's constantly lifting me up without me knowing.

"I know," my dad replies, locking his eyes with me.

His gaze drops from mine, moving to Evan and I have to take in a deep breath, so I don't start to cry. This is all I ever wanted from my dad. I just wanted him to *see* me. To understand me. To let me know that he can see how hard I've been trying to get him to realise that I'm capable of more than he thinks.

"Thank you, Evan," he says. Ev and I blink at him, neither of us knowing what to say or what he means. "Thank you for showing me what's been in front of me my whole life. I was too scared to get her involved and I didn't want to ruin her. It shouldn't have taken all this for me to realise that, but hearing about the way you have cared for her and looked after her, doing what I was unable to, made me realise that she is a lot tougher than I give her credit for. So, thank you."

I didn't even realise I was crying softly until I felt the salty tear drop onto my upper lip. I wipe at my face quickly, dropping my eyes to the ground. I don't know how much more my heart can take from this. It feels too full. Almost too much.

"You don't need to thank me, Mr. Voss," Evan says quietly. He reaches for my hand, and I give it to him, letting him hold me. I lift my head up and he's watching me, like always. "No matter how hard she makes me work to get it, I'm going to do anything to keep her happy and safe."

"Is that a promise you're making to me, Evan?" my dad asks seriously. My mom's gaze flickers between the three of us and I do the same.

He swallows. "Yes. That's a promise."

"Good," my dad replies.

"She could handle herself just fine without me, though," Evan says, smirking down at me. I'm glad he's finally got that in his thick skull. My dad smiles proudly. "She's vicious."

"Oh, I know," my mom laughs, and I stick my tongue out at her. She shakes her head at me before her whole face lights up as she looks at Evan. "And, Evan, the song you requested is on next, so you should probably head to the dance floor."

"You... What?" I ask, gawking at him. He ignores me, that slight smirk playing on his lips.

"Thank you Mrs. Voss," he says to my mom, nodding at her before twisting my hand into his chest and pulling me to the dance floor. It's already crowded, but we weave our way through, getting a spot where we can dance together.

The only lights are coming from the fairy lights above the shelter and from inside the hotel. Still, his dark green eyes glow with something I've never seen before. I wrap my arms around his neck, and he wraps his around my waist, pulling me into him, waiting for the song to start.

♫ FADE INTO YOU BY INHALER

I swear I almost pass out when I hear the open chords of the song start to play. It's one of those songs that you can't tell is a breakup song or a love song, but it can exist as both. This cover especially does something to my heart.

It's slow and peaceful and it makes me want to sleep. It's the perfect song to play in the background when I'm doing my homework or when I want to get out of my head for a while. And he chose this.

"Why did you choose this song?" I ask, resting my head on his chest as we sway to the music.

"It makes me think of you," he whispers, "it just feels like you. Like us."

I don't have to ask him what he means. I just understand it so perfectly that all I can do is keep my head pressed against the steady beat of his heart. He holds me close to him, his hands never leaving my body, even as we start to get shoved to the side with more sappy couples entering the dance floor.

Oh my God.

That's exactly what we are. We're a sappy couple. We're the kind of people I would see holding hands in a supermarket and wish that was me. We're basically Wren and Miles, unable to keep our hands off each other. We're everything I have wanted, but also everything I fear.

I want to be happy. I want to be that girl who blushes when her boyfriend texts. I want to be that girl who giggles over ridiculously stupid things for no reason. I want to feel everything he gives me right down to my core, no matter how much it hurts or feels different.

"Sorry to barge in." I open my eyes to see Kennedy and Wren stood at the side of us. Wren's eyes are wide, flicking between the two of us. I push off his chest, tilting my head to the side. "Wren's a little confused, as you can tell. She needs *this*..." She gestures between Evan and I. "...Clearing up ASAP."

"SCARLEY, girl, I've never seen you smile so much," Wren says when we get to the bar. I've tried explaining how everything happened, but it's so hard to do. It ends up with me shoving my face into my hands, my face burning red just thinking about it. Wren's face is bright with child-like joy, her eyes shimmering.

"Something's happening to me," I groan, wiping my hair out of my face.

"You could say that again," Kennedy mutters from beside me. I turn to glare at her, but she just laughs, looking back out at where Miles and Evan stand in a corner, chatting. "I'm loving this for you, Scar. I told you this from the start and now look."

I bark out a laugh. "But then, it sounded so ridiculous. Now it's so…"

"Real?" Wren says and I nod. "Yeah, I get that. You'll get used to it. I've never seen you so smitten."

"I know," I say, laughing at the ridiculousness of it all. "I hate it."

"No, you don't," Kennedy says, blowing a raspberry. "You're in your *Lover* era."

"Your time will come too, Kenny," Wren says.

"Oh, I know," she replies. "You deserve this, Scarlett. After everything that has happened in the last few months, this is good for you. Enjoy it."

I'll try. As much as I love to tease Evan and make him work for every angry kiss he gets from me, I also want what I see in the movies, in books and shows. I want to get dizzy by kissing him just because I can. I want to dance with him on a dance floor or in the rain. I want to smile when I see his name light up on my phone. I want to have everything I've dreamed of but been too scared to grasp.

I want it all.

46

SCARLETT

I TAKE off my earrings in the mirror, wearing nothing but a thin nightdress and black laced lingerie that I packed just for this trip. Everything about today has felt like a dream. One I'm not ready to wake up from.

Even better than a dream? Evan Branson leaning against the doorway, his arms across his chest in nothing but grey sweatpants. His eyes roam all over my body in the mirror, instantly making my whole body flush with heat. I blush too easily when he's around.

He's spent the whole night just doing that – looking at me and making my face burn.

"God, Branson," I groan, shaking my head at him in the mirror. "You're so obsessed with me. You need to stop looking at me like that."

"Can't," he whispers, slowly walking towards me as a grin crawls up his face. When he gets to me, he cages me in with his hands on either side of the vanity, kissing me on my shoulder lightly.

"I bet you wanted me the day you walked me home in the

rain. When you came rushing after me like I was a damsel in distress," I say, laughing. I giggle as his kiss tickles me on my shoulder, as he keeps his eyes locked with mine.

"No," he whispers. "Before that."

"When I accused you of stealing the whiteboard?" I ask, my eyebrows pinched together. He shakes his head lightly.

"Before that."

"What?" I gawk.

"When you shoved bacon in my face at Christmas in your apartment," he admits. If I thought my body was on fire before, I was wrong. This is exactly what it feels like to burst into flames.

"That was over a year ago, Branson. You're lying to my face right now."

"I'm not. In fact, it was probably way before that, but I don't want to scare you off when I've only just got you," he says, twisting me around to face him. Before I can process it, his strong hands have lifted me onto the bathroom counter, his fingers under the skirt of my dress as he rips off my panties in one motion. I gasp.

"Hey, I just bought these," I scold. He silences me with a kiss, pushing his hot, wet mouth to mine, letting me fall right into him, knowing he'll catch me. He pulls apart, his chest heaving as much as mine is.

"Good thing I prefer you without clothes on isn't it, Angel?" he says, slipping his hand to where I'm aching for him.

"I'm not your angel," I bite out.

"No. You're my fucking everything."

EVAN

"Keep your hands there, pretty boy," she demands, tightening her ribbon around my wrists.

I don't know how we got to this point so quickly. One minute I was finger-fucking her on the bathroom counter, watching her moan into my shoulder and the next, we're in the bedroom, I'm on my back as she straddles me, her pretty tits bouncing in my face as she ties her ribbon around my wrists, securing it to the headboard.

"You think I'm pretty?" I nudge my head up, trying to catch my lips with hers, but she tilts her head away from me.

"Something like that."

She leans up off my chest, fishing into the bedside drawer as she retrieves one of the condoms I bought. She rolls it on me and without any warning, with no teasing or edging, she slides my cock into her warm pussy, making me feel straight at home. As she sinks down, her body adjusting to my size, she braces her palms on my chest, rolling her hips slightly, causing her tits to fall further into my face.

"Fuck, Ev," she moans, throwing her head back. I'm hardly doing anything to her, unable to guide her with my hands, but she knows how to make herself feel good and it's a fucking sight. "Everything about you feels good. I hate it."

"I know you love it, sweetheart," I say through a desperate groan as she continues to ride me, her pace picking up. Using her palms to steady herself, she rolls her hips back and forth, pressing her clit onto me to cause more friction.

Her body creates the most obscene image as she gets lost in the moment – her head flying back, her back arched, her nipples hard peaks as she cries out my name. Her whole body is on display for me now, her golden skin glowing right in front of me. God, I want to touch her so bad.

"Scarlett, you're killing me," I bite out, but she doesn't stop. She continues to get herself off, not caring about the amount of pain I'm in. She starts to move faster, and I try to help by bucking my hips up, meeting her bounces, driving her closer to the edge.

"You've got to stop doing that or I'm going to come," she says, her sentence being broken up by pants. She slows down her pace and I slow down mine as she pressed her clit to my skin, rubbing herself against me.

They're something so maddening about not being able to touch her, but still watching her get off while riding me.

"I wish you could see yourself right now. You're being such a good girl for me," I say as her pace quickens, those brown eyes piercing mine. Her eyes gloss over, and she squeezes them shut. "What have I told you, Angel? You look at me when you come for me. Got it?"

A loud moan pierces through the air. "God...Evan..." Her words turn into a garbled moan as she reaches her climax, her body trembling as she collapses on my chest. I want to touch her, soothe her, tell her that she did a good job, but she hasn't untied my hands yet.

After a few seconds of uninterrupted silence other than her pants, she releases my hands from her ribbon.

She smooths her fingers over my wrists, kissing me there. "Was that good for you?"

"It would have been fantastic if I could've touched you," I say, finally grabbing her face and kissing her angrily.

I push her and she pushes back, constantly battling each other for what we want even though it's the same thing. Her body relaxes into me, and I finally get to use my hands to touch her everywhere.

TIME PASSES by in a haze as we shower — again — as the party still rages on downstairs. I don't know why we didn't stay out for longer, especially when our friends were enjoying themselves. I wouldn't have minded, but we were starting to get too touchy, and it didn't feel appropriate around her family. I swear I'd have her attached to me if I could.

For someone who couldn't stand me a few months ago, she clings to me like a koala as we lay in the bed, and I love it. I know that what she feels for me is deeper than we're both admitting, but I'm letting her come to terms with that in her own time. If it means we're going to spend nights like these, her legs wrapped around my waist as she rests her head against my chest as I stroke my hand down her spine, knowing it relaxes her, I'm fine with that.

"You're mine, right?" she whispers into my skin.

"I'm yours," I reply instantly.

She smiles, suddenly giddy and full of life, leaning up on my chest. "Mine," she says into my skin on my chest, kissing me there. "Mine," she presses again with another kiss. She lays back down on my chest, holding onto me tight. "All fucking mine."

"Are you branding me, sweetheart?"

"I don't want to lose you," she murmurs, her voice heavy with sleep. I brush her hair out of her face, smoothing it down.

"You won't. You wouldn't need to do this to prove that. You've had me for years, Scar. Fucking *years*."

47

EVAN

"HOW DOES it feel to lose, loser?"

No matter how many times I try to tell Scarlett something isn't a competition, she thinks I'm bluffing and turns it into one anyway. When I said we were going to be late to class to get our grades after sleeping in, she made it a mission to go back to her apartment and see if she could get to campus before me.

It's not that I let her win...

Okay, maybe I did.

Only because nothing beats the smile she gets on her face when she's won something. So that's the only reason why I'm sulking walking towards her outside of Anderson's office.

She stands with her hands in the air, one of her hands in an 'L' shape on her forehead as she scolds me for being late.

My stomach swarms with butterflies as I notice that her whole outfit is mine. She's wearing my sweatpants that she stole and my shirt that she took from my closet that says, *'Suck my Pianist.'* The clothes basically swallow her whole, the sweatpants band rolled down, and the shirt twisted into a knot at the side, showing off the sliver of her stomach and my favourite part, her tattoo.

She looks like mine.

I walk closer to her, shaking my head at her, while she continues to call me a loser. I drag her hand down from her forehead swiftly, interlocking my fingers with hers instead. "Not everything is a competition, Angel."

Her whole face lights up, those brown eyes staring right into mine. "With you it is. I told you I'd get here before you and I did."

"Great. Do you want a prize?" I ask, bored.

"You know what? I would lo-"

I silence her by kissing her deeply and she stumbles against the door. I'm pretty sure Anderson can see us from his office. If he can't see us, he can definitely hear the whimper that comes out of her as I press her against the wall, pinning her with my hips. I kiss her again, biting on her bottom lip before pulling apart.

"What was that?" she breathes, pressing her fingers to her lips.

"Your prize," I say, smiling down at her. "Now stop making up excuses just to kiss me. You're, like, obsessed with me or something."

"Or something," she mutters before turning around and opening the door to Anderson's office.

SCARLETT

I fucking knew it.

We came top of the class for our project, each of us getting A pluses, as well as receiving a call from the software developer, wanting to make *Hard To Tell* into a reality. We were both so giddy with excitement, telling each other how happy we were with the way it turned out that I couldn't even drive back home. I hate when I get like this. Where I get so excited and hot and bothered that I can't do anything, and I have to work off my energy.

"What are you doing tonight?" I ask him when we get inside my apartment building. "Do you wanna come over?"

"You should probably see what's going on inside," he says, nodding up to the elevator. Weird. I open my mouth to respond, but he turns around swiftly walking away from me. "Bye, Angel."

Sometimes I wonder why I live with these girls.

I knew Evan's weird goodbye meant something, but I didn't know exactly what. The second I open the door; the whole apartment is a mess. We usually create a lot of mess, but nothing compared to this.

The airing cupboard is emptied out so towels, tablecloths, and old shit we put in there when we moved in have spilled out onto the floor into the kitchen area. The kitchen is where most of the mess. There's a stand mixer on the countertop that wasn't there when I left this morning, the packaging on the floor while Wren stands over it, licking some sort of mixture off her fingers. The fridge door is opened, most of the contents emptied on the side while the Tupperware cupboard spills out onto the floor.

"What is going on...?" I ask, stepping further into the room. Wren turns around as if she's been caught, her cheeks red and puffy.

"Are you ready for Friendsgiving?" she asks. Has she been hit in the head or something? What the hell is going on?

"It's the start of May, Wrenny," I say gently, in case she is on the brink of a mental breakdown. She hardly ever bakes and she's not particularly good at it either.

"Is it?" she asks, chipper as ever. "Oh, well. We're all going over to Miles's for dinner so..." She shrugs innocently, sticking the spoon back in the batter.

"Who is *'all of us'*?" I ask, laughing at the absurdity.

We've been hanging out like always, so I don't know why she's pushing it. Since we came back from LA, Kennedy has been a little distant, but she usually gets like this around this time of year, given how far away she is from her family. It was a little weird that she didn't want to celebrate her birthday much this year, so we stayed in and watched a movie for her twenty-first. It was fun as always, but something has seemed off. Maybe that's why Wren's pushing this.

"Just Kennedy, Harry, Milesy, me and you, obviously and uh, Evan," she says, rushing her list.

I narrow my eyes on her. "Why?"

"I just thought it would be nice for us all to hang out now you and Evan are..."

"We're what?" I ask.

"He's your boyfriend, Scar. You can say it," she says, shimmying her shoulder at me for extra effect. That word is still so weird to me. I even considered not calling him anything, but there's nothing that he does that doesn't fit my requirements for a boyfriend. And he's annoyingly perfect at it.

"That doesn't mean I want to," I mutter.

"Can you stop being a grump for one night and enjoy this delicious meal that *your boyfriend* is putting together while I make dessert," she warns. I nod at her fierce tone. "Okay," she says it softer this time. "I've organised a seating plan, so be prepared."

I WISH she was more specific about being prepared because with the six of us, and although Wren made it clear she wants to see me and Evan 'in action,' she put us at opposite ends of the table as soon as we got here.

I wouldn't care that much if he didn't look so good. I just want to ruffle his hair, mess him up a little, take off that white button down and run my hands all over him.

Instead, he's sitting directly across from me at one head of the table, as I sit at the other. On his right, Kennedy sits next to Evan and Miles on her side, next to me. On my other side, Harry sits across from Miles, while Wren sits on Evan's other side.

"Baby," Miles presses as we start to eat the lasagne Evan made. "This seating plan is awful. I can't do this. Scarlett chews like an animal."

I kick him under the table, jabbing my heel into his shin and he winces. "If you want to complain, you can sit on the floor for all I care," I say.

This guy gets more and more immature as the days goes by. After the advice he gave me with Ev, I thought maybe he had grown up, but apparently not. He glares at me, but I roll my eyes.

"What's up with this seating plan, Wrenny?" Kennedy asks, wiping her mouth with her sleeve. I turn to look at Wren, ready to accuse her, but my eyes snag on Harry watching Kennedy. She's completely oblivious to the quiet, softie hockey player who is clearly head over heels for her. As much as they can say they're just friends, the kind of looks he gives her hold so much more than a platonic glance. "I mean, I'm not complaining, but splitting up the couples is brutal. Miles's veins are going to pop out of his forehead."

Wren carries on chewing her piece of garlic bread innocently. When she swallows, all of us watching her, she turns to Evan instead, placing her hand on his. "This lasagne is delicious, Evan. Did you make it from scratch?"

"Actually, I got-" he starts.

We're not doing that. At all. "Wren," I press. "What are you *doing*?"

She sits up straighter, pushing her blonde hair behind her shoulder before pinning me with a look. "Do you remember that time when you all said Miles and I couldn't keep our hands off each other?" I nod as the realisation slowly hits me.

When Wren and Miles started to date for real, they couldn't stop touching each other. After one of their games, all of us, excluding Evan, were in the living room and Wren was sitting in Miles' lap while they whispered disgusting things to each other, basically making out in front of us. After Ken pulled Harry away for their infamous seven-minutes-in-heaven debacle, I was left in the room with those two and it started to get less and less child friendly.

"So, you think Ev and I can't do that?" I ask, glancing at him. He looks so innocent, all put together as he slowly eats the food he made while everyone glances around the table. I want to kiss him so badly. Wren nods, clearly happy with her little genius plan. This is going to be more torture for her boyfriend than it is for mine. "We're not like you two animals. I can eat a meal across from him."

Wren shrugs as if to say 'We'll see' before digging back into her food. Miles has been fidgeting at the side of me for the whole meal and he's about to piss me right off if he doesn't sit still.

"Is this about self-control?" Miles asks and she nods. "You know I don't have a lot of that, baby." Harry starts to laugh. Even as the designated baby on the hockey team, he seems to have more sense than most of them combined. "Hey! You can't laugh, Butler. When you're in a relationship then you can talk. Until then, you won't know how completely devastating it is not to touch your girl."

"Yeah, I know what that's like," he mutters in response.

As the words leave his mouth his eyes connect with Kennedy's, and I swear time stops. The energy between them is radioactive, but for some reason, one of them seems to be giving it off more than the other. She smiles a little, dropping her gaze back down to her food while Harry's face burns red.

Strange.

"How are you holding up, Ev?" I ask causally over the table, taking a sip of my drink. He smiles wide, those perfect teeth showing.

"Great," he replies. "You?"

"Fantastic," I say, beaming. "Are you having trouble not touching me?"

He shakes his head, swallowing. "It's no big deal. I've been resisting you all my life. I can pretend again for one night." I press my mouth shut to hide the giddy grin that battles my face not to spread across my mouth, but I don't let it as the girls let out sitcom-worthy 'Awhs.'

"You've become such a softie," Miles murmurs to my boyfriend and I kick him again. "You too, Scarley." It's like he *wants* me to bruise his leg. I ignore him and continue eating my food.

"Can I say something?" Kennedy asks. Everyone's heads turn to hers, Harry's not moving from already looking at her.

"As much as you guys make me want to rip my hair out, you also make me laugh a bunch. So, thank you."

"Why are you thanking us?" Harry asks curiously.

"Well, you know what it's like to not be at home. But when I'm with you guys, I don't worry about that. I know I haven't been the most fun person to hang out with recently, but you never make me feel bad about it," she explains, dropping her gaze to the table.

"You shouldn't have to thank us for something like that, Ken," Wren says. "We've always got your back and you've always got ours. It's that simple."

"Yeah," she whispers before coming back to life. "I mean, where would you be without me manifesting you dating a hockey player so we could have an excuse to go to the games."

I laugh. "You manifested that?"

"Of course, I did. How else do you think they got together?" she explains, gesturing between the couple in question. "You'd be a shitshow without me."

"You didn't even like hockey," Wren retorts, laughing hard.

"You're a skater. Besties before testes and all that. But secretly, I love hockey," Kennedy says, waving her hand around in dismissal. She smiles wide, her dimples popping out as she looks at Harry. "Wouldn't want to miss out on watching my favourite player."

Harry's face turns completely red at the compliment. Even as a hockey goalie, he resembles more of a teddy bear than anything else. He gets all shy and nervous around Kennedy's loud energy, but when I catch them together they feed off each other, just becoming one huge ball of sunshine.

The way they're smiling at each other now? I don't know if friends just look at friends that way. Maybe I'm just projecting and getting antsy about not being able to touch Evan. Kennedy's thing is to overanalyse, so I'll leave that up to her.

We eat the rest of the meal talking about everything and nothing.

Wren tells us about her vacation this summer, while Miles sulks about not being able to go with her because his family are also going on vacation. They also tell us how they're spending half of the summer teaching kids how to skate at the local rink. Harry tells us about his family coming to visit him from Australia for a few weeks in the summer, while Kennedy tells us a story about what happened the last time her mom came up here from South Carolina, which ended in a lot of tears.

When everyone's done sharing and it's my turn, I don't know what to say. I don't have any plans for the summer anymore, other than working on new designs for *Voss*. I've not really thought about it at all. For once, I don't have a direction. At least when I'm at school, I know I'm working towards something. I have strategies in place, and I know I have a goal. Usually, I try to plan a solo vacation to give me some time to myself, but with a boyfriend, can I still do that? Are there rules now that mean I can't do things on my own or do we have to always do things together?

I stand abruptly from the table. "I'm going to the bathroom."

Evan stands too. "Me too." Wren shakes her head. "She's clearly in need of desperate help, Wren. I'm doing us all a favour here."

I roll my eyes at Evan's not discreet excuse as I move from the table and down the corridor to the only bathroom on this floor. I hear his footsteps a few behind mine, but I don't turn around. I make the quick decision not to go to the bathroom and instead walk out into the street, where the streetlights shine overhead as it starts to rain a little.

I need a second to breathe. I don't know why I'm panicking about this. I *shouldn't* be panicking about this. I've been in a relationship before. It wasn't a great one, but I managed it. So why does this one make me feel like I'm suffocating and nothing is even happening?

I can feel him before he actually touches me.

"Just give me a sec," I say, holding my hand up as I face away from him. "I think I'm having a panic attack or something."

I take in huge gulps of air, not knowing if this is working or not, but I need to do something. I can feel him moving behind me. Why is it always raining? Will focusing on that help? As the feeling in my chest tightens, I try to focus on the pavement, watching the rain fall down into the drain, but it doesn't help. Nothing is working.

"Can I- Will it help if I hold you? I can hold you really tight."

"You can try," I whisper.

The second the words are out of my mouth, he comes behind me, wrapping his huge arms around my chest, securing me, and holding me tight the way I need to, resting his chin on my head. I focus on breathing, making sure I don't run out of breath. My whole body feels heavy and sweaty, even with all the rain. But he's anchoring me. Keeping me safe.

"I've got you, Scar," he whispers into my hair. "I've got you."

"I know. I just... I don't know what's wrong with me," I choke out. "One second I was fine and the next... I don't know. I'm just worried when there's nothing to worry about."

He doesn't ask about what because I think he knows. "We're going to be okay, you know? If you keep trying to compare our relationship to everyone else's, you're never going to be satisfied. We don't need a plan for the summer to enjoy ourselves. If you want to go to Italy, walk around museums, go to New York…. Anything you want. We can do it all. Or we can stay here and do nothing. As long as I'm with you, close to you, I'll be okay. *We'll* be okay."

My heartbeat starts to settle again, and he starts to relax off me, his grip slowly loosening so I can breathe again. He twists us around, so my chest is to his and he crushes my face to his, kissing me on the forehead. How does he manage to make everything better? He just gets me. Sometimes I don't even have to speak, and he knows exactly what's wrong. I can give him a look and he'll just *know*.

When I start to breathe normally again, I open my mouth multiple times without saying what I want to say. There's no way we're going to move forward if I don't. I sigh, trying to muster up all the courage I need, and I step back from him. He still holds onto my shoulders, studying me curiously in the light rain.

Starting off strong, I say, "Don't ever quote me on this." He tilts his head to the side. "I feel like the luckiest girl when I'm with you. You listen to me. You make me feel smart. You take care of me even when I don't want you to. I've been so used to doing that on my own, only looking out for myself and pushing everything else away, and you took that part of me and cared for it so effortlessly. You never complain. You wait for me when I tell you I'm not ready. You just *get* me. And I get you. I couldn't ask for a better partner. And I know that word cringes people out, but that's exactly what we are: partners. Partners in crime, too."

My brain barely gets to process the fact that I said those words, let alone that his lips are covering mine. He grabs onto my face, holding me tight, kissing me so hard that I almost go dizzy. He's kissing me so hard that it's the force of a million kisses, telling me everything I never knew I needed to hear.

I'm proud of you and I've got your back, is all I can hear as he kisses the living daylights out of me. When we're still kissing and the rain has stopped, I can't tell if it's a tear coming from his cheek that I can taste or if it's the rain. I pull back from him.

"Hey," I say softly, brushing the tear that has fallen from his eye. "Why are you crying?"

"Because I'm happy about what you just said," he replies, doing his best and not to sound upset. He closes his eyes, tilting his head up to the sky. "Fuck, Scarlett. Don't say shit like that."

"Why?"

"Because I love you!"

"No need to shout, Ev," I murmur, laughing a little, but his face remains serious. My heartbeat roars in my ears, and I have to steady myself against his arms, making sure I don't slip or melt into a puddle at his feet. "You love me?"

"Of course, I do! Has that not been obvious? I think I've been so unhealthily in love with you my whole life, Scarlett. Since we were kids, there has been no one that I've loved as much as I love you. I love doing stupid things with you, I love it when you tell me to relax, I love it when you hold my hand when you don't even realise you're doing it. No one has ever made my chest burn just by looking at them. No one who has made me want to do better, be better, for them. I don't think about anything as much as I think about you, about us, about being with you. I would count down the minutes in class for a second to argue with you. I'd play your stupid games if it meant that I had your attention for just two seconds. I'd lay my soul bare for you, Scarlett. I'd let you pick me apart. I'd let you do absolutely anything to me. Because you're…" His voice wobbles. "You're *everything* to me."

"Why is loving me unhealthy?" I tease, tilting my head. The severity of what he said hasn't hit me yet. I don't know why that part is the only thing I'm caught up on.

"Because it's addicting. Even when you push me away, I still want more of you. All of you. All of the time," he says, his tone serious and deadly, thick with emotion.

"I want you too."

"Yeah?"

His smile almost makes me want to cry. He has the sweetest lined dimples that spread across his cheekbones when he smiles too hard. Sometimes he does it when he's being sarcastic or when he's trying to piss me off, but he's smiling like that now. Just for me.

My brain is refusing to process the words that just came out of his mouth. I'm still feeling dizzy from that kiss and now this is making me feel even more lightheaded. Evan Branson loves me. He doesn't just like holding hands with me or writing me songs. He doesn't like buying me two hundred thousand dollar paintings or whispering filthy things to me. He makes me feel smart and capable. He makes me want to work harder. He loves me. And I….

"I love you, Ev," I say, reaching out my hand to rest on his face. I watch him sigh as if he's been holding his breath for years. "If what we've been doing for the past few weeks is what it's going to be like forever, I don't want anything else. You make love seem fucking golden. You're *my* angel, Evan."

"I knew you didn't hate me." He grins.

"I knew you didn't hate me either," I challenge.

"Great." He steps closer to me.

"Good." I step closer to him.

"Perfect." His gorgeous ridiculous face is right in front of me now.

"What's wrong with you?"

"What's wrong with *you*?"

Then I kissed him again. And again. And again. Because he has me. And I have him. We're equals. We're partners. We're best friends. We're just *everything*.

And apparently, kissing in the rain is our thing now.

EPILOGUE

The Summer – Evan

"I'M STILL MAD AT YOU," she says. It still makes me laugh how she can say that with a straight face while climbing into my lap, wearing the shirt she stole from my closet and nothing else.

"Oh, come on, Scar. It was *one* episode. I can watch it again if you want me to," I groan, pulling her into me. We've been rewatching *Modern Family* and even though we've both seen it a million times, she plotted to kill me if I watched an episode without her. I didn't mean to do it, but it came on and it was a good fucking episode. "You can't stay mad at me forever."

"I can and I will."

"Even if I kiss you?" I say, trailing my hands underneath my — *her* — shirt.

"Even if you kiss me, Ev," she replies. She's gotten better at the whole 'your proximity does nothing to me' over the last few weeks. At the beginning, every touch was so sensitive, but as she's got used to it, she's also better at hiding how much I affect her and how much she loses control.

"You're still calling me 'Ev.' That's a good sign," I say, looking at the positives.

"That's because your name has too many syllables," she says proudly, holding up her head high. We've had this argument before and she somehow managed to win.

"It has two," I challenge.

"Yeah. Two too many," she says as if it's the most obvious thing in the world. I laugh at her as she continues to rub my shoulders gently.

"Scarlett, *tesoro*, you're ridiculous," I say.

"But you love ridiculous, don't you, Branson? You wouldn't be able to live without my ridiculousness. What's ridiculous is how you think *I'm* ridiculous," she rambles, sounding, well...ridiculous.

"Say 'ridiculous' one more time and your ass is going to be red and raw," I warn.

"Don't threaten me with a good time, Ev," she retorts, leaning into me as she whispers, "That." She kisses my neck. "Would be." She kisses my jaw until she gets to my ear as she rasps, "Ridiculous."

I'm about to go in to kiss her, finally tasting what she's been edging me on for since I got to her apartment, but her room door bursts open.

It's been harder than ever to get a moment of privacy in this apartment, but we still try every time. Kennedy and Wren don't seem to mind the whole 'walking in on your best friend while he sucks off her boyfriend' and it's slightly concerning.

Scarlett snaps her head to the door where Kennedy walked through. She's covering her eyes with one hand, her other arm searching aimlessly for Scarlett's closet.

"Jesus, Ken, what are you doing?" she asks.

"My eyes are closed," Kennedy squeals. "I'm just looking for the battery for my camera."

"Why would it be in my closet?" Scarlett asks.

"I dunno," she says, "A lot of stuff ends up in here."

"That's true," I say, kissing my girl on the neck, but she climbs off me, walking over to her friend. My button down is long enough to cover her ass, but if she's not careful she's going to flash someone. Me, hopefully.

"What's going on, Ken?" Scarlett asks. Kennedy turns to her, her eyes still squeezed shut. "I'm decent." She looks back to me, giving me a once-over. "He's decent. Just open your eyes."

She peaks behind her fingers first, not fully trusting us. When she sees it's safe, she drops her hand with a sigh, looking Scarlett in the eye as she says, "I'm going home."

"What do you mean, *home?* This is your home," Scarlett says, confused.

"I mean *home* home," she replies. I don't know if I'm supposed to be here for this, so I get up off the bed. As I do, Scarlett turns around, sending me a death stare and I sit back down. *Okay*.

"South Carolina home?" Scarlett asks.

"Yes."

"Why?"

"Only for the summer. I'll still be finishing fourth year, but then depending on how I feel... I might go back for good."

This doesn't sound good for any of us.

Without Kennedy, Wren and Scarlett would fall apart, which also means by proxy, Miles and I would fall apart. She's the literal glue to the group. She's funny without even trying and she is loud and chaotic, always trying to pull Wren and

Scarlett out of their comfort zones. She's been mine and Scarlett's biggest cheerleader since the first day I met her. Even I would miss her rudely barging in on us.

"Ken, talk to me."

She sighs, running her hands down her overalls. "Something hasn't been feeling right. It hasn't felt right for a long time. I just think spending the summer with my mom and Mia is the best option right now."

Scarlett shakes her head. "But that's where-"

"I know. That's why I also need to go back. He's gone. He can't ruin home for me anymore," she says. I don't know who *he* is, but he sounds like bad news. She pulls Scarlett into a hug, holding her tight while she stands there motionless. "I'll call you when I get down there."

"Okay," she muffles. When she pulls out the hug she says, "Stay safe."

"I will. Bye, Evan. Be good for Scar this summer or she'll leave you in Italy on your own."

Since the second school let out, we've been planning trips around Europe for the summer. Scar's content on not staying in Salt Lake all summer, which means we're not going to be here much as of next week. I can't wait for her to show me places where her family is from in Italy, and I can pretend I've never seen them before. It's going to be my new favourite game.

"I'll be on my best behaviour. Scout's honour," I say, beaming, holding up three fingers. She doesn't buy it because she points at me as she starts to walk backwards towards the door.

"Yes, so that that means no fucking in bathrooms while your friends are next door," she warns. I could have sworn no one heard us after my band performance, but apparently not. "Walls are thin."

"Ken, for the millionth time, we weren't-" I say.

She waves a hand, dismissing me as she slips through the door, shouting, "Have fun. And use protection!"

As Scarlett walks back to me, she's frowning. I reach out to grab her hand, pulling her into me so she falls into my lap again, her arms weakly linked around my shoulders.

"She's going to be fine; you know?" I say to her, knowing she needs the encouragement.

She sighs, looking back to the door where loud sounds of what Scar calls 'Kennedy Noises' sound outside. "I know, but she's my soulmate. There's a lot she's going back to."

"She can handle it, Scar. You just worry about yourself for now, okay?" I say, pulling her for a kiss. She dodges me just before they connect, climbing off my lap and falling back onto the bed. "What are you doing?"

"I'm still mad at you, remember?"

THE END.

ACKNOWLEDGMENTS

The hardest part about writing a book, for me, is knowing who to thank while also sounding as me and professional as possible. All I want to do is say, 'Thank you soooooo much!!! I couldn't have done it without you," but that doesn't seem like the most professional thing to do. Really, it seems insanely impossible to have such a short space to put into words how grateful I am for every single person who helped with this book and this series. But I'm going to try and give it my best shot.

Writing this book has been one of the most difficult yet rewarding experience of my life. Writing a mystery aspect was a lot more difficult than it need to be, but I'm hoping I managed to pull it off. This book contained roughly the same amount of side plots as book one but for some reason, incorporating Evan and Scarlett's journey separately was really difficult for me. There were so many days where I thought about scrapping the book and making it simpler, but then I say started to realise that the complexities this book holds is what makes it so special and unique. The long and gruelling process was completely worth it for you all to have read their story and to have it in your hands.

Now, this is the hardest part. From my supporters over on social media and my cheerleaders in person, it's so hard to put into words just how grateful and thankful I am to have had such a good support system.

Firstly, I'd like to thank my family for giving me the tie and space to create even if that meant I was stuck in my room for hours on end, screaming and giggling over stupid scenes. I know my friends would groan and tell me to stop when I'd say I have a new idea for a book but this one was the most fun to talk about. As much as Queenster deemed it a 'mafia romance' which is most certainly is *NOT*, I'll never forget the amount of laughs we had over certain scenes. So, thank you to my Queenie Boo, Christabel, Harriet, Ayela, Alannah, Eva, Sadie Amy, Ola, and Olivia for everything and for sticking by me as this book took over my life.

I never thought I would form an emotional bond and connection to people I met over a screen, but it happened. This book would definitely not be this book without Katie and Ella. We somehow found each other and became absolutely inseparable. Not only did they encourage me, send me their unhinged reactions to some of the scenes, but they made me feel so supported, loved, cared for, and seen. I've never felt more like myself like I am when I'm talking with them. I don't think anyone has been able to completely get me and understand me so easily than these two girls. You will always have such a special place in my heart, no matter what. My Prose Hoes.

Thank you to Emma for being there right from the beginning. Having you read this story whilst I was writing it was the greatest gift I could have ever asked for. You have always been right with me as I've written my current projects and this book would not be what it is without all your constant support and unique takes on scenes and chapters. You have been the best, most special friend anyone could ask for and I am constantly in awe of everything you do. So, thank you.

Thank you to all you readers who have chosen to pick up my book and read it. Everyone and their mothers say this, but I would not be where I am without you. Seriously. As an indie author, exposure online and in person is incredibly hard to get by and I could not get my books off the ground without the help of all of you for picking up my book.

And lastly, thank you to me. I have always been a perfectionist and have always tried to do a million things at once, constantly trying to raise the bar. It's hard being stuck in my head all the time, trying not only to please and satisfy myself, but others also. Being so young, I was constantly comparing myself to others, not feeling fully worthy or good enough. Slowly, I pulled myself out of that and gave myself some grace. Managing to write my sophomore novel has been a dream come true and would not have been possible without the hard work and dedication that I put into making it.

It's only up from here.

BOOKS IN THIS SERIES

Fake Dates & Ice Skates – BOOK 1

Wren Hackerly loves routines. She has always been a woman to stick by a schedule and work towards her end goal no matter the costs. The very last thing in her five year plan was to get caught in a fake dating plot with the one hockey player she just about tolerate.

Miles Davis is a rule breaker and a flirt - everything that Wren is not used to and does not want to get used to. It doesn't help that he's one of the most popular people to ever set foot on North University's grounds.

After much convincing, a few parties and an awkward family meeting later, Wren and Miles navigate the world of social media trolls and the harsh truths of living up to their potential. The more time Wren spends with him, she can slowly feel herself slipping out of the mould she has been in her entire life. For the most part, she kind of enjoys it, but there is a gnawing feeling like this is what is going to distract them from their goals. *When the line between what's real and what's fake begins to blur, will either of them admit to feeling things that aren't just pretend?*

Good Grades & Mystery Games – BOOK 2

Scarlett Voss is what girls at North University want to be but also what they fear. She's stubborn, confident and spends too much of her free time arguing with a certain blonde in all of her classes. She's grown up with money so she knows how it feels to be used for something other than her personality. So when a family mystery arises, Scarlett jumps at the opportunity to prove to everyone and herself, that she is capable of more than people think.

Evan Branson is the stuck-up, flirty boy who irritates Scarlett on a day-to-day basis, seeing how far he can push her until she cracks. It's no secret that he's a millionaire but that might be the only thing keeping him going after an embarrassing scandal involving a weeping Evan and a packet of Oreo's leads to him getting pushed aside from the family business. His one chance at getting back in with the Branson's is through a simple plan: Get close to Scarlett, find out more about her family and don't blow your cover.

When the two are paired up for an end of year project, an unlikely mystery tying them together and a final grade on the line, can they put their family feud and general hatred for each other to the side while they strive for a grade? How far are they willing to push each other to get what they want?

Summer Days & Great Mistakes – Kennedy's Book Coming 2024…

Printed in Great Britain
by Amazon